# Undertow

DISCARD

## Lorena McCourtney

Fleming H. Revell
A Division of Baker Book House Co
Grand Rapids, Michigan 49516

Published by Fleming H. Revell
a division of Baker Book House Company
P.O. Box 6287, Grand Rapids, MI 49516-6287
www.bakerbooks.com

Printed in the United States of America

Library of Congress Cataloging-in-Publication Data
McCourtney, Lorena.
        Undertow : a novel / Lorena McCourtney.
              p.        cm. — (the Julesburg mysteries ; bk. 3)
        ISBN 0-8007-5778-5 (pbk.)
        1. Models (Persons)—Fiction. 2. Oregon—Fiction. I. Title.
    II. Series: McCourtney, Lorena. Julesburg mysteries ; bk. 3.
    PS3563.C3449U53  2003
    813'.54—dc21                                           2003004011

Save me, O God,
   for the waters have come up to my neck.
I sink in the miry depths,
   where there is no foothold.
I have come into the deep waters;
   the floods engulf me.

Psalm 69:1–2

## 1

*N*ot the *New York Times.*
Not the *Chicago Tribune.*
*But it's mine, all mine,* Angie Harrison exulted as she fingered the computer printout of the new masthead.

*The Julesburg Herald. Established 1937. Twelve pages, publication every Wednesday, circulation 2,500, price 50 cents. Angie Harrison, editor and publisher.*

The front door to the office swung open. Ryan grinned at her and draped his elbows on the scarred counter. "Well, if it isn't my favorite newspaper editor, looking all smug and self-satisfied."

Angie returned her brother's grin. *I am feeling smug and self-satisfied. I've put the past behind me.* "Did you bring me some exciting tidbit of local news?"

"I saw Mark Higgins's terrier scrapping with Pete Dooley's mutt on the way over here."

"Great! My top news story for next Wednesday's edition. If I rush right out, do you suppose I can get a photo?"

Ryan smiled at her from across the counter. "It's good to see you looking so upbeat. Not so . . . tense as when you first got here."

Tense. A nice euphemism for nerves swinging from limp as jellyfish to barbed-wire tight, both wrapped around a feeling that she'd fled just in time to escape a trap closing around her. A trap of her own making.

"Except you think I may have jumped into this too soon," she suggested.

"Maybe," Ryan admitted. "You've only been here a couple of weeks. Being editor of a small-town newspaper on the Oregon coast is quite a change from the bright lights and glamour of a New York model's life."

"But newspaper work was my original goal, until I got sidetracked. Two years of college journalism, remember? And believe me, I've had all I ever want of bright lights and glamour."

Ryan's head tilted, and she knew he was considering the fervency of her statement. She'd never really explained to him why she'd abruptly abandoned New York and her modeling career. *Maybe because I'm still sorting through the reasons myself. Or just ashamed to bring it all out in the open.* "We'll talk about it one of these days," she promised.

"Okay. Hey, Stef says that tonight we're having a special celebration dinner in honor of your new venture. She's been in the kitchen, cooking up a storm all afternoon."

"Sounds good. I don't have any meetings to attend tonight. And I missed lunch, so I'm already starving." Angie rubbed her midsection.

"Good. Newspaper editors don't have to be as skinny as models."

*An attitude a world apart from Burke's.* Burke could spot an ounce of gain on her midriff and not hesitate to tell her to get to the gym and sweat it off.

"And you missed lunch today because . . . ?" Ryan added.

"I'm on to something important. I've just decided on my first big project for the newspaper. A special series. Something exciting."

"Digging up dirt on our local politicians?" Ryan speculated. "Investigating all of Julesburg's old secrets? Inciting our senior citizens to riot about the leaky roof at the senior center?"

Angie flipped an oversized paper clip at him. "I don't think you're taking my leap into journalism with the proper seriousness," she grumbled.

The phone rang. Angie picked up and took down a classified ad for an '82 Chevy pickup, 4-wheel drive, $1400 or best offer. She checked the caller's name against their list of deadbeats who didn't pay and couldn't find the name there. She said she'd bill him.

"Very professional." Ryan nodded approval. "And I'm sorry if it sounds like I'm not taking your new career seriously. Because I really do think it's great." He reached across the counter and squeezed her shoulder. "I couldn't be happier that you've found something that will keep you right here in Julesburg. We haven't seen enough of each other for much too long."

She couldn't disagree with that. Last year she'd planned on meeting Ryan and Stefanie in Japan for a vacation, but she'd let the chance for a spot in *Sports Illustrated's* swimsuit issue keep her from going.

"Okay, apology accepted," she said. "I'll even tell you all about my big idea at dinner tonight."

Ryan leaned across the counter and peered around the cluttered office. "You know, I've never been in here before."

"Then, by all means, come in and I'll give you the grand tour." Angie pulled open the swinging gate beside the counter and motioned him inside.

Ryan glanced at his watch. "A quick tour. I'm on my way out to Volkman Laser Systems for a meeting with the new owner. I'm running background checks on applicants for some key positions they have open."

"The tour won't take long. What you see is basically what you get."

Ryan grinned. "Basically, the place looks as if it could use a good housecleaning," he observed as he stepped through the swinging gate and dodged an overflowing wastebasket. Small mountains of paper skewered on holders or fluttering loose inundated the front desk. Lurking among them was the crust of a Danish roll and a half cup of cold coffee. "Maybe disinfecting."

Angie threw up her hands in pretend horror. "Oh, never! A sterile environment means a sterile newspaper. All this is essential clutter. Though we could use more space, that's for sure." She poked him in the shoulder. "And your office is no example to follow, brother dear. You may be Julesburg's premier private investigator—"

"Julesburg's only private investigator," he corrected. "'Premier' comes with that one-man territory."

"In any case, it looks to me as if your most difficult detective job may be to locate something in that disaster area you call an office."

They grinned at each other, pleased to be back to this companionable level of teasing after so many years apart.

Angie motioned around the room behind the counter. "Okay, what we have here are two computers, one old, one aging. This one by the front counter is mostly for business stuff. Advertising, subscriber accounts, and bills. But some copywriting. It's Madge Edelson's desk. That one over there is mine, for copywriting and all the other stuff, except ads, that goes in a newspaper."

At the moment, her computer was displaying a screen saver of an oversized pickup roaring through a mudhole, "mud" spattering the screen. *Pure Julesburg,* Angie had thought when she'd first seen it. She hadn't yet figured out how to change it to something a bit more soothing.

"A third computer, around the corner in the other room, is mostly devoted to ads. Becky Stroeber handles that."

"You have two employees? I'm impressed."

"Two part-time employees," Angie corrected. "Except that we all do a little of everything here. They both know more than I do."

"You'll learn. It's only your third day as an editor-slash-owner."

A squawk of chatter erupted from under a pile of papers cluttering Angie's desk. She scrambled to uncover the noise. "That's the radio scanner. It monitors police, fire, and ambulance channels," she said, turning up the volume.

Ryan smiled as they listened to an exchange between two officers about coffee at the Julesburg Café. "So you can race out and catch the breaking news as it happens?"

Angie put her hands on her hips. "Hey, sometimes important news happens in Julesburg. I've skimmed through some back issues of the *Herald*. A couple of big drug busts last year. Car wreck south of town that killed two people. The arson that destroyed the local plywood mill a couple years ago. Several murders in the past couple of years."

Ryan's teasing smile sobered. He had personal knowledge of the arson and one of those murders, as they both knew. "But it isn't as if we have a murderer on the loose, roaming the streets," he pointed out. "All those cases have been solved. And I'm hoping that's our quota of big crimes in Julesburg for a long, long time."

"But there's another, long-ago murder here that's never been solved."

"You *have* been digging around in Julesburg's secrets. You're not intending to get mixed up in that one, are you?"

"Maybe. Wouldn't it be an impressive coup for the new editor of the local newspaper to solve Julesburg's old murder mystery?"

"It's a thirty-year-old crime. Not exactly a hot trail to follow." Ryan paused, his forehead creased. Angie had the impression his concerns went deeper than the age of the crime.

"You're a detective," she pointed out. "How come you've never tried to run down the killer? Doesn't an old, unsolved local crime intrigue you?"

"I'm a PI. That stands for 'private investigator,' one who works for a living. Not 'playboy investigator,' dashing around and solving crimes for the fun of it." Ryan managed to sound lofty, as if mere curiosity didn't enter into his character or profession. "Although I have to admit to a certain . . . interest in that old murder. Sometime when there's a lull in the investigative business, maybe I'll look into it."

"And this lull might come . . . when, exactly?"

Ryan smiled wryly. "When arsonists run out of matches, for one thing."

Ryan, who had been a full-time arson investigator for a big insurance company before he opened his own private investigative agency, still traveled all over the Northwest, handling arson investigations for several insurance companies.

Angie collected a handful of loose papers from her desk and stacked them briskly. "Then I'll just have to unravel Julesburg's only unsolved murder myself," she said. "Murderer, beware. Angie Harrison is hot on your trail."

## 2

*A*ngie had tossed out the proclamation light-heartedly, but Ryan sounded unexpectedly somber when he said, "I really don't think that's a good idea."

"Why not? You're a believer in justice, aren't you, even if it's delayed?"

"Yes, of course, but—"

"Maybe an investigative gene runs in our blood, and mine's just now kicked in. A Harrison's gotta do what a Harrison's gotta do."

"Whatever," Ryan muttered.

They continued with the tour. Angie pointed to the bulky machine sitting in a corner in the second room.

"That's our copy machine, old but good. Unfortunately, we're so crowded in here that we can't get to it without crawling over one of these tables. Here's the file cabinets." She waved at the lineup of three metal cabinets that all looked as if they'd gone a losing round with a heavyweight boxer. "Fax machine, paper cutter sharp enough to double as a guillotine, flatbed scanner, waxing machine—"

"Waxing machine? You're planning to run a hair removal business on the side?" He dodged as Angie aimed a punch at his shoulder. "Okay, okay. My apologies for being annoying. So what does a waxing machine have to do with turning out a newspaper?"

"We're not exactly high tech here. See all these tables?" Angie motioned to the four large tables crowding the room. "That's where we do the page layouts. Most newspapers do them by computer now, but we're still a hands-on operation. The waxing machine is used to put wax on the back side of articles or ads so we can stick them to the layout sheets but still pull the pieces loose if they need moving. Then after everything is properly arranged, the layout sheets go to the printer. And out comes the newspaper."

"Your two years of college journalism prepared you for all this?"

Angie shrugged her shoulders. "In some ways. But they concentrated on the big stuff. The legalities of protecting your contacts. Libel laws. Very little mention of doing page layouts by hand, or how the inches of advertising affect postal rates when mailing the newspaper. Which can be really important to the finances of a newspaper this size."

"More complicated than I realized."

"Journalism classes also didn't tell me how to write a news article with one part of my head and keep track of the voices on the scanner with the other. Which usually sound like a couple of chickens cackling. Or how to collect payment from an advertiser who's three months behind on his bill. But Madge is teaching me."

"I'm sure you're a quick learner."

"I'm trying. There's lots of other stuff around. The little storeroom is full of supplies and things I haven't even looked at yet." Angie pointed to a couple of doors leading off to the back. "The big one has shelves of old *Heralds* going back to the dark ages. There's also a restroom and a hallway kitchenette where we make coffee. Want some? I think what's in the pot is today's brew. Definitely no older than yesterday."

"As appealing as that sounds, I'll pass for the moment."

Angie picked up the half cup of coffee from the front desk and dumped it in the hallway sink. "I'm not going to set the world on fire here, Ry," she said. "I know that. It's not cutting-edge journalism. But I'm happy with it. It feels . . . right."

"I'm glad to hear that." He looked at his watch. "I'd better get going. You can make it home on time for dinner tonight?"

Because of local meetings she was covering for the *Herald*, she'd been catching dinner at the Julesburg Café and hadn't been home before 10:00 the last two nights. "I'll be there. But first I'm going to look at a little house for rent on . . ." She picked up the scrap of newsprint she'd torn from last week's classified section. "Highland Street."

"Angie, you know you're welcome to stay at the house with Stef and me indefinitely. There's plenty of room. We want you to stay."

"I know. But I need a place of my own."

"Why not an apartment in that new building on Lighthouse Hill?"

"I've also had my fill of apartment living in New York. I want open space on the other side of my walls and floor and ceiling, not some couple shouting at each other over my head. I may even put in a garden."

"A garden," Ryan echoed. Another disbelieving shake of head. "Will wonders never cease? Just don't plant any zucchini. People will leave it on your doorstep as it is."

"I'll grow what I please, thank you."

Ryan's eyes rolled. "How come that doesn't surprise me?" he muttered. "Where did you say this house is? Highland? That's a pretty isolated street. How about if I come along and check out the security and fire safety?"

She showed him the ad. "At that rental rate, I don't think I can expect a doorman or high-tech security system."

Ryan frowned at the piece of paper in her hand. "Sis, if you're short on money, Stef and I can—"

"Don't worry. I could afford more. But I want to be working-class Julesburg. I think people will take more readily to a new editor on that basis."

Ryan still didn't look pleased, but he apparently decided to put a brake on any further advice. He pushed the swinging gate open. "Oh, by the way, Stef said that while she was out, someone left a message on the answering machine asking for you. But he didn't leave a name or number about calling him back."

Angie's fingers clamped around the scrap of paper in her hand. Burke? He'd called once before she'd arrived in Julesburg. Ryan hadn't known then that she was coming, so he'd told Burke that he had no idea where she was. But now that she was here . . .

She eyed her brother thoughtfully. Straight-laced Ryan balked at untruths, but if she asked him to, he'd probably tell Burke he still didn't know where she was.

No, cancel that. She wasn't going to drag Ryan into her past mistakes. She'd have to talk to Burke sooner or later. It wouldn't take him long to find out where she was. Her stock market account was with his brokerage firm, and she'd turned in a change of address. Actually, it was surprising he hadn't called again before now or even come roaring out here. She, not he, had ended their relationship, and Burke wasn't a man to let a woman upstage his dumping rights.

She must've had a funny expression on her face, because Ryan paused with a hand on the outer door. "Something wrong?" he asked.

She injected sunshine into her tone, the same way she used to put it into a smile for a photographer, no matter

14

how she was feeling inside. "Not a thing Stef's dinner won't cure."

"Okay. And will you think about coming to church with us on Sunday? You haven't been since you got here."

"I'll think about it. But this Sunday . . ." She just wasn't ready for church yet. She grabbed the first excuse that surfaced. "If everything goes right, I'll probably be moving into my new house that morning."

Lines momentarily cut between Ryan's dark brows, but all he said was, "Okay, see you at dinner."

Angie wrote up an article from the notes she'd taken at last night's school-board meeting. Both her part-timers were already gone for the day. She tidied up, washed out the coffee maker, and resolutely kept her thoughts away from Burke Davis.

He, along with New York and modeling, was in the past, part of what she'd walked away from. She had a new life now.

A middle-aged woman in purple polyester pants, her hair an amazing tomato red, met Angie at the Highland Street house. She introduced herself as Christine Daggert. Her biggest concern appeared to be that Angie, single and not unattractive, might move someone in to share the house.

"Once I rented it to a couple, seemed nice enough, but first thing I knew they had this whole herd of people with sandals and nose rings and kids living with 'em."

"I'll be here alone," Angie assured her. She tilted her head, listening. The house was a considerable distance from the ocean, but some peculiarity of topography or wind brought a faint boom of surf. Nice.

"And no illegal drugs. A friend of mine had some tenants set up an illegal meth lab, and she wound up having to have the place demolished."

"No drugs of any kind, guaranteed."

The house was old, but a far cry from Ryan and Stef's lovely Victorian. And a world away from her nineteenth-floor apartment in New York. One story, one bedroom, one bathroom with a rust stain in the tub. Combination kitchen and dining area, tired carpet, no garage. The house was also rather oddly arranged, with the living room in the rear and the main front door opening into the kitchen. An unexpectedly large picture window graced one side of the living room, but the view was of an abandoned car, its hood and trunk lids raised, half buried in blackberry bushes on the wooded hillside beyond the weather-beaten picket fence surrounding the backyard.

Angie peered through straggly lace curtains hanging at a bedroom window. It was, as Ryan had said, a rather isolated area. She could see only one small house, and it was at least two city blocks away. Except, of course, there were no city blocks measured out in this edge-of-town area.

*Good. I'm ready for some privacy.*

The house was furnished, more or less. The yellow-and-green plaid of the sofa was loud enough to get on her nerves, and the wavy bedroom mirror gave her an elongated forehead and double chin. But adequate for now, she decided. Not immediately having to acquire furniture would simplify things.

She signed the rental agreement and put up the first and last month's rent and a deposit. Mrs. Daggert inspected the check closely before saying Angie could move in whenever she wanted.

"I'll do it Sunday morning."

Angie had never been inside a grandma's kitchen, but the big old house her sister-in-law Stefanie had lived in most of her life smelled like what Angie thought a grandma's kitchen should smell like. She tilted her head and sniffed.

"Something chocolatey."

"Old-fashioned chocolate cake. From my mother's recipe."

Sherlock, Ryan and Stefanie's shaggy tan dog, ambled over to welcome her. Angie gave his big head the rough-housing he liked and sniffed again.

"Homemade bread?"

"Kneaded and baked by yours truly." Stef lifted a white dishtowel to reveal golden loaves.

"And sage?"

"It's in the stuffing to go with roasted Cornish game hens. Angie, your sense of smell is incredible!"

*The result of five years of food deprivation,* Angie thought. Sometimes about all a weight-watching model got from food was the scent.

Angie folded her arms and regarded her sister-in-law thoughtfully. Faded jeans, old sweatshirt, bare feet. Her brown hair was tangled in a messy topknot, escaping strands framing her face like dark parentheses. But she was there was no other word for it—glowing.

"And this awesome menu is just because I bought the local newspaper?" Angie inquired.

"Of course! Well, there is one other thing—" Stefanie broke off with an uncharacteristically breathless giggle. "I was going to hold off and make a big announcement when I served the cake, but Ryan already knows, and I just can't hold it any longer. Angie, I'm pregnant! I thought I was, and I went to Dr. Halmoose today, and he confirmed it."

Angie knew Stefanie expected her to be delighted. *I am delighted,* she thought as Stef looked at her expectantly. *This is wonderful for Stef and Ryan. They've been waiting and hoping.*

Yet just for a moment, something dark and painful ripped through her, something that made her stomach roil and her knees go weak. She made a frantic grab for self-control and the right words.

*Undertow*

"Stef, that's wonderful! I'm so happy for you. I'll be an aunt! Well, I guess I already am. Ted has two kids, doesn't he? But I've never met them." She realized she was babbling. Stefanie knew that since she was living in New York and older brother Ted in Seattle, she'd never met his children. She cut off the words and threw her arms around Stefanie. "How far along are you?"

"About three months."

Angie released her hold on her sister-in-law. "Everything's okay?"

"Healthy as the proverbial horse."

"What about Fit 'n' Fun?" Angie asked. Fit 'n' Fun was the local health club Stefanie had owned and managed for several years now.

"I'll probably lighten up my work schedule as time goes along, but Dr. Halmoose says there's no reason I can't hang right in there until I go into labor."

"Oh, Stef . . . shouldn't you lighten up before that? I mean, you don't want anything to go wrong."

Stefanie planted her hands on her hips. "This is what you say to the wildly happy pregnant lady?"

Angie managed a laugh and gave her sister-in-law another hug. "Of course, everything will go right. Ignore my worrywart tendencies. When do we get to vote on names?"

"Not before I have an ultrasound to tell if it's a boy or girl. And I'm not sure I want to find out. Whatever it is, this baby is a gift from God. And I figure if God wanted us to know these things in advance, he'd whisper it in our ears. Or send an e-mail."

*A gift from God.* Angie swallowed hard. "You're going to make a wonderful mother, Stef. Big, big congratulations." She didn't want to rush out of the room, but she had to get away, if just for a moment. "Where's Ryan? I want to congratulate him too."

"He was in the living room, making some phone calls."

18

Angie squeezed Stefanie's hand to emphasize her heart-felt congratulations, but in the living room she paused, hand on her chest, to reinforce her self-control. *The past is behind me.* She repeated the words as if they were an updated version of the feel-good mantra a guru she'd briefly patronized had tried to instill in her. *The past is behind me,* she repeated.

Ryan wasn't in the living room, but the phone on the end table by the sofa was ringing. Someone had called for her earlier that day. Burke? Could he be calling again?

*Okay. No big deal. I'll have to talk to him sooner or later.*

She crossed the room and braced herself as she picked up the phone. Stefanie and Ryan always answered with a casual hello, but Angie spoke more formally. "Harrison residence."

"Angie?"

She'd braced for Burke when she picked up the phone. But this voice saying her name with an edge of surprise was not Burke's. It almost sounded like . . .

No, surely not.

—3—

than gripped the phone on his office desk. He'd called the Harrisons' number in Julesburg, hoping Angie might be there but not really expecting she would be. And definitely not expecting her to answer the phone.

There was a moment's hesitation before she spoke, making him wonder if she'd recognized his voice, even though it had been close to two years since they'd last spoken. But then she said, "Yes, this is Angie," and there was no hint of familiarity in her tone.

"This is Ethan." He paused. "Ethan Kearney," he added, wondering if their relationship was so long ago and forgotten that the first name alone was not enough. And also, he had to admit, feeling a touch of resentment that she hadn't recognized his voice. Neither of which changed the big wave of relief he felt at hearing her voice and knowing she was safe.

A small, soft thud came over from her end of the line, as if she'd dropped to a chair or closed a door. He got up and closed the door to his own office, shutting out sounds of the computer store and the ringing of another phone.

"Ethan. How—how have you been?"

"I've been calling your apartment in New York for several days, but no one ever answered."

"My roommate has been working in Milan the last couple of months and won't be back for another week. I turned off the answering machine when I left. You were calling because . . . ?"

He thought back to a time when, if they hadn't seen each other during the day, they'd talk in the evening. Back then, they'd never needed a reason to call each other. *Okay, enough with the reminiscing.* "Kristi seems to be missing," he said.

"Kristi Yamori? Missing? What do you mean?"

"Her parents called me several days ago. As you probably know, she calls them every Sunday evening. When they didn't hear from her, they were worried. But they didn't want to be old-fashioned and overprotective, so they waited several days before contacting her landlord. Then he went into her apartment and told them the place looked okay, although maybe a little messy—"

"I can't imagine Kristi leaving her apartment messy. She's the neatest person I know."

"She also hadn't been picking up her mail. That made the Yamoris even more worried, but they waited another couple of days before getting hold of the company where she'd been working. Her boss told them Kristi quit her job quite abruptly a couple of weeks ago. They're trying to decide now if they should contact the authorities back there."

"Not contacting her parents doesn't sound like Kristi."

Ethan's thoughts exactly. For all her ambitions as an actress, Kristi was still a very dutiful daughter. "Quitting a job abruptly also doesn't sound to me like something Kristi would do."

A moment's silence, as if Angie were thinking that over. "She may have gotten an offer for a good part, something she had to accept right away or lose. Maybe something out of town, which would explain why she hasn't been at the apartment."

"Wouldn't she let the apartment go if she was going to take work out of town?"

"Not necessarily. An out-of-town acting job might last only a month or two, or she might be waiting to find out how long it would last. Good apartments are hard to find."

"That could explain it, I suppose," Ethan said, although he didn't feel convinced. "You don't think her folks need to contact the authorities, then?"

"I wouldn't say that. Actually, I think they probably should have the authorities check on her."

"That's my feeling too," Ethan said. "Kristi had said you and she saw each other occasionally, that you'd even helped her find the job and apartment. So that was why I thought you might know where she was."

"We didn't see a lot of each other, but I counted her as a good friend. A very dependable friend."

A certain emphasis on the word *dependable* made him wonder if dependable friends were not the norm in a busy model's life.

"So then, after I couldn't get hold of you at your apartment, I got to thinking maybe you and Kristi had gone somewhere together," he said, feeling a need to explain this phone call a little further. "Then I became concerned that something could've happened to both of you."

If his concern about her personally meant anything to Angie—which it probably didn't—she didn't let on. "Kristi will probably turn up in a day or two," she said. "I can't think she'd do anything foolish or dangerous."

"She's a sensible girl," Ethan said. "A really nice girl."

A moment of awkward silence. Ethan wondered if Angie was curious about his and Kristi's relationship before Kristi had left Phoenix to try for an acting career. But she didn't ask questions. What would his relationships in the intervening years matter to her, anyway?

"Do you know any other friends Kristi's parents or I might contact?" he asked.

"No, I'm afraid not. She had actor and actress friends, but I didn't know them. You'll let me know, though, if you hear anything more about her?"

"Yes. Of course. Look, I'm sorry I bothered you. I was just concerned."

"I'm sorry I can't help. It was . . . good to talk to you."

Truth? Or automatic good manners? Okay, he had manners too. He could chitchat. "You're in Julesburg on vacation?"

"No. Actually, I'm not going back to New York. I've quit modeling. I'm planning to stay here in Julesburg permanently."

"You are?" Ethan felt not so much astonished as blank. This was like hearing Bill Gates had decided to leave Microsoft and move to a one-palm-tree island. "And do what?"

"I've bought the local weekly newspaper, the *Julesburg Herald*. My first edition as editor and publisher will be out next Wednesday."

"Well, this is a surprise." He didn't disbelieve her, of course. He'd even heard a bit of pride in her statement. But he couldn't think this was anything more than a temporary whim. Not that ambitious, determined Angie often gave in to whims. Maybe her move was the result of an I'll-show-you argument with her stockbroker boyfriend.

Ethan finally managed to speak. "Well . . . uh . . . congratulations."

"Thank you. It was an impulsive decision," Angie admitted, as if reading his mind. "But a good one, I think."

*Okay, enough with the stilted politeness.* "What about your stockbroker friend?"

"Burke and I are . . . over."

"I see." He rubbed the sharp edge of his jawbone, what he always found himself doing when he was puzzled about something. "Is that the reason you decided to leave New York?"

"No!"

She was so vehement that Ethan remained silent, waiting for some further explanation. It was not forthcoming.

"Look, it's all kind of complicated," she finally said. "Actually, now that I think about Kristi a little more, I am worried. It really isn't like her not to be in touch with her parents or to quit her job without giving proper notice."

Ethan accepted the detour. "How long since you've seen her?"

"We went out to dinner together a couple of nights before I left New York."

"And you're sure she didn't say anything then about an acting offer or quitting the job she had?"

"No, not that I recall. I thought she was happy with the job. It was an investment company, as you probably know. Kristi was doing secretarial work, but she hoped to move into sales. She thought she could make a lot more money there."

"But you still think she may have quit the job to take an acting role?"

"I can't imagine why else she'd quit. Actually, now that I think about it, she did seem a little hyper at dinner that night. I remember wondering afterward if maybe there was a new man in her life, someone she wasn't ready to talk about yet."

"She could've impulsively taken off with a guy, then?"

"Possibly. Although, knowing Kristi, I doubt it," Angie said. "She just didn't do things like that. But she could also have been excited about the possibility of a new acting role and just didn't want to talk about it yet." Sounding self-conscious, she added, "Sometimes I've had that feeling. That if I talk about something I desperately want, then it won't happen."

24

Ethan couldn't remember ever having that feeling, but he didn't say so. Maybe it was what a woman he'd dated for a while had called "a girl thing." "This company Kristi worked for was connected with your stockbroker friend's Wall Street office?"

"No." She paused a moment as if reconsidering the answer, but she didn't change it. "The investment company is over in Jersey City. That's why Kristi was living over there. We didn't see as much of each other after she moved to Jersey," Angie added, "but I wanted to get together with her before I left New York, and she came over."

"Julesburg must be quite a change after life in the big city."

"A nice change."

Ethan digested that for a moment and then surprised himself probably as much as he surprised her by saying, "Hey, my brother married a girl from Eugene last year, and he's been working in a computer store there. We're buying it together and turning it into our first out-of-Arizona Kearney's Komputers. So I'll be coming up to Oregon sometime within the next couple weeks. Julesburg isn't more than a couple hours' drive from Eugene. I'm thinking maybe . . . ?"

He left the sentence dangling, hoping she would fill in with a breathless invitation. He was wrong.

"Still spelling computers with a K?" she asked.

"Yeah. My grandma says I ought to run it through a spell-checker. She says it's corny. 'Corny' not spelled with a K, as she points out. But it hasn't seemed to hurt business."

"You have . . . what? Two stores now?"

"Two in Phoenix, one in Scottsdale, another in Tempe, and one down in Tucson." He tried to sound modest, but he heard the pride in his voice. He felt his face redden. He'd worked hard, yes, starting with a part-time job in a computer store while he and Angie were both at Arizona

State University. A year after his graduation, while she was a sophomore, he'd bought the store and built from there. But he never let himself forget that the Lord was in control.

"Anyway, I'm going to be up that way before long," he said.

Was he waiting for her to fill in with an invitation? Angie hesitated, her throat suddenly full. Could there be a second chance for them? She clutched the pillow she'd grabbed when she'd recognized Ethan's voice on the phone.

*Oh, Ethan, if you knew the truth, would you want an invitation? Or would you shudder in disgust?*

She pushed the thought from her mind. *The past is behind me,* she told herself again. With a determined casualness, she said, "Give me a call when you're up this way, then, and maybe we can get together."

"I'd like that."

She sat there clutching the pillow after Ethan had hung up. Could he be generous enough to forgive how she'd walked away from him when the golden doors of a modeling career had opened for her . . . and all that had come afterward?

She'd often wondered what Kristi's relationship with Ethan had been back in Phoenix. Kristi had been offhand about it, but Angie suspected there might've been something more than friendship between them.

*Oh, Ethan, I hope she didn't do to you what I did.*

But sweet, elfin Kristi wouldn't have done that. Surely not. And surely her absence didn't signify anything serious.

Angie thought back to that last time she'd seen Kristi. They'd gone to a place called Hattie's, not one of the more trendy restaurants in New York but popular with a young crowd. Afterward, they'd taxied to Angie's apartment so Kristi could try on some clothes Angie wasn't taking with her. They were Mutt-and-Jeff difference in height, but Angie had thought some of her blouses might fit Kristi. Unfortunately nothing had fit, but they'd had a great time giggling and talking.

Kristi was the only person Angie had told about leaving New York, other than the modeling agency and a note for her roommate saying she'd pay her share of the rent until Cate found a new roommate. She'd mailed Burke's Dear-John letter from the airport, afraid that if he knew ahead of time, he'd try to stop her. She'd never settled with herself whether he would've been able to do it.

Now she wondered if Kristi could've had a romantic interest in her boss and had abruptly quit the job when the relationship went sour. Kristi had asked a lot of questions about him, Angie remembered, but she hadn't been able to tell Kristi much. She'd never actually met Jordan Riker and knew little more than his name. She hadn't wanted to rouse Burke's ire by asking personal questions about his partner in the investment company.

Burke and Jordan Riker had set up the company with headquarters in the Bahamas. She'd told Ethan just now that the company wasn't connected with Burke's Wall Street firm, and that was true, but the company was connected with Burke himself. He was always wheeling and dealing. She'd never really known what the business was about, other than that it had something to do with properties in Australia and that Burke had been in Sydney when Kristi was frantically looking for a job.

She'd never let Burke know she'd made a call to Jordan about a job for Kristi. Burke could build a jealous mountain out of the most innocent molehill, and he'd undoubtedly have accused her of some clandestine hanky-panky with his partner. At the time she'd also awkwardly requested Jordan not tell Burke about the call. Jordan had laughed. He'd gotten the message hidden under the request. "Burke's a great guy but about as trusting as an IRS agent, right?"

Right.

The food still smelled good when Angie sat down at the dining room table, but her appetite had fizzled. The more she thought about Kristi, the more uneasy she felt. Accidents happened. Sometimes even more terrible non-accidents happened.

At Ryan and Stef's house, they always said grace before dinner. Angie bowed her head and folded her hands in her lap until Ryan nudged her elbow. She dutifully clasped his hand and reached across the table for Stefanie's. She didn't object to this family ritual during the blessing. And she didn't object to the blessing itself. But somehow, for her, the whole thing just felt . . . fraudulent.

"Angie, you look a little upset," Stefanie said after the blessing, a dish of saffron rice in her hand. "Is something wrong?"

"That was Ethan Kearney on the phone." She glanced at Ryan, wondering if he remembered Ethan.

"I wonder if he was the one who called earlier today. We've kept in touch."

"You have?"

"Yeah. He's a great guy. We recognized each other's names when we were both working on a missionary outreach to Mexico." Ryan glanced at Stefanie, and Angie could tell that he'd told his wife about Angie's past relationship with Ethan.

She tried to dismiss an irrelevant and unwarranted twinge of disappointment that Ethan's keeping in touch with her brother had nothing to do with her. "He wanted to tell me that a mutual friend back in New York seems to be missing. He wondered if I knew anything about her."

Stefanie set the dish of rice back on the table. "Oh, Angie, I hope . . ." She shook her head, her smile rueful. "Out here in Hicksville, we tend to think of New York as overrun with murderers, with a mugging on every street corner. I know that isn't true, but still . . . missing. In a place as big as New York. That's scary."

"Ethan had tried to call me at the apartment. When he couldn't get hold of me, he got to wondering if maybe Kristi and I had gone somewhere together."

"Who is she?" Ryan asked. "A good friend?"

"Yes, she is. Her name is Kristi Yamori, and her family is active in Ethan's church in Phoenix. She did some acting in amateur productions and some television ads too. But her real love is theater. She decided to try to make it as an actress in New York, and Ethan put her in touch with me." That was the last time she and Ethan had spoken before today. "I couldn't be a lot of help to her, though. I know more people in modeling than the theater. But I have introduced her to some contacts, and she's gotten a few small, off-Broadway parts. She's a really sweet girl."

Even though they hadn't seen each other often, Angie had caught Kristi's short-lived performances whenever she could. "I can get you a ticket for opening night," Kristi had offered once. "Or maybe you'd rather wait for closing night? Hey, come to think of it, they're probably one and the same." Angie could giggle with Kristi as she never could with her sophisticated roommate, Cate, who weighed every decision, every relationship, every smile on how it would further her modeling career.

*Look who's criticizing whom,* a tart voice inside her reminded. *But I walked away from it,* she retorted fiercely.

"But Kristi hasn't made it big so far, I take it?" Stefanie asked.

Angie spread the paper napkin on her lap. She automatically slid half a miniature game hen onto her plate from the platter Ryan handed her.

"She ran out of money. She'd been working part-time, waitressing and this and that, like every hopeful actress. But her jobs and tryouts were always conflicting, so she decided she should get a full-time job. She was planning to save up money and then devote her time to making it as an actress. I helped her get a position with an investment firm, and then I loaned her money so she could get an apartment near the job. And she's paid me back every cent. She even wanted to pay interest." She looked down at the napkin in her lap. "Kristi is like that. But I wouldn't let her, of course. I told her just to let me in on a hot deal sometime."

"From what you've said about your friend Burke, you didn't need any hot tips on stocks," Ryan remarked.

True. Burke's financial guidance had been incredible. She had to give him credit there. His expertise was why, even with a high-maintenance lifestyle of $100 brow waxings, $400 facials, $450 haircuts, and $3,000 apartment, she still had a bank account and stock portfolio that barely showed a dent after buying the *Herald*. It was a nice safety net for the big life change she'd undertaken.

"Let's say a prayer for your friend Kristi," Stefanie suggested.

Angie felt panicked for a moment, but then was relieved when Stefanie didn't wait for her to come up with the proper words. If Kristi was in some kind of trouble, better the request for help and protection come from someone on more intimate terms with the Lord.

Angie could remember when she'd prayed every day. That was a long time ago. But maybe one of these days she would again be on those intimate terms with the Lord. After all, she'd turned her back on her old life. That was a first step.

"Lord, we ask that you watch over Angie's friend Kristi," Stefanie murmured. "We ask that you protect and guide Kristi and bring her back safely if she is in some dangerous position. And we ask that you be with her worried family and soon bring them the comfort of knowing she's safe. Amen."

Angie waited for a proper amount of silence and then spoke up. "Well, that should take care of everything," she said brightly. "And now, don't we have a couple of things to celebrate here?"

"Baby for us, newspaper for you," Ryan agreed.

Angie lifted her water glass. "So, congratulations to all of us."

They clicked glasses, Stefanie sloshing her water a little.

"Oh, look at me. If I'm this shaky and excited now, just think what I'll be like when I go into labor."

"What hospital will you go to? Dutton Bay?" Angie asked. Teasingly she added, "Or do you plan to rough it like some ol' wagon-train pioneer? Except that instead of taking a few minutes off from driving oxen, you'll take a short break between aerobics classes at Fit 'n' Fun."

"I'll head for the hospital as soon as I feel so much as a twinge," Stefanie declared. "I'd have made a lousy pioneer. And I'm taking no chances with our baby."

"Did Dr. Halmoose tell you when you can expect to feel the baby move?" Ryan asked.

Stefanie shook her head. "He said that it varies. Usually between the eighteenth and twenty-second weeks. But sometimes it can happen earlier. I know it's probably my imagination, since I'm quite a lot earlier than that, but sometimes I think I can feel little twitches already."

Twitches. The back of Angie's neck prickled. She ducked her head and whacked at the miniature chicken.

# 4

*R*yan and Stefanie went on talking about pregnancy and babies. Tests Dr. Halmoose wanted Stefanie to have. Getting enough calcium and folate. Angie concentrated on turning her Cornish game hen into slivers and rearranging them on her plate. She surreptitiously slipped a larger chunk under the table to Sherlock.

Stefanie reached across the table and tapped Angie on the wrist. "Hey, I'm sorry. Here I am, hogging the celebration."

"Buying a newspaper isn't quite on a level with having a baby," Angie said. The remark came out sounding petty, almost as if she thought Stefanie *was* hogging the spotlight. She tried to turn it into a little joke. "But I won't have to change its diapers."

"What's this big idea you were telling me about?" Ryan asked. "Some special series for the newspaper, you said."

Angie jumped into the subject eagerly, relieved to get away from pregnancy and babies. *I'll try my best to get over my attitude, though,* she vowed. Stefanie deserved enthusiasm, and Angie would give it. On Saturday she'd run over to Dutton Bay and buy a ton of baby clothes for her.

"I've been wandering around town, getting to know my territory. Talking to people and introducing myself and everything. And I've seen several old buildings that look as if they're just full of history and character, so I'm planning a series with an article about each of the buildings."

"Sounds like a great idea," Stefanie agreed. "Use lots of names. People will buy more copies if they see names they know in the paper. Especially their own."

Angie nodded. "There's the brick building Fit 'n' Fun is in, of course, with that wonderful old cupola on top. It was a brewery once, right?"

"Right. A long time ago. I think Prohibition was what did it in as a brewery. My grandfather said a local delegation went back to Washington, D.C. to talk to their senator, but they had a few too many drinks beforehand. Which resulted in a . . . ummm . . . boisterous sort of behavior that weakened their argument against Prohibition."

"Oh, that'll make a great story!" Angie twirled her fork with excitement. "I've also been looking at that old Victorian house down by the motel. The one with a gift shop and a beauty shop in it now."

"Better do it fast," Stefanie advised. "I think the termites holding hands with the carpenter ants is all that's keeping it up right now."

Angie laughed. "And then there's the most fascinating building in town, of course," she said. "The Nevermore."

Site of the town's long-ago unsolved murder, the theater sat on Julesburg's main street, its wood-shingled sides mossy and weather-beaten, a few cryptic letters still clinging to the marquee. Totally nondescript except for that vertical NEVERMORE name sign still straight as a knife blade, and the double front doors painted a garish bloodred.

Stefanie put her fork down and dabbed her mouth with a napkin. She shot Ryan a sideways glance, one of those looks that said something between married couples, the interpretation of which was closed to outsiders.

"Angie, I think your idea of doing an article about the history of the old buildings around town is really great." She sounded as if she were choosing her words carefully.

"But?"

"But I really wish you'd just . . . ignore the Nevermore. There are plenty of wonderful historic places without it. How about the old lighthouse that Lighthouse Hill is named for? It isn't used anymore, but it's still standing."

Sure. The lighthouse was a great idea. But . . .

"I can't ignore the Nevermore. It's the most interesting building in town. And with that murder to spice up the story, well . . ."

Angie started to look to Ryan for support but then remembered he hadn't shown any enthusiasm about her interest in the old murder.

"The Nevermore isn't known for being kind to those who show an interest in it," Ryan said now, as if he were also phrasing his words carefully.

"I don't understand," Angie said. She remembered a real estate company's FOR SALE sign tacked on the theater. "Is it owned by some local big shot, and you think writing about the murder will step on his toes or interfere with a sale? Maybe some businessman who'd be unhappy enough to stop advertising with the *Herald*?"

"Actually, the owners live out of state. California, I think," Ryan said. "At one time they'd planned to move here and reopen the theater, but Mike at Julesburg Realty says the husband was badly burned in an odd electrical accident."

"So why not write about it?"

Another glance exchanged between Stefanie and Ryan. Angie sometimes found herself envious of those intimate husband-and-wife exchanges. But now they were merely frustrating.

"I know this will probably sound foolish, but so many people connected with the Nevermore have had terrible misfortunes," Stefanie said.

"Misfortunes can happen to anyone," Angie pointed out. "Sooner or later, they do happen to everyone. Besides, you don't really believe that the Nevermore had anything to do with those things."

"Well, no, not exactly. But some people think the woman who owned the theater at the time of the murder put some sort of curse on it that brings disaster down on anyone associated with it."

"You mean the place is supposed to be haunted? Oh, I love that! The Ghost of the Nevermore."

"No, not a ghost," Stefanie said. "No one has ever seen or heard anything unusual there. It's just that . . . bad things happen to anyone connected with the theater."

"It is kind of a creepy place," Ryan said. "The woman who owned the place committed suicide right there in the lobby."

"You've been inside?"

"I went there once with a friend who was thinking about buying the place and turning it into offices. And Stef, of course, actually went to movies there."

"How did the woman do it?" Angie asked.

"There's a big mirror behind the candy counter. She hung herself right in front of it," Stefanie said. "So she could see herself, people say."

"It's . . . spooky to look in that mirror and think about this woman looking at herself as she died," Ryan said. "Look too long and you start thinking you might even be able to see her dangling there right behind you." He laughed as if he felt self-conscious about admitting such a thing.

"I heard she was into some kind of spiritualism for a while," Stefanie added. "Trying to contact the dead, séances, all that weird kind of stuff. Some of the more far-out stories say she stirred up some evil spirit who decided to attach itself to the theater."

"And that's it?" Angie asked. "Some old murder happens there and a few people have bad luck, and suddenly everybody gets all superstitious about the place?" That her smart, sassy sister-in-law could be included among the superstitious was incredible. That her brother—practical, no-nonsense Ryan—apparently held some misgivings about the old theater was even more incredible.

"Is this kind of thinking, um, Christian?" she asked.

Stefanie sat up straighter, as if the question was a reality punch to the spine. She and Ryan exchanged glances again. "Dabbling in superstitious nonsense isn't, that's for sure."

"So . . . ?"

Stefanie smiled and lifted her hands. "Okay, chalk it all up to pregnant-woman hormones on a rampage. I've had this strange craving for pickled pigs' feet too."

"Pickled pigs' feet?" Angie repeated. "Yuck." She eyed the salad dressing suspiciously. It was the only item on the table that she figured could conceal unknown ingredients.

"It's safe," Stefanie assured her.

"Good." Angie's appetite had revved up, and she scooped up a forkful of saffron rice.

Ryan grinned. "Maybe the raging hormones are catching. Although I'll skip the pickled pigs' feet, thank you. It's just that we care about you, little sis. We worry about you. We're so glad you're here, and we want you to stay and be happy. Marry some logger or fisherman or high-tech laser whiz. Produce a herd of kids to play with ours."

A herd of kids. Angie blinked. Her appetite took another nosedive. She sidestepped a hard landing with another question. "So what's this ghost-that's-not-a-ghost supposed to have done to give the Nevermore such a bad reputation?"

Stefanie gave her a rundown. "A man inherited the theater from his cousin, the one who killed herself—Amelia Swarthout was her name—and he also committed suicide. Then there were later owners or people connected with the theater who suffered a variety of calamities and disasters. There was a fire in the upstairs projection room. No insurance, so the people dropped whatever project they had in mind. A supper club idea that fell flat—"

"And was a dumb idea to begin with," Ryan commented.

"And some bigger disasters. A heart attack killed one man. Another owner's son was on a commercial fishing boat that overturned at sea, and his body was never found. Another married couple had arranged to buy the place but was killed in a freak boat accident. And then there's the current owner, who was burned so badly in a peculiar electrical accident."

"And the two wonderful young women, twins, actually, who started to buy the theater only recently. One of them was murdered," Ryan added.

That was one of the murders Angie recalled reading about when she was skimming the stacks of old *Heralds*. "It's a sobering list," she admitted. "But still . . ."

"Still just a string of unfortunate coincidences," Stefanie agreed.

"But you'd prefer I skip the Nevermore in my series."

"I guess I do," Stefanie admitted. "Maybe it's like a curve on a road where several bad accidents have happened. If you're prudent, you think about those accidents and slow down when you come to the curve. Or take a different route and avoid it completely."

There was a big difference between a dangerous curve on a road and the string of bad-luck coincidences surrounding people connected with the Nevermore. But Angie didn't want to say that her brother and sister-in-law were wading in the deep end, so all she said was, "Even if there is a so-called curse, just writing a history

37

of the Nevermore would hardly be connection enough to earn my way onto the bad-luck list."

"You're gonna investigate and write about the Nevermore and the murder, aren't you?" Ryan grumbled.

Angie gave an exaggerated sigh. "Okay, come right out and say it. Sister Angie is stubborn, headstrong, pigheaded—"

"You journalists do have a way with words," Ryan said with a grin. "No need for me to add anything to that wonderfully descriptive list."

"But what's that old motto? Neither snow nor rain nor heat nor gloom of night shall deter me from my—"

"That's the postman's motto," Ryan scoffed. "Not—"

"I'm a postman of sorts. I deliver the news."

"Which means you're going to go ahead with including the Nevermore in your series."

"Of course, I am. It wouldn't be a comprehensive series without it."

Her sister-in-law reached across the table and squeezed Angie's hand. "Just be careful, okay?"

Angie nodded, even though she felt a bit foolish agreeing to be vigilant around a weather-beaten old movie theater, even one with bloodred doors.

# 5

ngie raced out to cover a chimney fire in a
duplex the following morning. She got a photo
of one of the firemen carrying the family dog
to safety. If nothing better turned up, it would make the
front page of next Wednesday's *Herald*.

On Saturday she had the film developed at a one-hour
photo stand in Dutton Bay. She knew big newspapers
used something more high tech than the 35mm camera
that had come with the *Herald*, but the color prints looked
good. Madge had showed her how to use the scanner to
change photos to sharp black-and-white prints ready to
be waxed to a layout page.

Next she went to a newly opened Wal-Mart and picked
up items for her new living quarters. Stefanie had said
she had plenty of extra dishes, silverware, and pans to
give her, but Angie bought bedding, a heavy throw to
hide the plaid of the sofa, towels, and a toaster, plus a big
sack of baby things. She didn't select the baby items piece
by piece, just told the clerk she wanted a lot of nice things
for a newborn and took what the clerk handed her.

She felt guilty that evening when Stefanie raved about
her choices, but she managed to accept the enthusiasm without confessing her limited involvement in the selection.

_Undertow_

On Sunday morning, while Stefanie and Ryan were at church, she hauled her belongings over to the house on Highland. There wasn't a lot to move. She'd left most of her expensive clothes in the New York apartment, telling Cate in the note that she could have them or toss them or whatever.

She then decided to leave the putting-away until evening. The fall day was sunny with only a few puff-ball clouds scattered across blue sky—perfect for a walk on the beach. She picked up Sherlock for company, leaving a note for Ryan and Stefanie that she'd borrowed their dog.

She took off her shoes and spent all afternoon on the long curve of sand and rock south of Julesburg, walking, jogging, and tossing sticks for Sherlock. Or just standing back when sand flew as he went into a frenzy of digging. One dig produced a rotting fish skeleton, another an equally smelly dead seagull.

"Sherlock, you need to learn to be more selective," she scolded. "Think treasure, not dead stuff."

Next time the energetic dog obliged and dug up a waterlogged tennis shoe. This was an improvement, and she patted him on the head. "Good dog."

When they were both tired, she collapsed on the sand with her back against a log, her face and bare toes lifted to the sunshine.

"So I'll probably freckle," she said to Sherlock. "So what?"

With a lazy flop of tail, Sherlock agreed. So what?

Several hours later, she dropped him off at the empty house. Church was long over, but Stefanie and Ryan had apparently gone somewhere for the afternoon. On the way to her new home, not being prepared to jump into the role of cook and household goddess just yet, she stopped at a pizza place called Website X and picked up a vegetarian sub for dinner. Back at her house, she

40

thought she'd make a cup of coffee from the packet of instant she'd appropriated from Stefanie's kitchen, only to discover the house furnishings did not include a microwave. Worse yet, she then discovered she didn't even have electricity. With a sinking feeling, she dashed to the phone. Dead.

"I can't believe this," she muttered. Her first inclination was to retreat to Stef and Ryan's place until she could arrange for the civilized necessities. Who could live without electricity and phone? And a hot shower?

On second thought, she decided that was the old Angie's attitude. The new, I'm-in-Julesburg-now Angie washed sand out of her toes with cold water, then drove to the Shop 'n' Save and bought candles and matches.

She was glad she did. She enjoyed a relaxing evening sitting on her back step, eating her submarine sandwich and listening to the distant roar of surf. The remnants of a sunset lingered in the west, the undersides of incoming clouds streaked with rose and gold. A squirrel slithered through the picket fence and industriously investigated pinecones in the weedy grass. A thorny bush, so scraggly it was almost leafless, still displayed two perfect pink roses. A snag silhouetted on the ridge of a nearby hill looked like some ancient finger pointing to the sky.

Or to God?

It had been a long time since she'd felt inclined to talk to the Lord. She'd been in beautiful spots all over the world, spots more stunning than this by far. But there was something about the simple beauty here that made her more conscious of what God had created than she'd ever been at those more exotic locations.

*Thank you for bringing me here, Lord. You know I'm working on myself, don't you? I'm getting my act cleaned up. Just give me time, okay?*

Angie didn't have a chance to start looking into the history of the Nevermore on Monday. It was a madhouse of a day.

First, she had to call about getting the electricity turned on and the phone hooked up at the house. She'd planned to ask for an unlisted phone number, but at the last minute opted for a regular number and even changed the masthead on the *Herald* to list her new after-hours phone number. If Burke wanted to find her, he would, whether or not her phone was unlisted.

People rushed in during the day with last-minute ads to beat the deadline for the week's edition. Becky had called in sick, so Angie wrestled with the computer to turn out an attractive display ad for the local beauty shop. The old computer wasn't much newer than the ones she'd worked with back in college, but its age also meant it wasn't totally beyond her technical capabilities. She unpacked boxes of grocery ad inserts, searched for the copy of an ad that Reedy's Hardware and Variety wanted to run again, and placated a man who was outraged about a previous classified ad that listed his old Ford van at $150 instead of $1,500.

"Old rusted-out piece of junk is barely worth a buck fifty, let alone $1,500," Madge muttered when he left, refund in hand.

What Angie was thinking was that maybe she should've bought the old van herself. She hadn't owned a car in New York—not worth the bother, since taxis and limousines were so much more convenient—and Ryan had helped her pick out the compact Corolla over in Dutton Bay. Which was before she realized she'd be hauling around 2,500 copies of a weekly newspaper.

Yet for all that hustle and bustle of activity, Angie knew from studying the accounting records that the *Herald* needed more advertising for good financial health. The previous owners had managed with whatever advertising business came through the door, plus a few phone calls to local businesses, but she'd have to pound the streets to sell ads if this was going to be a profitable enterprise.

In her "spare" time, she worried about Kristi, thought about Ethan, and wondered about Burke. Had he simply accepted the end of their relationship? He liked wearing a high-profile model on his arm. He liked long, golden hair, sexy clothes, and paparazzi popping flashbulbs when they were out on the town. She hadn't been the first. But once she'd abandoned modeling and New York, maybe he'd just written her off and picked up a new arm ornament. He'd definitely have no use for a small-town newspaper editor working the wrong side of a camera.

But she knew quiet acceptance wasn't Burke's style. She shivered, remembering his possessiveness. The scene he'd made one time when she had lunch with a guy from college who'd looked her up. The way he sometimes showed up at a photo shoot, aggressively "checking things out." For a long time she'd been flattered by his jealous attention—until she figured out that the possessiveness was more about control than love. Ego would surely get in the way of acceptance of her leaving; if a relationship ended, he had to be the one to end it.

Even so, she worried considerably more about Kristi than Burke. Ethan hadn't called back. Was that good news or bad? Good, because it meant nothing terrible had happened to Kristi, or he'd have called. Bad, because it also meant Kristi hadn't turned up yet.

Tuesday was page-layout day, also hectic. By the fourth time she'd rearranged the front page, she felt like tossing all the headlines and news articles into the air and letting them land where they may.

"It's like trying to put a jigsaw puzzle together," she grumbled to Madge as she cut an inch off a syndicated column about gardening to make room for the senior citizens' lunch menu on page two. "Except I don't think all the pieces are from the same box."

"I make patchwork quilts in my spare time, the complicated kind with a zillion little pieces," Madge said. She nodded toward the page layout where she was filling a blank space with a joke from their filler collection. "There's a certain similarity."

Neither of them got out of the office until almost 9:00 that evening.

On Wednesday morning Angie ran the page layouts up to the high-speed printer in Coos Bay, collected the 2,500 completed copies a couple of hours later, rushed back to the office to do the grocery ad inserts, distributed the copies to stores in Julesburg and the surrounding area, took mail subscription copies to the post office, and finally plopped down in the seat of her Corolla. *Am I out of my mind? I paid real money to own this business, just so I could bounce around like some steel ball in a pinball machine?*

But at the end of the day, after a call from Ryan telling her the issue looked great and another call from the beauty shop owner reporting they'd had more appointments than usual after the ad came out, she felt good.

*As good as seeing your face on the cover of* Cosmopolitan? asked the little voice inside her that had long ago stopped acting as conscience and now served more as resident cynic.

*Yes. Better.*

And never mind that she hadn't fulfilled that once-burning ambition to be on the *Cosmo* cover. That too was behind her.

On Thursday morning, things quieted down. Madge didn't work Thursdays, and Becky was taking care of the front desk. Angie followed a police conversation on the radio scanner for a car accident, which turned out to be a non-newsworthy fender bender. When she returned to

44

the office, she started searching through old issues of the *Herald* to see what she could dig up about the Nevermore and the murder, but then she decided to save that for bedtime reading at home. She figured Becky was too young to know much about the Nevermore's past, but she asked anyway during their coffee break.

Becky was guiltlessly enjoying an apple fritter with her coffee. Angie hadn't yet reached that level of food freedom; she was just sipping coffee. Black. But she wasn't doing anything drastic to stay slim these days either.

"I've never been in the old theater," Becky said in answer to Angie's question. "I can't even remember back to when it actually *was* a working movie theater. But my folks used to go to movies there when they were in high school. The local making-out hangout, I guess. But for as long as I can remember, it's just been a rundown old place somebody every now and then has had big ideas about remodeling. Turn it into offices or a mini-mall or civic building or something."

"But some disaster always happens."

"Seems that way." Becky dunked a chunk of fritter in her cream-laced coffee.

*And the girl doesn't have an extra pound on her,* Angie marveled. She knew models who would kill for a metabolism like that. And skin, if you wanted to get cosmetic-ad rhapsodic, like wild roses and cream.

"So what do you think of the old stories about the place being cursed or haunted or something?" Angie asked.

Becky's brown ponytail swung as she laughed. "Does anybody really believe that stuff?"

"But the stories don't die."

"Well, a lot of bad things have happened to people who got involved with the place," Becky admitted. "I guess you won't find anyone who's been around Julesburg for a long time particularly eager to buy it."

"Nobody believes the superstitions. But they play it safe and avoid involvement anyway?"

"That's about it."

"I wish I knew who all's owned it over the years, so I could actually check into what happened to them." Angie was mostly musing to herself, but to her surprise Becky came up with a practical answer.

"The title company up in Dutton Bay could check ownership records at the courthouse. My folks recently bought some acreage, and right away the title company found some peculiarity about an old mortgage in their search of the records. But I suppose it could cost a lot. Maybe you could figure out how to do it yourself."

Finances, even if the *Herald* was not exactly a money machine, were not an issue. Thanks to Burke, there was that safety net. "I'll contact the experts and leave it to them."

Becky set her cup down. "Angie, would it bother you if I ask something about modeling and how you got started?"

"No, of course not."

"I just got the impression you'd had . . . maybe an unpleasant experience or something and came here because of it. And would rather not talk about it."

"I've walked away from modeling, that's true. But I don't mind talking about modeling as a job." She looked at Becky more closely. An attractive, slender, wholesome girl. But not model material.

As if reading Angie's mind, Becky laughed. "No, no, not me. Aaron and I are going to get married and take over his dad's commercial fishing boat. It's my cousin Stacy, up in Coos Bay. She wanted me to ask about how you got started."

"Well, as a teenager I won a few beauty contests." Angie laughed. "Miss Demolition Derby at a stock car race track. Miss Desert Rose Mall. I'd enter anything. Then in college I got in a contest that was bigger and more important, and as the winner I got my expenses paid to the finals in Dallas. A woman from a big modeling agency was there. She invited me to come to New York, and I did. And I was on my way."

"That's all there was to it?"

"Well, first they had to make me over. Hair too curly, eyebrows too bushy, thighs too jiggly. For a while I wondered why they'd wanted me, given how wrong I apparently was."

"But you had the right basics."

"I guess. And then I spent most of a year in France and part of a year in Japan. I worked my buns off, getting experience and learning the ropes, before they gave me the chance to start modeling in New York. You definitely have to put career before everything else."

*And be willing to give up a lot. A lot.*

"Maybe my cousin could make it. She's tall and gorgeous. She was Crab Queen at a local festival last year."

Angie smiled at the familiar sound of that. She'd been Miss Cotton Candy once. "It isn't as glamorous when you actually get into modeling, unlike what most people think. There's a lot of getting up before dawn and sitting and waiting that's really boring. And the competition is incredible, with a lot of backstabbing. Unless you're one of the really big supermodels, there's also a lot of rejection. It costs a fortune to live in New York too. And except for a few very special models, it's not an occupation that's going to last a lot of years."

Such warnings wouldn't matter to Becky's cousin, of course, if she really had her heart set on modeling. Angie had heard those warnings too, but once she'd realized that having her face and body on covers and in magazine and TV ads was actually within reach, nothing else mattered. She'd have crawled over hot coals—or the backs of anyone who got in the way—to make it.

"Could you tell me the name of the modeling agency you were with, so I can tell Stacy?"

Angie hesitated. She didn't want to be unhelpful to a young hopeful. But neither did she want to send the girl down the route she'd taken. Yet a name was no magic door; hundreds of girls showed up at the agency every year, and most never got past the receptionist. She scribbled the name on a piece of scratch paper and handed it to Becky. "My name won't do her any good as a reference there," she warned. "I'm not exactly on their A-list these days."

Their coffee break was just about over, so Angie briskly turned to the phone. She'd jotted down the number of the real estate company on the sign tacked to the old theater, and now she called and made arrangements to see the inside with a sales agent named Estelle Reeves. A half hour later, they met at the red doors.

Up close, Angie could see that runny ridges had globbed the paint, giving it an unpleasant, dried-blood appearance. But which, as Angie pointed out to herself with a mental kick at her gory imagination, only indicated a sloppy painter, not some bloody-fingered ghost.

Estelle Reeves turned out to be middle-aged and trim, her hair cut smartly short and sleek and tinted an attractive champagne blond. Her boots were high-heeled, the collar of her jacket stylishly upturned.

"I really appreciate this," Angie said as Estelle turned her back on a spike of wind and put an oversized key in the lock.

The gorgeous weather of the previous weekend had changed to low-hanging clouds, dismal spatters of rain, and an erratic wind. Angie had already told the woman what her interest in the theater was and that she wasn't a potential buyer. Estelle had been cheerfully cooperative anyway.

48

"Maybe the publicity will help sell this turkey," Estelle said. She smiled. "Pardon. I mean this awesome example of early Julesburg architecture. I just can't imagine why someone decided to put this kiss-of-death paint on the doors."

Estelle's husky voice and down-to-earth manner unexpectedly complemented rather than detracted from her stylish appearance. A woman who could tell a risqué joke or two, Angie suspected.

With a grimace of distaste when she touched the red paint, Estelle pushed the door open and felt for a light switch. Angie followed her inside. The dim light revealed a lobby with red carpet, decidedly threadbare, wallpaper that perhaps had once been gold-flecked but was now a leprous yellow, and a huge mirror behind a curved candy counter.

Angie stopped short as she stared at her reflection. The mirror gave her eyes an unnatural brilliance, her cheeks a skeletal gauntness. The lobby lights suddenly flickered, and hints of movement wavered in the shadowy corners behind her.

*Ryan was right,* she thought. It didn't take much imagination to picture a lifeless body dangling from a rope just beyond her left shoulder. A little more imagination and she might feel that rope tightening around her own throat.

*Get off it, girl,* she scoffed. *It's just an old mirror, not some window into the past.*

Then she changed her mind. *No, remember this peculiar feeling. Get it into the article. Great spooky ambiance.*

Estelle didn't appear to be affected by any ambiance. She waved a hand in front of her nose. "Wow. This place needs a good airing out and a dose of Lysol spray, don't you think? Smells as nasty as a closet full of my grandson's dirty sweatshirts."

49

Angie realized she'd been rubbing her throat and lowered her hand. "There are all kinds of superstitious stories about this old place. You've heard them, I suppose?"

"Oh, yes, all those old wives' tales. The murder. The suicides. The disasters that happen to anyone who gets involved with the theater in any way." Estelle rolled her nicely lined eyes.

"I take it you're not impressed?"

"We've had the place listed ever since I started working at the agency about a year ago, and I've shown it several times. That's involvement, isn't it? But unless this ghost is currently fixated on breaking fingernails—" Estelle frowned at a miniscule split in one of her immaculate, French-manicured nails—"I haven't had any disasters to speak of."

"What sort of people want to look at this place?"

"Oh, touristy types mostly. On a rainy day, getting a guided tour through local property often strikes people as a great way to spend an hour or two. And the idea of owning a rundown theater in a small coastal town seems to start lots of people dreaming. But common sense apparently intrudes before they plunk down any money."

A flicker of motion made Angie peer cautiously behind the ornate counter. A skinny gray tail was disappearing into a pile of oddly assorted items. A length of old red velvet fabric, a shard of porcelain sink, bits of wallpaper, and a letter J that looked as if it might've hung on the marquee at one time.

"A good general housecleaning wouldn't hurt, along with that Lysol," Angie said.

Estelle nodded. "How's that for melodrama?" she said as she pointed to the clock over the red velvet curtain draping the doorway into the main part of the theater. It was stopped exactly at midnight. "The witching hour."

"I understand that the current owner had a peculiar electrical accident, and that's why they want to sell it," Angie said. She lifted her eyebrows. "Part of the curse?"

"The guy was using some huge, long metal ladder to rescue a neighbor's ferret—a ferret, mind you—from a tree and hit a power line. Roasted him like a hot dog. Strikes me as more stupid or careless than peculiar. And definitely not the work of some spook reaching a long arm down to southern California. Assuming spooks even have arms."

*Now here's a woman not inclined to either superstition or gra tuitous sympathy,* Angie decided. No ghost would ever dare to haunt Estelle Reeves. "Would you mind if I take some photos?" she asked.

"Photo away. Maybe you'll catch the spook on the prowl."

Angie took several shots of the old lobby. A criss-crossing of boards blocked the stairs going up to what she assumed was a projection room. Had the old fire damage never been repaired?

Estelle pushed the velvet drape aside, and they moved into the sloped seating area. The theater had been quite grand in its day, Angie realized. Seats padded with red velvet, muted lighting from gold sconces high on the walls, gold satin curtain concealing the screen.

"I wonder where in here the man was murdered?" Angie asked. "And why?"

"I have no idea."

"Do you know who he was?"

"Fiancé of the strange woman who owned the theater, or so I've heard. Although I'm not sure if she was strange before the murder or got that way afterward. I understand she used to dress up in costume and roam up and down the aisle, emoting lines from *Gone with the Wind.* Before she committed suicide, that is. I don't think anyone claims to have seen her doing it since then."

"I wonder why it's called the Nevermore. It isn't exactly one of your usual movie-theater-type names."

"Beats me."

"I wonder if there's anyone still around who knew the woman? And the man who was murdered?"

"Oh, I'm sure there is. Probably a number of people, actually. You might try an elderly lady named Myrna Bettenworth. She's been around here since Year One, I believe. She recently listed the lot adjoining her house on Howard Street with us. A bit of a jungle right now, but a few hours with a bulldozer could fix that."

Angie snapped several more photos, then asked, "Can we look around in back, behind the screen?"

"Help yourself. I won't go with you, if you don't mind. You've heard of werewolves? Last time I was here I saw a creature back there that looked as if it might qualify as a were-rat. No, I'll just stay right here and see if I can fix what the spook did to my fingernail." Estelle dug an emery board out of her purse and settled on a wrought-iron stool from the cashier's cage.

Angie made her way down the worn aisle and up the steps to the stage. She ducked behind the slithery curtain. Up close, the gold satin was dull and shabby around the edges, soiled along the bottom. One end drooped, as if the entire thing might collapse at any moment. No lights were on in back of the curtain and the screen, but she fished out the tiny keychain flashlight she kept in her purse. Its slender beam of light illuminated the bulky shape of a metal monstrosity with large, cylindrical appendages leading off into the shadows. Some sort of old-fashioned furnace, she decided. It was set in a pit, apparently so heavy that the raised floor couldn't support it. Three steps led down to a narrow pathway around the furnace as access for maintenance and servicing.

The raised floor back here behind the screen was uneven, perhaps warped by moisture, and she stumbled several times over twisted boards and trash. It looked as if this had been the dumping spot for everything from discarded rags to a section of battered movie seats.

She heard a couple of rustles but didn't spot anything of the rodent genre. A back door that she at first thought was locked turned out to be, on closer inspection, nailed shut. This door also appeared to be the only one available for emergency exit—definitely not a situation that would sit well with modern building and fire inspectors. And neither would all that trash.

Indeed a creepy place, with or without the ominous reputation. Not one she'd care to stumble around in on a dark night. Actually, she realized, she'd had enough of the Nevermore's ambiance. The stale air felt as if it still held some of Amelia Swarthout's last breaths.

She hurriedly snapped a few more flashbulb photos and headed back up the aisle. At the entrance to the lobby she grabbed the velvet drape, yanking it aside as Estelle had done, so she could pass through.

And instantly was plunged into blackness.

## 6

*A*ngie froze as the heavy old velvet drape enveloped her like a shroud. She knew what it was, and yet a peculiar feeling that it wasn't just a hunk of rotting fabric, that it was a thing alive with evil, paralyzed her muscles. Her head reeled as if from some unknown blow. She couldn't see, couldn't move.

Her mind dipped into a slow spin. Disorientation tilted her sense of direction. She tried to stretch out her arms, but they wouldn't move. They felt weak and useless against the strength of the heavy velvet trapping them against her body.

A musty scent, like something long dead, clogged her nostrils. Disorientation turned to panic. *I can't move! I can't breathe!*

The panic overcame her frozen muscles. She flailed against the shroud, battling it with a frenzy of fists and elbows and knees and feet, fighting her way up from the depths, ramming through the suffocating weight.

She scrambled out from under the drape and gasped for breath. Estelle stood there gaping at her, emery board in hand.

Angie swiped a hand through her hair, panic shifting to a wave of embarrassment as she eyed the tangle of red velvet at her feet.

It was, after all, nothing more than an old velvet drape. No reason to go at it like something out of an old Three Stooges comedy.

There was also, she now saw, nothing mysterious about the drape's collapse. The doubled velvet fabric was attached with brass rings to a metal rod, and her yank had flung the metal rod out of its holder. The heavy metal rod must've been what walloped her on the head.

All very everyday and normal.

She explored the top of her scalp cautiously but found no lump forming. Even though it felt as if a baseball bat had thudded down on her head, the thick velvet drape had padded the blow of the metal rod.

So no damage done—except to her nerves.

"Well, that was a bit spooky," Estelle observed. "Are you all right?"

Angie cleared her dry throat. "I don't know what got into me. I've never been claustrophobic, but I felt like . . ." *Like what? Like something had hold of me and wouldn't let go.*

She wasn't about to admit to that flurry of wild imagination, though. She brushed at a few velvet fibers that had sifted onto her shoulders and quelled an urge to abandon the lobby and rush headlong into the fresh air outside.

"I'd better put the drape back the way it was."

"Oh, don't bother. Just kick it over there behind the counter with that other pile of stuff." Estelle inspected Angie shrewdly. "Some people would be inclined to sue over something like this, you know. Traumatized by collapsing drapery. Terrible mental anguish and all that."

Angie managed a laugh. "Sue who? The spook?"

She dragged the wrought-iron stool over to the doorway. As she stood on the padded top, she could see now why the brass rod had fallen. Again, nothing mysterious. A holder that was supposed to keep the rod in place was broken. She'd just yanked the drape too hard.

But it would still work. Estelle lifted one end of the rod, and together they manhandled everything back into place. The drapery was fully as heavy as it had felt holding her down. *No wonder I thought I was suffocating. The thing feels solid enough to stop bullets.*

She climbed down from the stool and wiped her hands against her thighs. "I guess I've seen all there is to see. What's the price?"

"Just over a hundred thousand." Estelle's tone implied the owners would come down in price. "Actually, it's a sturdy old building. And a large, well-located lot, one of the best in town, if boom times ever come to Julesburg."

"Fat chance?"

Estelle laughed. "Probably. Although I've made a decent living selling real estate since we came here last year. Not getting rich, of course, but not bad. New people are always moving in. Or out. You looking to buy, now that you own the *Herald*?"

"Just renting for now. But maybe later."

"Well, let me know when you start thinking about buying, and we'll get you into something suitable. Prices are down a little right now." Estelle patted her perfect hair. "I'm looking forward to your piece about the Nevermore," she added.

Angie smiled. "If the spook doesn't zap me before I get it written."

That afternoon she attended a play at the elementary school and used as many names as she could when she wrote up an account of it. Parents bought newspapers, after all. She also started her get-out-and-sell-ads campaign. She talked the Julesburg Café into a display ad that listed their daily specials, and the gift shop into enlarging its ad from business-card size to four by five inches.

And the bluntly named Second Hand Stuff store, which had never advertised in the *Herald* before, agreed to a small tryout ad.

After doing that, she called Stefanie at Fit 'n' Fun to get the dates of the long-ago murder and suicide so she could look up appropriate issues of the *Herald* to take home and read. Early seventies was as close as Stefanie could come on the murder, early eighties on Amelia Swarthout's suicide.

Angie had no difficulty locating a couple of issues that referred to the suicide, but she could find nothing at all about the long-ago murder. What she did find was that issues from four months in 1972 were missing. She could already see that early issues of the newspaper tended to treat unpleasant news rather circumspectly, but surely murder couldn't have been completely ignored. She figured the missing issues must be the ones containing accounts of the murder and follow-up investigation. Odd.

She ate a good lingcod dinner at the Julesburg Café, then caught a meeting of the city council in the same building that housed the town library. This was the former location of Julesburg's city police department, Ryan had said, but last year the council had voted to do away with the two-man city department and contract with the county sheriff's office for police protection.

The meeting was dull and routine but blessedly brief, and Angie was home by 8:30. She showered away the dust from the theater still clinging to her hair, slipped into pajamas, and settled into bed with an armload of old *Herald*s on the floor beside her.

The account of Amelia Swarthout's suicide was not as stilted as the treatment of some other local tragedies, but it stuck to bare facts and detoured the sensational.

The outside door of the Nevermore had been locked, it said. Amelia's body, hanging in the lobby, was discovered by Neila Moore, a young woman arriving for her job as ticket seller. No mention was made of the murder in the theater years earlier. A follow-up article indicated there had been minimal investigation into the death. Amelia had left no note, but her affairs were in order, and there was apparently no doubt that she'd taken her own life. The only photo was of the outside of the Nevermore. In black and white, the color of the doors was not discernable, but otherwise the building appeared much the same as it did now. Then, as now, there was something oddly menacing about the bold slash of the upright sign with its inexplicable name.

An obituary in the next issue listed a cousin as Amelia's only living relative and gave respectful treatment to the prominence of her parents in the community. Warren and Althea Swarthout had "preceded their daughter in death," although no dates were given. If Amelia had ever been married, she apparently was not at the time of her death. Angie caught a subtle implication that she had never married, even though her birth and death dates indicated she was in her early fifties when she died.

Since issues of the *Herald* that covered the earlier murder weren't available, she'd brought home a random selection of other issues, hoping to run across something useful. She did find an account of the fire in the projection room, but no cause was given, nor was the owner at the time named. In an earlier issue, she found a picture of Amelia at a ceremony honoring her large donation toward buying a fire truck for the town. The photo was taken from too far away to tell much about the woman, other than that she appeared tall and almost skeletally thin. The bouffant style of her hair and the shiny material of her dress looked a bit cocktailish for the occasion.

Angie made mental notes for the following day. *Ask Madge what she knows about the murder, contact the title company in Dutton Bay, and try to see Myrna Bettenworth, the lady Estelle had mentioned.*

She was yawning and ready to turn out the light when the phone beside her bed rang. She glanced at her small digital clock. 11:10 already? She was surprised at how long she'd been engrossed in the old newspapers.

Surprised too by such a late call. Ryan and Stefanie usually didn't stay up past ten. Burke, maybe?

Her nerves jittered as the phone rang again, but she set aside speculation about the caller and simply spoke a brisk hello. A news tip could arrive at any hour.

"Angie, I'm sorry to bother you this late. This is Ethan. Ryan gave me your number."

Apprehension thudded in her throat. "You've heard something about Kristi?"

"Yes."

## 7

'm sorry," Ethan said. "It's not good."

Angie clenched her fist around the phone cord. "What happened?"

"The authorities back East called Kristi's parents last night. They've been holding the body of a young woman they hadn't been able to identify. The Yamoris flew back there this morning, and they called me just a few minutes ago. The body is Kristi's."

"Oh, Ethan, no."

"They'd tried to reach me earlier this evening, but I wasn't home because of an emergency at the Scottsdale store. That's why I'm calling so late. Mr. Yamori was too shaken to tell me much in the way of details, but there's no doubt about one thing. Kristi was murdered."

Angie hugged her knees to her chest. All she could do was repeat the same helpless words. "Oh, no . . ."

"She was found in an alley behind a vacant building in a rundown area. I don't know if the authorities think she was murdered there or killed elsewhere and . . . and dumped there."

Angie's stomach felt as if she'd just dropped twenty stories in a free-fall elevator. Kristi. Sweet, elfin Kristi. With the snappy, dark eyes that sometimes bubbled with mischief, sometimes burned with indignation. Kristi giggling, Kristi doing one of her wild imitations or telling a new "lightbulb" joke, Kristi throwing her heart into an acting role that wasn't worthy of her talent. Kristi dead. Murdered.

"How . . ." She couldn't swallow past the constriction in her throat. "How was she . . . ?"

"Stabbed. She'd been dead at least a week, maybe longer, when she was found. And then the body was in the morgue for even longer than that because they couldn't identify her. They connected with the Yamoris through the missing person report."

"It must've happened within a few days of when I last saw her."

"It looks that way."

"Does this mean someone deliberately removed anything that would help identify her?"

"Possibly," Ethan said. "Although not necessarily. If someone stole her purse, all her identification went with it, of course."

"Someone murdered her . . . stabbed her . . . to steal her purse?"

"Also possible. But it appears that taking the purse may have been more incidental than the real point of the crime."

She sensed something behind Ethan's words. She pulled a blanket over her cold shoulders and massaged a foot that had gone numb and icy. "Are they saying she was sexually assaulted?"

"That's something else I'm not clear about. But I'm afraid it's probable, given the circumstances."

Raped. Murdered. Left in a dirty alley. The coldness in Angie's foot crept up and settled in the pit of her stomach.

"Do they have any suspects?" she asked.

"Yes, there's a suspect. Which doesn't actually make him identifiable, unfortunately. And they don't have him in custody."

"I don't understand."

"I don't keep up on big-city crime back East. The local newspaper is full of enough of it happening right here in Phoenix. But I understand there's a serial killer in the New York area who leaves a specific mark on his victims."

"Yes, there's one they've been calling the Question Mark Killer. He's killed four or five women. Although so far he hasn't drawn the nationwide notoriety some serial killers do. He always carves a question mark on his victim's shoulder—" Angie broke off as she suddenly realized that Ethan was making a connection between Kristi and this mutilating killer. She shook her head in frantic protest. "This killer always picks up his victims in a bar! He couldn't have gotten to Kristi. She never—"

"Kristi had a question mark carved on her right shoulder. Mr. Yamori saw it. He said it appeared so . . . carefully done." Ethan made a strangled swallow. "Like something the killer was proud of. And took pleasure in doing."

Carved. In Kristi's flesh. Angie shuddered as her protest collapsed.

"Angie, are you okay?" Ethan asked. His voice had turned sharp, as if he could see her there in her bed, limp and drained like some boneless creature washed up by the sea.

Angie looked at her right hand, pale against the purple zigzag comforter she'd bought for the bed, her tendons corded into ridges. Was she okay? No. This murder had happened three thousand miles away. Kristi had been dead for two weeks or more. Yet for Angie it was as immediate as if Kristi were outside her window, crying for help.

*Oh, Kristi . . .*

She remembered the two of them laughing over something odd Kristi had ordered for that last dinner together. Kristi always liked to try new things. What was it that time? Eggplant mousse. They'd studied the yellowish puddle on the plate and giggled. Had that eagerness for the new somehow led Kristi into danger?

She saw a vision of a knife plunging into her body, a murderous hand carving a twisted line into her delicate shoulder . . .

*No, no, no!*

Yet what she managed to whisper to Ethan was, "Yes, I'm okay."

Ethan hesitated as if he doubted that, but he didn't press the point. "Do they know anything more about this killer other than that he leaves this mark on the shoulder of his victims?" he asked.

Angie forced her thoughts to turn away from her sickening vision of Kristi's death. "I remember an artist's sketch in the newspaper. It was of a man someone had seen in a bar with one of the victims."

Angie had to admit she hadn't paid much attention to the sketch. The killer may have claimed four or five victims, but his New York world had not been her world. She'd felt no personal danger from him. Which was no doubt what Kristi had thought.

"Look, Angie, I know what a shock this is for you. It's late. I'll let you go now. We'll talk again in a day or two, okay? Maybe I'll know more then."

"No, don't go!" A peculiar sense of panic whipped through her. "Maybe there's been a mistake. I mean, if the body was . . . mutilated, couldn't there have been a mistake?"

"Her parents identified the body, Angie. They were stunned and shaken, but they knew their own daughter." His tone was gentle, not impatient with her frantic protest.

"It's just so hard to believe."

"Hard for both of us to believe. Because we don't want to believe it."

"But Kristi was always so careful. So upstanding. I can't imagine her getting into a situation where this could happen. She didn't party or go to bars or do anything wild. How did this killer find her?"

"Good question."

Kristi had been working long hours at the investment firm, Angie remembered. Had she worked late and gotten careless going home, maybe even stopping for a late-night snack at a bar because it was the only place open? No, that didn't jibe. Ethan had said she'd quit the job, so she couldn't have been going home from it.

"Hopefully we'll know more after the police investigate further," Ethan said.

"Did this happen near her apartment, I wonder? Or close to the office where she worked?"

"Actually, I think it was the New York authorities who called the Yamoris. So it sounds as if it probably happened over there rather than near her apartment or job in New Jersey. Or at least she was found in New York."

"I suppose she could've been in New York trying out for a new acting part."

"That's definitely possible. We'll just have to wait for more details." Ethan paused. "Are you okay?" he asked again.

"I feel . . . guilty."

"Guilty?"

Guilty because she'd helped Kristi head down the ambitious path she herself had taken, even loaned her money so she could keep going. "Kristi was so sweet and naïve and . . . nice. I should've told her to forget about acting, to turn around and run back to Phoenix as fast as she could go." *To run back and marry you, Ethan.*

Guilty because she'd been too wrapped up in her own plans and fears that last night she and Kristi were together. If she'd been more observant, maybe she'd have seen some hint that Kristi was dissatisfied with her job and considering making some change in her life. A change that put her into the orbit of the Question Mark Killer.

"There's plenty of guilt to go around," Ethan said. He sounded grim.

"I can't imagine that you encouraged her to go to New York."

"No. But I did give her your name. So she had a contact there. And proof that success was possible—" Ethan broke off sharply. "Angie, I'm sorry. I didn't mean that the way it came out. I'm not thinking too straight. I'm sure Kristi would've headed for New York whether or not she had you to contact. I'm just glad you're in Julesburg now, far away from all this. You've rented an apartment of your own?"

"A little house, actually. I'll probably buy something later on."

"You're really planning to stay in Julesburg, then?"

A definite note of skepticism in his voice, Angie thought.

"I'm in for the long haul. In fact, I'm working on something special for the newspaper, a series about the historic old buildings here in town. There's this old theater—" She broke off, suddenly squeamish about the Nevermore and murder and suicides. Death and murder seemed all around her now, much too up close and personal. She changed direction and added, "Ryan thinks the old buildings are a good idea for a series."

"Good. Keep busy. Don't dwell on this, okay? Kristi knew the Lord. Whatever happened here, she's safe with him now. And they'll get the killer sooner or later."

"Is there anything I can do?"

"No, I don't think so. Unless you can remember something that might be relevant."

"I'll try."

Angie drew the blanket closer around her shoulders after they said good-bye and hung up. A wind had come up, and overgrown bushes scratched against the side of the house.

Did she believe what Ethan had said about Kristi being safe with the Lord now? Yes. Kristi may have slipped away from regular church attendance once she left Phoenix and her family. She may have drifted out of the habit of asking a blessing before meals, but she still read her Bible. And she'd never done anything even close to the things Angie had done to blast an unbridgeable gap between her and the Lord.

But to leave this life when she was so young. So full of passion and energy and fun.

Angie got up and went to the kitchen. The scratching bushes sounded unpleasantly like fingernails scraping the boards. *Ryan said this place was too isolated . . .*

*Irrelevant,* she chided herself. But sleep now felt as if it existed only on the far side of another planet. Would a cup of tea help? She stood there looking at a carton of chamomile tea bags Stefanie had given her, but all she could see was Kristi. Kristi with her fragile shoulders and big heart.

Had this murderer conned her by asking for help? Deceived her with some phony line? Kristi wasn't foolishly trusting, but she was so softhearted, so willing to help anyone who was down or in need. Several times she'd let some stray actress "between jobs" move in with her temporarily. And she could get really indignant about injustice or unkindness. Angie had once seen her jump all over a surprised jogger who was jerking his dog around in Central Park. Yet she could also be mischievous, even a little outrageous. Her imitation of Dolly Parton could almost make you believe her petite body had Dolly's curves, that her sleek black hair was poufed and blond. And she wasn't cowed by opinions just because they came from someone with authority. An important agent had once told her she should have breast implants,

66

and she'd told him she could get along just fine with the equipment God had given her, thank you.

*Oh, Kristi, Kristi, how could anyone do this to you?*

Angie went back to the bedroom without any tea. At the moment, tea seemed . . . frivolous. And the past not nearly as far behind her as she'd wanted to believe.

She climbed into bed. A few newspapers were still scattered across the comforter. She picked one up to put on the pile beside the bed, and then she saw what her hand was touching. The photo of the old theater.

The Nevermore.

A chill slid through her hand and up her arm. It clogged her throat like a shaft of ice.

She was involved with the Nevermore. And her friend Kristi was dead.

## 8

*T*he thought was so preposterous that Angie slammed the newspaper halfway across the room. It landed in a tented heap, the photo of the Nevermore ripped as if an earthquake had struck the building.

*Get a grip, girl.*

Kristi was not involved with the old theater, and her death had happened three thousand miles away. No possible connection.

But some of the catastrophes of the past had happened to the loved ones of those involved with the Nevermore. And they hadn't happened at the theater. The woman who lost her husband to a heart attack. The son who disappeared at sea.

No. The timing made a connection impossible. Kristi had been dead before Angie bought the *Herald,* before Angie had even heard the overblown tales of murder and suicide and curses and ghosts. The most fiendish of spirits could hardly preplan a murder to coincide with Angie's peripheral connection with the Nevermore and then reach a misty hand across the country to motivate the Question Mark Killer.

The evil was within the killer himself, and it didn't originate with any rundown old theater in Julesburg, Oregon.

The next morning she patched the ripped page with Scotch tape and returned the borrowed copies of the *Herald* to the storeroom.

"Hey, Madge," she said as her coworker arrived for the day's work, "do you know anything about the four months of missing copies from 1972? I'm wondering if those issues have something to do with the murder in the Nevermore, since I couldn't find any other issues that referred to it."

Madge smiled as she slipped a letter opener into a piece of the morning's mail. "You're thinking the Nevermore's spook crept in and did away with them? Some furtive ploy to hide the facts about the murder from inquiring minds?"

*Why not?* Angie thought wryly. Last night, alone in her bedroom, with bushes scratching like misshapen fingers against the outside wall, it hadn't seemed unreasonable to suspect a connection between the old theater and Kristi's death.

"Sorry to disappoint you," Madge said. "The fact is, the *Herald* wasn't published during those four months."

"Why not?"

"The owner and editor was the man murdered at the Nevermore. So publication ceased rather abruptly and didn't start again until a new owner took over."

The news of this onetime close connection between the *Herald* and the Nevermore jolted Angie. She glanced around the cluttered room. "Was this the *Herald's* office back then?"

"I suppose. Some of the dust in the storeroom looks as if it's been here that long. Actually, though, I don't really know. The murder happened several years before Ed and

I moved here, so all I know is rumors and gossip. Although we were living here by the time the old gal hanged herself."

"I heard she was supposed to marry the man who was murdered. Did she commit suicide because the man she loved was dead, I wonder? And she finally decided she couldn't live any longer without him?"

"You're saying she mourned him to death? Killed herself for love?"

"It's possible. Maybe the name of the theater has something to do with his death. Nevermore she'd see the man she loved."

Madge laughed and stabbed a bill onto a metal skewer. "On some soap opera, maybe."

"Oh, come on. Love like that is possible in real life."

Madge tilted her head and gave Angie a shrewd inspection. Angie hadn't known it before she bought the *Herald,* but Madge and her husband had wanted to buy the newspaper themselves. They'd been trying to scrape up the money for a down payment when Angie showed up with cash in hand. Madge was too bighearted a person to hold a grudge, however, and her generous help and advice were invaluable to Angie in getting started.

Now Madge said teasingly, "Why, Angie Harrison, I do believe you're a closet romantic. Dying for love. Who believes in that these days? I'll bet you save the heart-shaped boxes from Valentine's candy, don't you? And the two straws from a Pepsi you once shared with your first sweetheart."

Okay, she used to be that kind of sentimental saver. But it had been a long time since she kept a drawer full of romantic mementos. The corsage Ethan had given her for an Easter dinner back in college had long since disappeared. In recent years, her idea of savable mementos had run more to the fourteen-karat variety.

Angie just smiled and ignored the tease. "Do you know anything about this man who was murdered?"

"No, not really. Offhand I can't even remember his name. But it must be on the masthead in issues before those missing four months."

Angie started for the storeroom, stopped to answer the phone and take a "hot news tip" about the Do-Si-Do Square Dancers Club doings, and then dug into a stack of old *Heralds* with earlier dates than any she'd taken to the house. She grabbed one and squeezed between the tables they used for layouts to spread it out.

"Yes, here it is. Editor and publisher: Harry Llewelyn."

"I suppose I've heard the name, but it doesn't ring any bells," Madge said. "I never met him, of course."

"Do you know a woman named Myrna Bettenworth? The real estate woman who showed me around the Nevermore yesterday mentioned that Myrna had probably known Amelia Swarthout."

"You went in the Nevermore?" Madge reared back in her swivel chair, almost overturning it. A cowlick popped up in her gray hair. "For goodness sakes, why?"

"I guess I haven't told you. We're going to do a series about the old buildings in Julesburg. Starting with the Nevermore." When Madge didn't say anything, Angie turned to look at her. "No comment?"

Madge straightened her chair. "I suppose it could be an interesting series."

Restrained enthusiasm at best. "So you believe those old stories about terrible things happening to anyone who gets involved with the Nevermore, and we'd better stay away from it?"

Madge snorted and slashed open another envelope. "I believe all that nonsense just about as much as I believe our property taxes are going down, my hips are getting smaller, and politicians are becoming more honest."

Another one of the I-don't-believe-this-stuff-but-I-don't-want-to-get-involved crowd. Angie smiled and tossed out a challenge. "How about working there, then? We need more room. I'm thinking about buying the Nevermore and moving the *Herald* offices over there."

"You have got to be kidding." Madge swiveled the chair and looked Angie full in the face. "Right?"

Angie had tossed out the idea on an impulse mostly to tease Madge. But now that she thought about it, why not? They definitely needed more space than they had in this cramped office. She could probably get the old theater at a bargain price. Cancel all that superstitious nonsense—and put the incident with the drape in the dumb-accident category where it belonged—and the old Nevermore could be turned into a fine, spacious, centrally located office.

"Hey, maybe I could even have an apartment built into the rear of it!" Angie added. "There's plenty of space. And I'd be right there on top of the news twenty-four hours a day. If Julesburg grows, maybe someday we'll even go daily."

Madge was staring open-mouthed, as if Angie had just sprouted two heads and both were speaking drivel, when the radio scanner suddenly chattered.

Angie turned up the volume and deciphered the chicken squawks to be a report of a break-in on Howard Street. She dashed to the city map posted near her computer to locate the street, grabbed the camera, and ran to her car.

She got to the scene of the crime in time to snap a photo of a scruffy-looking guy in handcuffs rounding the corner of a newer-looking house, a sheriff's deputy behind him. She didn't get much out of the deputy, just that she could obtain information about the arrest from the police log later. The sheriff's department faxed a copy of the log over every Monday anyway. From what Angie had heard, the printed version in the *Herald* was one of the newspaper's more avidly read features. Julesburg residents liked to keep track of their neighbors.

Angie started to head back to the office, then changed her mind. Hadn't the real estate woman said Myrna Bettenworth lived on Howard Street? Of course, the proper thing to do would be to call and set up a formal appointment. But Julesburg tended not to stand on formalities. She picked out a house next to a vacant lot with a Julesburg Realty sign stuck in it and grabbed a pad of paper and a pen that she always kept in her car. She walked up the driveway and knocked on the door.

"Come on in," a voice called. Behind the woman's voice Angie could hear the murmur of a male voice on radio or TV. "Unless you want to wait five minutes for me to get up and come to the door."

Angie hesitated. A woman, elderly and apparently alone, simply inviting in someone who knocked on the door? She must've, as Estelle Reeves had said, lived in Julesburg since Year One. Angie tentatively pushed the door open.

"I'm looking for Myrna Bettenworth."

The woman didn't seem disturbed to see a strange face at her door. "I'm Myrna. If you're selling something, I'm not buying. But come on in anyway."

"You really should be more careful about letting people in," Angie said. "There's been a burglary a few doors away from here."

"Are you here to burglarize me?"

"No . . ."

"Then come on in."

Angie stepped inside and closed the door behind her. The room was on the dark side, crowded with heavy furniture, and felt a bit too warm. Faint scents of Ben-Gay and peppermint hung in the air. Myrna, her hair white and her hands knobby with arthritis, sat on a heavy sofa with doilies draped like lacy growths across its arms and back. A cane lay on the floor beside her. What Angie at first sight had thought was a round pillow turned out to be a white cat curled up beside the woman.

The male voice was coming from a cassette player on a heavily carved end table beside the sofa. It was intoning, "In God I trust. I will not be afraid. What can man do to me?"

"See?" Myrna said, apparently offering the words as proof that it was okay to let strangers in. She reached over and pushed a button to turn off the tape. "The Psalms. One of my favorite books. Along with Proverbs. And Luke. Well, Genesis too, of course. And I'm always going to Isaiah." She smiled. "Come to think of it, I guess they're all my favorites. It's the complete Bible on tape," she added by way of explanation. "A friend gave it to me. I forget about how much my arthritis hurts when I'm listening." She patted her knee.

Angie didn't want to get trapped into a biblical discussion. Hastily she explained herself and her articles about Julesburg's old buildings. Midway through the explanation, Myrna motioned her to a seat in an overstuffed chair across from the sofa.

"So I'm wondering if your memory goes as far back as when the Nevermore was built," Angie said at the end of her explanation.

"I was just a girl then but, oh yes, I remember standing down there on the sidewalk with eyes as big as sand dollars, watching some big, noisy piece of machinery lift the name sign into place. Though it was the Rivoli back then, of course, not the Nevermore." Her nose upturned with a sniff as she spoke the Nevermore name, as if the change, no matter that it was years old, still had not earned her approval.

"Do you know who built the theater?"

"No. But Twila Mosely might." Myrna tipped her gnarled fingers together and smiled as if she cherished the memory. "Those marvelous ruby red seats and sparkly gold walls. The best popcorn in the world—a giant carton of it for a nickel. The first movie I saw there was a Shirley Temple movie, I remember, and oh, how I wished I was that little curly-haired girl who could sing and dance."

Myrna laughed, a surprisingly earthy chuckle from one who looked so fragile. "Now, if I could just remember what happened yesterday as well as I can remember that popcorn and movie, I'd be in great shape. Twila brought me a new pair of pantyhose, and I can't for the life of me remember where I put them."

Angie was less concerned about yesterday's pantyhose than she was the long ago. "Can you tell me anything about Amelia Swarthout?"

"I knew her, of course. But she and her family had lots of money, and I was just one of the girls working at the cannery."

"Cannery?"

"Fish cannery, down by the jetty. Belonged to the Swarthouts. It's been gone a long time now."

The cat shifted from round-pillow shape to an elongated pelt of white fur. It opened blue eyes and regarded Angie with the superiority of a queen looking down from her throne, then deigned to jump down and inspect her more closely. Angie leaned over and scratched the cat on the throat, and the superiority dissolved into an ecstasy of an eyes-closed purr.

"This is Clementine," Myrna said.

*I wouldn't mind having a cat,* Angie thought irrelevantly. Then she got back to the subject at hand. "I'm under the impression Amelia never married."

"That's right. Oh, dear, I probably shouldn't say this, her come to such an unhappy end and all, but Amelia was . . . well, plain. Tall and skinny with a long, bony face. And long, bony feet and elbows. And, oh my, the biggest ears you've ever seen. Then to make it even worse, she always wore those huge, dangly earrings—" Myrna broke off and pressed a veined hand to her throat. She smiled apologetically.

Angie was afraid an attack of guilt was going to stop Myrna from going on. She reached for something to encourage her. "But Amelia was a wonderful person?"

There was not, however, a rush of agreement from Myrna.

"She had her good points." Myrna tapped her lower lip as if searching her memory for one of those points. Her eyes brightened. "Amelia was a wonderfully generous woman, she really was. Whenever the town needed something, she always contributed. Any group raising money for a project for the school could count on her. She never went to church, but she often sent money."

"I saw in an old issue of the *Herald* that she contributed money toward a fire truck for the town."

"Yes, and she bought new uniforms for the entire boys' basketball team one year." Myrna sounded relieved that they could agree on this admirable character trait.

"I'm sure Julesburg appreciated her generosity."

"Well, you can be sure they knew about it. She always made sure everyone knew when she made a donation." Myrna touched her mouth with her fingertips after the tart words spilled out. "Oh, dear, there I go again. Unfortunate words just seem to be flying out of me today. I hope the Lord isn't listening. But then, he always is, isn't he?"

Angie reached across the dark carpet and patted Myrna's hand. "I don't think anything you say about Amelia at this late date is going to matter. I get the impression she maybe didn't socialize with people much?"

"She was kind of stuck-up and superior, even when we were all in grade school. Then her folks sent her off to some fancy boarding school, and when she came back, she really looked down on all of us."

"Including potential local suitors?"

"Yes, except . . ." Myrna's gaze drifted somewhere beyond Angie's right ear as she looked into the past. "At least that's what I always thought. Now I look back and wonder if I was unfair. Maybe, even as a little girl, she was more shy than aloof. Or perhaps dreamy is the word. She was there at the theater every night, you know, and sometimes I think she just watched too many silly movies and got her head crammed full of too many fool ish, romantic fantasies."

"Local guys paled in comparison to the handsome hero up there on the silver screen?"

"Yes. Exactly! In the movies, some dashing hero rode into town and fell in love with a local maiden. Usually a beautiful maiden, but if she was plain, she took off her glasses and let down her hair and turned beautiful. And maybe Amelia thought that would someday happen to her too."

"But in a way, isn't that what did happen? Here was Amelia, at least forty, plain and lonely, and Harry Llewe-lyn fell in love with her. And if he hadn't been killed, maybe they would've married and lived happily ever after, just like in the movies. Did you know him?"

"No. My husband and I moved up to Portland for a few years in the seventies. Harry bought the *Herald* after we left and was dead by the time we came back."

"I wonder if he was dashing and handsome, like some young reporter in a movie?"

"Well, could be, I suppose." Myrna sounded indulgent, as if her opinion of Angie matched that of Madge's: closet romantic. "But from what I heard, Harry was just about as plain as Amelia. And a widower with a small child to boot. I always figured that by that age, Amelia had decided she'd have to settle for whatever she could get, that her knight in shining armor wasn't going to gallop in after all." Myrna sighed. "But he was a good man," she added. "Harry Llewelyn was a very good man, and he died protecting Amelia, he did."

"He protected her? How?"

"He picked Amelia up every night after the theater closed. I guess he worried about her going home alone with the night's receipts. With good reason, apparently."

Angie leaned forward, intrigued with this new spotlight on Harry Llewelyn as hero rather than murder victim. "What happened?"

"Amelia was just locking up for the night at the theater. It was a Saturday night, and that was always the big-crowd night at the movies, of course. Harry knocked, and she let him in. But another man pushed in right behind Harry. A man wearing a disguise over his head, a bag or something, so all she could see was his eyes. He had a knife and demanded money. I guess Amelia didn't give it to him fast enough, and when he threatened her with the knife, Harry tried to protect her and got stabbed for his trouble. Then the man grabbed the money and got away."

"And was never identified or caught."

"That's right. Julesburg's only unsolved murder."

Angie paused from frantically scribbling down notes on a pad of paper. "Harry sounds very brave. A man giving his life for the woman he loved. The first of the tragedies connected to the theater, wasn't it? It must've been very difficult for Amelia, losing a man like that."

"Yes, I imagine so."

"And there were no suspects?"

"Well, I heard the police suspected a new man she'd hired as projectionist a few months before the murder. But I think it turned out he'd already left Julesburg before it happened."

"Who was running the projector that night?"

"Amelia, probably. She'd been around the theater long enough to do everything from fire up that old oil furnace to fix the popcorn machine if she had to. And even if she was skinny, she was strong as a mule. She could bodily throw some misbehaving kid out of the theater. And she wasn't reluctant to do it. Actually, she hated to hire anyone to do anything she could do herself. She could be pretty stingy that way."

"An unusual woman."

"If by unusual you mean strange, yes. And stranger still after the murder. You've heard about her wandering around the theater, talking like she was Scarlett in *Gone with the Wind*, I suppose?"

Angie nodded.

"And then, by the time we moved back to Julesburg, she'd changed the name of the theater to that awful Nevermore."

"Did she have any close friends I might talk to? Someone who actually lived here at the time of the murder?"

"Well, there's several of us still around who knew her when we were girls. But Lillian Feldman is the only one I think you could call a close friend. Also tall and skinny and uppity. Two beanpoles they were, looking down on the rest of us."

"This Lillian still lives around here?"

"She's in the Laurel Cove Nursing Center over in Dutton Bay now."

"Can she have visitors?"

"On a good day Lillian is sharp enough to beat any contestant on *Jeopardy* or that millionaire program. That's what Twila Mosely says, and she still visits Lillian once in a while. On a not-so-good day, Twila says Lillian's a bit fuzzy. I'm not sure what she means by that. Maybe it's just Twila being nice instead of saying that on some days Lillian is nutty as a bag of peanuts. Twila's not one to say anything bad about anyone."

*Unlike me,* Myrna's half-guilty, half-mischievous smile seemed to add.

"Maybe I'll try to see Lillian, then." Angie made a note of the name. Lillian Feldman. Laurel Cove Nursing Center. "I understand the cashier at the theater found Amelia's body. A woman named Neila Moore?"

"Oh yes. Neila. A wonderful girl. She died of breast cancer at least a dozen years ago."

"I'm sorry to hear that." Angie stood up. "Would you like me to bring you a copy of my article about the Nevermore when it's published in the *Herald*?"

The cat had jumped back onto Myrna's lap, and the woman frowned as she stroked the white fur. "There's an old saying," she murmured. "About sometimes it's better to let sleeping dogs lie."

Angie halted. "You're saying I shouldn't dig too deeply into the Nevermore's past? Do you think there's something to those old tales about bad luck for anyone who gets involved?"

Myrna waved a scornful hand. "All those old tales about curses and mean spirits? I'd as soon suspect Clementine here of turning into a witch when she goes out at night."

"Then . . . ?"

"Somebody killed Harry Llewelyn. Who's to say that someone isn't still around?"

"But it was so many years ago."

Myrna's shoulders lifted in a "so what?" shrug, as if time were irrelevant.

"Isn't it more likely the murderer was a transient, if the police were never able to track him down?" Angie suggested. "Or someone who's long since left and moved to . . ." She picked a state at random. "Illinois?"

"And maybe it wasn't a transient. Maybe it was some young kid right here in town. Someone from a good, respectable family who just thought he'd pull a wild stunt for some quick cash. Only it soured and turned into a killing. But he's still here, all grown up and respectable now."

Angie felt a chill at the thought.

"You look like a bright young lady to me." Myrna's gaze scanned her shrewdly. "Determined too. The kind of young woman who just might dig around until she uncovers something from a long time ago. Something someone is not about to let be uncovered after all these years."

# 9

ngie drove over to Dutton Bay on Saturday, but it was a frustrating trip. The one-hour photo finishing shop was having equipment problems, and she had to leave the film from the Nevermore for later pickup. The title company wasn't open on Saturdays, and the nursing home said Lillian Feldman was too under the weather for visitors. Because Julesburg no longer had a police department, she drove over to the county seat in another small town and inquired at the county sheriff's office about records of the old murder at the Nevermore. More disappointment. Some records had been transferred when the Julesburg police department closed, but no one seemed to know if records from as far back as the Nevermore murder still existed or what might have happened to them in the transfer if they did exist.

The one thing she managed to accomplish was to get a cell phone and sign up for an account.

The day was too rainy for beach walking when she got back to Julesburg, so she went to Fit 'n' Fun and worked off her frustrations on a weight machine and treadmill. She peeked in the office and was concerned when Tina, Stefanie's assistant, said Stef wasn't feeling well and hadn't come in that day. She ducked through the rain to the other end of the building and opened the door to Ryan's office.

He gave her a little wave. "Be with you in a minute." He clicked the mouse while he watched the computer screen. "Just checking out the references for one of the applicants at the Laser Systems company."

"You can do things like that on the computer?"

"This guy has great references. From companies that don't appear to exist." Ryan shook his head. "Beats me how the guy thought he could get away with all this."

Angie inspected Ryan's office while she waited. There was an intriguing oil painting on the wall, a wistful, old-fashioned girl standing on a windswept point overlooking the ocean. A couple of awards. A sea of paper clutter. Self-righteously she decided that, in comparison, the *Herald*'s office could be considered efficient and orderly. Finally Ryan tapped a key on the computer and leaned back in his chair.

"Well, little sis, what's with you today? Out searching for breaking news?"

"Right now I'm wondering about Stef. Tina said she wasn't feeling well."

"She had some mild abdominal cramps last night."

Cramps. Angie forced herself not to close her eyes. Or touch her own abdomen.

"Dr. Halmoose didn't think it was anything to worry about, but he said she'd better stay home and take it easy for a day or two."

"And you're not worrying?"

"I wouldn't say that," Ryan admitted. "But don't tell Stef."

"I'll run by and see her before I go home."

"Okay, that sounds good. Hey, how's your series about the old buildings coming?"

"I've found out a few things. But it's mostly frustration."

She thought about telling him of Myrna's warning that the Nevermore killer could still be in Julesburg and might not appreciate her mucking around in the past. She decided against it. Ryan had enough to worry about with Stef's pregnancy. She also didn't see any point in telling him about her ridiculous encounter with the velvet drape in the theater. Or that she was giving serious thought to buying the Nevermore. She kept thinking about all that space.

"Did Ethan call you? I gave him your number the other night."

"Yes." Angie sagged into a chair. So far today she'd managed to keep too busy to let her mind dwell on Kristi. "My friend Kristi's body was found. She was murdered."

The words still felt vaguely unreal. Murdered. It was difficult to apply the finality of that word to bubbly, full-of-life Kristi. She'd had a terrifying dream last night. Not about Kristi or the murder, just some dark and frightening thing about tunnels and clutching vines. Or maybe, in some convoluted way, it *was* about Kristi, and how frightened Kristi must've been when she'd been attacked. Or maybe it was just another version of those nightmares she used to have in France . . .

"Angie, I'm so sorry." Ryan reached over and held her hand.

"I keep feeling . . ." Angie hesitated, uncertain about the odd niggling in the back of her mind. "Feeling like maybe I know something, maybe something important, but I just can't quite grab hold of what it is."

"About the murder? Or the killer?"

"I don't know. Maybe both. But I don't know how that could be." She explained what Ethan had told her about Kristi's death and the mark on her shoulder. "Apparently the authorities don't have a clue about who this guy is. But I can't think my friends back there included some psycho who likes to carve his signature on women."

"Psychos don't come with identification tags. Look, I have an Internet friend on the New York police force. I'll see if I can find out anything from him. By the way, your stockbroker friend called the house last night."

Angie stiffened. "What did you tell him?"

"Not your phone number."

"Good."

"But I did tell him I'd pass along the message that he'd called. And if you wanted to talk to him, you'd call him. Okay?"

Burke didn't have to interpret that to mean she was in Julesburg. But she knew that was exactly how he'd interpret it.

So what? If he wanted to get her number from information and give her a bad time, she could take it. If it would soothe his ego, she'd gladly let him think he was breaking up with her.

"Okay, thanks."

The tilt of Ryan's head asked a question.

"No, I'm not going to call him," Angie said.

"Want me to get tough if he calls again?"

*Good ol' Ryan. Still protecting me, just like he always has.* "Just tell him the same thing. That if I want to talk to him, I'll call. But don't hold his breath waiting."

Angie gave Ryan her new cell phone number and left him to his detective work. She drove by the house to see Stefanie, who was indeed taking it easy on the living room sofa, TV rumbling and Sherlock flaked out on the floor beside her.

"Can I do anything for you?" Angie asked. Stefanie looked unnaturally pale, and one hand rested protectively on her still-flat abdomen.

"I'm on the prayer chain. But I can use all the extra prayer I can get."

"Stef, I don't understand this. Do you know what's wrong? You felt so good a couple of days ago."

"It's just a temporary glitch." Stefanie reached over and squeezed Angie's hand. "Don't worry. Tina has everything under control at Fit 'n' Fun, and a woman from church is coming in to do cooking and housework for the next few days."

Angie squeezed her hand back. "I just don't want anything to happen to my little niece or nephew. Or you."

"Don't worry. I'll do anything I need to keep this baby safe. Stand on my head or eat foul-tasting healthy stuff or take to my bed for the next six months if I have to. Whatever it takes."

Whatever it takes. Yes, that was the kind of mother-to-be Stefanie was. What a mother-to-be should be.

On the way home Angie made an awkward attempt at a prayer. *Take care of Stef, please, God? I know I don't have any right to ask anything of you, but this is for Stef and Ryan. And they're . . . your people. And take care of their baby. They want this baby so very much. And so do I.*

As if *that* pulled any weight with the Lord.

On Sunday she attacked weeds in the backyard. And had a visitor. It squeezed through the ramshackle pickets of the fence, its voice more plaintive squeak than meow.

"Oh, my, look at you," Angie said, dismayed by the poor creature's skinny body. The cat was orange, only half-grown, and wary in spite of its thinness. It wouldn't let her get close enough to touch, although it followed her to the door.

She didn't have cat food in the house, but she did have a can of tuna and some milk. The cat devoured both on the back steps and lost some of its wariness. By that evening, it was inside the house. And by that evening, it, or she—Angie had made a gender determination—had a name. Keyhole. "Because you're little and scrawny enough to slide right through one," Angie told her. By Monday night Keyhole was firmly ensconced on Angie's bed. Her meow was still a bit squeaky, but she could purr up a storm.

Angie had to laugh. On Friday she'd had a passing thought that she wouldn't mind having a cat. Presto, one arrived. Would that all wants were so efficiently granted!

Monday, Tuesday, and Wednesday were so hectic that Angie only had time to check on Stefanie by phone, but she was relieved to hear that the cramps were gone and Stefanie was feeling fine again. Angie also grabbed a minute to call the title company in Dutton Bay. They could do a search on past ownership records of the Nevermore, but they said it could take two weeks or more. Angie planned to run the article in the *Herald* before that, but she decided the catastrophes connected with association or ownership might make an interesting enough story for a follow-up.

"Just do it as soon as you can, then," she said.

"This could get expensive," the woman warned.

"That's okay."

"If you're planning to buy the property, the research we do to furnish title insurance guarantees a clear title, you know."

*Buy the Nevermore. Am I serious about that idea?* "Right now I'm just checking things out. I want to know specific names of former owners."

First thing Thursday she called the nursing home in Dutton Bay and got an okay to visit Lillian Feldman that afternoon. She was just closing the office door behind her after lunch when a battered yellow pickup pulled into the Herald's small parking area. She stopped short as a stocky figure stepped out.

It had been five years since she'd seen him, but he still had the same muscular, athletic build he'd had when he wrestled in college. Still the sea blue eyes and thick brown hair and solid jawline. Not handsome enough to stand out in a crowd, but good-looking, with an air of solidness that she now knew was far more important than ad-campaign looks and TV charisma.

Her voice squeaked just like Keyhole's when she said his name. "Ethan."

Ethan returned her one-word greeting. "Angie."

He didn't know why she'd left modeling, but it certainly wasn't because her looks were failing. Same long-legged, slim figure, same long blond hair, same sky blue eyes. There was maturity in her face that hadn't been there before, but it showed only in her gaze, not in lines on her face. She was always smiling in her magazine ads, the smile that had dazzled him and various beauty-contest judges before she'd crashed New York.

Just now the smile was more tentative than dazzling. "I—I wasn't expecting you so soon," she said.

"I've been in Eugene for several days on the computer-store purchase. I should've called before I came over, but . . ." He didn't want to say the real reason he hadn't called—that he was afraid she'd change her mind and tell him not to come.

"That's okay. I'm glad you're here."

The words were welcoming, but her look was still wary, as if she might take off at a high lope down the street.

*Angie, I'm not here to make accusations or pick a fight or rehash the past. I just wanted to see you again.*

He tried to defuse the tension between them with small talk.

"My brother's pickup." He nodded to the yellow truck beside him. It sat high on oversized tires, the battered door still open. "Since he moved up here, he likes to get out and barrel around in the mud."

He saw her stiff shoulders relax fractionally. "A favorite southern Oregon pastime, I think," she said.

88

"Did I catch you at a bad time? You look like you're about to go somewhere."

"Yeah, I have an appointment over in Dutton Bay."

"Well, maybe I could ride along? I have a little more information about Kristi I thought you'd want to know." He stopped short, realizing he was pushing things and bargaining unfairly. *You let me come; I'll tell you what I know about Kristi.* He backtracked. "But I can hang around town until you get back. Maybe we could get together for dinner?"

"That's a long time to hang around. You can come along with me, but you'll be stuck waiting in the car while I talk to this woman. If you don't mind that—"

"No problem."

They slid into her compact Corolla. A copy of the *Julesburg Herald* lay on the passenger seat, and Ethan looked it over as Angie drove north out of town. There was a photo of a scene from a school play on the front page, and farther down another photo of a ceremony giving a local senior citizens' volunteer an award. Inside were columns of church news and various other small-town doings, police log records, display ads, a crossword puzzle, and a half-page of classified ads.

"It's just twelve pages now. But I'm hoping to increase it to sixteen within a few months. And up the advertising."

"I like it. It's . . . homey. Like front-porch news. I'm glad you're doing this."

Her sideways glance asked, *As opposed to what I've been doing for the past five years?* But she didn't toss the challenge into the air. All she said was, "So tell me the news about Kristi."

"There's nothing new on catching the killer. And unfortunately, he's killed again. The body of another woman with a question mark carved on her shoulder was found in the Queens area just a couple of days ago."

"He killed someone else, and they still don't have any more leads? You'd think the authorities could turn up *something.* He's killed six or seven women now!"

"There may be details or clues they aren't telling the public," he said, trying to lessen her obvious frustration. "And there's one thing different about Kristi's killing," he added. "It's not much consolation, considering how she died. But she wasn't sexually assaulted."

Angie's fingers flexed around the steering wheel as if she felt a small flow of relief. Then she glanced sideways at him again. "I'm glad. But that's odd, isn't it? Considering what he's done to his other victims?"

The same thought had occurred to Ethan. He was grateful that Kristi had at least been spared the additional horror of sexual attack. Yet, as Angie had said, odd.

"Did he rape this latest victim?" she asked.

Ethan nodded. "The police opinion, according to the Yamoris, is that Kristi fought back, fought hard, and apparently was killed before the man had a chance to make that kind of attack on her. Her body was bruised, and she had a broken finger. She had also scratched her attacker. There was flesh under her fingernails."

"DNA that can identify the killer?"

"Yes. If they ever get a suspect."

"I hope they nail him. I want them to nail him so bad!" Angie's knuckles turned white as she clenched the steering wheel.

"You haven't remembered anything Kristi said that might be helpful?" Ethan asked. "About quitting the job or anything?"

"Nothing. Although I keep feeling as if there might be . . . something. Something I just haven't been able to pin down yet. Or maybe that's only wishful thinking. Or guilt that I wasn't more observant." She swallowed. "Where is Kristi's body now?"

"The authorities have released it, and services are scheduled for Tuesday in Phoenix."

"I'll send flowers. In fact, I could fly down." She gave him a tentative sideways glance.

"They're keeping it small. Just family and very close friends."

Angie was quiet for a moment. "I guess I've wondered—" She cut off the question, but he could guess what she'd started to ask.

"About Kristi and me?"

"Yes."

"We dated a few times early on, and I cared about her. A lot. But it was a big brother/little sister kind of caring. Which doesn't mean it hurts any less than if we were involved some other way."

They rode in silence for several minutes, the coastal highway lowering almost to sea level in places, rising high on forested bluffs or massive headlands in others. Angie pulled off the highway at a viewpoint area.

"You've never been to the Oregon coast, have you?"

"No." *But that isn't why I came.*

"This is a particularly spectacular view."

They got out of the car together and stood at the guardrail looking down on pounding surf. The tide was in, and waves roared up the cliffs and fell back in froths of whitewater and misty spray over the rocks. Driftwood battered the shoreline and swirled around the offshore rocks. A thick log tumbled like a toothpick fallen into a boiling pot. Some unseen force beneath the churning surface suddenly dragged it under. Ethan watched, expecting the sea to spew it out again, but it vanished as if some underwater monster had swallowed it.

"Kind of puts us in our place, doesn't it?" Angie gripped the guardrail as if she felt caught in the undertow too. "I look at all this, and I feel . . . insignificant."

*Undertow*

"But you're not insignificant. None of us are, at least in God's eyes. Each of us is valuable to him."

He saw a movement of her throat, as if she'd made a convulsive swallow. She abruptly turned and headed back to the car.

In Dutton Bay, Angie turned the Corolla into a parking lot where a shield-shaped white sign with carved blue lettering identified the sprawling building as the Laurel Cove Nursing Center. Angie got out, leaving Ethan to read the *Herald,* but a moment later she returned and leaned down to peer in the window.

"You're going to get cold sitting out here. Why don't you come with me?"

A drizzle had joined the chilly air, but temperature wasn't the reason he slid out and followed her. He didn't know how much time he had with her, and he wanted to take advantage of every minute available.

# 10

The Laurel Cove Nursing Center was a low, flat-roofed building with gray siding trimmed with blue shutters and had a great view of the ocean. Concrete walkways lined with metal railings wound among evergreen trees and shrubs and wooden benches in sheltered nooks. A colorful wind sock whirled in the breeze, and flowers decorated some of the interior windowsills. Two cats, apparently residents, sat on the sheltered front steps, washing themselves leisurely. Ethan did occasional nursing home visits for his church, and this was definitely one of the most inviting of such homes he'd seen.

Angie asked for Lillian Feldman, and a receptionist directed them to a room down a hallway angling off toward the ocean side of the building.

The door to room 128 was open, but Angie tapped to announce their presence. "Mrs. Feldman?"

An oversized TV dominated the wall across from the bed, but the sound was turned down on several over-excited people hopping around on a game show. The cheery yellow-and-white patchwork quilt on the bed looked handmade, and a spray of shooting stars pressed between layers of stained glass hung at the big picture window. Family photographs and cards, one a childish scrawl in crayon, decorated the windowsill.

Ethan didn't know if the elderly woman had been readied for this meeting or if she always looked this way, but she was quite nicely turned out. Spiffy, as his grandmother would say. Fluffy pink bed jacket, white hair curled to a frothy confection and decorated with a pink bow, eyes smoky with eye shadow. He finally got an inkling what this meeting was about when Angie explained her interest in the old theater in Julesburg.

"I'm hoping you can give me some information about Amelia Swarthout and the early days of the Nevermore for my article."

"Amelia's been gone so long now," the woman murmured. She turned her face to the window, apparently indifferent to answering questions posed by an eager young reporter. Outside the window, two seagulls sailed by, coasting on the wind.

Ethan could feel Angie's disappointment that the interview was headed toward an instant dead end. He didn't know who Amelia was, but he'd noticed the striking sign on the Nevermore when he first drove through town. On sudden impulse he leaned forward and said, "I'll bet you had all the young guys in Julesburg begging you to go to movies at the Nevermore back then."

Lillian straightened against her pillow, her watery blue eyes coming to life. "It was the Rivoli back then." She laughed. "Oh, my. I did have so many beaus. There was one special seat I liked, the best seat in the theater. Amelia called me the Princess of the Back Row."

Ethan still didn't know exactly what Angie was after here, but with a nod of encouragement from her, he led Mrs. Feldman—Lillian, as she insisted he call her within a couple of minutes—through personal memories, some connected with the old theater, some not. He teased her and let her tell him about old boyfriends. And she actually gave him a flirty flutter of eyelashes now and then.

Angie didn't seem to mind that the conversation wandered here and there. She whispered an occasional question for him to pass on to Lillian and discreetly took notes.

"Amelia never did marry," Lillian said in answer to a question whispered by Angie. "And she and I weren't as close after I married."

In an unobtrusive voice Angie said directly to Lillian, "But Amelia was engaged to Harry Llewelyn. She must've been heartbroken when he was murdered right there at the theater."

Ethan did a double take. *Murder? At the Julesburg movie theater?*

"Maybe," Lillian said airily. She gave Ethan a playful sideways look, as if she hadn't noticed the question came from Angie. He could see a hint of the old Princess of the Back Row in the flirty gesture.

"Maybe?" he repeated.

"There was another man in Amelia's life. One not many people knew about."

"But you knew, of course. Who was he?"

"His name was Vance Spohn. Amelia hired him to run the projector. And then fell in love with him."

"Really." Ethan looked to Angie. He could tell this bit of information was a complete surprise to her.

"Tell us something about him," Angie whispered, and Ethan repeated the request to Lillian.

"Oh, Vance was something, all right. Remember Rhett Butler in *Gone with the Wind*? Vance could've been his younger brother. Mustache and all. And a flashy dresser. You should've seen him strut in those fancy Italian leather shoes. Whoo-ee! He wasn't buying them on a projectionist's salary, I can tell you. Or that ruby set in a big black chunk of onyx that he always wore on his finger."

"But Amelia's relationship with him wasn't an open one?" Ethan asked.

"Well, it wasn't a total secret. Some people knew they were up there in the projection room—what do they call it now?—making out? But they weren't, you know, an official couple, going out to dinner or dancing at the Elks Lodge. But I think Amelia cared a whole lot more about Vance running out on her than about Harry getting himself killed. The police kind of suspected Vance in the murder for a while. I sure do."

Ethan noted that Lillian put the suspicion in the present tense, as if time hadn't changed her mind. "They suspected that something happened because of a rivalry between Vance and Harry over Amelia?" Ethan looked at Angie again, lifting his eyebrows to tell her he was losing his way here.

Angie leaned forward. "But it was a stranger, or at least someone disguised so Amelia couldn't identify him, who forced his way into the theater and tried to rob her that night. And Harry was killed protecting her."

"So Amelia said."

"But . . . ?"

"I always figured Vance killed Harry. In fact, I have no doubt about it. But the police, I guess they believed Amelia's story." Lillian didn't hide her scorn.

"But why would Vance kill Harry?" Angie asked. "It sounds as if he could've had Amelia if he'd wanted her. He didn't need to do anything that drastic to get rid of his rival."

"Well, because Vance was after her money, of course. Why else would a good-looking young guy like that romance an older, not very attractive woman such as Amelia? Harry Llewelyn may not have been any ball of fire, but he wasn't dumb. He could see what Vance was after. So Vance was afraid Harry would make Amelia see that he, Vance, was only after her money. So Vance killed

Harry to keep that from happening." She folded her hands in her lap as if it all made perfect sense.

Angie frowned. "But Vance didn't stick around to claim her or her money as a prize. And didn't the authorities determine that he'd left Julesburg before the murder?"

"With fancy-boy Vance, I wouldn't be sure of that." Lillian nodded. "He was a slimy one."

"But Amelia said there was an intruder," Angie reminded Lillian. "A man with a bag or something over his head. And a knife."

"Amelia wasn't above stretching the truth. Or downright making things up. She knew Vance killed Harry. But she didn't want Vance caught, no matter what he'd done. She told me once he was the love of her life. So she protected him with that robber-with-a-knife story. I think she thought Vance just took off temporarily, until the . . . you know . . ." Lillian paused as if searching for an appropriate term. "Until the heat was off. Then he'd come back. Or she'd go to him."

"But he didn't come back."

"No. And after a while she started getting strange. Or stranger. Because a lot of people thought she was strange to begin with."

"Wandering up and down the aisles in her *Gone with the Wind* costume?" Angie said.

"Exactly. But she finally decided Vance wasn't coming back after all," Lillian added. "That was when she changed the name of the theater to the Nevermore. And started going in for more weird stuff. Séances, contacting the dead, palm reading, crystal balls, tea leaves. I wouldn't be surprised if she was looking at goat entrails, if she could've found someone who did that. I'd have to say our friendship kind of went downhill somewhere along in there."

"And then she killed herself."

Lillian's fragile figure jerked ramrod straight. "That wasn't my fault!" she exclaimed as if she thought Angie was holding her responsible for Amelia's death. "Just because I had reservations about keeping up a friendship with someone who started acting loony—"

"I'm sorry," Angie soothed. "I didn't mean to imply anything."

Lillian leaned back against her pillows. "I was never so all-fired certain she did kill herself, actually. She was bitter and sour and unhappy. But suicide . . . I don't know. It was just so unlike Amelia. She always kept herself up. Always had her hair done before wandering around in her fancy ballgown. And her nails were always perfect. Don't people depressed enough to commit suicide let themselves go?"

"But if it wasn't suicide, then what?"

"Someone killed her and made it look like suicide."

"But why would anyone want to kill Amelia?"

Lillian let out a long sigh. "Amelia knew Vance Spohn killed Harry. She protected him with that wild story about the robber with a knife. But he chickened out on marrying her. Maybe he had some other lady with even more money lined up. Then he was afraid Amelia would be vengeful enough to turn him in. So he came back and took care of her to make sure that didn't happen."

Lillian was getting tired, Ethan could see. The charcoal shadow around her eyes had turned to garish smudges of old ashes, and her true, narrow lipline showed within the lush curve of pink lipstick. Angie apparently saw the tiredness too. She stood and leaned over to press Lillian's hand, where the blue veins stood out like map lines.

"Thank you so much, Lillian. You've been a wonderful help. Maybe we can come back to see you again sometime."

Lillian looked to Ethan as if for confirmation that the "we" included him. He nodded as Angie started toward the door.

98

But he didn't follow right away. He was wondering about a detail Angie hadn't questioned. "What became of the knife that killed Harry?"

Angie stopped short and looked back at Lillian from the door.

"I don't know that I ever thought about it," Lillian said. She shrugged. "Maybe it was still sticking in Harry when the police got there, for all I know. Ask them."

"It's so long ago that the records about the murder seem to have been misplaced somewhere along the line. But I think I have enough information for my article for the *Herald* anyway," Angie said. "Wait, there's something else I forgot to ask you about. I understand Harry Llewelyn was a widower and that he had a small child. I wonder what became of it?"

"The child?" Lillian sounded lost now, as if the past were fading into a mist. "I don't know. I think some relatives showed up and took him. Maybe a sister or somebody."

Ethan kissed Lillian's cheek, bringing a smile to her mouth and a faded-rose blush to her cheeks. Angie asked one more question before they left.

"What do you think about all the old stories about Amelia putting a curse on the Nevermore or bringing in some ghostly spirit?"

Angie spoke as if she expected a disclaimer of belief, but that wasn't what she got. Lillian twined her forefingers in an odd little circular motion. Her voice was unexpectedly clear and hard when she spoke.

"We owned the theater for a short time in the eighties, my husband and I, after Amelia died. We were going to reopen it as a theater and start showing movies again. The young people in Julesburg haven't much to do for entertainment, you know. But within a month Mack had a heart attack. And within a year he was dead."

## 11

ngie could tell Ethan was confused by the interview with Lillian Feldman. Back in the car, she filled him in on details about the history of the old theater, Amelia Swarthout, the murder of Harry Llewelyn, and the bad-luck stories about anyone unwise enough to get involved with the place.

"And I need to thank you for dragging new information out of Lillian for me. Without you, the interview would've been finished in about two minutes." With a teasing smile, she added, "You and your inimitable charm."

Ethan grinned and puffed out his chest. "When you've got it, flaunt it."

"And you flaunted it very well. Thank you."

"What was all that *Gone with the Wind* stuff about?"

Angie filled him in on that peculiarity of Amelia's. "It makes a weird sort of sense now, knowing Vance Spohn resembled Rhett Butler in the movie."

"It should make an interesting piece for the newspaper," Ethan said. "I certainly noticed that Nevermore sign first thing when I drove through town."

"Kind of grabs you, doesn't it? And those awful red doors. They make me think of dried blood every time I see them."

"Have you been inside?"

"Yeah, and it's kind of a creepy place. You should've seen me panic when the big old velvet drape across the aisle door accidentally fell down on me. I fought like a wildcat."

After that conversation, they fell into silence. Angie mentally reviewed the interview with Lillian as they drove across town to the shopping center where the photo-finishing shop was located. Lillian had indeed provided helpful new facts, but Angie doubted that her speculations were any more realistic than Myrna's. The little old ladies of Julesburg probably had too much time on their hands, and definitely too much imagination. Myrna thinking the intruder who'd killed Harry was still around and willing to kill again. And Lillian suggesting a projectionist named Vance had come back and done Amelia in with a fake suicide, afraid she was going to spill the beans about his murdering Harry.

She also thought about sad, abandoned Amelia. Living in loneliness, changing the name of her theater from the Rivoli to the Nevermore as a monument to a lost love. Earlier Angie had thought that lost love was Harry Llewelyn; instead it was the projectionist who had walked out on her.

And poor, lonely Lillian. Ethan had obviously been the high point of her day. Or month. Angie was glad he'd come into the nursing home with her.

She parked the Corolla in a diagonal slot at the shopping center. Earlier rain had puddled the uneven asphalt, but the sky was clearing now. Wind kept rearranging the patches of blue sky around the clouds, turning continental blotches to ink-blot tests and then to pale windows of stained glass.

Ethan waited in the car while she ran inside to get the photos. When she returned, she found that he had picked up two hot mocha lattes at an espresso wagon nearby. He handed her a steaming Styrofoam cup.

"Ummm, great. Just what I need."

She took a sip before opening the photo envelope. She studied each photo, then passed them on to Ethan. The interior shots of the Nevermore had turned out surprisingly well from a technical viewpoint. The flash had lit up all the corners. But the photos would definitely not make a winning sales tool for someone such as Estelle Reeves. Every flaw showed. Curls of peeling wallpaper Angie hadn't noticed when she was in the theater. Stains on the ceiling. A crack across one corner of the big mirror. Shards of porcelain lying just inside the open restroom door. If you didn't experience the mysterious ambiance of the theater in person, it was just a rundown old building.

"That popcorn machine looks like something out of a Stephen King novel," Ethan observed. "As if it might start spewing killer popcorn out of thin air."

"Maybe that's the ghost's home base. If you're suddenly surrounded by a scent of old popcorn, beware." She sniffed meaningfully, and Ethan laughed.

"I sense a certain . . . umm . . . lack of respect for the Nevermore's resident entity," he said.

"Want to know something really wild?"

He gave her a sideways glance. "I'm not sure. Do I?"

"I'm seriously thinking about buying the Nevermore myself. We're crowded like toes in a tight shoe in that office we're in now, and I think the old theater could be remodeled into a great office. I'm even thinking maybe I could have an apartment built back where the screen and stage are now."

"All the old tales don't scare you?"

"Hey, I survived getting lost in the Bronx. On foot. In high heels. After that, one little Julesburg spook with a hunk of velvet drapery isn't going to intimidate me." *At least not for long,* she qualified, remembering how she'd almost turned into a believer when she was trapped inside that claustrophobic velvet.

Ethan laughed again and went back to the photos. She handed him one that showed the big furnace looking like a many-armed metal monster crawling up out of a cave.

"I'd have to get that old heating system torn out, of course, and something modern put in."

"In the meantime, you could use this pathway in the pit around it as a jogging trail for exercising," he teased. "I wonder what the door is for?"

"Door?"

He handed back the photo, and Angie had to peer closely to see the faint outline of a small opening built into the outside wall of the pit encircling the old furnace. She couldn't see a knob or latch. Maybe, like that rear outside door, it had been nailed shut. If it even was a door.

"Probably full of ancient plumbing and wiring," she said. "And creepy-crawly things."

"It might be interesting to prowl around in that old building."

"I'll let a remodeling contractor do the prowling, thank you."

"You're really serious about buying?"

"I'm not sure." Angie tapped the steering wheel. *Am I?*

"You don't have any thoughts about moving on with journalism? Working on a big city newspaper, maybe?"

"I'm just taking it one day at a time for now." She briskly stuffed the photos back in the envelope. "Another thing I should've warned you about. I need to do a little shopping while I'm over here."

"I can handle shopping."

*Ethan Kearney, you could handle almost anything. Except the one thing I never intend to tell you.*

They finished their lattes, then drove out to the edge of town where Wal-Mart was located.

"I told myself I wasn't going to have a TV in Julesburg," Angie said as they walked along the wall of myriad screens all showing the same game show. She had the peculiar feeling of having been dropped into a cloning experiment. "I told myself that it's just a big time waster. But it's harder to disconnect from the . . . umm . . . cultural core of our modern world than I realized."

"I don't have much time to watch mine. News and a few sports games, and that's about it."

Angie glanced up at him. "I don't even know where you live now."

"I bought a house last year. In the Paradise Valley area north of Phoenix."

He said it without inflection, but Angie swallowed. They'd looked at a house together in Paradise Valley once. Dreaming more than shopping, really. If they'd married then, they wouldn't have been able to rake up a down payment on so much as a tin-roofed shack. But he probably didn't even remember looking at that house together.

Yet a sideways glance at the small frown of concentration on his face told her he did remember.

She selected a medium-size TV and added a small microwave from another section of the store. An employee wheeled the boxes out on a cart, and he and Ethan wrestled them into the Corolla. Angie looked at her watch. Almost 5:00.

"I'd better get back to the office and make sure no crises have arisen while I'm away." She hesitated, uncertain on two counts. She didn't want Ethan to rush off when they got back to Julesburg. But she also didn't want to make him feel as if he were under some obligation to spend more time with her. He'd been pleasant and friendly, but maybe he'd seen enough to tell him there was nothing left between them.

The other reason she hesitated was more mundane—her cooking skills were hardly impressive enough to invite him to a home-cooked dinner. Back in college she'd done some cooking when she'd shared an apartment with a couple of other girls, but her minimal skills had definitely deteriorated. Since she'd become a model, eating at home had usually consisted of a bowl of cold cereal or take-out Chinese.

Ethan tossed a question into her indecision. "Maybe we could have dinner at the Singing Whale when we get back to Julesburg? It looked nice."

"I'd like to, but I won't have much time. There's a town planning commission meeting I have to cover tonight. Big discussion about turning a couple of residential lots into commercial."

"Maybe pizza, then?"

He apparently did want to spend more time with her, and the thought lifted her spirits. "Website X, yes. That would be great."

"But maybe we'd better unload this stuff first?"

"Right."

They drove by the *Herald*'s office first. Becky had locked up, but Angie ran inside to see if there were any messages. She didn't find anything. So she grabbed the radio scanner to take home.

Ethan followed her to Highland Street in the yellow pickup. Getting the big box holding the TV out of the car and into the house turned into a comedy of errors. The box stuck like a cork in a wine bottle. When it popped free, Angie fell backward on her bottom. Ethan skinned his knuckles on the doorjamb. Keyhole took one look at the whole scene and headed for a tree.

"I'll get a Band-Aid," Angie said as soon as they wrestled the bulky box to the living room.

"Maybe we should rescue your cat first."

"She's been up that tree before. She knows how to get down."

"Does this remind you of anything?" Ethan asked unexpectedly as he looked at the packing boxes.

It didn't at first, and then the memory hit her. "That time you were helping me move from one dorm to another, and you had that tiny little Volkswagen. And I had all those boxes and boxes of stuff—"

"And we were wondering why people were looking at us and laughing as we drove down the street—"

"And then we discovered a box on the roof had come open, and we had a bra and pantyhose flying like flags in the breeze."

They looked at each other and laughed.

"We had good times, Angie," Ethan said, his voice husky.

Angie nodded, something catching in her throat. "Lots of good times."

She headed for the medicine cabinet in the bathroom but detoured when the phone rang. She still had a smile on her face when she answered it. "Hello?"

"Angie," the voice said. "You're sounding all upbeat and cheerful."

"Hello, Burke." She dropped to the sofa, wishing she'd ignored the ring. Now, of all the inappropriate times for Burke to call. She braced herself for an inquisition.

"You're a hard woman to get hold of. Your brother wouldn't give me a clue about your whereabouts. Did you tell him I was your neighborhood stalker or something?"

"He's a good brother. So how did you get this phone number?"

"I figured a gorgeous model showing up in a town the size of Julesburg would be big news. So I called the local newspaper. And lo and behold, guess what I found out?

106

Quite a change, Angie, from model to newspaper owner and editor. A nice young woman helpfully supplied me with your home phone number."

"You didn't need to go to all that trouble. I'm listed with Information."

"Look, I'm getting off to a bad start here. Story of my life, right? We need to talk, Angie. Really talk."

The change in his voice from faintly mocking to urgent but gentle surprised her, but she kept her response cool. "I don't see any point in going into some big discourse on all the reasons I left modeling and New York, if that's what you're after. It's all . . . irrelevant now. Over and done with."

She was aware that Ethan was standing there looking uncomfortable, listening to her end of the conversation. Yet he didn't politely excuse himself and leave the room. She thought about suggesting he go get the microwave from the car but changed her mind. Maybe it would be better if he heard this.

"There's more to talk about than that," Burke said. "Your leaving has opened my eyes. And shaken me up. Badly. I'm flying out to San Francisco tomorrow morning on business. I'll rent a car as soon as I'm finished and drive up to Julesburg."

*Vintage Burke. He doesn't ask. He states.* "No, don't do that. I don't want you to come here."

"You're not alone, are you?"

Angie wasn't aware she'd given the slightest hint of that, and sensitivity wasn't a character trait she'd ever attributed to Burke. But apparently he'd picked up on something. Or more likely he'd simply made a suspicious stab in the dark. Many were the times she'd had to explain why she wasn't at the apartment to answer the phone, where she'd been and with whom. And more than once he'd checked out her answers.

"Don't come, Burke," she repeated. "I don't want to see you."

"Angie, I don't get it." The gentleness flipped back to a more familiar impatience. "I don't recall us having a big fight. Did I miss something? Do something?"

*Actually, it was what I did. What I was going to do if I stayed.* She glanced up, and her eyes met Ethan's.

"The way you picked up and left, it almost looked as if you were running scared," Burke added.

Yes. Scared. Scared of what she'd become. Scared of where she was headed. Sometimes even a little scared of Burke and his jealous possessiveness.

"Just drop it, Burke. It doesn't matter. Look, I have to go now. I have a meeting to cover for the newspaper in a few minutes."

"I'm coming. I'll be there by Sunday."

She slammed the phone down, harder than she intended. Could she just disappear from Julesburg for a few days?

Ethan suddenly became very busy. He pulled out a pocketknife and started slashing open the TV box.

"I'll get that Band-Aid—"

"No, my hand is fine." Ethan swiped his knuckles across his thigh and stuffed the knife back in the pocket of his khakis. "Look, I'm sorry. It was rude of me to stand here and listen. When I realized it was your stockbroker friend, I guess my manners took an exit."

"That's okay."

"But you have to know I'm curious about why you gave up modeling and left New York. Apparently that's what Burke wanted to know too."

Angie thought about detouring this conversation. Ethan was too gentlemanly to insist on knowing. And she didn't have to tell him. But if there was ever to be anything meaningful between them again, she had to tell him.

## 12

et's make coffee," Angie said. "Though it will have to be instant. I forgot to buy a coffeemaker today."

"Instant's fine."

The microwave wasn't unpacked yet, so she heated water on the kitchen range, set out mugs donated by Stefanie, and added an oversized spoonful of instant to each. She needed a caffeine jolt.

Ethan sat at the table, and she carried the steaming cups to it. The house was chilly, and she didn't remove her jacket.

"This isn't a pretty story," she warned.

"You don't have to tell me anything—"

"I want to tell you. I need to tell you."

Ethan nodded. "I appreciate that."

She took a sip of coffee before beginning. "My leaving New York and modeling was something that had been building for a long time. I kept telling myself everything was great with my career and Burke . . . but it wasn't. The proverbial straw that broke the camel's back, I suppose you could call it, was a party Burke and I went to. There was cocaine off in a side room. I'd known cocaine and other drugs were available at parties, but I'd never tried any of them."

She sucked in a deep breath, wishing it could cleanse more than just the air in her body when she blew it out. "But I did try the cocaine that night. I was feeling down. My contract with Golden Angel shampoo wasn't renewed. I had been up for another important cosmetics advertising campaign, but another model got it. Although none of that is excuse for what I did."

She suspected that Ethan was thinking, *You could've turned to the Lord,* but he said nothing, just sipped the dark coffee she'd made so strong it burned with an acid aftertaste.

"Burke showed me how to sniff it. And I . . . liked it. It made me feel strong. Invincible. The disappointments didn't matter. I felt like Supermodel of the Universe."

"That's one of its dangers, I hear." Ethan's tone was neutral, unaccusing. But he didn't offer soothing platitudes, and she respected him for that.

"Burke also introduced me to a man at that party. An older man, a magazine publisher. He wanted me to do a big layout in his magazine. Very big money, he said. They'd do it as a mystery-celebrity feature, not even handle it through the modeling agency. I'd be wearing a mask so I couldn't be recognized or identified." She took another breath and looked directly into Ethan's eyes. "And that's all I'd be wearing."

The shock flared in Ethan's eyes. "What did Burke think?"

"He told me to go for it. That I had the body and I . . . should show it off. That the mask would make it fun, and no one but him would know it was me. And he'd be proud of me."

At the time she'd been surprised that Burke would react that way; she'd have thought his jealous possessiveness would make him demand that she turn down the offer instantly. But now she could see that his willingness to let her pose nude was simply an extension of his possessiveness. Others could look, but only he could touch.

"So . . . ?"

"I told the publisher I'd think about it." She ground the cup in circles on the table, digging so hard the cup slipped and sloshed. "I didn't say, 'That's outrageous, I'd never do anything like that. Get away from me, you sleazeball.' No, I said, 'I'll think about it.'" Her voice gritted on the words.

"And?"

"I did think about it. By the next day I'd almost decided to do it. Why not? Good money. Anonymous, but an ego boost. It would please Burke. But that night, I woke up in bed. I had a peculiar feeling of not knowing what time it was or where I was. My heart hammered. My head throbbed like a dozen drums were pounding inside it. I had rivers of sweat running down my sides. The sheets were soaked with it. Then my leg cramped, and the pain seemed to go all the way from my toes to my heart."

She paused and braced herself with a gulp of coffee. "I didn't hear some big voice shouting at me, but the words were there. Like some tabloid headline screaming across my mind *You're going down, Angie. Down, down, down.* And I knew it was true. Angie Harrison was going down. I already wanted another snort of cocaine. And I knew I'd want more after that. Another and another and another. Then all the things I'd done over the past few years started rushing up at me, just as if they were spewing out of a pit. All the compromises I'd made to get where I was. Turning my back on God. And you. Betraying the agency that gave me my start to jump to a more prestigious one. The tactics I used to keep from gaining weight. The ambition that made nothing else matter. My . . . relationship with Burke.

"I knew I had to get out before I did the even worse things I was . . . tumbling toward. Before I posed nude. Before I was trapped by cocaine. Before I lost all sense of right and wrong. I didn't stop to plan or think things through. I just ran."

Ethan reached across the table and touched her hand. "You did the right thing this time. You ran before you were trapped. What you did took strength and courage. I'm proud of you."

Angie also felt a moment of pride. She'd given up a career and lifestyle that would send most women into green spirals of envy. Money and travel and clothes and glamour, admiration and attention, fancy restaurants and opening nights.

She saw no condemnation in Ethan's eyes, not even for her relationship with Burke. He was willing to do what she had done with her mistakes and wrongdoings—put them all in the past.

Yet the bubble of pride burst in an explosion of shame. She hadn't told him all of it. And when she did . . .

She remembered his comment when she spoke of feeling insignificant in relation to the immensity of the sea and surf. *"Each one of us is valuable to the Lord,"* he'd said.

*Exactly. Each one.*

This was the end, right here, right now. It had to be. Better to let the brief spark of their relationship die, with good feelings of friendship, than kill it with hate and disgust.

She jumped up. "You know, I don't think I'm going to have time for pizza before that planning commission meeting after all."

She lifted her wrist to make a point of looking at her watch. She couldn't make out the numbers through eyes that had gone blurry, but it made a meaningful gesture. "I—I need to shower and change . . . and everything."

Ethan looked bewildered. "Angie, I don't understand. I thought—"

"It's been great seeing you again." She turned on the high-wattage smile the photographers loved. "I'm glad you came. Now if you'll just excuse me."

Ethan hesitated, as if he wanted to argue, but he finally gulped the last of his coffee and stood up. "I'll just stop over and say hello to Ryan and Stefanie before I head back to Eugene, then."

"I'm sure they'd like to see you."

Ethan rubbed the solid jut of his jawbone. Then his stubbornness asserted itself. "Angie, I was angry with you, very angry, for a long time, and I can't say I'm not shaken by everything you've told me tonight. But my feelings for you never died, and I'm still hoping—" He stopped, leaving his hopes hanging, his look questioning.

Angie clenched her teeth so hard her jaw ached. He was a good man, a generous and forgiving man. The best. Living out his Christian beliefs even now in his willingness to forgive the past. Her own hopes rose. Was it possible, through some miracle, that they *could* start out fresh?

"I don't deserve you, Ethan."

"Does that mean you're thinking we may have a chance?"

He wanted to make that start. She could see it in the forward tilt of his body and his direct gaze. She wanted that start too. But he still didn't know all of what she'd done.

"I'm not sure what I'm thinking," she said honestly.

"Have you taken all this to the Lord, Angie?"

The question caught her off guard, but she knew she should've expected it. Ethan was a man who took everything to the Lord.

"The Lord and I aren't in close communication these days."

"He didn't abandon you—"

"I never said he did! I know what I did. I abandoned him. I considered myself a Christian, but I put my selfish wants and ambitions ahead of him. I'm not blaming God for anything."

Ethan took a step toward her. "Then come back to him. He wants you back."

"I'm trying, Ethan. I'm trying to get back to him. I'm cleaning up my life. I've broken with modeling and Burke, and I've turned my back on the ambition that led me to make so many wrong choices."

"He doesn't demand that we clean up our lives before we come to him. Remember that old hymn? 'Just As I Am.' Then he does the forgiving and cleansing. It's what grace is all about, his gift, not something we earn."

"I'm working on it, okay?"

"Okay. I'm coming back up to Eugene in a couple weeks or so. I'd like to come to Julesburg too."

Angie stood there, torn between asking him to come see her again and the weight of responsibility that she had to tell him more. And then he wouldn't come. He'd despise her.

When she didn't say anything, he pulled a Kearney's Komputers card out of his pocket and tossed it on the table. "My business, home, and cell phone numbers are all on there. Unless I hear otherwise from you, I'm coming."

She shoved the card in her jacket pocket without looking at it.

Angie unpacked the microwave and found a place on the kitchen counter for it, but she skipped dinner. She gathered the notebook, pens, and tape recorder she'd need for the meeting. By that time Keyhole was over her scare and wanting in the house. Angie got back in her good graces by offering a half can of tuna, still the cat's favorite food. Keyhole was curled up on the bed by the time Angie left the house again.

The planning commission met in the city council room behind the library. The discussion was heated, loud enough to drown out the voices that raged inside her.

"We need more commercial zoning. We need jobs!" the applicant for the zone change pleaded with passionate conviction.

"We must stop changes like this before they destroy our small-town livability!" an opponent roared with equal conviction.

In the end, the commission waffled, and the matter was tabled for "further evaluation."

Angie resisted an urge to drive by Ryan and Stef's house to see if a yellow pickup was parked outside. She was almost certain they'd invite Ethan to stay the night. Would he do it?

She arrived home wishing she'd left lights on inside. In the darkness, the house inspired a vague feeling of uneasiness. *Gotta get some potted plants for the front steps. And get the bulb replaced in that outside light above the front door.*

Yet she wasn't without a welcoming committee. Keyhole curled around her legs, purring companionably as she stuck the key in the lock.

"Fine watch-cat you make," Angie grumbled as she opened the door. "You'd hide in a tree at the first sign of trouble."

Inside, she fed Keyhole again. Then, even though she wasn't hungry, she slapped peanut butter and jelly on bread for herself. She slammed shut the three open cabinet doors on her way to the refrigerator for a glass of milk.

Still eating, she dropped to the sofa, the nerve-jarring plaid now concealed by a conservative blue spread. *A blue that shows every orange cat hair,* she thought as Keyhole jumped up beside her. She smiled and ran her hand over the cat's arched back.

"Never mind. Your company is worth any number of stray cat hairs." After finishing the sandwich and milk, she went back to the kitchen and peered into the freezer section of the refrigerator. She didn't know what she was looking for, but she wanted *something.*

*Well, I am getting messy,* she thought as she straightened the plastic sacks of vegetables crammed into a corner. One was even broken, spilling Chinese vegetables all over the freezer section. She scooped everything back in the bag.

Whatever she was hungry for wasn't there. She gave up. "Okay, cat, let's go to bed."

In the bedroom, she stripped down and slipped into pajamas. The pillow was on top of the purple zigzag bedspread. *Now that's odd,* she thought, pausing for a moment before she threw back the covers. She always tucked the bedspread over the pillow, never left the pillow on top.

A blast of uneasiness hit her, a feeling that she was not alone.

*Ridiculous. Nothing larger than a leprechaun could hide in this tiny house.*

Even though she felt foolish doing it, she lifted the spread and peered under the bed. She opened the closet door and shoved the hangers aside so she could see the floor and all the way to the back wall. The small house had no other hiding places.

Yet the feeling persisted. Now it was not so much a feeling of not being alone as it was the feeling that someone had been there. She looked around the bedroom again. That bottom drawer of the bureau. Had she left it shoved in crooked like that?

She walked slowly through the house. A corner of the blue spread covering the sofa was tossed back, revealing one of the cushions, and she was always careful to keep that ugly plaid hidden. It was almost as if someone had been looking under the cushions.

*So what am I saying, that someone has been in the house?*

No way. Nothing had been stolen; other than today's purchases, nothing was worth stealing, and both the new TV and the microwave were still here. She'd rented a safe deposit box at a bank in Dutton Bay and deposited her good jewelry there only a few days after she'd arrived in

Julesburg. Although a burglar wouldn't know that, of course. And she hadn't put everything in the safe deposit box.

She dashed to the bureau in the bedroom. Top left drawer. Diamond stud earrings, the only genuine gem jewelry she'd kept out to wear.

Right there in the drawer, just where she'd left them.

Obviously she'd just left the house in a messier state than she'd realized. She'd never claimed to be a Martha Stewart–type housekeeper.

She turned to her bed. Keyhole was already there, kneading the pillow into proper consistency. Time she hit the sack too.

Angie stopped short at the foot of the bed.

She could be mistaken about the open drawers and the pillow. Even the disorganized freezer and the exposed sofa cushion.

But she wasn't mistaken about this.

Keyhole had been inside the house, sleeping on the bed, when Angie went to the meeting. But the cat had met her *outside* the door.

## 13

ngie returned to the front door and studied the lock. She knew little about locks, but this one appeared no-nonsense, not like one of those flimsy things a TV detective could outfox with a quick wiggle of a credit card. The bolt made a satisfying thunk when she turned it from the inside. To lock it from the outside, the key had to be inserted and turned.

Had she done that this evening when she left the house? Or had she been distracted by the jarring ending to her reunion with Ethan and neglected to do it?

She opened the freezer again. Now she was almost certain someone had poked around in there. A gourmet burglar, hoping for lobster or filet mignon? No, a burglar who knew some people thought a freezer was a safe place to hide valuables, the last place an intruder would look. But in reality, it was probably one of the first places an intruder would look, according to what Ryan had once told her in a brotherly lecture about security.

Was this a random burglary? Or was she a target because some local crook figured an ex-model from New York would have expensive stuff lying around? But that didn't make sense. The rooms had been searched subtly, leaving only minimal traces of entry. Surely not the way some crook in a hurry would do it. And surely a burglar would have seen those diamond studs in the drawer.

Keyhole, who'd followed her, jumped up on the coffee table to get her attention. Angie picked up the cat, then studied the magazines and papers strewn across the scarred wooden surface. Had she left them scattered like that?

Maybe.

Maybe not.

But why would a burglar paw through this stack of trivia? Surely he wouldn't have expected to find valuables buried among magazines and junk mail. Of course, since she had no home filing system yet, there were a few important items mixed in with the miscellany. A copy of the rental agreement on the house. A curt letter from the modeling agency and a statement from Burke's brokerage company about her stock market account. Some notes to write up for the seniors' column in the *Herald*.

But none of it was important to anyone but her. She put Keyhole down and separated out the papers that should be saved. At the bedroom door a thought occurred to her, and she looked back at the coffee table.

Notes.

She had taken notes during her interviews with both Myrna Bettenworth and Lillian Feldman. Could the burglar have been looking for those?

She scoffed at the idea. How could they be important? Both Myrna and Lillian had offered facts and speculations new to her, but surely nothing that could pinpoint a killer.

But the man who'd killed Harry Llewelyn didn't know that . . .

Could he think she might have uncovered incriminating new evidence? Was it possible one of the elderly women actually *had* given her important information?

But committing burglary to hunt for her scribbled notes seemed far-fetched. If a killer was worried about what Myrna or Lillian knew, he could've gone after one or both of the women years ago.

*Girl, your imagination is running wilder than those two old ladies on skateboards. No one's been in here. You're simply a messy housekeeper. With a bad memory about irrelevant details.*

*But then how did Keyhole get outside?*

*She probably slipped out when I was locking the door as I left the house, and I just didn't notice.*

*Exactly.*

She went out to the car and retrieved the interview notes from where she'd left them on the backseat. By now she'd convinced herself there was nothing to be uneasy about. Although she did make certain the front door was securely locked after she closed it behind her, and just for good measure she also checked the door from the living room into the backyard.

No lock with a sturdy, no-nonsense bolt back there. This lock was little better than the fastener on a cheap suitcase, and the door itself no more sturdy than the door to the closet. And there, on the carpet right in front of the door, was a sliver of wood. Weathered white on one side, freshly broken on the other. Angie picked it up with a stomach-jarring sense of recognition.

A splinter from the picket fence, like what might break off if someone crawled over the fence to get into the back-yard. And then came through the back door.

Her imagination wasn't running wild now. She was certain of it. Someone had been in the house.

She ran to the phone. Maybe Ethan was still over at Ryan and Stef's—

She put down the phone without dialing. No. No way could she run to Ethan for help. She had no right to ask him for anything.

But she could call Ryan.

No, if Ethan was there, they'd both come rushing over.

Obviously, she should've taken Ryan up on his offer to check out the house for security. He'd have noted that flimsy door right away. But it was a little late to think of that now.

*Okay, no need to panic. The intruder has come and gone; no reason for him to return.*

But just to be safe, she wrestled an overstuffed chair in front of the door.

When Angie unlocked the office the next morning after a night worthy of a veteran insomniac, she half expected to find that it also had been searched. As far as she could tell, however, nothing had been touched. She considered calling the police to report the burglary at the house, but since nothing had been taken or damaged, she doubted they'd consider it important. She did call the landlady about installing a new, more sturdy door and lock, but Mrs. Daggert didn't feel the situation warranted the expense.

*Well, I do.*

She called the local hardware store, then contacted a man they recommended. He said he could come over to take measurements first thing in the morning and then have a new door and lock installed first thing next week.

She was dialing Stefanie's home number when Madge arrived. Angie welcomed the woman with a fingertip wave.

"Your friendly neighborhood editor just calling for a pregnancy update," she said when Stefanie picked up. She made checkup calls often, so this one was nothing unusual. It was, after Stefanie said she was fine, easy to then ask casually, "Did Ethan stop by to see you and Ry last night?"

"Yes, he did. I'd never actually met him before, and he seems like a great guy. And aren't you impressed that he drove all the way over here from Eugene just to see you? I am."

"Did he go back to Eugene last night?"

"We tried to get him to stay in the guest room, but he wanted to get back and spend a little more time with his brother. He's flying home to Phoenix tomorrow."

"He wants to be there to offer whatever help he can to Kristi's parents. The services are Tuesday."

"Yes, he mentioned that. It also sounded as if you really hooked his interest in the Nevermore. And what an intriguing meeting you must have had with Lillian Feldman! She used to be what passes for high society here in Julesburg."

"Yes, she was helpful. I think I'll have the first article in the series ready to run in the *Herald* next Wednesday."

"That's your only interest in the Nevermore?" Stefanie asked.

Angie caught the meaningful inflection in her sister-in-law's voice. "Ethan told you that I'm thinking about buying it, didn't he?"

"He mentioned it. Then he realized it was something we didn't already know and felt embarrassed that he'd said anything."

"It's not as if it's a secret," Angie said. "But I suppose you're now going to give me a big lecture. If I get involved with the Nevermore, I'm sure to be sucked into some disaster."

There was a moment of silence, as if Stef was indeed considering a lecture, but then she laughed. "I'll leave lecturing to your big brother. When is Ethan coming back?"

The question caught Angie off guard. "I'm not sure," she said. She thought of the card she'd stuffed in her jacket pocket. Ethan had said to call him if she didn't want him to come. She wasn't sure what she'd do.

At least she didn't have to worry about Burke arriving for another day or two. Perhaps by then she could think of some way to avoid him. Or maybe he'd even change his mind about coming.

Wrong.

## 14

The former owners hadn't kept the *Herald* offices open on Saturday, but Angie had decided that in the interests of encouraging business, she would do so. On this first Saturday, which she expected to be quiet, she wanted to work on the Nevermore article. She drove over to the office right after meeting with the carpenter at the house about the new door.

First thing she did was call Twila Mosely, the friend Myrna had mentioned who was also a contemporary of Amelia Swarthout's. Twila was informative and helpful and her memory excellent. She knew the name of the Nevermore's builder, although he was long dead now. She also knew several other owners' names and what had happened to them.

Twila lived up to Myrna's comment that she never said bad things about anyone. Her only response to Angie's somewhat slanted questions about Vance Spohn was that she understood he was a capable projectionist. Twila remembered that Harry Llewelyn had a small son, and she, like Lillian, thought some relative had come and taken him. Unlike Myrna, with her warning that the murderer might still be lurking in Julesburg, and Lillian, with her theory that Vance Spohn had returned and murdered Amelia with a contrived "suicide," Twila had no theories to offer. She said people connected with the Nevermore had suffered an unusual number of misfortunes, but she hoped someone would find a worthwhile use for the old theater one of these days.

Angie decided, for the time being, to keep to herself that she was considering doing exactly that, although she did make up her mind to talk to Estelle Reeves again.

Twila went on to offer one interesting new fact: Amelia had been a dedicated diary keeper.

"She started it when she was a little girl in grade school, before she went away to that fancy boarding school. I remember at recess or lunchtime most of the girls would be playing hopscotch or jacks or jumping rope, but Amelia would be sitting over on the steps with her little diary. She always kept one hand curled around the page as if she was afraid someone might see what she was writing. Then when the bell rang she'd lock up her book with a key she kept on a chain around her neck and walk off with her nose stuck up in the air. I always figured she was spying on us and writing it all down so she could get us in trouble."

Angie smiled. "Were you doing something that you could get in trouble for?"

"Probably. You know kids. I stuck out a foot to trip her once. Then I felt guilty and tried to make up for it by giving her a package of gum and asking her to come to Sunday school with me."

"Did she come?"

"No. She always had to help her folks clean the theater on Sunday mornings. They really made her work."

"Do you think she continued keeping a diary or journal in later years?" Angie asked.

"I'm sure she did. When we were both grown and past childish foolishness, we became friends of sorts, and she told me she'd lived such a fascinating life that it would make a wonderful book. She said she had everything written down, and that someday she'd get it all properly organized for a book or movie."

"From what I've learned so far, her life sounds more sad and lonely than fascinating," Angie said.

"I'm afraid that's true. Amelia was a . . . dreamer."

"I wonder what became of her journals?"

"I've wondered too. Although I'd guess she may have destroyed them before she hung herself. Her will stipulated a closed casket at her funeral, and she'd already told me she didn't want people staring at her when she couldn't stare back. I suspect she also may not have wanted her life stared at from the pages of a journal, before it was properly organized, that is."

Angie could sense that Twila was running out of things to say. She set down the pencil that she'd been taking notes with. "Twila, thanks for all your help. Is there anything else you can think of to tell me about Amelia before I let you go?"

"Well, I can think of one other minor point that might interest you. Amelia's parents suffered an unpleasant demise considerably before the murder. They were killed when a tree on the edge of the parking lot at the Nevermore blew over in a storm and crushed them in their car."

The information sent Angie's thoughts in a new direction: Had the Nevermore's curse started long before the murder and suicide?

After typing up the notes she'd taken while talking to Twila and reviewing her other notes, Angie began work on the article. She started it with Myrna as a little girl watching the big sign go up. Then the deaths of Amelia's parents. The murder, the young boy left fatherless, the suicides, the strange string of misfortunes. She worked steadily until an internal rumble told her it was past time for lunch. These days she paid attention when her stomach said it was time to eat.

She was just pulling the final page of the first draft out of the printer when the office door opened. Her muscles instantly tensed. Burke. With flowers. Smiling as if he'd just called another turn of the stock market and as if they'd never had that hostile conversation on the phone. Her nerves screeched as he held the bouquet of deep red roses across the counter.

"Peace offering," he said.

She collected the pages from the printer and paperclipped them together. She didn't return the smile or take the flowers. "I wasn't expecting you so soon."

*I was hoping you'd never show up.*

"I left San Francisco as soon as I finished my meeting yesterday. Drove part of the night, stopped to sleep at a motel for a few hours, and drove the rest of the way this morning. That coastal highway is beautiful. But slow as an old wagon trail. Lots of twists and turns."

Whatever hard hours Burke had put in driving didn't show. He still had a Mazatlon tan, and his teeth flashed white in an easy smile. He wore laid-back tan slacks, a suede jacket with knit cuffs, and Italian boots. Casual but not inexpensive, Angie knew. The kind of man for whom "tall, dark, and handsome" could be a trademark. She could still see what she'd seen in him when they'd first met at a party in New York. With relief she also realized the zinger effect was gone.

She swallowed and braced herself. "Okay, that's enough small talk, Burke. If you came here to rant and rave about my walking out, let's get it over with."

"Something you're writing for the newspaper?" He nodded toward the pages in Angie's hand.

She didn't realize until then that she'd rolled the papers into a tight cylinder. She set the roll on the front desk and smoothed the pages flat. "That's my job now."

His glance flicked around the crowded office. "You run the whole show on your own?"

"I have a couple of part-time employees." She folded her arms across her chest. "I like it here," she added. "I like the town. I like the ocean. I like being near my brother and his wife. I like owning the newspaper. I like my cat."

"Sounds like big competition for one old boyfriend from New York." His tone and smile were teasing.

Angie lifted one shoulder in a shrug.

Burke's expression turned serious. He put his elbows on the counter and leaned toward her. "Angie, your leaving really shook me. I've been doing a lot of hard thinking since then. I think I've figured out what our problem is."

"And that would be . . . ?"

"Me."

The statement surprised her. She'd expected an outline of her shortcomings. Had Burke been doing a meditative self-examination and turned over a new leaf?

Doubtful. Definitely doubtful. And at this point, how many new leaves he turned over didn't matter. She shook her head.

"You're just not getting it, Burke. It's over. Modeling, you and me, everything."

"You won't even listen to what I have to say? This isn't like you, Angie. You were never unfair."

She heard the reproachful tone and knew he was trying to manipulate her. Yet the word *unfair* hit a hot button. She should've had the courage to break off with him in person instead of doing it the snail mail way. He'd called the day she and Kristi were going to dinner, wanting to see her. She'd gaily told him it was girls' night out, just her and Kristi, and never said a word to reveal that she didn't intend to see him again.

Yes, that probably had been unfair. She leaned up against the desk. "Okay, say what you have to say."

"Not here. I haven't had lunch." He smiled and touched his lean midsection, the six-pack of toned muscles he didn't mind showing off. A would-be pickpocket in Cozumel had once been rudely surprised when Burke flattened him with a karate kick. "I can't plead my case on an empty stomach. If you've already eaten, come have coffee with me. I saw a place while I was driving through town that didn't look too bad. The Singing Whale?"

Uneasily feeling as if she were compromising herself but determined to see this through, she finally nodded. "I'll go wash my hands."

In the tiny restroom, she sloshed water on her hands and face and pressed her palms hard against her temples. She looked at her reflection in the tiny mirror and reluctantly ran a comb through her hair. She'd intended to have it cut before Burke arrived, maybe even tinted darker. It was he who'd suggested adding those silvery highlights, and he'd always liked her hair long and loose, flowing over her shoulders. Maybe because it also gave him a convenient handle to grab, as he'd once done when he didn't like the way she was dancing with another man. She'd intended, with a cut, to make plain that what he liked or wanted didn't matter to her now. Yet here he was, and here was her hair, still long and loose. With sudden determination she dug a rubber band out of a drawer and skimmed the long strands back into a severe ponytail.

If Burke noticed the hair restyling when she returned to the front desk, he didn't mention it. He was reading the article about the Nevermore. "Hey, this is wild! Murder. Suicide. Curses and evil spirits! Sounds like a psychic carnival. Who'd have thought it of a little place like this? And very well written too."

She didn't want to feel it, but she did. A butter-melting-on-toast warmth from the praise. But all she said was a tart, "And you've suddenly turned into a literary expert?"

All she'd ever known Burke to read was sports and the stock market page.

He smiled. "I know what I like when I see it." His gaze grazed her from head to hips, and his eyes added, *And I like what I see right now.*

The lunch hour was past, but the Singing Whale was still busy. A convention of antique dealers staying at the adjoining motel, Angie remembered. She'd written a piece about them for the *Herald*. A trio with their name labels still on was actually singing in a corner booth, which seemed a bit frisky for antique dealers.

She deliberately ordered a cheeseburger and fries to let Burke know she'd abandoned the dietary limitations of a model. He ordered a steak sandwich. Rare.

"Wine?" he suggested. Then he smiled. "Although I'm not sure what's correct with a cheeseburger and fries."

"A 7Up, please," Angie told the waitress. "Regular, not diet."

"Not a bad place at all," Burke commented approvingly after the waitress had gone. They were sitting in the glassed-in alcove raised above the level of the main dining room. The VIP tables. Apparently the hostess had awarded Burke that status. "Food good?"

"Excellent." The Singing Whale had a top rating as a coastal restaurant, and it was a shame to order a cheeseburger when they had such outstanding fish and crab dishes. But she had a point to make.

Burke reached across the table and squeezed her hand. "It's so good to see you again, Angie. You're looking terrific. I've missed you."

"You're here with an agenda," she said bluntly. He managed to look briefly reproachful, but she didn't back down. "What is it?"

"Well, first I have to admit I come with some bad news. So I may as well tell you and get it over with. You remember that little Asian friend of yours, the actress? You introduced me to her one time after we went to a play she had a small part in."

Angie straightened in the chair. "Kristi Yamori."

"She's dead. Murdered."

"I know. I . . . I've been very upset about it."

Burke lifted a dark eyebrow. "I didn't realize it would make the news out here. But maybe, since a serial killer is involved—"

"A mutual friend told me. So you just happened to see it in a newspaper back there and remembered her name?"

"No. I did see something in the news about the serial killer killing again, but I'm afraid I didn't pay any attention to the name. But she was working for an investment company over in New Jersey, as you probably know, and I know the owner slightly."

"Actually, I helped her get the job there. I called Jordan Riker for her."

"That's what Jordan told me just recently." Burke skewered her with that narrow, penetrating gaze with which she was all too familiar. The gaze that asked suspiciously, *Just how well do you know him?*

Which was exactly why she hadn't told Burke about calling Jordan Riker at the time. She'd been afraid he'd misinterpret and do exactly what he was doing now: Come up with a wild and totally unwarranted suspicion about a personal relationship between her and Jordan Riker.

"I never actually met him," she said. She heard the defensive undertone in her voice and gave herself a mental kick. *You don't have to explain to him.* But neither did she want a matter of zero importance to escalate. There were more important issues at stake.

"You and I had flown down to the Bahamas for a few days a year or two ago. I thought it was supposed to be a vacation, but I spent most of my time at the swimming pool alone while you were in our suite with Riker setting up this investment company. I never actually met him, though," she emphasized.

Burke made a show of hanging his head. "Guilty as charged. I always let work take up way too much of the time we should've had together."

"Burke the workaholic."

"I'm sorry, Angie. No wonder you walked out on me." He reached across the table and caressed her cheek lightly.

Angie shrugged. Burke could, when he wanted, put considerable charm into an apology. At one time it had an effect on her. But not now. "I came into the bedroom through the sliding door that opened onto the pool area one time while you were in conference with him. The two of you were arguing about something, and I heard him saying how hard it would be to hire trustworthy people. I knew Kristi was as trustworthy as the sun coming up, and she had secretarial experience, which was why I called Jordan about her getting a job there."

Burke lifted his head and smiled engagingly. "I've seen the error of my ways, Angie. I'm a changed man. On top of that, I got out of the company within just a couple months, so all that work on the Bahamas trip was mostly an exercise in spinning my wheels."

"I got the impression from Kristi that it's a very successful company."

"Right. I probably should've hung in there. But I got into the deal with Jordan mostly because I knew his family back in Texas. Shirttail relatives, more or less, and I felt kind of obligated to help him out when he came to New York. Like you did with your friend Kristi. But I was also under the impression Jordan was a solid, intellectual-type guy with a background in accounting. Right away I discovered that under his wimpy exterior, what Jordan liked to do best with his number-crunching talent was bet on the horses. Or anything else that moved. Being in partnership with some irresponsible gambler wasn't my idea of a sound investment, so I bailed out. But apparently he's either a very successful gambler or he gave it up, because the company is doing great."

"You lost money when you got out?"

Burke grinned. "Well, no."

She could've guessed that.

He cleared his throat. "But to get back to your friend. I don't talk to Jordan often, but I happened to call him about an IPO I thought might interest him. He was all shook up about your friend. Apparently she was a really nice girl and a hard worker. Then she quit, and he didn't think anything about it until a couple weeks later when the police showed up. Somebody had just identified the body, I think. She was pretty well carved up, as you probably know, and he found that really hard to take. He mentioned her name at the time . . . and I'm embarrassed to say I didn't recognize it even then. But when he said something about her being Asian and an actress on the side, things finally clicked in my head. It was a terrible thing to have happen to her."

Angie swallowed, pushing back that vision of a knife carving a question mark in Kristi's delicate shoulder. "Did he say why she quit the job?"

"I don't know that we discussed it. Although it sticks in my mind that he thought she was leaving New York."

"I've wondered if she was involved in a personal relationship with him. And maybe quit when the relationship soured."

"I don't think so. He didn't mention it. But could be, I suppose. I don't think men talk about relationships as much as women do. It's pretty much sports and the stock market with the guys I know."

*And maybe the best source of good cocaine?* Angie added, although she let the accusing question remain unspoken.

"You didn't know she was planning to quit the job?" Burke asked.

"No. I saw her a couple of nights before I left New York, and she didn't mention it. Though I keep thinking maybe she told me something important, and I just wasn't paying attention."

Burke tapped the table with his knuckles, as if he were debating saying something.

"What is it?" Angie demanded.

"I hate to say anything about this. Riker felt bad even thinking it, considering what happened to her. And she was your friend. But he thinks she may have taken some confidential company information with her when she left. Probably on computer disks."

"Kristi wouldn't do that!"

"A competitor might pay a lot of money for those records," Burke said. "Don't starving actors always need money?"

"I don't care what they'd pay. Kristi wouldn't do it. She was honest. I was with her one time when a store accidentally missed charging her for a blouse, and she went right back and told them about it."

"Hey, don't get mad at me. I'm just telling you what Riker said."

"He's wrong. Did he say anything to the police about this?" The idea that Kristi's reputation might be besmirched made Angie's pulse pound with indignation.

"I don't know. But I doubt it. I got the impression he felt bad enough just thinking she might've done it. And unless she sold the records before the killer got her, they probably won't turn up anyway."

Angie hesitated. She remembered Kristi asking her a couple of weeks earlier about a good place to rent a safe deposit box, and Angie had named the bank where her own box was located. Would Kristi have put stolen records there for safekeeping, with the idea of capitalizing on them? No. Never.

Burke caught her hesitation. "Did you think of something?"

Angie shook her head. "I just get to feeling really bad about Kristi sometimes."

"They'll get her killer one of these days. He can't keep getting away with murdering women like he does."

The waitress brought their food. Angie took a bite and then put the cheeseburger back on the plate.

"You know, I'd forgotten it until now, but I tried to call Kristi the night before I left and didn't get an answer. She lived over in Jersey City, but her body was found in New York. What if she never made it home from that evening we went out for dinner together? What if the killer got her that very night?"

"But she hadn't quit the job yet when you saw her, had she?"

"That's right. She hadn't." Angie leaned back in her chair, relieved. She didn't want to think there was something she should've done that night, something that would've changed the course of Kristi's life.

"Angie, I can see how bad you feel about this, and I don't want to rush you. But you're right. I did come here with an agenda. And right at the top of it is that I want you back."

"No."

His gaze narrowed, but he managed to put tease in his voice when he said, "Well, now, you don't have to beat around the bush about it. Just come right out and tell me what you really think."

Angie refused to let the tease affect her.

"Okay, I've lived in New York for years," he went on. "But sometimes it starts looking like a good place *not* to live. We've had the World Trade Center tragedy. We have a killer running around mutilating women. Who knows what else? Julesburg isn't exactly my style . . ."

Even Angie had to smile at that understatement.

"But I've been thinking about transferring to our San Francisco office."

"Leave Wall Street?"

"If I can persuade you to make the same move."

Angie was momentarily too surprised to repeat her unambiguous no. "What would I do in San Francisco?"

"Be my wife."

"Wife?" Angie echoed. A french fry, almost to her mouth, dangled from her fingers.

"This is why I say our biggest problem has been me. Me and my unwillingness to make a permanent commitment. But I'm past that, Angie. You've made your point by walking out. I was angry at first, but now I thank you for it. You've made me realize what I'm missing without you and that I don't want to lose you. I'm asking you to marry me."

This was indeed a new leaf for Burke. Unlike most of the people they knew in New York, who all seemed to have at least one marriage behind them, Burke had dodged marriage vows from the very beginning. He'd come from a tough, working-class background in Texas, raised by parents who bounced beer bottles and each other off the walls regularly. Not exactly walking advertisements for wedded bliss. He'd clawed his way through college, started as a trainee with a stockbroker in New York, and dedicated himself to making money. As much and as fast as possible.

Early on, she had indeed been troubled by his aversion to a marriage commitment and, thinking his jealous possessiveness proved something, had played a few games trying to get him to commit. She'd learned the danger of that when he rammed his Jaguar into the taxi she was in when he thought she was going out with another man. By the time of that last party, she was grateful they weren't entangled in marriage and that she could simply walk away.

"I'd intended to make more of a production number out of this. Wine and candles and the whole romantic scene. But I can see you're not going to give me much time here, so cheeseburgers and 7Up will have to do."

He reached in his pocket and, with a perfect fifties' movie flourish, set a small, black velvet box on the table and flipped it open.

## 15

The diamond was at least five carats, blazing with an inner fire. Emerald-cut diamonds, small only in comparison with the size of the center stone, flanked it on either side.

Burke was not unaware of her recent fondness for glittery mementos.

Yet, oddly, where once she'd have been thrilled by the ring, now she only felt embarrassed. Embarrassed for Burke that this was the only way he knew how to reach out to her—or to any woman, probably. Embarrassed for herself that once she could've been bought with this diamond.

"Burke, this is very sweet of you. And generous. But—"

"But it isn't the most important part, is it?" He reached both hands across the table and encircled her fingers. "Because the important part is the words that go with the ring."

"Please, Burke, don't—"

"I love you, Angie. I find the actual words difficult to get out. I've never said them, you know. Whatever relationships I've had in the past, I've never said them. But I'm saying them now, and I mean them with all my heart. I love you."

She looked at him and swallowed. How many times had she tried to wheedle those words out of him? Did he mean them now? She tilted her head and studied him. Serious lines cut between his dark brows, as if his future happiness or despair hinged on her response. Yet for all his seeming sincerity, a strong undercurrent of doubt flowed through her. Was Burke even capable of love?

And whether or not he was capable of it no longer mattered.

"Burke, I appreciate everything you're saying and doing. You're making this really difficult for me."

He leaned back and smiled. "How difficult can it be to say yes and let me slip this ring on your finger? I thought we might drive right on down to Reno and get married. Unless you want the white gown and champagne reception and all?"

"No, it isn't that." Carefully she closed the ring box and slid it back toward him. "I'm sorry, Burke. You came all this way and everything, but—"

"But you're turning me down?" He leaned forward in his chair, tight lines suddenly etched around his mouth, as if this were a response totally beyond belief. The beauty contestant turning down the crown.

"I'm sorry," she repeated. She shook her head. "It's just . . . over, Burke."

He leaned back in the chair. "Oh, come on, Angie. Get real. Who are you trying to fool? You don't belong in this burg, and we both know it. You're going to mold and rot here. What do you want that I'm not offering?"

*Ah, the real Burke has returned. This is the Burke I know.* "It isn't that I want anything—"

"A house? You can't be happy in that dump you're living in. I always figured you were the penthouse type, but if it's a big house you want—"

"If I want a big house, I can buy it, Burke. Your financial expertise in the stock market has left me very well fixed. It's me I'm not satisfied with. Me I'm working on changing. I don't like what my ambition did to me and what I became. I want to find the person I used to be before . . . everything."

"None of us can turn back time."

"But we can walk away from the past."

"Some things can't be walked away from."

"I've walked away from you, Burke," she said softly. "And I'm not turning back."

"Is that guy you were involved with before I met you mixed up in this? The computer nerd in Phoenix?"

The question didn't surprise her. The ever-suspicious Burke. Though she was surprised he remembered Ethan's existence.

"No," she answered.

He grabbed the ring box and jammed it in his shirt pocket. He stood up, yanked out his wallet, and threw a couple of bills on the table. He grabbed the suede jacket and started to stalk away, shoulders rigid. Unexpectedly he stopped and wheeled to face her.

"I really think you should reconsider this. It's important."

She shook her head slowly. This time, after a long, lips-compressed appraisal, he didn't look back when he strode away.

Angie sat there, her cheeseburger mostly uneaten, her greasy fries congealing, her hands wrapped around the cold glass. She'd never expected to feel sorry for Burke Davis, but at this moment she did. He hadn't a clue about what was really important in life. Why had he bothered with this charade? Because he couldn't stand the fact that she'd dumped him, and he figured he'd manipulate her until he chose the proper moment to dump her. Was it worth even a ring and marriage to prove his control and superiority? Was there truth in anything he'd said?

Yes, she reflected, it was probably true that he'd never told any other woman he loved her. It was a matter of ego and pride with him, she suspected. He could get what he wanted without saying the words other men resorted to. Yes, he'd bitten the bullet and said them today, but she'd heard no depth of love behind them. Only . . . words. Calculated words. They were Plan Two, in case the ring didn't work.

Only in his somber expression and those final words—*I really think you should reconsider this*—had she seen and heard an unexpected hint of truth and regret. Maybe it was only then that her decision had finally gotten through to him.

The unpleasant confrontation left her feeling edgy, but by the time she walked back to the office, the edginess had turned to relief. It was over. Burke had come, tried everything from diamonds to declarations of love to derisive anger, and she hadn't caved. Today wrote finis to the past.

The article and a photo Angie had taken from an angle that elongated the Nevermore name to a menacing dagger came out in the following Wednesday's edition of the *Herald*.

Ryan immediately called to tell her it was great. So did Twila Mosely. Angie took a copy to Myrna Bettenworth, and in spite of her warning about letting "sleeping dogs lie," the elderly woman's eyes lit up when she saw her name right there at the beginning of the article. Several people Angie didn't know also called, one man rambling on about how he'd once considered buying the theater but right away his dog got run over and he figured that was bad omen enough right there. Even the carpenter who installed her new door and lock commented on it. On Thursday morning the grocery store called to say they'd run out of copies. Angie contacted the printers in Dutton Bay and had another one hundred printed.

That same afternoon an older man in a slightly rumpled brown suit came into the office. He introduced himself as Warren Beasley. They shook hands over the counter.

"Associated Press. I work out of Coos Bay, but I get down this way once in a while. I heard the *Herald* changed hands not long ago and thought I'd stop in and say hello and offer my good wishes and congratulations."

"That's very nice of you. I appreciate it."

"I knew the former owners fairly well. Also the owners before them." Warren Beasley picked up a *Herald* from the stack on the counter. "Ah, the Nevermore. I see you're digging right into Julesburg's old skeletons."

"I'm planning to do a series of articles about all the old buildings here in town. Although I doubt any of the others are as fascinating as the Nevermore."

Beasley dug in his pocket for change to pay, but Angie waved off his money. "Professional perk. One journalist to another." She smiled. "Although that may be elevating my status somewhat higher than it deserves."

He inspected the front page through the bottom half of his bifocals. "This looks good. Crisp and snappy. The Dolangers were great people. Hard working and conscientious. But they never quite got the hang of headlines."

"I'm trying to learn."

"You know, eight or nine years ago I did a piece about various unsolved crimes here on the coast. Not nearly as in depth as what you have here, but I looked into that old murder at the Nevermore. Maybe I'll dig it out and see what I have." He lifted his gaze from the front page and smiled at Angie. "You going to solve that old murder and bring the killer to justice?"

Angie smiled back. "I just might do that."

"I made a little effort to locate—" Beasley broke off and ran his gaze down the article until he came to the name. "This guy. Vance Spohn, the projectionist. He was under suspicion for a while. But I didn't have any luck finding him."

Angie considered telling him Lillian's theory that Vance had returned and faked Amelia Swarthout's suicide. But it was too far out even to mention. She certainly hadn't mentioned it as a possibility in the article. Not only too far out but too libelous.

"I've wondered if maybe Spohn wasn't his real name," Beasley added. "I think he was kind of a drifter. He'd have to be . . . what, now? In his late fifties, I suppose. From the information I picked up, he was considerably younger than Amelia Swarthout."

Angie did a quick calculation and nodded in agreement with the time frame. She also thought of Myrna's theory—a killer who was a kid at the time of the murder, now a respectable adult right here in Julesburg. That person, if he existed, would probably be younger than Vance Spohn, maybe in his mid or late forties now. She was still wondering if such a person might have been interested enough in her notes to break into her house. Could he have been afraid that she might dig deeper and collect enough disparate facts to figure out some hidden truth?

Yet if he read this article, he'd have to realize she hadn't uncovered anything new.

"I also tried to find the son of the man who was murdered," Warren Beasley went on. "But I didn't get anywhere there, either."

"I can understand why. It was all so long ago. Even the police don't seem to know what became of the old records."

Warren Beasley smiled and pushed his glasses higher on the bridge of his nose. "Well, maybe you'll be the one to figure it all out."

On Sunday afternoon, a bright day after a week of dreary rain, Angie headed to the beach for a hike. She thought about taking Keyhole. Why shouldn't a cat enjoy beach walking as much as people and dogs? But Keyhole was apparently off on important cat business or too smart to get dragged into a beach walk, so she didn't answer Angie's kitty-kitty call.

At the beach, Angie took off her shoes, tied the laces together, and slung the shoes over her shoulder. The day held a fall crispness, the boom of big surf and a bank of ominously dark clouds offshore suggesting a storm brewing out in the Pacific. Kelp lay in long strands on the shore, the big bulbs squishy underfoot. She strolled leisurely, digging her toes into the sand, peering into tide pools, pouncing on an occasional agate or other beach treasure.

As she walked past Wandering Creek, the cell phone she'd tucked into the pocket of her windbreaker rang. She perched on a big log stranded in sand to answer it.

"Angie, hi!" Stefanie sounded excited. "Hey, have you looked at today's *Oregonian?*"

Portland's *Oregonian* was the largest newspaper in the state. The *Herald* would fit into its classified ad section.

"No, I'm just down here walking on the beach."

"I figured you might be, since you didn't answer the phone at the house. Hey, this is buried on an inside page, but it's about you and Julesburg and the Nevermore!"

*The AP guy. He doesn't waste time.* "What does it say?"

"It starts out, 'Does a sleepy little town on the Oregon coast have its own *Amityville Horror?'* Remember that *Amityville Horror* movie about the murders and other strange and awful things that happened in some old house back East somewhere?"

The short article hit the highlights of the Nevermore's past, adding a bit of information from Warren Beasley's earlier research that Angie hadn't discovered. The police officer who had done the main investigation of the murder had died in a shoot-out with a bank robber in Portland the following year. In total, however, the article was more about the arrival of a new editor at Julesburg's weekly newspaper, an editor Beasley described as energetically dedicated to digging into the Nevermore's strange history. It ended with what she'd said when he asked if she was going to solve the old murder. "I just might do that."

Angie laughed. "It makes me sound so spunky."

"Well, actually, you are kind of spunky."

The first part of the week was hectic, as usual. A half dozen interesting letters came in about the Nevermore, and Angie decided to publish them all. She was so busy she didn't get around to calling Estelle Reeves until Wednesday evening, when the next issue was safely on the stands.

Estelle said that Angie could look at the Nevermore again. "Come pick up a key whenever it's convenient. If I'm not here, Mike will give you one. Just go on over and wander around to your heart's content. The owners won't mind. Just watch out for that killer curtain."

Angie had just hung up the phone when it rang again.

"Hi, Angie. Ethan here."

He sounded friendly and brisk, as if their parting was not forgotten but took a backseat to more important matters.

"I'm glad to hear from you," she said. Did that sound like the understatement it was? "I've been wondering about the service for Kristi."

"So many people wanted to come that the Yamoris opened the church to everyone. It was a beautiful service. Kristi was much loved." She heard the catch in his voice, and it touched her. Somehow she doubted if Burke had ever in his life had an emotional catch in his voice.

"Have you heard anything more about the investigation?"

"That's why I called. There's been an arrest. A man who was seen in a bar with the woman who was killed after Kristi. I thought you'd want to know. Although I don't know how much they actually have on him."

"They have DNA from Kristi's fingernails!"

"Right. Though it'll take a couple of weeks or more, I think, to run DNA tests on him. The arrest may be mostly a way to detain the suspect until the results come in. Oh, something else. Your name was in the newspaper down here."

"It was?" For a moment all Angie could think was that some tabloid had invented an overblown scandal out of her leaving modeling and breaking up with Burke. Had they latched on to her one-time waltz with cocaine too? She braced herself.

"Maybe the local Chamber of Commerce ought to promote the Nevermore as a big tourist attraction."

Angie went blank for a moment. "Oh, the Associated Press piece about Julesburg and the Nevermore! Their man stopped in the other day. He'd researched the murder himself several years ago. I didn't realize the news release would show up so far away."

"AP stuff goes all over the country, doesn't it? I suppose it just depends on which newspapers pick it up. Hey, maybe an important movie producer will see it and come clamoring for a screenplay from you."

Angie laughed. "Yeah, right. With a million-dollar contract clutched in his hand. Wait—isn't that a Ferrari I hear pulling up outside the door right now?"

"I don't know about a Ferrari, but sometime within the next few days a beat-up old yellow pickup will be pulling up to your door again."

The casual statement ended on enough of an upswing to turn it into a question. *How do you feel about my coming?* Angie didn't hesitate. "I'm looking forward to it."

A movie producer didn't arrive the following afternoon. But someone else did.

## 16

&stelle had another appointment, and Angie spent over an hour by herself in the Nevermore on Thursday morning. She turned on every light she could find, including one that still worked in the old popcorn machine. No just-wakened spook charged out to meet her.

She climbed around the boards blocking the stairway and inspected the upstairs. Exposed beams below the charred floor were almost burned through in places, overhead beams collapsed or cracking. An ominous creak when she stepped onto the floor sent her backpedaling immediately. She knew little about building construction, but she suspected the entire upstairs level would have to be demolished.

No matter. She didn't need an upstairs anyway.

The theater was on its best behavior today. The mirror didn't show peculiar reflections. The lights didn't flicker ominously, and the drape didn't attack her when she slipped around it to enter the main seating area.

It was just an ordinary old building badly in need of repairs. Perhaps, if you wanted to get maudlin—and anthropomorphic—even a building lonely for human companionship. And with possibilities, great possibilities. An office here would have a front-row seat on Jules-burg's main street.

The only time she felt uneasy was when she stepped down into that concrete pit surrounding the old monster of a furnace. She flicked the narrow beam of her little flashlight along the circular path, trying to dispel an irrational feeling that something could be lurking in the shadows on the far side of the furnace. Aiming the beam upward, she saw a naked bulb, apparently burned out, hanging from a cord that disappeared into spiderwebbed rafters. She spun the beam to a corner when she heard a scurrying sound, but saw only a pile of old concrete building blocks.

She circled the pathway around the furnace twice before spotting the opening cut into the outer wall, along the way stumbling over a pile of oily rags that suggested old maintenance problems with the furnace. She'd never have known the little door was there if the flash of her camera hadn't hit it at just the right angle when she was taking those photos.

Just as the picture showed, there was no latch or knob, although a tiny screw hole indicated where one may have once been. Now the door was only an almost indiscernible square cut into the waist-high wall, its edge matching a seam where boards joined. She tried to pry the door open with her fingers and got nothing for her efforts but two broken fingernails. Estelle Reeves's fingernail-fixated spook? She'd left her purse under the seat in the car and didn't even have a fingernail file to use as a tool.

No matter, of course. The movie screen and everything back here behind it would have to be torn out. Plus a ton of trash hauled off. But she was certain now that her idea for an apartment in this section of the theater was indeed workable. Haul off that old furnace, install windows and skylights to lighten up the gloom, make a private entrance into the parking lot, and it could be a great place to live.

*Read my mind, ghost of the Nevermore. It's time to move on. Angie Harrison is movin' in.*

She returned the key to Estelle, had two slices of pizza at Website X for lunch, and got back to the office just as Becky was leaving for the day. They met on the sidewalk outside the door.

"Some guy was here about a half hour ago looking for you," Becky said. "I tried to get him to tell me what he wanted, but he said he had to talk to you."

"Nobody you know?"

"No. But there are lots of people I don't know. Julesburg isn't as everybody-knows-everybody as some people seem to think small towns are."

"You're sounding philosophical today." *And a bit grumpy.*

"Yeah, sorry. I just found out Aaron has been sneaking around, seeing some woman who moved here a few weeks ago to work for Volkman Laser Systems."

"Oh, Becky, I'm so sorry."

"Maybe I'll move to Portland. You just picked up and left a career in New York, and it's working out fine for you."

"Well, check it out with Aaron before you do anything rash, okay? Things aren't always what they seem on the surface."

Angie was just unlocking the office door when a blue sedan with a Nevada license plate pulled into the tiny parking lot. A big guy stepped out of the car, shoulders hunched against the drizzle that had just started. He wasn't overweight, definitely not fat, but he had a sleek, well-fed polish. A big-steak man, she decided. But no couch potato. A deep tan, sun-streaked gold hair with a cultivated wave, tan slacks and a pale blue polo shirt under an expensive windbreaker. Not here to place an ad to peddle an old pickup.

"Hello. I'm looking for the editor. Angie Harrison, I think her name is."

"That's me. Come inside and get out of the rain."

Once inside, Angie pushed through the swinging gate. The stranger stood at the counter.

She slipped off her jacket. "So, what can I do for you?"

"Help me find a killer, I hope." He smiled. Great teeth. "My name is Steve Llewelyn."

It took a moment for the name to register with Angie. She stopped short in the process of hanging her jacket on the stand beside the gate. *It's true,* she thought. *A jaw actually can drop.*

"Llewelyn? You're—"

"Harry Llewelyn's son." He smiled. "Are you as surprised to see me as I am to be here?"

"Yes, I certainly am."

Angie inspected him more closely. Mid-thirties, she guessed, with a confident air of success. Impeccably groomed, although his aftershave or cologne was a little heavy for her taste. A thick gold ring studded with an impressive diamond decorated his right hand. Very well-kept hands.

"You saw the Associated Press piece about the Nevermore and the murder in a Nevada newspaper?" she asked.

He looked startled. "Uh, yeah, how'd you know that?"

"Just a guess."

"Well, seeing that article was pure luck. I've been working in the Middle East for several years, and I just returned to the States a few weeks ago. I'm in the process of buying a car dealership in Vegas."

Angie supposed she shouldn't be surprised that the article had shown up in Las Vegas. Ethan had seen it in a Phoenix newspaper. A combination of murder, a haunted old theater, and a spunky editor apparently appealed to a wide audience. Yet she was surprised—and gratified—that what had started with her article in the tiny *Julesburg*

*Herald* had reached out to a man who'd been so affected by what had happened here long ago. A small miracle of sorts, actually.

"I'm sorry about your father. You must've been very young when he was killed."

"I barely remember him. I don't even have any photos. They were all lost in a house fire."

"The Associated Press man who wrote that article said he tried to locate you several years ago, but he didn't have any luck."

"I'm not surprised. We moved around a lot. And then, like I said, I've been out of the country in recent years."

She was curious about what he'd been doing in the Middle East, but he didn't volunteer information, and asking seemed a bit nosy. "A couple of people told me that relatives came and got you after your father's death."

"That's right. My grandparents."

"Someone thought it was an aunt."

"Oh? No, it was my grandparents. Wonderful people. Gram and Pops, I always called them. But they're both dead now. They died in the house fire."

A dismaying thought suddenly occurred to her. "I hope reading the newspaper article wasn't how you found out that your father had been murdered?"

"No, I've always known that. Gram and Pops didn't like to talk about it, but once in a while when Pops had a little too much to drink, he'd start rambling on about how the police had never found the . . . well, I'll censor what Pops called the killer. But he was bitter. His son murdered, and no one ever brought to justice for it."

"Did he ever offer any ideas about who he thought did it?"

Steve shook his head. "Never did. I guess it's odd, since they didn't talk about my father much, and I never really knew him, but from as far back as I can remember I've always had this . . . I don't know what you'd call it. A passion, maybe? A passion to someday come back here, find out who killed him, and bring the murderer to justice. When I read that piece in the newspaper, I knew this was the time."

Angie reached under the counter and grabbed a *Herald* from the small stack of last week's issues. "Just about everything I know is in here," she said when she handed it to him. "I don't want to discourage you about finding the killer, but everything happened so long ago that even the police records have disappeared."

"Did someone want them to disappear?"

The question startled and then impressed Angie. A half hour in town and he'd already come up with a thought that had never occurred to her. Maybe he *could* track down a killer.

Steve Llewelyn spread the front page on the counter and started reading. The phone rang. Angie answered it and said yes, she'd be glad to cover a meeting of the Julesburg Save-the-Wetlands committee next Monday.

"Killed with a knife," Steve murmured as he read. "I didn't know that. I always assumed he'd been shot."

"Somehow a knife seems to make it more personal."

"Yes. Exactly. The killer has to actually touch his victim, not just stand across a room and pull a trigger." He pulled back from the newspaper as if he found this aspect of his father's death particularly repugnant. "Although I guess dead is dead, no matter how it's done."

Steve shook his head when he finished the article and refolded the newspaper. "Curses and evil spirits have always seemed like a darker version of the tooth fairy and Easter bunny to me. But reading about the misfortunes of all these people connected with the Nevermore makes you wonder, doesn't it?"

Even as he talked to her his gaze roamed the room. She had the feeling he could turn his back and instantly name forty objects visible here in her office. And he probably could describe her to the last detail as well, she decided when his blue eyes returned to her. It was a vaguely disconcerting feeling.

"How long do you intend to be in Julesburg?" she asked.

"I'm not certain. As long as it takes to find the killer. Or convince myself that bringing him to justice isn't possible."

"How do you intend to go about finding the killer?"

"You're familiar with the town and the facts. I figure you're curious enough to want to know who the murderer is or you wouldn't have gone this far." His eyes were shrewd but his smile beguiling when he added, "I thought we might join forces."

"Actually, I'm doing a series on all the old buildings in Julesburg."

"Each with its own murder?"

"No. The others are just old buildings." She didn't mean to downgrade them in comparison to the Nevermore but knew she had.

He smiled again, as if that answered his question about how he'd find the killer: She was too curious a woman not to work with him on this.

"Okay, I'm interested in the murder and in finding the killer," Angie admitted. "But I don't really know how to dig any deeper than I already have."

She hesitated, wondering whether to tell him about Lillian Feldman's and Myrna Bettenworth's conflicting theories about the killer. And the fact that her house had been searched, possibly by someone looking for her notes.

Detouring that, she instead said, "I imagine you're interested in seeing the Nevermore. It's for sale, and I'm sure that if you contact the real estate office, someone will be happy to show you around."

"I'd definitely like to see inside the theater." He lifted blond eyebrows. "I don't suppose I could talk you into coming along? You surely know more about the place than any real estate agent."

"I'll check with Estelle."

Angie called Julesburg Realty again, and Estelle said she'd meet them at the theater with the key. When Angie told her who was interested in seeing it, Estelle gave an impressed whistle. "Think he's a potential buyer?"

"Who knows?"

And it was a thought that unexpectedly worried her. She wouldn't feel right trying to buy the old theater if Steve Llewelyn wanted it, but she was more and more feeling like she wanted it for herself.

Angie locked up again, leaving the clock sign on the door with hands arranged to indicate she'd be back by three o'clock. Steve Llewelyn followed her in his car to the theater. Estelle came flying up the street just as they were parking at the curb. She didn't even get out of the car, just rolled down the window and leaned across the seat to hand Angie the key. Angie made quick sidewalk introductions.

"You can do the tour by yourselves, okay?" Estelle said. "I have to make an emergency run up to the title company office in Dutton Bay and do CPR on a deal before it falls through."

Angie hesitated. Steve Llewelyn seemed nice enough, but she hadn't known him more than fifteen minutes and wasn't sure she wanted to close herself up in the Nevermore with him.

"Maybe we'd better do it another time, then," he said.

Realization that he so quickly recognized her wariness and was sensitive to it relaxed her moment of uneasiness.

"Just keep the key in case you want to take a later look," Estelle said. "We have another one at the office." She zoomed off, not waiting to see if they were going inside now or not.

Angie turned and unlocked the door. They were here. She may as well give him the tour. By this time, when she stepped into the shabby lobby and felt for the light switch, the old theater felt almost familiar.

"You've been in here before?" Steve asked.

"I had to see it for the article. And then I came back just this morning because I'm thinking about buying the place myself."

"You are? What in the world for?"

"I could turn it into offices for the newspaper. We need more space." She laughed lightly. "Although maybe not a smart move on my part, given the disasters that have happened to most of the other owners."

"I wouldn't put much stock in that. In my opinion, we pretty much make our own luck."

It wasn't, she thought with a quick glance at him, just a casual comment. It sounded more like a life philosophy. "But if you're interested in buying the Nevermore—"

He threw up his hands. "Me? No way. All I want to do in Julesburg is find my father's killer."

Angie looked at their reflections in the mirror, where the crack seemed to be growing larger. "I never did find out where your father was actually killed, but I think it must've been here in the lobby."

Steve walked around sizing things up, his observant gaze flicking from the boards blocking the stairway to the chunks of old sink visible in the restroom. What did it feel like to step into a strange place and know that this was where your father had met his violent death? Steve Llewelyn didn't appear to be overcome with emotion, although he exuded a restless energy as he peered behind the counter.

"If the killer followed him in when Amelia Swarthout opened the door, it would have to have happened right here," he agreed.

"Yes. Except . . ."

"Except?"

She hesitated but then decided he was entitled to know everything, even the far-out stuff. "There were a few things I didn't put in the newspaper article." She told him about Lillian Feldman's theory that the projectionist, Vance Spohn, had killed Harry Llewelyn, and why. "And if that was the way it happened, the murder could've taken place anywhere in here."

"Maybe even somewhere else, and then the body was moved here so Amelia could spout her intruder-with-a-knife story?"

That was another intriguing thought that had never occurred to her. A murder committed somewhere other than the theater. She smiled. "You have a devious mind. A valuable asset when investigating murder."

He returned the smile. "Thank you. What else wasn't in the article?"

Not much got by Steve Llewelyn. Okay, she'd gone this far, she may as well tell him the rest of what she'd heard. She told him about Lillian's idea that Vance Spohn had come back and rigged a fake suicide to kill Amelia. She laid out Myrna Bettenworth's suspicion that the killer was still in Julesburg, upstanding and respectable now. And perhaps willing to kill again to protect his status.

"Interesting. A local person who had the power and opportunity to make those police records disappear."

Another thought that hadn't occurred to her.

"So what we have here," Steve reflected, "is the possibility that it could be dangerous for anyone who starts digging too deeply into all this."

"Oh, I don't really think that. Basically, I think it's just two little old ladies with wild imaginations." She paused. "Except that my house was searched."

"Searched? As in ransacked? Vandalized?"

"No, actually it was a very subtle search. Just a few items out of place that made me realize someone had been there. And nothing was taken, even though there were a few things that could've been pawned or sold."

"What do you think the person was after, then?"

"I've wondered if someone was worried about what I'd learned from Lillian and Myrna and was looking for my notes from the interviews. I suppose someone could presume that, as a newspaper reporter, I would have taken notes. But the notes were in my car, not in the house when it was searched."

"Intriguing. And a very strong possibility, I'd say, that your notes were exactly what they were looking for." He turned to look at her, blue eyes thoughtful. "Are you freaked out?"

"No. . . . Well, maybe I was a little the night I realized someone had been in my house. But I've had my door and lock changed since then."

"You live alone?"

Angie felt another flicker of uneasiness. Steve Llewelyn seemed pleasant, in a high-powered sort of way. But this wasn't information she cared to give out to a man who was still a stranger. She detoured the question by smiling and saying, "I have a watch-cat."

"Hey, how about that? So do I."

"Really?" Angie was surprised. Steve Llewelyn didn't strike her as a man who'd let a cat inside his door. Which showed what you got for judging a man on the basis of his cologne or his sleek good looks.

"His name's Macho Man. Big, ears-chewed-off tom. Would've eaten anything including old shoe leather when he showed up at the door. Now he wants the fancy stuff in cans."

They smiled at each other with the camaraderie of owners of strays-cum-royalty. They were standing in the center aisle now, and Angie had been about to suggest they leave. Instead she said, "There's a place in back of the screen I'm curious about. If you don't mind stumbling over a lot of trash and stuff . . . ?"

"Would it be okay if I look around upstairs first? That's where the projectionist would probably have spent most of his time."

"Be careful. The floor looks unstable."

She heard several creaks overhead as she waited, but he made no comment when he returned. She led him down the aisle and behind the gold satin curtain. In the pit around the furnace, she targeted the beam of her tiny flashlight on the faint seam line between the door and circular wall. Steve knelt in front of it and ran his fingers along the edge she pointed out.

"I think maybe it's nailed shut," Angie said.

"I don't see any nails. Maybe it's warped with moisture and age. Why do you want it open?"

"Good question," she admitted. "Just curiosity, I guess."

Steve didn't argue with the logic of feminine curiosity. He took the flashlight and climbed the three steps up to the stage level. After digging around in the contents of the trash, he returned with a length of metal rod.

He rammed the rod into the seam, metal briefly screeching against wood, and levered the door open. The old hinges squawked in protest, and an unpleasantly moldy, earthy scent blasted out to meet them.

Angie waved a hand in front of her face. "Yuck. Close it up, quick."

To her surprise Steve took her flashlight and crawled through the opening, his broad shoulders barely able to make the squeeze. She was curious enough to get down on her knees and follow him. He swiveled the flashlight beam around the large area that was much too low to stand upright. The concrete floor under the huge oil furnace did not extend here. Above were heavy joists of rough-cut lumber holding up the stage floor; below, raw earth. Upright braces scattered here and there provided further support for the floor, plus a tangle of pipes and wiring that Angie suspected would give any building inspector nightmares. And enough spiderwebs to stock a horror movie. Another pile of old rags lay near the outside concrete wall that was part of the building's foundation.

"Looks like it's just a crawl space, same as most houses have," Steve said after they'd both crawled out of the opening.

Angie swiped at a spiderweb tangled in her hair. "I don't know why I was so curious."

"If you're thinking about buying the place, it's smart to check out everything."

Steve pushed the small door shut, but now it stubbornly refused to stay shut. She showed him the concrete blocks piled in a corner, and he carried one over and braced it against the door.

Back in the lobby, Angie asked, "Does being here give you any feeling of . . . I don't know, connection with your father in some way?"

"You know, it does. It really does. It's an awful thing, growing up knowing someone deliberately snuffed out your father's life. And it happened right here. I guess I have to say that being here reinforces my determination to find out who murdered him."

Steve told her he was staying at the Sea Haven Motel, which was just outside the south end of town. He invited her to dinner at the Singing Whale. After a moment's hesitation, she accepted. She had to admit her feminine curiosity was in high gear here also.

They met at the Singing Whale at seven, and she was right about one thing: Steve Llewelyn was definitely a big-steak man. His rare sirloin covered most of the plate and made her shrimp scampi and baked potato look almost skimpy. He was also an interesting man and widely traveled, although he never did reveal what he'd been doing in the Middle East. His special interest was scuba diving, but he didn't try to dominate the conversation with talk about himself and his accomplishments. He was, without being nosy, also curious about her, and a good listener. She was both pleased and relieved that when she finally admitted she'd been a model, he appeared interested but not awestruck.

"I understand many people who live in New York wouldn't live anywhere else, but I've been there a couple times and hated it," he said. "Las Vegas is growing like a weed, but there's still a lot of open space around it."

"A good friend was murdered in New York, not long after I left." Angie didn't know why she'd brought that up, except that Kristi was never far from her mind.

"I'm sorry to hear that."

Steve's words were ordinary, but there was interest and concern in his gaze, and Angie found herself telling him about Kristi and her senseless murder. "She was killed with a knife too. The killer carved a question mark into her shoulder." The vision still made her shudder.

Oddly, the fact that they both had lost people to violent deaths created an unexpected bond between them. How many people had been close to someone whose life had been ended by the brutal savagery of a knife? But Steve had lost his father that way, just as she'd lost Kristi.

At the end of the meal, when they were drinking coffee, Steve pulled a pack of Marlboros and a lighter out of a pocket. He shook a cigarette out of the pack and flicked the lighter but didn't touch the flame to the tobacco. He glanced up at Angie.

"I'm sorry," she said, "but I think this is a no smoking restaurant."

He laughed and tapped the cigarette back into the pack. "Don't worry. I'm not going to light it. I've quit. I just do this little test of willpower every now and then."

Angie shook her head. Strange, but admirable.

After dinner, he asked if she'd show him where Myrna Bettenworth lived, because he wanted to talk to her. By then she had lost her wariness of him, and they took his car, leaving hers in the restaurant's parking lot. After showing him Myrna's little house, she guided him on a quick tour of the town.

Back at the Singing Whale's parking lot, she said, "Julesburg has only one cemetery, and I don't know who, if anyone, keeps a record of where graves are located. The only way to locate someone in it may be to wander around until you spot the grave."

"Cemetery?" He sounded blank.

"Your parents are probably buried here in Julesburg, aren't they?"

"Oh. Yeah, right. And I certainly want to visit the graves while I'm here," he said, although she had the impression the thought hadn't occurred to him until that moment. "I'll check it out tomorrow. I don't suppose you'd have time to go with me?"

"You know, I've never been there. It might make an interesting feature article for the *Herald*. I can probably get away tomorrow afternoon."

"Great. Then I guess the next thing is to plan strategy, how I'm going to flush out a murderer."

"Well, there is one idea I've thought about following up," Angie said. "It's kind of far out, but Lillian mentioned this person, and if you could find her, it's possible you could learn something helpful."

He smiled. "How about *we* could learn something?"

"Well . . ."

"Think what a story you'll have for the *Herald* if we run down the killer."

She smiled. "Okay. We."

## 17

ngie spent Friday morning promoting ads to various businesses around town. Website X took out a quarter page to advertise their new calzones. Reedy's Hardware agreed that it was a good time of year to play up winterizing your home. She got a polite turndown from the owner of the local RV park but signed up the new South Julesburg Storage Units for a regular once-a-month ad.

Angie enjoyed the contacts with people, but at the same time she realized she was warily measuring every-one of a certain age group against Myrna's suspicions of a young killer grown up and respectable. Could one of these people have searched her house, concerned about those notes? The RV park owner was the right age, and not eager to talk to her. Simply because he didn't want to buy an ad, or for some other reason? Al Reedy at Reedy's Hardware was much too old, but his son Jeff, about the right age, came out of a back office to compliment her on the Nevermore article.

"And next week you're running an exposé on the killer's identity, right?" he said jokingly. But was he joking? Or jumpy?

*Get off it,* Angie chastised herself. *Next thing, you'll be thinking the chef at the Singing Whale is spiking your scampi with arsenic so you won't uncover his unsavory past.*

She dropped her clipboard and pen onto the front seat of the car, annoyed at herself for throwing a paranoid party. On the way back to the office, she saw a car with a Washington state license plate parked outside the Nevermore. Spotting a middle-aged couple looking at the real estate sign jolted her. The man was motioning with big gestures. Big ideas for the old theater? Wouldn't it be just her luck that the Nevermore was for sale for months, and she dallied just long enough for someone to buy it out from under her. She called Estelle Reeves as soon as she got back to the office.

"I want to make an offer on the Nevermore. Can you write it up right away?"

"You just bet I can!"

Estelle lost some of her enthusiasm when she heard the low amount of Angie's offer, but she agreed that the remodeling Angie had in mind would be expensive. And cash talked. Estelle said she'd have papers ready for Angie to sign late that afternoon.

The first thing Angie said when she slid into Steve's blue sedan later that day was, "I did it! I made an offer on the Nevermore."

Steve smiled. "And the ghost or whatever it is hasn't zapped you yet?"

"Well, I haven't actually signed the papers. And the day is still young."

Angie directed him to the hillside cemetery on the east side of town. The wire fence surrounded several acres, but the cemetery was more serviceable than showy, much of the area unused and weedy. A white arch and gate decorated the entrance, but the road was unpaved. Headstone choice was unregulated, and Angie and Steve wandered among monuments ranging from a simple metal plate set flat in the ground to a grand, head-high memorial of rose granite topped with a bell. Angie found Canfield graves that belonged to Stefanie's parents, but nowhere did they spot the Llewelyn name.

"If your mother wasn't buried here, maybe your grandparents took your father somewhere to be buried beside her," Angie suggested.

"Could be. They never said."

The occupied area was cared for but not manicured, and Angie liked the waving meadow grasses and hedges of native azalea and rhododendron bushes. Serene. Comforting. An undeveloped back slope was different, however. It fell off into a steep ravine choked with heavy brush and blackberry bushes and an unfortunate accumulation of discarded grave decorations and tree trimmings. Here Angie felt uneasy. Somehow the ugly, trash-strewn area made her think of Kristi's body lying abandoned with the garbage in a dark alley. She also didn't like the way Steve had moved up and draped an arm around her shoulders. She'd agreed to be partners in investigation, but this was a bit too much.

"Whoo-ee, it's a climb up here, isn't it?"

Angie turned out from under Steve's arm and saw a middle-aged woman carrying an armload of dead flowers up the hill toward the gulch.

"I'm always sad when the fresh flowers of summer are gone and I have to start using imitation ones," the woman chattered amiably as she discarded the dead blooms. "But I found some lovely yellow daisies at Wal-Mart that look almost real and just last and last. Inexpensive too."

Angie murmured something in polite response, and she and Steve headed back for the car parked near the gate. "I'm sorry we didn't have any luck finding your parents' graves," she said.

Steve pulled out a cigarette, lit it, then seemed to become aware of what he was doing. He dropped the barely burned cigarette and scrunched it beneath his heel.

"You mentioned yesterday that there was someone else we should try to locate, someone this woman at the nursing home mentioned to you," he said as they approached his sedan.

"What she told me was that Amelia Swarthout developed an interest in the occult after your father was killed. Séances and crystals and palm reading and such. If we could locate the spiritualist or palm reader or whoever it was she was going to—"

"You're thinking, what? That Amelia thought some hocus-pocus crystal ball reader could put her in touch with my father, and he'd announce who'd killed him? That's garbage." Steve jammed the key into the car door lock, the impatient gesture suggesting he'd expected something more worthwhile.

"True. Garbage. But I just thought . . . I don't know. Don't people confide in their spiritualists? If Vance Spohn did kill your father, and Amelia knew or suspected that, maybe . . ." Angie smiled as Steve opened the door for her. "Okay, grasping at straws, I guess. It would probably be better if you just jump in and do your own investigation without being distracted by my wild ideas."

"Hey, I didn't mean that." Steve's eyebrows lifted in alarm. "I need your help here. Where do we find this woman who might know who Amelia's spiritualist was?"

"Laurel Cove Nursing Center over in Dutton Bay. Her name is Lillian Feldman."

"Great. Let's go."

"I have to go back to the office now, but you might be able to see her yet today if you drive on over."

"I'd rather wait until you can go too."

Angie glanced at him sharply. Was there something meaningful in that comment? The last thing she wanted was some unexpected romantic interest from Steve Llewe-lyn, and that arm around her shoulders had felt a little too friendly for comfort. But as he knelt down beside a rear tire, absorbed in his study of the tread, she decided she was imagining a personal interest that didn't exist. *Your femme fatale days are over, remember?*

"Tomorrow afternoon, then," she said. "I want to keep the office open in the morning. I'll call the nursing home to see if Lillian can have visitors before we make the trip."

Steve suggested dinner again, but this time she turned him down. When she got back to the office, she checked in with Madge, who was sending out renewal notices to old subscribers. They'd had a dozen new subscriptions come in since the Nevermore article. Madge said the title company in Dutton Bay had called to say they were mail-ing over the information Angie had requested. Since things were quiet at the Herald, Angie decided to run over to Fit 'n' Fun and, if Stefanie wasn't too busy, see if she could come up with names to go with Myrna's sus-picions. Paranoid or not, she was curious about who might fit the profile of juvenile bad-boy back then, solid citizen now.

It turned out to be an unproductive errand. Stefanie was in Dutton Bay leading the twice-weekly acrobics ses-sions she conducted for seniors at the nursing home. Ryan's office was locked up and his cell phone number was posted in the window, which probably meant he was working somewhere up or down the coast for the day. She decided to borrow Sherlock for a beach walk, but when she got to the house, she found Ryan's pickup in the driveway.

She knocked on the door and rang the bell. Sherlock bounded around the side of the house to greet her, but no one answered. Then she heard odd clunks and thuds coming from somewhere and walked around the house to investigate. What she found was a dirty, disgruntled

Ryan backing out of an opening in the foundation under the side of the house. Sherlock sniffed at him as if to make certain this bedraggled person was really someone he knew.

"The detective business must be slow if you're investigating the underside of your own house," Angie said.

"What I'm investigating is termites. And I found them. I'm going to have to call an exterminator." Ryan swabbed a network of spiderwebs off his shirt. A live spider dropped off his pants leg. He picked up an oblong section of plywood that covered the opening in the foundation and fastened it back in place.

"I think maybe this ought to be a screen instead of a solid board," he muttered. "Maybe it needs more air circulation under there. I think the foundation must've been added a long time after the house was built. See? It's modern concrete blocks."

"This is a really fascinating conversation, termites and all," Angie said, "but if you'll excuse me, I'm just going to borrow Sherlock and go for a walk on the beach."

"Hey, wait a minute. Before you go, I want to ask you something. I'm leaving tomorrow morning to investigate a fire up in Yakima. I'll have to be gone several days. I was wondering if you'd come stay with Stef?"

"Of course. I'll be glad to. But . . . ?" She tilted her head questioningly.

"She's been fine. Don't worry. And she'll probably clobber me for suggesting someone should be here with her. 'I'm not sick, I'm pregnant,' she keeps telling me." He took off his shirt and shook it, scattering specks of dirt and an aroma of musty earth. "But I'd feel better if you were here with her while I'm gone."

"Leave it to me. I'll come over like it was my own idea."

"Good. Oh, I was also going to tell you. I've exchanged a few e-mails with my friend on the police force back in

New York. There's been an arrest in the Question Mark murders."

"I know. Ethan told me."

"You're keeping in touch with him?"

"Actually, he's coming up again, probably within the next week or so."

"I'm glad to hear that." Ryan nodded approvingly. "Ethan probably also told you that at this point the evidence against this guy is on the flimsy side, but DNA tests should prove something definite."

"I hope so."

"My friend Hirsch was also telling me something else, though it's not really connected with the murder. He said he had a friend who invested money with that company Kristi worked for. There was supposed to be a guaranteed monthly income, something to do with a ranch in Australia, and it was doing great for a while. But all of a sudden the payments stopped, and now he's just getting a big runaround from them."

"Really? I'm surprised. Burke seemed to think the company was doing great." But he'd also mentioned Jordan Riker's gambling tendencies. Maybe that had finally caught up with the company's financial operations.

"Well, maybe it's nothing. You know how it is after that big Enron scandal. Everybody's suspicious of everything. You . . . uh . . . keeping in touch with Burke too, since he was here?"

"No. He got it through his head that we were finis, kaput, au revoir."

"Good."

"But there are a couple of other things. Remember Harry Llewelyn, the man who was murdered in the Nevermore?"

"How could I forget, given the scintillating write-up in the illustrious *Julesburg Herald*?" Ryan grinned.

Angie ignored the tease. "His son showed up yesterday. He saw the AP piece in a Nevada newspaper."

"No kidding!"

"He's determined to find out who killed his father. And there's something else. I've made an offer to buy the Nevermore." She laid that second item on her brother in a rush, hoping to sneak it through unnoticed.

Fat chance.

He stopped in the process of putting his shirt back on. "You're not serious. Why would you make an offer on the Nevermore?"

She explained her plan to remodel it as both office and apartment. "I suppose I should've consulted with you first," she admitted.

"Of course. Little sisters should always consult their big brothers before making important decisions. I thought we settled that a long time ago after that little fiasco with your bedsheet-as-parachute scheme."

"I promise not to parachute off the roof of the Nevermore."

"I suppose I'll have to be thankful for small favors, then. Though I'd have suggested consulting a contractor for a bid on remodeling before rushing in to buy the place."

"I saw some people looking at it. I was afraid they might buy it out from under me. These things happen, you know. And I made a really low offer."

"Maybe you won't get it, then." He sounded optimistic. "So let's not tell Stef just yet, okay? No need worrying her about something that may not happen. She's a bit paranoid about the Nevermore."

"I noticed."

Angie and Sherlock took their beach walk, and on the way home she stopped by the real estate office to sign the prepared papers on the Nevermore purchase and write a check for the earnest money.

She had some second thoughts as her pen poised above the signature line. *What if there really is something to the Nev-*

*ermore's curse? Am I playing with my destiny here, signing up for disaster? Or maybe just making a really dumb investment?*

No. This was a sensible and practical investment. The Nevermore's past was coincidence and superstition. She signed her formal name, Angel M. Harrison, with an extra flourish.

The owners had ten days to accept or decline.

"If you get it at this price, it'll be a fantastic bargain," Estelle said as she stapled papers together.

"Of course, the drawback is that the spook and the killer curtain come with the deal."

"Some people would pay extra to get a resident spook," Estelle shot back, and they both laughed.

The following morning Angie called the nursing center and learned that Lillian had had a bad night and it was not a good day for a visit. She passed the word along to Steve when he came by later. He suggested a drive up the coast, but she pleaded work to catch up on. She still had the uncomfortable feeling that Steve Llewelyn's interest in her might include a personal element that went beyond the investigation of his father's murder.

She was glad she'd stayed in the office when Ethan called late in the afternoon.

"You're calling from Phoenix?"

"I'm calling from Eugene. On my cell phone while walking toward this yellow monster my brother calls a pickup."

"I hadn't expected you back in Oregon this soon."

"Turns out there was a lost comma in this purchase agreement, and I had to rush up here immediately to find it." He spoke seriously, but she heard the grin in his voice when he added, "If you don't find that explanation believable, give me a minute and I'll think up another one."

The adolescent flip-flop of which her heart was still capable surprised her. "You're coming over?"

"Unless you tell me I can't."

"How about if I warn you that Ryan is off on an arson investigation, and I'm staying with Stef until he gets back. Which means you'll get my cooking for dinner."

"I like to live dangerously."

"See you in a couple hours, then."

Angie went by her house after locking up at the office. She picked up some overnight things, fed Keyhole, and left the cat inside for the night.

Stefanie was expecting her, although she grumbled that she'd never felt better, didn't need a baby-sitter, and wished Ryan would lighten up. She held her pants tight against her abdomen and angled her profile to Angie. "Do you think I'm showing yet?"

Using all her imagination, Angie thought she might detect a centimeter of bulge. "Oh, definitely showing," she said.

The yellow monster turned into the driveway just before 7:00. Stefanie had insisted on cooking dinner herself, and spicy scents of spaghetti and garlic bread filled the house. But Ethan didn't seem to notice the scents when Angie opened the door. He just stood there looking at her, and she gave in to what she wanted to do and stepped into his arms for a hug.

"I'm glad you had to come up early to look for that comma in the contract," she said.

Dinner was lively. Ethan told about the eccentric lady who'd sat next to him on the plane, nibbling on what looked tasty until she informed him she was into all-natural food, and these were chocolate-covered ants. Angie related the news of the unexpected appearance of Steve Llewelyn. She didn't ask Stefanie for names to fit Myrna's profile of a potential killer, not wanting to weigh down the upbeat evening with heavy stuff. Stefanie talked about baby names, saying she was leaning toward Grady if the baby was a boy. Ethan and Angie looked at each other and groaned.

"Okay, okay," Stefanie grumbled. "It's not written in stone."

After dinner, Angie shooed Stefanie into the living room, and she and Ethan cleaned up the kitchen and loaded the dishwasher. Angie told him then about her decision to make an offer on the theater but asked him not to mention it to Stefanie yet.

"She's a little hyper on the subject of the Nevermore," Angie added. "So what do you think? Did I do a really dumb thing?"

"Are you asking my opinion of the Nevermore as an investment? Or if I think there's something to those old stories about disasters happening to anyone connected with it?"

"Either. Both. Whatever."

Ethan looked as if he was about to make a crack about spooks, but then he turned serious. "If it were me, I'd take it to the Lord and ask for his guidance."

That figured. "Did you take coming here to Julesburg . . . and me . . . to the Lord for guidance?"

His voice was sober and a little husky when he said, "Yes, I did."

They had a great evening. They played Monopoly with a board so ancient the fold in the center was almost worn through. They drank hot chocolate—Stefanie was staying away from coffee—and nibbled blue tortilla chips Ethan had brought. Ryan called, and he and Stefanie talked for a good fifteen minutes, even though he'd left just that morning.

At 10:00, having won most of the Monopoly money, Ethan yawned and said it was time to head for his room at the Sea Haven. He stood up and started sorting Monopoly money into piles. "So, how about if we all get together for church tomorrow?" he suggested.

Angie stopped in the process of dumping tiny Monopoly houses and hotels in their box. Church. They all knew she hadn't been inside a church in years. She searched for an excuse. "Oh, I don't think so. I have . . . uh . . . laundry to do—"

"Hey, great idea!" Stefanie interrupted. "Ethan, you come here for breakfast. I'll fix bacon and French toast with blueberry preserves, and we can all go to church from here."

"I was thinking I'd take both of you out for breakfast at the Julesburg Café so you wouldn't have to cook," Ethan said. "Then we can head for church from the restaurant."

"We'll let Angie decide," Stefanie said. They both turned to Angie expectantly.

Angie had been about to vote for the Julesburg Café, so Stefanie wouldn't have to cook, but she stopped short. "Wait a minute. I see some fine print here. I get to choose about breakfast. But both choices include church afterward."

"I didn't notice that," Stefanie said, all innocence. She looked at Ethan. "Did you notice that?"

"Well, we have to have breakfast before we go to church," he said, as if it were a simple matter of logic.

Angie crossed her arms over her chest. "You're ganging up on me," she accused. "A conspiracy. Two against one."

"A loving conspiracy," Stefanie said.

Ethan nodded. "So how about it?"

Angie tapped her fingers against her elbow. Yes, she planned to reconnect with God one of these days. She planned to start going to church again. But not this soon. She was still putting her life in order.

But why not? Why delay longer? She'd made the final break with Burke. She could honestly say that the ambition that had driven her to make so many wrong choices was behind her. She and Ethan were feeling their way toward a new relationship.

*The past is behind me.*

She uncrossed her arms. "Okay, breakfast at the Julesburg Café. They have awesome cinnamon rolls." She stopped, deliberately leaving them hanging for a moment, before she said, "Church together afterward."

Stefanie hugged her and Ethan grinned. She walked with him to the back door, and he drew her outside to the steps.

"I'm glad, Angie," he said.

"I'm glad too." And she was. She felt an unexpected rush of joy for the closing of the chasm that had long stood between her and the Lord. And for the reopening of the gates that had long been closed between her and Ethan.

He wrapped his arms around her and pulled her close. Fog covered the house in cool mist and blurred the lights from nearby houses. His body felt warm and familiar. Like home. She lifted her face, and he kissed her. A kiss of hope and renewal and welcome, yet with passion like the glow from a moon not yet risen, a promise hiding just beyond the hills.

"I still feel the same as I always did about you," he whispered.

Caring that had survived betrayal. Forgiveness so deep that it blotted out the wrongdoing and made saying the words unnecessary.

Yet truth interrupted her sweet delight in the kiss. *Ethan, I'm not worthy of this! You don't know . . .*

"Ethan, I—"

"Shh." He put a fingertip to her lips. "I'm not asking for anything. No rush. No decisions or commitments."

He kissed her again, and his warmth wrapped around her, a shelter from the coolness of the night and the storm churning inside her. She returned the kiss, reveling in both the newness and familiarity of it, trying to make it shut off the words that ran like an endless banner across her mind.

*You have to tell him.*

*No! The past is behind me. Behind us. It doesn't matter now.*

"I'll see you in the morning," she whispered.

It was a plan that lasted until 2:30 A.M.

## 18

ngie left the guest room door open when she went to bed. Stefanie's bedroom was down the hall, with a small storage room between the two rooms. They called their good nights back and forth like girls at a slumber party.

Angie woke once to the sound of wind howling around the corner of the old house, rain spattering the window. She snuggled deeper under the covers, feeling warm and safe and . . . the thought lingered somewhere on the edge of consciousness as she drifted back to sleep . . . loved.

She woke again some time later, briefly disoriented by the oblong shape of dim light that marked the doorway to her bedroom. They hadn't left any hall lights on when they'd gone to bed . . .

She peered at the red digital figures of the clock on the nightstand. 2:25. She jumped out of bed when she realized that the light was coming from Stefanie's bedroom. She ran down the hallway. Stefanie's door was open. The bathroom door was closed, a line of light shining beneath it. Sherlock was parked beside the door, whining softly. Angie tapped on the door.

"Stefanie, are you in there? Is everything okay?"

"I—I don't know."

"May I come in?"

"The door's . . . unlocked." The words came on a gasp.

Angie opened the door. Stefanie stood at the sink in her nightgown, her arms braced on the counter, her head slumped between her shoulders. Sherlock crowded close to her.

"Stef! Are you sick to your stomach?"

"No, I just *hurt*. I woke up a few minutes ago with an awful cramp—" Stefanie broke off as another cramp hit her. She held her abdomen with one hand, and Angie could see a dot of blood where she was biting her lip to keep from crying out.

"Here, sit down."

Angie lowered the padded lid of the toilet seat and guided Stefanie to it. Stefanie's face looked gray, years older than when she went to bed. Then Angie looked at the spot on the floor in front of the sink where Stefanie had been standing. Blood. Blood fresh and red, pooling like something from a horror movie. Blood on Stefanie's feet and the hem of her nightgown.

Angie didn't wait, didn't ask more questions. She ran into Stefanie's bedroom and dialed 911.

"We need an ambulance right away. Now! My sister-in-law is pregnant, but she's cramping and bleeding. Hemorrhaging, I think." The woman asked calm questions. What's the address? How long had this been going on? Was she vomiting? Dizzy? Headache? Angie knew the questions were probably important, but they infuriated her anyway. "Just send an ambulance," she begged, then hung up and ran back to the bathroom.

Blood was seeping out from under Stefanie's legs now, soaking her nightgown, dripping to the floor around the stool. She gasped and leaned forward as another cramp ripped through her. Drops of sweat stood out on her forehead.

Angie yanked the linen closet open and tumbled towels to the floor as padding. She held Stefanie by the waist and eased her onto the towels. Stefanie didn't resist. Then she ran to the bedroom for a blanket to cover her.

The blood! So much blood. And no way to stop it.

Where, where, where was that ambulance?

Surely it didn't have to come all the way from Dutton Bay! Hadn't she seen one parked near the fire department? But maybe it was no longer in use. Would it be faster to try to take her in the car? But she couldn't move Stefanie alone.

Ethan. Ethan was here!

"Ryan," Stefanie said weakly. "Get Ryan."

"Ryan's gone, remember? He's up in Washington."

"Call him . . . cell phone . . ."

Angie couldn't remember the number. She ran down the stairs and dug frantically in her purse. Her address book  had she written Ryan's cell phone number there? She scrambled through the pages. Yes!

She'd just started to dial when she heard the wail of the ambulance siren. *Thank you, Lord!* She slammed the phone down. No time now. She ran back upstairs and grabbed Stefanie's robe off a chair by the bed. In the bathroom she found Stefanie curled in a fetal position on the tangled towels. She knelt beside her and pulled the robe around her shoulders.

"Help's coming, Stef. I can hear the ambulance. It's almost here. Just hold on."

"Ryan . . ."

"I'll get hold of him just as soon as I can. Just hang on. Pray." She swallowed. "I'm praying."

And she was. Not in conscious words but with every beat of her heart. *Save Stef's baby. Save Stef's baby.*

Tears and cold sweat mingled on Stefanie's twisted face. "I'm losing my baby!" She clutched her abdomen again, as if by holding on hard enough she could stop it from happening.

Angie grabbed one of the towels and swabbed Stefanie's face.

"They—they'll do something when they get here." Words she didn't believe. Not with so much blood. She wrapped her hands around Stefanie's. "Pray, Stef. Just keep praying. Help is almost here."

She heard the ambulance wail to a stop in the driveway and ran downstairs again. Sherlock followed, frantic to help. The circling light made colored flares through the windows. She ran to the back door.

"Here! This way!"

The two rumpled-looking paramedics ran to the door, one of them carrying a folded stretcher. Angie led them upstairs, stumbling over Sherlock as she and the dog collided. One man wrapped a blood pressure cuff around Stefanie's arm. A moment later he shook his head.

Angie's heart sank. Was Stefanie's life in danger too?

They didn't bother with further preliminaries. They eased Stefanie onto the stretcher. She reached out a hand to Angie.

"You'll come?" Stef managed to whisper.

"I'll be right behind you in the car. As soon as I get hold of Ryan."

While the men eased the stretcher down the steep stairs, Angie threw on the jeans and sweatshirt she'd taken off earlier. She caught up with the stretcher at the back steps and held Stefanie's hand all the way out to the ambulance, desperately willing strength and love into the grip. Rain pelted them, and she hunched against the stinging drops and the wind, trying to shelter Stefanie with her body. Sherlock ran alongside and would've jumped in the open rear doors of the ambulance if one of the men hadn't blocked the way.

"I don't want to lose my baby," Stefanie pleaded as the men lifted the stretcher into the ambulance. "Please save my baby."

"I'm praying," Angie whispered as their hands separated. She saw Stefanie's body jerk as another spasm of cramps hit her.

Angie stood in the steep driveway as the ambulance backed down the hill. At the street it swung in an arc, and the siren opened up again. She grabbed Sherlock's collar as he went into a frenzy of leaping and dancing and whining at the sound.

She tried to collect her thoughts as she ran back to the house. *Get my purse. Find Stefanie's purse for the insurance card and whatever other information the hospital might need. Call Ryan.*

Ryan answered the cell phone as if he were sleeping with it on the pillow beside him. She told him what she knew. He didn't waste words. "I'll start home right now."

"How long will that take?"

"Seven and a half or eight hours coming up here. I'll make it back in seven. Or less."

They were both silent for a moment. What could happen in seven hours? What had already happened?

"I'll see you at the hospital, then," Angie said.

She found her jacket, turned off the lights upstairs, collected the purses, and gave Sherlock a reassuring hug before she went out the back door. She knelt beside him. "It'll be okay, guy," she whispered. But his pleading amber eyes got to her, and she couldn't close the door on him. "Okay, you come along," she said.

They ran to the car through the wind and rain, hard drops battering them from both above and below as the rain bounced back from the concrete walkway. Sherlock jumped into the seat the moment she opened the passenger's side door.

The overhead streetlight was swinging in the wind when she reached the highway that was also Julesburg's main street. The street was deserted, not a car moving on it. Her windshield wipers whipped crazily, fighting a losing battle against a fresh onslaught of rain. Outside town, she pressed on the gas, caught between a frantic desire for speed and a back-of-the-mind warning that she wouldn't do Stefanie any good if she had an accident.

She had to stop at an all-night gas station in Dutton Bay to ask for directions to the hospital. When she arrived there, she expected blazing lights at the emergency room, but only a dim glow showed through the glass doors. She slid into a parking space, told Sherlock that this time he really had to wait, and ran inside.

She stopped at the emergency room desk. Questions. Forms. Paperwork. *But what's happening to Stefanie and her baby?* Angie wanted to scream. But she didn't waste her energy. She just gritted her teeth and continued filling out forms.

Finally the woman motioned her to a lineup of un-padded seats along a wall. "We'll call you when the doctor can tell you something or you can see her."

Angie stumbled to a seat and slumped into it.

There was nothing to do then. After what seemed like hours of frantic activity—although the clock showed only 3:45—all she could do was wait. And think.

And remember.

## 19

than came up out of sleep thinking his alarm clock was going off. It took him a moment to realize the sound was the phone beside his bed. He sat up, his eyes groggily searching for the motel room's digital clock. 5:35? Who would call at this hour?

He shoved the phone to his ear. "Hello?"

"Ethan, it's me, Angie."

"What's wrong?"

"I'm at the hospital with Stef." Her words were gaspy and muffled by sobs.

"Hospital? What—"

"She's lost her baby."

"No. . . . You're sure?"

"I'm sure. I just talked to the doctor. But I—I knew even before he told me. They've given her something, and she was almost asleep when I saw her a few minutes ago."

"I don't understand. What happened? She was fine when I left the house last night."

"She got terrible cramps and pain in the middle of the night. And bled and bled . . . I've never seen so much blood!" She stopped short. "I've got to go back to the house and clean it up."

"We can take care of that later."

Her voice suddenly turned crisp, as if she had just grabbed hold of an island in a sea of helplessness. "Yes, I'll go clean it up. I can do that!"

"Did you drive your car to the hospital?"

"My car?" she repeated. "My car. Yes, my car is here."

She wasn't thinking clearly, that was obvious. And she was definitely in no condition to drive anywhere. "Tell me more about what happened."

"She was cramping and bleeding at the house. I called 911 for an ambulance, and they came and brought her here. But there was nothing the doctor could do. She'd lost so much blood, they had to give her a transfusion. Oh, Ethan, the baby is gone! It was a baby, and now it's . . . gone."

She sounded desperate, on the edge of falling apart, and then the phone clunked and rattled and blasted into a storm of static.

Finally her voice returned. "I—I'm sorry. I dropped the cell phone. I'm so shaky—"

"I'll be there as soon as I can. You stay right there. Don't try to go anywhere."

"But there's nothing you can do—"

"Just give me directions."

"I shouldn't have called you. It's not even daylight yet. But I felt so . . . so alone here . . ."

He wished she'd called him the moment she and Stefanie had wakened in the night, but he didn't say that. Recriminations were the last thing she needed at this point. Not that his presence would've changed the outcome, but maybe he could've lessened the trauma for her.

"I'm glad you called me. I want to be with you. Now, the directions?"

She gave him garbled instructions to the hospital in Dutton Bay, and he repeated the command that she was not to go anywhere.

"What about Stefanie? Is she okay?"

"I was worried, but the doctor said she'd be . . . fine." The last word came out on a choked gasp, and the despair returned to her voice. "Can anyone be fine after something like this? She's going to be devastated."

Ethan didn't try to soothe her. She needed more than words over a phone. Neither did he ask her to clarify her disjointed directions to the hospital. Stefanie might be fine, safely under medical attention, but Angie sounded close to collapsing.

"Just hang on, hon. I'll be there."

He pushed the glass doors of the emergency room open, and the first thing he saw was Angie curled in a chair at the far end of the sparse room. The hospital was old, not designed for the visitor comfort some newer ones offered. An overhead fluorescent light sputtered.

He thought she was sleeping when he approached. Her legs were drawn up under her, her eyes hidden by the long hair falling across her face. Blood smeared the arm of her pink sweatshirt. He knelt beside her.

"Angie?" he whispered.

She lifted her head, her eyes open as if she might never sleep again. The despair that had been in her voice on the phone was written in the ashy color of her face and the bottomless depths of her eyes. He thought of things to say. Platitudes that arose out of some subconscious well, even though he'd never personally known a woman who'd suffered a miscarriage. *Everything will work out. Stefanie is okay, and that's the important thing. There'll be another baby.*

He didn't say the words. There might've been a certain truth in them, but in the midst of loss, they were meaningless. He put his arms around her, and they stayed that way for long minutes, foreheads locked together.

Finally he said, "Let me take you home, hon. You can't do anything here now. We'll come back later, after Stefanie is awake again."

"No. Ryan is coming. I called him. I want to stay until he gets here. Stefanie might wake up and need someone."

He heard the stubbornness in her voice and knew arguing would be a waste of breath. She'd apparently forgotten her earlier determination to go back and clean up the blood at the house, and he wasn't going to remind her. "Then let's get some breakfast. Is there a cafeteria?"

"I don't know."

He kissed her on the forehead and went to the front desk. The woman said the cafeteria was closed on weekends.

It was Sunday. The day they were planning to go to church, the three of them together, a day of new beginnings for Angie. He didn't question the Lord's workings, but at the moment he had to admit he was at a loss to understand this night's happenings. Stefanie's baby gone. Angie's return to the Lord interrupted.

He realized then that the woman behind the desk was telling him about a small restaurant a block away that would be open now. He returned to Angie with the information.

She shook her head. "I don't want to leave."

"Please? You need breakfast." He brushed the hair away from her face. "Do it for me?"

He hadn't meant anything special, just words to coax her, but she looked at him strangely, as if the small request had some unexpectedly deep meaning for her. She nodded and stood up. He put his arm around her shoulders and guided her out the door and across the parking lot to the yellow pickup. The sky was lightening on a clear day, pale streaks of pink in the east. Last night's storm had passed over. They walked by her car along the way. It was parked askew, as if she'd slid to a panicked stop.

"Hey," he said as a shaggy head popped up. "Sherlock's in there."

184

"Oh, he is, isn't he? I'd forgotten. He was so frantic about Stef that I brought him along." She pulled out from under Ethan's arm and managed a shaky run to the car.

He followed and heard her murmuring words of comfort to Sherlock as she rubbed his big head. She let the dog out, and he made a quick dash to the weedy grass beyond the parking lot.

"We'll bring him something to eat too," Ethan said when Sherlock jumped back in the car.

Once at the restaurant, Angie opened the folded menu and looked at it as if the words were printed in a foreign language. Ethan closed his menu and ordered scrambled eggs, toast, juice, and coffee for both of them.

She took a sip of water and a deep breath as they waited. She even looked around, and he saw her note an elderly woman in a prim little hat. *Good,* he thought. *She's pulling herself together.* Then she spotted the smear of blood on the arm of her sweatshirt. She held out her arm and stared at the stain with a look of horror.

He reached across the booth and clasped her hand. "It's okay," he soothed, but she shook her head, tears filling her eyes.

"It was a baby, a gift from God, and now it's gone."

They were the same words she'd said before, with the addition of the phrase about God. Was she blaming God? She dropped her head and buried her face in her hands.

Shocking and tragic as the miscarriage was, Angie's reaction seemed almost overmagnified. She, whom he'd always thought of as strong and independent, seemed ready to break. He knew what a sensitive and caring person she was, how back in college she'd faithfully visited a little girl with leukemia in a local hospital, how broken up she'd been when the girl died. But hard as that loss had been for her, she hadn't taken it nearly as personally as she was taking this. Of course, this baby was her niece or nephew, he reminded himself. And back then, she'd had her faith in God to lean on.

Was she somehow blaming herself, thinking if she'd wakened and gotten Stefanie to the hospital sooner, the miscarriage could've been stopped? He started to reassure her that she must not put that burden on herself. Then a disturbing new thought occurred to him.

"Angie, you aren't thinking that this is somehow connected to your decision to buy the Nevermore?"

"Connected?" She looked up from the bloodstained sleeve she'd been staring at. Her eyes were wide and bloodshot, and her lips formed a silent *oh*. He realized this was a thought that hadn't occurred to her, and he kicked himself for bringing it up.

She leaned forward. "The Nevermore's evil spirit might have done this?"

"No! If you're thinking that, don't," Ethan said. "It's a ridiculous myth. A foolish, dangerous myth. What happened to Stefanie has nothing to do with you or some rundown old theater."

Angie nodded, but he didn't know if she was agreeing with him or with some conclusion she'd reached in her own mind. He expected questions now. Where was God in what had happened? Did he cause Stefanie's loss or allow it to happen? Why did he send children to some people who didn't want them, and withhold them from couples who did?

The waitress brought the food and coffee. He was relieved to see Angie start eating, even though her movements seemed more mechanical than conscious. As if her mind were elsewhere and her body numbed, operating on a robotic level.

"Stefanie would've done anything to keep this baby," she said suddenly. "Anything."

"Most mothers would."

"Yes." Then, so softly he could barely hear her, she said, "It isn't fair, Ethan. It just isn't fair."

Angie didn't say anything more in words. Tears spoke for her, running down her face, falling silently on the abandoned plate of food.

But he wasn't certain what they were saying.

than stood in the doorway, holding the scrub bucket he'd just emptied downstairs. Angie was kneeling on the bathroom floor, swabbing up the last smears of blood. She leaned back on her heels and tossed the rag in his bucket, and he saw the tears streaming down her face.

"I wish you'd let me do this," he said.

"I'll be done in a minute."

She poured extra-strength bleach straight from the jug on the tile, and the scent rose in an acrid vapor around her. Together they'd already cleaned the bloody spots on the carpet in Stefanie's bedroom and changed the sheets. Now Angie worked doggedly, the scrub brush grinding round and round, as if she hoped that if she scrubbed hard enough, she could scrub away what had happened.

Ethan was still troubled by the intensity of her reaction to Stefanie's miscarriage. He could understand her being sad and disappointed for her brother and sister-in-law. He could understand wanting to help. He felt bad too. He knew how much Ryan and Stefanie had wanted this baby. And any baby, even one barely formed in its mother's body, was a special creation of God's, and its loss deep cause for mourning.

But this . . . this despair of Angie's seemed out of proportion.

*Or am I just being callous and insensitive?*

Yet Angie had seemed so different ever since this morning. At first she'd clung to him there at the hospital as if she desperately needed him, but then she'd seemed to withdraw into some dark world of her own. If only she could take her suffering to the Lord! Then another troubling thought occurred to him.

"Angie, are you angry with me about something?"

She looked up, a startled expression on her face. Her skin was still unnaturally pale, puffs of blue shadow under her eyes. "Oh, Ethan, no! You've been wonderful. I'm sorry if I gave that impression. It's just that everything is so . . . awful. I'm having a hard time coping with it." She looked at her hands. He could see they were clean, wrinkly even. And thoroughly disinfected from the bleach. She stood up and scrubbed them in the bathroom sink anyway.

"Do you want to go back to the hospital?"

"No, I don't think so. Ryan is the one Stefanie needs now, and he's with her." She dried her hands on a towel, then tossed the towel in the dirty clothes hamper as if the single touch had contaminated it. "I want to go home and take a shower. And poor Keyhole has been locked in the house since yesterday."

"How about if I bring something over to eat later?"

"I'm not really hungry."

"I have to drive back to Eugene tomorrow morning, and I'm flying home in the afternoon."

She managed a smile. "The Komputers are calling?"

"I'll stay longer if you want. I can manage it." Not easily. He had a presentation to make Tuesday morning about setting up the complete computer system for some new insurance company offices in Tempe. But no sale mattered more than Angie, and he hated to leave when she was so down.

"I appreciate that. But the first part of the week is so busy at the office, and I have a meeting to cover Monday evening. I'll be okay."

He had to admit he'd have liked her to say, "Yes, stay! I need you." But it would do her good to keep busy with her work.

"I love you, Angie. You know that, don't you?"

He hadn't really intended to say that yet. He was still wary of scaring her off. He especially hadn't intended to say those words in a bathroom doorway, with a scrub bucket dangling from his hand. But the words just came out. "I tried really hard not to for a long time. Sometimes I thought I'd made it. But now . . ."

She didn't look elated by his declaration. Neither did she appear angered or unhappy. She just looked distant. Pensive. As if she'd taken a dozen mental steps backward to some secret hiding place. Suddenly she seemed to make an effort to turn on an upbeat attitude and said, "Give me an hour or so and then come on over to the house, okay?"

"Okay. I'll bring food."

He went back to the motel, showered, shaved, and put on clean clothes. The motel was almost deserted on this Sunday evening, only a blue sedan at the far end of the parking lot. A pair of crows squawked from the forested hillside rising steeply behind the motel, and seagulls circled overhead. A scent of sea hung strong as the mist in the air.

He picked up calzones and salads at Website X and arrived at Angie's house just after 6:00. Keyhole rushed in ahead of him when Angie opened the door. She looked refreshed, in body at least, wearing clean jeans and sweatshirt, her hair freshly shampooed and fragrant and a touch of lipstick brightening her face.

"Ryan called a little while ago," she said as she pulled Styrofoam plates from a cupboard. "He can bring Stefanie home tomorrow. They have to do a D and C first."

Ethan was unsure what a D and C was, but he decided not to ask. He figured it was better if Angie didn't fixate on details.

She got sodas from the fridge and set them on the table. The TV was on. He suspected she'd been using the noise to block out whatever thoughts kept that haunted look on her face. Now she flicked the remote to turn the TV off. She ate the spicy calzone as if she were determined not to disappoint him with a lack of appetite.

"Umm, this is really good." She peered at the ingredients tucked into the crispy shell. "Pepperoni, ham, cheese, green peppers, tomatoes, onions." Then as if to make certain when she ran out of ingredients that the conversation wouldn't turn to painful subjects, she added, "Tell me about your brother's new wife."

So he told her about Kerri and her art talent and the house his brother and Kerri were buying. He didn't tell her Kerri was five months pregnant, her ultrasound showing every indication of a healthy baby.

When it was time to go, he put his arms lightly on her elbows as they stood at the door together. "I know this has been hard. I can see it's really gotten to you. Can you take it to the Lord? He can help."

"I don't think the Lord and I are ready for a . . . happy reunion after all."

"Are you blaming God for Stefanie's miscarriage?"

"You told me not to blame it on some malicious spirit from the Nevermore!" The tart comment sounded facetious, argumentative, and challenging all whipped into one. Her back went straight and stiff as a soldier snapping to attention.

He smiled and made a deliberate attempt at teasing. "Are you trying to pick a fight with me?"

The soldier stance collapsed. "Maybe I am," she admitted. She pounded his chest lightly with her fist. "I just feel so angry and helpless and frustrated and depressed, and maybe I do just want to let off steam with a big fight."

"Maybe you need a workout at Fit 'n' Fun. Or, if you prefer, I'm available as a punching bag."

"That's a good idea." She smiled and dropped her hand, as if only then aware she was hammering on him. "Fit 'n' Fun, I mean, not punching you. Because I don't want to fight with you, Ethan." She looked into his eyes. "I really don't. You're a great guy. The best. And you deserve the best."

Complimentary as the words were, they made him uneasy. "Somehow this sounds like the preliminary to, 'So can't we just be friends?'"

She smiled again, but he couldn't tell what she was thinking. "Just let me think about things, okay?"

Monday morning, after a terrible dream about blood and babies that had left her awake much of the night, Angie was late getting to the office. Two people were at the counter, and Madge was fielding their complaint about a billing. The day didn't improve. A phone call from a mail-delivery subscriber irate about a newspaper arriving mangled. The copy machine going temperamental and slashing black lines across pages. The only bright spot was that Becky was happy because she and Aaron had worked out their problems.

"I took your advice and checked things out with Aaron, and we're okay now," she told Angie. "Maybe you ought to start writing a lovelorn column."

The Lovelorn Angel? Angie shook her head. Not with her record of mistakes.

Ethan stopped in to say good-bye at around 9:00. He pushed through the gate and came to where Angie was at her computer working on an article about the grand opening of a new gift shop.

"I don't suppose Ryan has brought Stefanie home yet?"

"He called. They've done the D and C, but they've decided to keep her another day."

"Probably a good idea. How is she?"

"As well as can be expected, I suppose. This was a real heartbreak for them."

Ethan reached out and took her hand. "You'll keep in touch?" he asked. When Angie nodded, he added, "I'll be back again within the next couple weeks."

"You're expecting another lost comma?" She worked on a smile to accompany the question. She was far from feeling upbeat this morning, but she'd had so many problems and kept so busy that she hadn't had time to dwell on Stefanie's loss.

"I'm expecting I'll just be wanting to see you again."

He looked as if he might lean over and kiss her, but he settled for a squeeze of hand on her shoulder. Angie was relieved. She'd wanted Ethan's kiss. She'd wanted to be back in the relationship they'd once had. And for a short while she'd seen the glorious possibilities. But since Stefanie's miscarriage, she'd watched those possibilities sink, dragged under by the weight of the past.

The phone rang as Ethan gave her a little good-bye wave from the door. She picked up the phone and found out this evening's Save-the-Wetlands meeting was cancelled. *Good.*

*Or maybe not so good,* she thought a moment later when the phone rang again and it was Steve Llewelyn saying he'd arranged for them to see Lillian Feldman this evening. Now she didn't have an excuse not to go with him.

Angie tapped a pencil against her chin. She really did want to find out the truth about what had happened to his father that night at the Nevermore. But she wasn't totally comfortable with Steve. He'd never done anything improper or unpleasant, but he was just a little too . . . what? Pushy?

*Don't be silly,* she chided herself. Steve was, after all, the kind of guy who took in an old stray tomcat. And he was trying hard to quit smoking. Both were character assets of which she approved.

She turned down Steve's dinner invitation but agreed to see Lillian with him that night. Madge returned from the post office with the mail, and Angie looked over the title company's report showing the Nevermore's former owners. She recognized a few names. Lillian Feldman and her husband. The Reedys, who now owned and operated Reedy's Hardware and Variety. Odd. What had they intended to do with the old theater? And had anything bad happened to them? Wally Greer, manager of the local bank, had also had a brief ownership. The list didn't include people she'd heard about who had started to buy the theater but hadn't actually done so because of interrupting tragedies. All things considered, it was not a particularly helpful document. She went back to work on the article about the new gift shop.

She worked until almost 6:00 that evening, picked up a take-out calzone for dinner, and was ready when Steve arrived at quarter to seven. She thought he'd probably spent the day talking to people and seeing what he could dig up about his father's death, but apparently he'd been sightseeing instead. He'd visited the lighthouse at Cape Blanco, driven up the river to the county seat, and hiked partway up Humbug Mountain. "Maybe we could hike to the top later this week," he suggested.

"Maybe."

The first thing Lillian did when they arrived was look at Steve Llewelyn and say bluntly, "Where's that nice young man who was here before?" She sounded cantankerous this evening.

"He couldn't come this time. But here's someone I know you want to meet." Angie touched Steve's arm. "This is Harry Llewelyn's son, Steve. He came back to Julesburg because he wants to find out who killed his father."

Steve stuck out his hand. "I'm glad to meet you, Lillian."

She frowned, as if she didn't appreciate the use of her first name. She gave Steve's hand an unenthusiastic fingertip shake. Angie expected her to come right out with an accusation against Vance Spohn, but she seemed unexpectedly sulky without Ethan's presence.

Angie tried to encourage her. "My discussion with you a while back about Amelia and the Nevermore was very helpful."

"Well, it was all so long ago."

"Yes, it was. But I've been thinking about the fact that Amelia was going to someone for séances. We think this person might be able to give us helpful information. I'm wondering if you can remember her name and maybe how we could locate her?"

"It's been fifteen or twenty years ago now," Lillian muttered. "And I don't know how that charlatan could help you. I should think by now she'd have given up trying to hoodwink people with those phony séances."

"So you don't know her name or where she is?" Steve said. He was slouched in a hard chair that was too small for him. One heel jiggled impatiently.

That wasn't what Angie had gotten out of Lillian's comment. She heard something more personal. Tentatively she said, "She couldn't contact . . . someone you wanted to contact?"

Lillian's knobby fingers played with a frayed thread on the bedspread. "I hate to admit I even went to her. It seems so foolish now. But I was so lonely after Mack died, and I thought if I could talk to him . . ."

"What happened?"

"Oh, she went through all this mumbo jumbo, and then the lights dimmed way down and the table moved. Then she started talking in this deep, deep voice." Lillian's own frail voice deepened in contemptuous imitation. "And I was supposed to believe that was Mack talking through her? No way. It wasn't him. I got up and walked out."

"Without paying her?" Steve asked.

"Madame Zorrich might be a fraud, but she wasn't foolish. She made you pay first. But at least I had the good sense not to go back to her. I don't know how many times Amelia went."

"Do you know where we might find Madame Zorrich?"

"She was in Coos Bay when Amelia went to her, but she'd moved up to Newport by the time I went. No telling where she might be by now. Maybe she's on the 'other side' contacting people on this side." Lillian's voice dripped with scorn.

"Was Zorrich her real name?" Angie asked.

"I think so, but it's hard to say. She had a heavy accent, which I'm pretty sure was as phony as her black hair. Though she was quite foreign looking."

"How about a first name?"

"I never heard one."

"How old was she?"

"She was probably in her forties when I went to her."

Angie made small talk with Lillian for several more minutes, even though Steve's jiggling foot and the way he got out his cigarette lighter and tossed it from hand to hand told her he wanted to get away. As soon as they were back in the car, he said, "What a place. Old people all have that certain smell, you know? The whole place reeks of it." He lifted his sleeve and sniffed, as if afraid some of the scent clung to him.

196

"I didn't notice anything. Lillian was wearing a rather nice perfume, in fact."

Steve shrugged and dropped the subject. "So it looks like a dead end with Madame Zorrich, doesn't it?"

"It's not a common name. I'll see if my brother can do anything with it. He's sharp on the computer."

"Didn't somebody tell me he investigates fires or something for some insurance company?"

"He has his own business as a private investigator now. Harrison Investigative Services. Although he still does a lot of arson and fraud investigation for several insurance companies."

"A private eye?" Steve sounded surprised. "Julesburg seems an unlikely place for a private investigator."

"He keeps busy."

Steve stopped at a couple of viewpoints on the way back down the coast. The moon was out now, and he said the views of surf and offshore rocks were spectacular and that she should come see them. But the strain of the last couple of days was getting to Angie. Her energy had faded to dishrag level, and getting out of the car took more effort than she could muster. She just leaned her head back against the seat and closed her eyes.

By the time they got back to the house, the long-ago murder was slipping off Angie's mental list of priorities. Other thoughts she'd been avoiding crowded in on her now.

Ryan would be bringing Stefanie home tomorrow. The house would look the same as it had before, no physical stain of blood and the tragedy that had happened. But inside the hearts of Ryan and Stefanie and Angie, the loss would always be there. The scent of the powerful bleach she'd poured on the bathroom floor lingered with her, as if it had burned into her brain. But it wasn't enough to take away the raw scent of blood that also still lingered in her brain. Nor was it strong enough to take away the thought that ran endlessly across her mind.

How could she ever have thought the past was behind her? Even Burke, without a philosophical bone in his body, had said that some things can't be walked away from.

And tonight the past felt like a weight on her mind and body and soul, dragging her down, pulling her under.

*The past is not behind me.*

yan brought Stefanie home at midday on Tuesday. Angie was tied up with the layouts for Wednesday's *Herald,* but she went to the house as soon as she finished at 8:00.

Stefanie was sitting on the sofa in the living room. She looked physically normal, her color good, but the pain of loss made luminescent pools of her eyes when her gaze turned from the Bible in her hands to Angie. Angie didn't say anything, just wrapped her arms around Stefanie's body, now so vulnerable in its slenderness.

Angie felt the drip of Stefanie's tears on her shoulder, felt her own tears trickling down her face. Ryan came down from upstairs and sat on the other side of Stefanie, his body protectively close.

"Oh, Stef, I'm just so sorry," Angie whispered. "So very sorry."

"Thanks for being here. Thanks for cleaning up. Thanks for everything."

"Ethan helped. Are you feeling okay?"

"I'm not hurting."

Angie knew that was true only of physical pain.

"The doctor says this won't affect future pregnancies, and there's no reason the next one won't go fine," Stefanie added. She sounded as if she were speaking words she'd memorized. "I'm young and healthy, he says."

Platitudes. But platitudes could be true, Angie reminded herself. "That's good to hear."

She didn't stay long. Ryan followed her out through the kitchen.

"Thanks, sis," he said.

"Is there anything I can do now?"

"No, I don't think so. People have been bringing food." Ryan motioned to a pan of homemade cinnamon rolls and a pie on the kitchen table. "We've been talking to the Lord about everything. We're okay."

Any connection between what had happened to Stefanie and Angie's connection with the Nevermore apparently hadn't occurred to him, and she was relieved. She wished the troubling thought wouldn't keep circling around inside her own head. It was foolish and preposterous to think her connection with the Nevermore had anything to do with this tragedy. Just a coincidence in timing.

Another tragic coincidence for the Nevermore.

"Are you going into the office tomorrow?" she asked.

"Probably. I'm working on locating a man on an inheritance matter for a lawyer in Dutton Bay."

"While you're on the computer . . ." Angie took a scratch pad out of her purse and scribbled the name "Madame Zorrich" on it. "If you have time, see if you can locate this woman, will you?"

Ryan looked at the name. "I doubt you're going in for palm reading or crystal balls, so this must have something to do with that old murder at the Nevermore."

"Maybe. That's what I want to find out. This is the name of the spiritualist who conducted séances for Amelia Swarthout. I think she'd be in her late fifties or sixties now. I'm hoping she's somewhere in the area."

"The son from Nevada is still here?"

Angie nodded. "Staying out at the Sea Haven."

"Nice guy?"

"Seems okay."

"You're seeing quite a lot of him, aren't you?"

"We're trying to find out who killed his father."

"Ethan is still in love with you, you know."

Angie finally caught the drift of her brother's conversation. "Steve Llewelyn is not a potential candidate for the position of brother-in-law, if that's what you're thinking," she said.

Ryan smiled. "Good. I'm pulling for Ethan. He looks like great brother-in-law material to me."

*Yes. Great brother-in-law material. But don't count on that little fantasy coming true.*

Wednesday was a normal day . . . as Wednesdays go. Hectic. Even more so than usual because the printer in Dutton Bay broke down and was two hours late getting the *Herald* out. Angie was ready to drop by the end of the day. She took home a chicken Caesar salad from Website X for dinner.

Ryan called while she was sitting cross-legged on the sofa and eating her salad, Keyhole purring beside her. He had information about Madame Zorrich.

"Already? I'm amazed! What did you find out?"

"Her first name is Marie. She's sixty-six years old. Apparently no longer in the séance business, unless she's doing it on the side. She has a gift shop in Brookings now."

"How did you find out all this?"

"That's what we expert detectives do, m'dear. Actually, this didn't take much detective work. Zorrich isn't a common name, and a little foray into phone numbers did it. Only three Zorriches in all of the 541 area code in Oregon, and two of the names were male. A little further digging, and I had a birthday and the information about the gift shop. Although there is no assurance, of course, that this Marie Zorrich is the Madame Zorrich you're looking for."

"We'll check it out."

"You and the Llewelyn guy?"

"That's what he's here for. To find out who killed his father."

Ryan hesitated a moment. "I did a little checking on him too. Took a run out to the Sea Haven, in fact, and picked off his car license number."

"What in the world for?"

"Detectives are curious."

"So what did you find out?"

"Not much," he admitted. "It's a more common name than Zorrich. From the license I tracked down the fact that the car's a rental, and that's about it. No phone, no nothing."

"He's been working outside the country for several years. He's just now buying a car dealership in Las Vegas."

"That might explain it, then. I could find out more if I had a date and place of birth or a Social Security number."

"If you got Marie Zorrich's birth date, why don't you just look up Steve Llewelyn's too?"

"I tried, but some are in the database, some aren't. Actually, there were several Steve Llewelyns listed, but none appeared to be in the right age bracket."

"You're suggesting, then, that I pickpocket his wallet and go through it for information?"

"You're being facetious, right?"

"In all honesty, I'm not that curious about Steve Llewelyn," Angie said. Actually, if he weren't Harry Llewelyn's son, with a big stake in uncovering the killer, she'd avoid him. Even if he did have a cat named Macho Man. She didn't like his opinion of old people or the attitude he'd shown at the nursing home. She also had the feeling that he'd jump their relationship to a much more intimate level if she'd give him so much as an eyelash flutter of encouragement.

Yet they both wanted to track down the murderer, so she called Steve at the motel and passed along the information Ryan had dug up about Madame Zorrich. She thought Steve would probably be eager to drive down to Brookings the following day, but he said he had some fax and phone matters to take care of with the purchase of the business in Las Vegas.

Angie was tied up covering an art exhibit at the school and a Cranberry Growers' barbecue on Friday, so they settled on Saturday for the trip down to Brookings to locate Marie "Madame" Zorrich.

She didn't get home from the barbecue until almost 4:00 on Friday. The event had been held on the grounds of a cranberry processing plant about ten miles south of town, with old-time fiddlers for entertainment, a taste-boggling assortment of foods made with cranberries, and an awards ceremony. Angie had it all on tape so she could get the names right for the newspaper. The weather had been unusually balmy for fall, and people were talkative and friendly. Angie was still getting compliments about the Nevermore article, along with questions about her progress on finding the long-ago killer

She parked the car in the driveway and grabbed her notes and tape recorder from the passenger's seat. Oh, and she had leftover cranberry-glazed chicken and cranberry cake that someone had insisted she bring home. She grabbed her keys from the ignition, dropped them in her jacket pocket, and opened the rear door of the car to retrieve the carton of food. Keyhole strolled out from the front steps to meet her, tail a lazy upside-down J curled over her back.

"Are you coming to meet me because you're glad to see me, or do you just smell this chicken?" Angie inquired. She slammed the car door and started toward the house, balancing Styrofoam carton, notes, tape recorder, and purse.

Two sounds, close enough together to be one.

A gunshot.

And a sound Angie had never heard before but instinctively recognized.

The whine of a bullet missing her by inches.

## 22

The Styrofoam carton clattered to the gravel drive-way. Angie ran for the house, scattering notes and tape recorder. Another gunshot. This time she didn't hear the whine. Her blood thundered loudly in her ears as she frantically grabbed for the keys in her pocket.

She shoved the door open, slammed it, and fumbled with the deadbolt. She leaned against the door, breathing as if she'd just run up a mountain. *Who? Why?*

She jerked away from the door. Wood might not stop a bullet. She pressed her knuckles to her mouth, trying not to panic, and edged toward a window. Could she see the shooter? Then fear rose above curiosity, and she ducked low and crept to the most sheltered spot in the house, the bedroom doorway.

She stood there, muscles rigid, ears straining.

Only the hammer of her heart and rasp of her breathing.

No more shots. No rustle of footsteps around the house. No squeal of a car taking off. Not even a wind rattling the bushes against the house. The world seemed to have stopped on a held breath.

Was the gunman still out there, hiding, waiting for another chance at her?

Keyhole had scooted inside with her. The cat's orange hair stood out in an electrified ruff, tail twitching as she crouched behind Angie's ankles. A minute inched by in a flicker of red numbers on the digital clock in the bedroom. Two. Five.

Then a car passed on the road outside at normal speed, and the world started moving again. Angie tiptoed to the kitchen window. Two boys were riding by on bicycles, one drinking from a straw poked into a soft-drink can, a big dog following them. The dog detoured into her yard and did away with the scattered pieces of chicken and cake in a few enthusiastic chomps.

All so ordinary.

Had she made a mistake? Maybe the sound had been a car backfiring somewhere, and her imagination had given the ordinary noise some wild interpretation.

No. She hadn't imagined the whine of the bullet.

Cautiously she moved to the phone. She hesitated, finger poised over the buttons. She hated to bother Ryan, with all the worries he already had. Should she call the police? But unless a patrol car happened to be cruising in the area, it could take them twenty minutes or more to get here.

*Ethan. I want Ethan.* But he was a thousand miles away in Phoenix.

She reluctantly dialed Ryan's number, knowing he'd be furious if she didn't, and told him what had happened.

"Have you called the police?" he asked.

"Not yet."

"Do it. Use 911. I'll be right over."

"I'm not sure you should come. Whoever did the shooting might still be out there somewhere."

"I'll be careful. I have a gun too."

Angie made the call to 911. The operator's begrudging attitude gave the impression the policeman's wages were coming out of her own pocket. But she said they'd send an officer.

Ryan arrived just after she put the phone down. She watched through the kitchen window as his pickup pulled into the driveway and stopped behind her car. He didn't get out immediately, but when he did, he ran to the house, gun held close to his side, head swiveling as he tried to watch all directions. Angie opened the door to let him in.

He gave her a hug. "You okay, sis?"

"Scared stiff. I've never been shot at before."

He peered out the kitchen window. "Any idea which direction the shots came from?"

He didn't try to convince her that her imagination was running amok, that she hadn't actually been shot at. Which was what she suspected the 911 operator had thought. She appreciated Ryan's faith in her.

"Probably from up the road to the east. There aren't any houses that direction. Okay, you don't need to say it. You told me this place was too isolated."

He nodded acknowledgment but didn't belabor the point.

"I suppose I should've told you about something else that happened earlier," she added reluctantly. "Just a few days after I moved in, someone got inside and searched the house when I wasn't home. I don't know that the two incidents are connected, but—"

"You're right. You should've told me. How'd he get in?"

She motioned to the door to the backyard. "The old one was pretty flimsy. I had it replaced."

He examined the new door and lock. "Looks secure. Was anything taken?"

"I've never found anything missing. I know it probably sounds far out, but I keep wondering if the person was looking for notes I'd made on interviews about the Nevermore murder. I suppose I should also have told you one of the people I interviewed thinks the killer may still be in Julesburg. And not happy about someone digging into the past."

"Burglary and gunshots suggest more than a simple unhappiness," Ryan said. "More like someone could be really worried about what you may uncover."

"What I'm wondering now, is someone trying to warn me off investigating the murder further? Or is someone actually trying to kill me?"

"Good question."

Ryan prowled the interior of the house as they waited for the officer to arrive. Angie suspected her brother was about to start investigating outside by himself when the police car pulled onto the shoulder of the road in front of the house. No lights were flashing or siren wailing. The officer got out and paused by the open police car door, surveying the area for a minute before heading toward the house.

Angie watched from a kitchen window as Ryan went out to meet the officer. He scooped up her fallen tape recorder and notes along the way. The two men conversed for a moment before coming to the house. Ryan handed her the items he'd picked up in the yard and made introductions. She knew he had occasional contact with the police because of his investigative work, but she had the impression he and this Officer Randall hadn't met before now.

The officer asked Angie questions and took notes. He was middle-aged and friendly, a bit paunchy, the kind of easygoing, nice guy she figured would show up at schools to talk to kids about obeying the law and staying away from drugs.

He took down names and addresses for both Angie and Ryan. Then he started with the questions. What happened here? Did she see anyone or hear anything other than the gunshots? A vehicle, maybe? How long had she lived here? Did she live alone? Had she received any threats? Any prior problems here or at the newspaper? He nodded as he made notes of Angie's nervous answers. She also told him about her house being searched.

"Anything taken?"

"I don't think so. I think both the searching of the house and this shooting today may be connected with a long-ago murder here in Julesburg that I've been—" She broke off. She'd started to say investigating, but she instinctively knew the officer wouldn't approve. She already knew Ryan didn't. "That I've been looking into for a newspaper article."

The change of wording didn't help. The officer's concerned demeanor changed to a disapproving scrunch of eyebrows. "Murder is the province of the authorities, not private citizens," he said.

"I know, but this was years ago, and the police have long since given up on—"

"Was a police report made about the break-in of your house?"

"No. It didn't seem . . . I mean, I'm sure the house was searched. Whoever was inside let my cat out. But since nothing was taken . . ." She floundered, thinking how insubstantial, perhaps even frivolous, all that sounded.

"Are there deer in this area? And other wildlife?"

The question seemed odd to Angie, but she was relieved to get away from remarks that verged on accusations. "Several deer hang around, and squirrels. And I saw a skunk once."

"Kids around here, sometimes they like to get out and take potshots at squirrels and birds with their BB guns. A BB gun, you might not know, isn't really—"

"I know what a BB gun is! Ryan had one when we were kids. And whoever shot at me wasn't using a BB gun. I heard the bullet whine right by my head."

The officer didn't argue, but Angie could see he wasn't convinced. He closed the notebook and tucked it in his pocket. "I'll take a look around outside."

Ryan went with the officer. Angie watched from the window as they walked up the gravel road together, then back down the other direction. Ryan motioned toward the old car buried in blackberry bushes, apparently suggesting it as a place where the gunman could've hidden. The officer shook his head.

"We didn't find anything," the man reported when they returned to the house. "No empty bullet casings that had been ejected from a gun. No signs of where anyone had been standing waiting to shoot at you." He cleared his throat. "I'm inclined to think it was kids—"

"I told you, it was *not* a BB gun!"

"Kids could've been hunting with something bigger. A .22 maybe. Or it might even have been an adult, shooting within city limits when he ought to know better. And I'm not doubting the bullet whizzed right by you, if you say you heard it. But if you haven't had any threats and no enemies, I just can't think it was anything but a stray bullet. Which is bad, of course." His voice went stern. "Very bad. If we can find out who's shooting around here, we'll nail 'em. But I don't think you have to worry that it was someone deliberately aiming to hit you." He paused almost delicately. "Although sometimes we see relationships that have gone sour turn ugly . . . ?"

He quirked an eyebrow, leaving the suggestion open-ended. Angie just shook her head.

"I don't think you have anything to be concerned about then." In a kindly voice he added, "Sometimes people who are accustomed to city living come to a little place like Julesburg and have trouble making the adjustment. The noises are different, and the houses, like this one, sometimes much more isolated." He smiled tolerantly.

*Okay, I get the picture. I'm a city girl with jittery nerves, one who wouldn't know a BB gun from an assault rifle, and I'm stewing over kids taking potshots at a squirrel.*

"Thanks for coming."

"Maybe it would be a good idea if you go stay with your brother for a few days until you . . . ah . . . feel more comfortable here. And stay away from those murder investigations," he added sternly. "That's our job."

*Yeah, a job the authorities blew thirty years ago.*

"I'm going to look around some more," Ryan said after the officer had gone. He headed for the door.

"I'll go with you."

She was just retrieving her jacket from where she'd dropped it on the sofa when the phone rang. She ran to it with a sudden guilty thought. *Stefanie. Worried about Ryan. We should've called her.*

But it wasn't Stefanie's voice. "Angie, are you okay?"

"Yes, I'm fine."

"Don't go outside," Steve Llewelyn commanded. "Stay away from the windows. Someone just shot at me. They may be after you too."

Angie dropped to the sofa. "Shot at you? Where? How? What happened?"

"I was just getting out of my car here at the motel. The bullet missed me by inches. It hit the car door right beside me. I'm inside now, but I'm so shaky I can hardly hold onto the cell phone." She heard a rustling sound, as if he'd moved the phone to a different hand and ear.

"Have you called the police?" she asked.

"I wanted to warn you first."

"I don't need a warning. The gunman has already been here. He took two shots at me. I guess I should've warned you."

"What?"

Angie elaborated on what had happened at her house.

"This is connected with the Nevermore, then," Steve said. "I thought it might be, the minute it happened. Now I'm sure of it."

Angie agreed. Investigating the old murder at the Nevermore was the only thing she and Steve Llewelyn had in common. The gunman must've gone directly from her place to Steve's motel.

"Look, we need to talk about this," Steve said.

"Call the police first. An officer just left here. Maybe you can get him out to the motel before he leaves town."

"I'll call you again as soon as I can."

Angie hesitated. She knew her brother was going to echo the officer's advice that she stay at his house for a few days. At the moment, much as she hated to admit being scared, she was inclined to accept. But she didn't want Steve calling the house or coming over there and possibly upsetting Stefanie more than she already was.

"How about if we meet at the Julesburg Café at 7:00?"

"Good. I'll see you then. And I'll call the police now."

Outside, Angie reported Steve's call to Ryan. He scowled but didn't comment. He called Stefanie on his cell phone, and then they searched around the house. They found nothing to suggest the gunman had come that close, no trampled weeds or footprints in the damp area by a leaky faucet. But it was almost dark now, not an ideal time for picking up small details.

Ryan fought his way through the brush to the abandoned car and decided no one had been near it in years. They walked to the top of the hill to the east, where Highland met Rigby Road, and Ryan concluded that this was probably the gunman's vantage point for the shooting. He pointed back toward the house.

"There's a clear view of the driveway from here."

Dusk softened the house's outlines, but Angie's white Corolla stood out like some overgrown mushroom against the background of dark brush.

"Where I was a sitting duck. It's a wonder the shooter missed me. What did the officer think about this spot?"

"We didn't come this far. I think he had his mind made up from the beginning that it was just a stray bullet, not someone shooting at you."

"I'm not sure he was convinced there even was a shot."

Ryan didn't disagree. "From here, the gunman would've had to use a rifle and maybe a scope to have much hope of hitting you. A bullet from a handgun would probably travel that far, but it would lose accuracy at this distance."

"So the fact that he missed me says . . . ?"

"I'm not sure."

"But wouldn't he have been concerned someone would see him parked or standing here waiting?" Angie asked. "It looks pretty risky."

"Neither of these roads has much traffic. He may've figured if he had bad luck and was seen, he'd just give it up for today without taking a shot. Or maybe he knew about what time you'd be getting home and that he wouldn't have long to wait."

"I don't know how anyone would know that," Angie said. "I got home earlier than usual today, because I went to the Cranberry Growers barbecue—" She broke off, startled by an unexpected thought.

Ryan put it into words. "Unless someone knew when you left the barbecue and made a beeline to beat you here."

"But everyone was so nice. So friendly."

"You're coming to the house for tonight. Maybe several nights." He paused. "Maybe permanently."

Angie silently rejected his last opinion. She wasn't going to intrude on her brother's life indefinitely. But she didn't argue about tonight or several nights. "Can I bring Keyhole?"

"Okay by me, and Stef likes cats. Although you'll have to work it out with Sherlock."

Ryan waited while Angie packed an overnight bag and scooted Keyhole into the cat carrier. She'd bought it because she was intending to take the cat to a vet for spaying in a few days.

"Hey, in all the excitement, I forgot to tell you something," Ryan said. "I've been in e-mail contact with my cop friend in New York. He says the authorities there are sure they have the right guy in custody for the Question Mark killings. The last victim was sexually assaulted, and material taken from her body matches his DNA."

"They got Kristi's killer?" Relief swooshed through her. "I wonder if Ethan knows?"

"They figure they've got the Question Mark killer all right, but this doesn't necessarily settle anything about Kristi's murder. That's the strange part, because DNA from the scrapings under her fingernails doesn't match this guy's."

"I don't understand. What does that mean?"

"It's a strong indication the man in custody didn't kill her."

"But she had the Question Mark killer's carving on her shoulder!"

"Which could mean a different killer was trying to make it look as if the Question Mark killer had done it. And it might've worked, if Kristi hadn't gotten her fingernails into him."

"So now what?"

"They keep looking for another killer."

At the house, Stefanie welcomed both Angie and Keyhole, and Sherlock took a tolerant attitude toward the feline visitor. Keyhole immediately started prowling and within minutes had everything from laundry room to upstairs storage room checked out. Stefanie hadn't gone back to work at Fit 'n' Fun yet, but she was up and around and cooking. Angie skipped dinner, however, still feeling stuffed from the afternoon barbecue.

Steve's blue sedan was parked at the Julesburg Café when she arrived at 7:00. She took a long look around before getting out of the car. On her way to the café's entrance, she got a look at the rear door of Steve's sedan under the parking lot lights. She brushed her hand across the neat hole and shivered.

How close had she come to having a neat hole drilled in her?

nside, Steve lifted a hand to wave her over to a booth. The café was warm, with the fragrant scent of its specialty, clam chowder. She slid into the vinyl-covered seat across from him. He reached across the table and squeezed her hand.

"I guess there's one thing we can be grateful for," he said.

"What's that?"

"That our gunman is a lousy shot. If he weren't, we could both be dead."

"It's possible they were warning shots telling us to back off on our investigation, rather than someone actually trying to kill us. Maybe he meant to miss."

"You think so? Then maybe I'm wrong, and he's an extremely good shot. In that case I'm glad he didn't miss his target, because about a foot to the right and he'd have wiped me out."

The waitress arrived. Without looking at the menu, Angie ordered a small bowl of clam chowder and coffee. Steve opted for a T-bone steak and french fries. He was casually dressed this evening, in jeans and a plaid shirt, but the wave in his hair was carefully tended.

When the waitress was gone, Steve braced his elbows on the table and leaned forward. "Personally, I think the misses were definitely accidental. I think this guy wanted to take both of us out."

"Which suggests he may try again?"

"A strong possibility."

"Did the police officer come to the motel?" Angie asked.

Steve nodded. "The bullet had gone right through the car door. He retrieved it from inside the car."

"Good. Can't they get all kinds of information from bullets, maybe even identify the gun it came from?"

"Well, the officer didn't say much, and I don't know anything about guns and bullets. But what I saw looked like a mangled blob. Maybe going through metal like that messes up markings or whatever."

"Do you know where the shot came from?"

"Probably on that wooded hill up behind the motel. There aren't any houses up there. Apparently no one in the motel heard the shot, although I don't know how they could've missed it." He shook his head. "The gunman must've come directly from your place to mine," he added, voicing her own thought.

"It's possible more than one person is involved."

"I hadn't thought of that," Steve muttered. "Another worry."

"The shot sounded loud and close?"

"Actually, I'm not sure if I heard the gunshot or just the whack of the bullet hitting the car door. You don't exactly keep things straight when you're scared out of your wits. First thing I knew, I was down on the ground, trying to crawl around the car to hide." He motioned to his clothes, apparently changed after the incident, and smiled ruefully. "Not my finest hour, I'm afraid."

"I wonder if the police will be able to tell if the bullet was from a rifle or handgun? My brother thinks the gunman shot at me from too far away to be accurate with a handgun."

"Really? That's interesting. If he had a handgun, maybe that's why he missed me too."

"We'd better hope he doesn't get smart and buy a rifle."

Their coffees arrived in white mugs. Angie clasped hers with both hands. She was having difficulty keeping her hands from shaking.

"None of this seems quite real. It's hard to imagine someone actually shooting at me." She hesitated. "I keep wondering if it's . . . connected with the Nevermore."

"Of course, it's connected with the Nevermore! There's a killer out there who's afraid we're going to identify him. That's what I told the officer."

"That isn't the connection I'm wondering about." She gave him an abbreviated version of Stefanie's miscarriage. "That, along with someone shooting at me . . ."

"You mean you're thinking it's connected with the Nevermore's curse? Some ghost or something?"

Angie smiled self-consciously. "On a rational basis I know that's far-fetched. But sometimes it looks as if I'm another in a long line of people connected with the Nevermore who've had strange misfortunes. First, my good friend back in New York was murdered. Then Stefanie's miscarriage. Now this. Alive only because of a gunman's bad luck or poor choice of weapons."

"I'm inclined to think the first two are just unfortunate coincidences," Steve said. "And this last one, that was the killer's finger on the trigger, not some ghostly appendage."

"Well, what did the police officer have to say?"

"I don't think he totally ruled out that someone shot at me—"

"He shouldn't, considering that I'd just been shot at too!"

"But he seemed inclined to think it was a stray bullet from someone poaching deer or shooting squirrels up there in the woods. Apparently that's not uncommon around here. I told him I thought it was connected with my father's murder at the Nevermore, but he was skeptical."

"Did he have any comments about the murder?"

"No. Basically he just said I should trot on back to Nevada and let the police take care of murder investigations. What about you?"

"Pretty much the same thing. He thinks I'm a nervous city girl with an overblown imagination."

"He'd probably have thought 'big imagination' about me too, but that bullet in my car was solid proof of something. I asked him if I could have it as a souvenir of Julesburg, but he said no, that they'd definitely see if a lab could do anything with it. So I'm pretty sure he wasn't ruling out someone deliberately shooting at me. He spent quite a bit of time in the woods, looking for the casing."

"Nothing?"

"Nothing."

"The rental agency probably isn't going to be happy with that bullet hole in the door when you turn the car in."

"Rental agency?" He looked at her in surprise. "How'd you know that?"

Angie felt her face flush. "My brother is very protective. He did a little checking on the car."

"And me?"

"He didn't find out anything about you." Angie smiled, trying to defuse a situation that suddenly felt tense. She couldn't blame Steve for reacting with a certain hostility. She wouldn't want someone prowling into her personal life on the Internet. "You're a man of mystery."

"I don't appreciate someone snooping around in my personal life. I'm financing the purchase of this car dealership, and I don't want some strange inquiry to mess that up."

"Could it do that?" Angie asked.

"I don't know. These things can be rather sensitive."

"I doubt Ryan plans to take his inquiries any further, but I'll make sure, just in case."

"Thank you." Steve took a long gulp of water. "Are you scared, what with all this shooting going on?" he asked after he set down his glass.

"I'm staying with my brother and his wife for a few nights."

The food arrived. Steve flooded his french fries with ketchup. The clam chowder smelled tantalizing, although Angie still didn't have an appetite. By now, she suspected the cause was lingering jitters more than overindulgence at the barbecue. And the sight of that puddle of blood-red ketchup didn't help.

"This doesn't mean you're going to back out on buying the Nevermore, does it? Or stop investigating my father's murder?"

"I'm not sure."

Steve's oversized chunk of rare meat dipped in ketchup stopped halfway to his mouth. "I'm surprised. You haven't struck me as the kind of woman who'd scare off that easily." He sounded reproachful.

"Fearless newspaper reporter determinedly digs for the story, no matter what the dangers?" Angie smiled. "I suppose I should ask what Lois Lane would do in this situation."

"Now I feel, to keep in the spirit of things, that I should duck into the nearest phone booth and don my Superman outfit."

"Except phone booths are so open-airish these days. A bit inconvenient for major garment changes."

"Didn't you ever wonder what ol' Clark Kent did with his regular clothes? Did he have a special hideaway pocket for them? Or did he put his Superman outfit on over his nerd suit?"

The foolish little exchange lifted Angie's spirits and put her in a calmer state of mind. "I'm not backing out on buying the Nevermore. Or investigating the murder."

"Good. Then we need to think about a certain point." Steve's steak was already almost demolished. A real speed-eater. "Is this person worried about what we already know or what he's afraid we may find out?"

"I can't think we know much now."

"I agree. So the attempts on our lives are probably meant to stop us from investigating further."

"From going to see Madame Zorrich?" Angie looked up from her chowder. "But who would know about that?"

Even as she asked the question, Angie gave a small inward groan. At the barbecue, she'd put a lighthearted spin on their plans when she talked to people.

"I'm afraid I may have mentioned it a couple of times," Steve said before she had a chance to confess. "I went to see Myrna Bettenworth today—"

"Myrna surely wasn't out there shooting at us!"

"No, but she's a talkative old gal. Who knows who she may've told that we're going to see Madame Zorrich tomorrow? Or who they may have told? And then I was in the bank, talking to one of the officers when my ATM card jammed, and . . . I don't know exactly how the subject came up, but I mentioned it to him too." Steve shook his head as if appalled with himself. "I didn't realize I was such a big-mouthed jerk. Now I remember I also got into a discussion with a guy at that store that has a little of everything—"

"Reedy's?"

"Right. And this guy who works in there was really interested in the Nevermore and the murder."

Angie also remembered Jeff Reedy's interest from when she was soliciting ads for the *Herald*. And the family had taken a brief stab at ownership of the Nevermore. A connection with the old theater—and the murder?

"I did a little blabbing today too," she admitted. It had seemed natural, there at the barbecue when people discussed the Nevermore article with her, to tell them she had located Amelia's old spiritualist and was planning to see her tomorrow.

"You wouldn't think some cranberry grower would be hiding a knife-killing in his past," Steve said. "I always associate cranberries with turkey. Not murder."

"There were a lot of people besides cranberry growers there. The barbecue was really a community event. I remember talking to an older guy from the bank, Wally Greer. He knew Amelia. His son wasn't there, but I'm pretty sure he'd be about the right age to have been a teenager at the time your father was killed."

"An old man who felt he had to use a gun to protect his son from nosy and dangerous outsiders like us? And maybe with enough of a local 'in' to make police records disappear?" Steve speculated.

Angie nodded uneasily. "I chatted with Estelle Reeves from the real estate agency too. I probably mentioned Madame Zorrich to her. And the Cranberry Growers Association president was very interested in the Nevermore article. The Associated Press guy who wrote the article about the Nevermore also showed up for a few minutes."

"All so respectable. People you'd never suspect of involvement in a murder."

"And I talked with a local CPA who has a scholarly interest in local Indian history. He mentioned an old Indian tale about local spirits, and I know I said something about Amelia's interest in contacting the dead. And that I planned to talk to her spiritualist." Reed McIvers, the accountant, was also the right age to have been a teenager when Harry Llewelyn was killed, and he'd lived in Julesburg most of his life. He seemed an unlikely suspect, though. "I guess I hate to think one of those friendly people could've tried to kill us," she added.

"You don't know, of course, who may've been eavesdropping on your conversations. Someone you weren't even aware of. Someone not so friendly."

True.

Angie skipped dessert, but Steve had a big slab of kahlua cheesecake. They parted with an agreement to meet at the *Herald* office at 8:30 the following morning.

The phone was ringing when Angie got home.

"Good news!" Estelle Reeves said. "The owners down in California just called. They're accepting your offer on the Nevermore. I'll do the paperwork to get the escrow started immediately. You're making a wonderful buy."

*Am I?*

The day was cloudy, but the sun broke through occasionally on the drive down to Brookings. They took Steve's car, and the air made a peculiar whistling noise through the bullet hole, an unpleasant reminder that someone hadn't wanted them to make this trip. Angie had considered calling ahead and making an appointment with Marie Zorrich, but she'd decided that might result in a flat turndown. This way they at least had a working chance to see the woman.

They found the Dancing Dolphin Gift Shop just off the main street in Brookings. A display of shell and rock wind chimes tinkled around the door. Inside, the shop smelled faintly of sandalwood, and Angie noted a stack of incense sticks in various fragrances on a shelf. She didn't see anyone who resembled the black-haired, "foreign looking" Madame Zorrich whom Lillian Feldman had described.

A thirtyish woman was busy with a customer. An older woman with a matronly figure and gray hair was straightening a display of glass figurines. An enameled pendant and earrings, both in elegant black and white, dramatized her stylish black dress. Her shoes were thick-soled black flats, however, as if she wasn't willing to sacrifice comfort for style in the foot area. Angie approached her.

"Hi. I'm looking for Marie Zorrich."

"That's me." The woman gave her a friendly smile. She had gone a little overboard with the eyeliner and mascara, but her lipstick and blush were nicely muted. She looked well-preserved for her age. Her voice, Angie noticed, showed no trace of accent.

"I'm Angie Harrison from the Julesburg newspaper, the *Herald,* and this is Steve Llewelyn, Harry Llewelyn's son. We'd like to talk to you, if you have a few minutes."

The Llewelyn name didn't draw any reaction from Marie Zorrich. Her gaze shifted between them, puzzled but still friendly. "Sure. Have I won the lottery or something? Come on back to my office."

She led them through a rear doorway into a cubbyhole of an office with a desk, a filing cabinet, and jumbles of papers piled in baskets. She found a couple of chairs in a nearby storeroom and crowded them around the desk.

She folded her hands on the desk, put an attentive look on her face, and waited for one of them to take the initiative. Angie pulled out a copy of her Nevermore article and handed it across the desk. The woman took quite a long time reading it closely. She looked up at Steve once, apparently at that point connecting his name with the murdered man in the article. Her dark eyes were bright and shrewd within their frame of black eyeliner.

"I don't see why you've come to me," she finally said. She handed the newspaper article back to Angie.

"Steve wants to find out who killed his father."

"I certainly don't know. I was still living down in L.A. when the murder happened."

"But you were Amelia Swarthout's spiritualist. When you were Madame Zorrich, she came to you numerous times to conduct séances to contact Harry Llewelyn."

The woman didn't deny that she was Madame Zorrich, but her eyes narrowed at the mention of her past occupation. "How did you find out about that?"

"It came up in one of the interviews I did for the article."

"So what do you want? I don't do séances or read palms now. So if what you have in mind is doing a séance to contact Amelia Swarthout—"

"Oh, no, that isn't what we want," Angie said hastily. "We're hoping you can give us some information that would help us identify Harry's killer."

Angie shot a sideways glance at Steve. He took the hint and leaned forward. "If you could tell us about those séances between Amelia and my father . . . ?"

"You think that in a séance Harry told Amelia who stuck a knife in him?" Marie Zorrich asked. "And now Amelia can tell you? Or you want a direct line to Harry?" The questions came in a faintly mocking tone.

"Well, I . . . uh . . . doubt any of that is possible," Steve said, "but we'd appreciate anything you could tell us."

"My grandmother had Gypsy blood, or so she said, and she conducted many, many séances. Her clients believed they were real, and so did I. She said she'd teach me how to contact those on the 'other side.' I don't know now if she was faking all along or if I was just a poor student, but I never did learn how to actually contact anyone. Although I learned fast enough that real contact wasn't necessary and that I could make pretty good money faking it. And that's what I did." Marie Zorrich leaned back in her swivel chair, arms folded across her chest, chin lifted in defiance.

"Faked the moving table? Faked the voices talking through you?" Angie asked.

"Faked everything."

Angie had never believed in the ability to communicate with the dead, but the blunt admission of fakery startled her. Although the admission was not, she recognized instantly, accompanied by guilt. The words held a certain satisfaction, as if Marie Zorrich was proud of the accomplishment.

"How about the accent?" Steve asked. "Did you fake that too?"

"I imitated my grandmother's accent. Hers was real."

"Why did you quit?" Angie asked.

"I finally just got tired of it all. Tired of creepy people who wanted to talk to the dead. Tired of the endless act. Would you believe I was even sued once? I decided I just wanted to live a normal life. Which is what I'm doing now." She motioned toward the front of the gift shop with a nod of satisfaction.

"I can understand that," Angie said.

"Although people who came to me regularly, especially Amelia, sometimes I thought they came not so much for the séances as for the company and someone to talk to."

"Lonely people?"

"Amelia was. Sometimes I'd pretend to do a séance but tell her no one was answering today, and then we'd just sit and drink tea and talk."

"Did you talk about my father's murder?" Steve asked.

"Amelia never said much about the murder. It didn't seem all that important to her. Mostly she liked to talk about her childhood. She must've been a very lonely little girl. She had an incredible memory for movies she'd seen. She could describe movie scenes from thirty years ago. She'd read a lot as a girl too. She said she had a special 'hidey-place' where she liked to go and read. But what she liked to talk about most was the books and movies she intended to write."

"Someone else also mentioned that. Her life story, I think she wanted to do."

226

"Well, more than that. She had all kinds of ideas, some about her actual life, others pure imagination. 'Amelia and the School Bullies.' 'Amelia's Adventures in Boarding School.' A romance about a handsome pilot going to a small town on a secret mission and falling in love with a plain young woman who became beautiful through his love. I think she may have intended to write about the murder too, but she was cagey about that."

"You remember a lot, considering how long ago it was," Steve said. "It would seem you'd remember *something* she said about the murder."

Angie didn't think that a particularly helpful remark. Nor was Steve's obvious impatience helpful. Somewhere he'd acquired a paper clip, which he was methodically straightening and bending.

"I may have faked séances, but there's never been anything wrong with my memory, especially where Amelia is concerned," Marie snapped. "She was special to me, and I have no doubt our talks were very comforting to her. And I can tell you one thing."

"What's that?" Angie asked.

"It wasn't Harry Llewelyn Amelia was trying to contact."

# 24

t wasn't?" Angie asked in surprise. "You mean Amelia wanted to contact her parents?"

"Well, she did talk to them a few times."

"Talk?" Steve's voice held a sneer.

Marie ignored him. "I had them tell her they were in a good place, very happy and comfortable, and they wouldn't object at all if she sold the old theater and moved away from Julesburg, that it would be a good idea if she did do that." She looked over at Angie. "You don't need to look so horrified," she added tartly.

"I'm not horrified," Angie said. "Just surprised that you'd suggest something so . . . life changing, I guess. Was moving away something she asked about?"

"No. I just suggested it. Lots of times I could see exactly what people needed. I could've told them myself, in my own words, but they needed to hear it from whatever dead soul it was they were trying to contact. So I let that person tell them. I figured Amelia would be better off far away from that creepy old theater and whatever had happened there."

"But she didn't listen to what her 'parents' had to say?"

"No. She killed herself there at the theater, as you know. But that was some time after she stopped coming to me."

"So if Amelia wasn't trying to contact Steve's father, who did she want to talk to?" Angie asked.

Marie frowned and fingered the enameled pendant hanging on her ample chest. "I don't know."

"I thought you had such a great memory," Steve said.

"It isn't lack of memory. Amelia wouldn't tell me."

"How can you call someone from beyond the grave without a name and identity?" Steve scoffed.

"When it's fake, you can do anything," Marie snapped back. To Angie she added, "Amelia said he'd know it was him she wanted to talk to, and if he wanted to talk to her he would. She told me to tell him she loved him, no matter what."

"No matter what," Angie repeated, puzzled. "Those were her exact words?"

"Exactly."

"So what did you have this unnamed person tell Amelia?" Steve asked.

"The whole business with him made me uneasy," Marie said. She straightened ballpoint pens in a blue mug. "It was . . . peculiar. I've never encountered anyone else so secretive in that way. Always the first thing they say is, 'I want to talk to my dead husband, Arnie,' or 'I want to talk to my sister Sally.' Usually I pretended to Amelia that I couldn't reach this person, because it's hard to fake someone when you don't even know who you're faking. But once in a while I'd have him say he loved her and missed her too. Along with the usual 'I'm fine, happy,' etcetera."

"When Amelia was 'talking' to him, did she ever ask specific questions about anything that had happened before his death?"

Marie shook her head. "Amelia was a strange one. She not only believed the dead could be contacted, she believed she could sit there and talk to this person by mental telepathy."

*Undertow*

Steve snorted. "If she could do that, what did she need you for?"

"She believed I was the channel or bridge who could open up the communication, and then she could take it from there."

Steve rolled his eyes.

"And she never did try to contact Steve's father?" Angie asked.

"Actually, she did a couple of times. I told her he didn't seem to be available. I didn't want to encourage Amelia's growing . . . mental aberrations. I was also afraid she'd imagine him naming someone as his killer and then make a lot of trouble for some innocent person."

"How very ethical of you," Steve said.

*If eyes could send someone off to another dimension, Steve would be gone,* Angie suspected. She couldn't understand why he was being so unhelpful. "So you never discussed who might've killed Harry?" she asked Marie.

"No."

"Did she ever mention a Vance Spohn?"

Marie looked off into space as she searched her memory. "No, I don't think so. Doesn't jiggle any memories, anyway."

"There's gossip from long ago that Amelia was in love with him even though she was supposed to marry Harry Llewelyn. He worked in the theater as a projectionist. Perhaps quite a ladies' man, from what we've heard. There's also some suspicion he might've killed Steve's father, in a rivalry between the two men over Amelia."

"Over Amelia?" Marie Zorrich's heavy eyebrows lifted. "Well, I suppose that's possible. Maybe this Vance is who she was trying to contact, then, the one whose name she wouldn't tell me."

"But Vance wasn't dead," Angie said. "He just walked out on her."

230

"Really? Puzzling, then. In all honesty, I'm surprised to hear Amelia had two guys on the string. Her personality wasn't exactly scintillating. And she was hardly beautiful."

"But she was rather wealthy," Angie said.

"I'm sure Madame Zorrich knew that," Steve cut in.

Marie ignored the insinuation. "Perhaps she didn't want to believe this Vance walked out on her and convinced herself he was dead," she suggested. "People have done stranger things. And Amelia wasn't the most stable person in the world."

"Did you predict the future for people?" Angie asked.

"Usually not. Too many pitfalls when things don't come true. Though sometimes, when it really seemed important, I'd have the person on the other side give a warning about the future. I was always very careful never to do any harm," Marie added, her tone defensive. She stood up, signaling the interview was over.

Angie got up too. "We really appreciate your talking with us." She set a business card on the desk. "Would you give me a call if you think of anything else that might be helpful?"

Back in the car, Angie jumped on Steve about his attitude toward Marie. "What were you doing? We were trying to get information from her, not antagonize her."

"I'm sorry," Steve muttered. "Patience isn't my strong point. And old people get on my nerves. Especially someone like her, conning people with all that séance garbage."

"You'd better develop both patience and tolerance if we're going to get anywhere finding your father's murderer. Anyone who knows anything is going to *be* old."

"I guess."

Steve tried to get her to have dinner with him that evening and hike up Humbug Mountain on Sunday, but she gave him excuses about being busy with Ryan and Stefanie.

"Remember to tell him to stop snooping around about me," Steve muttered.

After Steve dropped her off at the Herald, she checked her mailbox at the post office. Along with some junk mail there was a letter from Cate, her former roommate in New York. She'd sent Cate her new address, and now Cate was telling her she should pay part of a previous electric bill and complaining that it was "rude of you to go through my things before you left." Angie shook her head. Theirs had not been the most harmonious of roommate relationships, but what was *that* about?

On the way home she stopped at a place called Second Hand Stuff and bought a shovel, rake, and some small gardening tools from a haphazard assortment displayed on the sidewalk. Then, with Keyhole's "help," she spent the remainder of the afternoon working on the yard.

When the sun sank behind Lighthouse Hill, she quit work and went inside. She called Ryan and told him she'd be over later, just before bedtime. She knew he'd have preferred her to come now, and he made her promise to call him if she heard so much as a squeak around the house that evening.

After talking with Ryan, she skimmed out of her clothes and into the shower. It was then, with hot water peppering her back, that something Marie Zorrich had said hit her. Something that had passed right over her at the time.

*A hidey-place.*

## 25

*A*melia Swarthout had had a secret place as a child where she'd go to be alone to read and dream.

And Angie knew where that hidey-place was.

She hastily dressed in old jeans, a sweatshirt, and a heavy jacket. In the kitchen she grabbed her big square flashlight out of a bottom cabinet. She was closing the front door behind her when a white sedan pulled into the driveway. Damp autumn darkness had already fallen, obscuring the interior of the car, and she warily stepped back inside the doorway, leaving only a crack to peer through. It wasn't until the male figure stepped out of the car that she recognized him and felt a flood of relief.

She opened the door. "Ethan! What happened to the yellow monster?"

"It's stranded in my brother's driveway. Carburetor problems, he says." Ethan could rebuild a computer from cyberspace up, but the internal combustion engine had always been a mystery to him. "So I picked up a rental. You dodged back in the house like you thought I was going to give you a hard sell on encyclopedias. Is anything wrong?"

"There were a couple of gunshots here yesterday. I'm a little edgy."

"Gunshots? What happened?"

They'd been walking toward each other, and now Ethan put his hands on her arms. His concerned eyes grazed her face from eyes to throat. "Are you okay?"

"I'm fine. The police think it was probably some kids out shooting at squirrels or birds, and that a couple of stray shots just happened to come this way. Or that maybe it was my city-girl imagination that there even was a gunshot at all."

"But there were shots?"

"I heard a bullet whine right by my ear. I wasn't imagining that. Although I suppose it could've been a stray shot. But a bullet also missed Steve Llewelyn in the parking lot of his motel a few minutes later."

"Stray bullets coming one right after the other in two different locations doesn't seem likely," Ethan said.

"My thought exactly. Although I guess the police don't think it was anything more than coincidence."

"You think this has something to do with your probing into that old murder at the Nevermore?" Ethan asked.

"It has to be. There's no other reason someone would be after both Steve and me. We're just not certain if this someone was actually trying to kill us or if the shots were meant as a warning to stop our investigation."

"The police investigated both here and at the motel?"

Angie nodded. "They took the shooting at the motel somewhat more seriously, I think. At least with a bullet hole in his car door and the actual bullet in his car, Steve obviously wasn't just imagining a gunshot."

Ethan glanced around, and Angie was aware of the concealing darkness of the brushy woods around the house. An army of snipers could be out there planning an ambush.

"I don't think it's a good idea for you to be here alone," Ethan said.

234

"I stayed with Ryan and Stef last night. I'm planning to go over there again later this evening." She leaned into him and gave him a hug. "I'm surprised to see you back in Julesburg this soon."

"We missed our date for church last week, remember? I thought we'd give it another try tomorrow morning."

Angie had put the whole situation with God and Stefanie's miscarriage and her own unsettling realization about the past on a back burner, determinedly squashing the thoughts whenever they arose. She didn't want to argue about church with Ethan now. She dodged his question and pulled out of his arms, a bright smile on her face.

"Hey, you got here just at the right time! I'm on my way to check out something important. Want to come?"

"Big news scoop for the *Herald*?"

"Maybe."

Angie flicked the flashlight on to test its strength. The glow lit up the yard. Ethan motioned to his rental car, and she ran around to the passenger's side.

"Where to, spunky young reporter?"

"The Nevermore."

He gave her a sideways glance as he backed out of the driveway. "Really? What's happening there?"

"It's not what's happening. It's what may be there." She smiled at his puzzled lift of eyebrows. "You'll see. If there's anything to see."

She was out and opening the garish doors of the old theater before Ethan even had his rental car locked up. She knew her haste was foolish; if there was anything hidden in the Nevermore, it had been there for a couple of decades now and surely wouldn't disappear in the next few minutes. But that didn't curb her eagerness. Ethan had never been inside the Nevermore before, but she didn't take time to give him a guided tour.

"By the way," she tossed over her shoulder as she shoved aside the drape across the opening to the aisle, "the place is almost mine. The owners have accepted my offer." The drape tumbled down again, but this time she managed to fling the velvet shroud aside before it enveloped her. She kicked it toward the candy counter. *You're on your way to the dump,* she informed it with satisfaction.

Ethan followed her down the aisle and up the steps to the stage level, where the gold satin curtain concealed the screen. *Another item headed for the dump.* It looked just as close to collapse as the aisle drape. Behind the curtain she flicked the glow of the flashlight around the accumulation of trash, the light catching a shine of beady eyes.

"I know it doesn't look like much now, but it's going to make a great office for the *Herald* and a wonderful apartment for me."

"I admire your imagination, because I'm afraid all I see is a mice-infested relic."

She led Ethan by flashlight to the pit around the multi-armed furnace and pulled the leaning concrete block away from the small door. This time it swung open of its own accord, letting out the same rush of musty-cave scent.

Angie got down on her knees and aimed the flashlight toward what she'd earlier thought were old rags piled near the foundation. She hesitated, her confidence momentarily rattled as shadows leaped and swooped with each twitch of the flashlight beam. Would a little girl really have chosen this dank atmosphere and dark isolation as her hidey-place? And come back to it as an adult to hide her secrets? *I wouldn't!*

But strange, lonely Amelia might.

Angie crawled toward the pile, Ethan following.

"I hope you know what you're doing," he muttered. "Isn't this the part of the horror movie where the human-eating lizard pops up through the ground?"

236

"Human-eating lizards stay away from Julesburg. Too many macho guys with high-powered hunting rifles."

At the lumpy pile of rags, Angie squatted back on her heels and fought a sudden assault of claustrophobia. The space was large in area, but the stage floor overhead so low that it felt like a hovering weight ready to collapse and crush them in a rubble of old lumber. Hastily, anxious to get out of there, she poked at the pile with a forefinger. Rotten fabric crumbled at the touch, but her finger hit something hard underneath. A black spider scurried out of the folds. Angie looked around for something with which to push the disintegrating fabric aside, but she saw nothing. She braced her squeamish nerves, but before she touched the bits of fabric again, Ethan brushed them away with a sweep of his forearm. Underneath was a metal-reinforced wooden box about two-thirds the size of a footlocker, rusty hasp fastened with a padlock.

"You want to see what's inside?" Ethan asked.

"Oh, yeah."

He yanked the padlock, but it was frozen with rust and didn't give. He changed position to brace himself and slammed it with his heel. The padlock crumbled under the blow. He lifted the lid of the box, and Angie looked down on exactly what she'd hoped she might find.

*There must be thirty or forty of them, all shapes and sizes!* Small, thick diaries with rusted locks. Larger notebooks and journals, some plain, some fancy. Angie opened one, its pages stuck together in clumps, and saw faded, spidery handwriting filling the pages. She felt a thrill of connection with the past, as if Amelia herself were standing in the wings, waiting to speak and reveal her secrets.

"What is all this?" Ethan asked.

"Amelia Swarthout's old diaries and journals." She briefly explained about the meeting with the spiritualist and how the woman had mentioned Amelia's old hidey-place. "It didn't mean anything to me at first, but then I knew this space under the stage had to be it. And then I just hoped that her hidey-place was where she'd hidden her old diaries too."

"You think her diaries will tell about the murder?"

"Amelia couldn't ignore it, could she? It had to be a turning point in her life." *Or maybe a dropping-off point.*

The bottom of the old box had rotted to crumbling wood, and Angie wished now that she'd thought to bring sacks or boxes in which to carry the journals. Those lying against the bottom of the box, where the wood had rotted, were too badly disintegrated to be worth taking, but she and Ethan made several trips taking the others to the tiny doorway. Then they both filled their arms to carry everything out to the trunk of the car. Angie tilted her head back as she carried her stack, trying to keep her nose away from the unpleasantly musty scent of the old pages.

Back at the house, Angie spread newspaper on the living room floor and laid the journals and diaries in a single layer on it. The box had, at least, protected them from depredation by mice. And they weren't actually damp. They wouldn't have survived this long in a truly damp condition. But they definitely needed some warmth and deodorizing.

Ethan called the Sea Haven to make certain he could get a room there for the night. Angie made coffee, and then, both sitting cross-legged on the floor, they started trying to separate the old pages and decipher the faded writing.

Angie glanced only briefly at the diaries with rusted locks. From what Twila had said about Amelia keeping a locked diary during her school years, Angie figured these were the oldest records. A quick glance into one told her she was correct. The old pencil writing was little more than illegible shadows now, but here and there a word came through. *School . . . bullies . . . Someday I'm . . .*

*hate them.* She moved on. She'd come back to study Amelia's unhappy girlhood at a later time.

"Here's one that's dated 1969," Ethan said. "It's not too readable, but I can make out some words about 'roast beef' and 'asparagus.' And something about trying a different brand of coffee."

Poor Amelia. Was she reduced to keeping track of what she ate for meals?

Angie removed a rusted paper clip from a journal, leaving a stain on the page. This one was dated 1950-something. The last numeral had faded. "What we need is 1972. That's when the murder happened. Or maybe 1971, to see what she says about Vance Spohn. I'm not sure when he showed up."

Occasional mention was made of Harry Llewelyn, most of it impersonal, as if he were merely a business acquaintance. Angie found no account of a marriage proposal, although she assumed it was lost in one of the faded sections. Surely acquiring a fiancé was an important event in Amelia's life, even if it wasn't the romance of her dreams. The mentions Amelia did make of Harry were mundane, though. She and Harry had eaten pork chops at the Julesburg Café. She would have to rearrange the bedroom furniture in her house after they married. He had escorted her to a Christmas play at the school, a "tedious affair."

Angie found only one mention of Harry's son, and that was not by name. *"Harry's little boy is such a whiny child. Perhaps . . ."* Faded section. *". . . live with Harry's sister."*

Amelia obviously had no intention of taking on the job of raising a small boy herself.

Then Angie came across a blurred but even more telling line about Amelia's relationship with Harry Llewelyn. *"Harry is always—"* Faded section. *". . . so dreary and bor—"*

The last word had faded into nothingness, but the meaning was plain. This was a marriage of desperation, not a happy love affair. And then, in handwriting changed from spidery to forceful, so forceful the turquoise ink had survived the years intact, Amelia wrote, *"I've found it. Love! My own true love at last!"* What followed was a rapturous account of how she and "VS" were destined for each other.

"I think she's just met Vance Spohn." Angie passed the journal over for Ethan's inspection.

He read it and nodded. "Sounds like it."

There were many more blissful references to Vance, and they were better preserved than much of the material, as if the power of Amelia's emotions had strengthened the very ink with which it was written. Her woman-in-love excitement danced off the faded pages. Vance had brought her a rose. She had given him a ruby ring that had belonged to her father. Alone in the projection room, often they had held hands and watched the movies together.

About that time, a peculiarity began. The journals that were kept on an orderly day-by-day basis ended, and the writing changed from first to third person. *"She was so happy that she danced in the moonlight,"* Amelia had written. And on a more prosaic note: *"She went to the store and bought veal chops because those were his favorite, and she made lemon pie with mounds and mounds of beautiful meringue for him. Theirs was a love as two people have never loved before, a love for all eternity."*

She showed it to Ethan.

"Not afraid of melodrama, was she?" he said.

"I think it's kind of creepy," Angie said. "Writing about events as if she were standing outside herself watching them happen."

"Do you think she's writing about herself here?" Ethan asked. He read Angie a paragraph about a man watching a woman walking on the beach and instantly falling in love with her.

"Sounds like wishful thinking to me," Angie said.

She opened another notebook and read faded bits of a short story that she suspected had its basis in real life, about a young girl's rejection by a clique of schoolgirls. But the story veered into the realm of horror fiction as the girl set fire to the school and watched with satisfaction as flames engulfed her helpless classmates trapped in an upper window.

Then Angie read a sketch about a woman who fell from a cliff into the sea and was swept away in an undertow, her body never found. Angie read it to Ethan.

"Here's the ending: *'And each year her brokenhearted lover returned to toss roses into the sea, one rose for each year she was gone.'* That one certainly can't be true, at least not of Amelia and Vance. I'll bet no one ever suspected what an odd romantic imagination she had."

"Or what murderous thoughts she had about doing away with her childhood enemies," Ethan added.

"I wish she'd just stick with the facts on a day-by-day basis, the way she did in her earlier journals. With this stuff, you can't tell what's true and what's her imagination." Angie sniffed her fingers and wrinkled her nose after she closed another musty notebook. "So far we haven't come across a single word about the murder."

"No. But of course, her account of the murder might be in one of those journals that were disintegrating in the bottom of the box."

True. Unfortunately.

They stopped to eat grilled cheese sandwiches and minestrone soup from a can, then returned to the journals. Angie's back began to stiffen, and she was about to suggest they give it up for the night when she saw something that made her sit up straighter.

Underſtow

This section actually had a title, as if Amelia had definitely written it as a story: *"Love and Jealousy."* Angie read it through. Lines were faded and missing, but the story was startlingly plain.

A beautiful woman was in love with a younger man. She was so beautiful she could've been a movie star, but she had chosen instead to live a private life running a theater in a small town. These two had loved before, in another life, and now they were together again, blissfully happy. But another man who was in love with the woman and mad with jealousy killed her beloved. He buried the body in a secret hiding place beneath the theater. But the woman found out, and she avenged the death of the man she loved by killing the man who killed him. She made it look like a robbery, and no one ever suspected the truth. *"But soon,"* the story ended, *"my beloved and I will be together again. Someday very soon."*

Angie just sat there for a moment, stunned. Here it was. Amelia's account of the murder. Written in fanciful third person. But that last sentence, with the switch to first person, said it all. "She killed Harry. Amelia did it."

"What?"

"Amelia killed Harry. It's all right here."

Ethan took the notebook and read it. "This could be just one of her story-writing attempts. Some of her other stuff certainly isn't fact. And this bit about being lovers in some previous life . . ." He shook his head. "But . . ."

"But?"

"But the rest of it has a ring of truth, doesn't it?" He turned the page and read further. After a few more pages he handed the journal back to her. "Except take a look at version two."

This story had a different title: *"Nevermore, My Love."* But it started out the same. Beautiful woman. Breathtaking love affair. Except this time the loved one was characterized differently. This time he was a handsome

242

rogue who seduced and then betrayed the heroine with another woman. In a rage of hurt and anger, she killed him. She was then heartbreakingly sorry, but it was too late. He was dead. She buried him where she could always have him near. Then a man she had once planned to marry found out what she had done. He, vindictive because she had rejected him, was going to turn her in. So she pretended a robbery and killed him also. The ending was the same: *"But soon, my beloved and I will be together again."*

"Now what do you think?" Ethan asked.

"I don't know whether to think Amelia Swarthout had a sick and morbid imagination or was nutty as a fruit-cake."

"Or a murderer. Maybe even a double murderer."

"I guess there's one way to check it out," Angie said. "The stories agree on one point."

"Yeah. There's a body buried under the Nevermore."

e should probably get in touch with the authorities," Ethan said.

"I suppose. But . . ." Angie hesitated, remembering how the officer had acted when she'd told him she'd been shot at. He already thought she had a boogeyman-in-the-bushes mentality, and she could picture the reaction if she called in claiming the Nevermore hid a long-buried body. If the authorities did a search and found nothing, her credibility would be zero. Not a good situation for a newspaper editor.

"I think I'd rather check it out first to see if there is anything buried there." She looked at her watch. "Then we can contact the sheriff's office immediately if we find anything."

"You want to go over there now?" Ethan asked.

Angie hesitated again, then smiled. "Well, no, I guess not. The Nevermore is creepy enough without going there in the dark of night to dig for a body."

"How about tomorrow afternoon? We could have breakfast at the Julesburg Café, go to church, and then jump into the role of amateur sleuths searching for a body. We should probably take along a properly chilling musical accompaniment. Maybe the old *Twilight Zone* theme?"

Angie laughed and shook her head. "You think this is all pretty far out, don't you?"

"To be honest, I don't know what to think. If we look further in the notebooks, we may run across version three in the saga of Amelia. Maybe this one will be Vance Spohn killing Harry Llewelyn and taking off for South America. With Amelia planning to follow. Not that I think this is a joke to be taken lightly," Ethan added hastily. "Harry was murdered, and you may have been shot at, and that's definitely serious stuff."

"I know. It's just that sometimes it does start looking kind of slapstick. Spooky old theater, eccentric woman, buried body, bumbling amateur detectives."

Ethan laughed. "Well, even bumbling amateur detectives have to be prepared. We'll need something to dig with. Maybe we can borrow a shovel from Ryan?"

"I'd just as soon not tell Ryan and Stefanie about this yet. I have some garden tools we can use."

"Okay, sounds good. So I'll meet you at the Julesburg Café . . . say, 9:00? And then we'll go on to church?"

Angie had been hoping he'd forget that detail, but there it was. She brushed a spiderweb off an unread journal, stalling for time. Yes, she could go to church. Sing the hymns and praise choruses, close her eyes during prayer, listen to the sermon. Pretend everything was just fine between her and the Lord.

And know she was a phony, an imposter, an outsider who had no right to be there.

The words, the reverse of what she'd been telling herself ever since she'd left New York, lumbered across her mind. *The past is not behind me.* The past was right here, dragging her down, pulling her under.

"I don't think I'm ready for church yet," Angie muttered.

"Going to church isn't really the point; I know that. You can start or renew a relationship with the Lord without that formality. Right now, in fact."

245

"Don't push me, Ethan."

He shook his head. "I don't get it. I have the impression you want to come back to the Lord. Last week you were willing to go to church with Stefanie and me." He leaned back against the table. "Now you're holding back again. Why? What's going on?"

Angie got to her feet. She felt as if she were pushing her way up through air that had turned unnaturally thick and heavy. She was still holding an open journal, and she set it carefully on the table. "I thought, when I left modeling and Burke, that I'd walked away from a life I'd come to realize was wrong. I walked away from a *me* I didn't much like anymore. You know about the ambition that dominated my life and took me astray. And my wrong relationship with Burke. I've told you all that."

He'd never held that relationship against her, however much it may have hurt him, and he didn't pursue discussion of it now. It was a generosity and self-control that spoke more than any words.

"There's that old saying that church isn't a museum for saints, it's a hospital for sinners," he said.

Angie rubbed a finger on the faded page of a journal. "I think what I need is more like a scrubbing machine. To scrub out the past."

"The past can't be scrubbed out. Wrongdoings can't be undone. But we can ask the Lord to forgive us for whatever we've done. It's that simple."

"No, it isn't that simple!" Angie slammed the journal shut. "I don't even feel worthy of asking for forgiveness yet. I wanted to clean up my life so that when I came to him, the Lord would know I'm sincere. So he could see I'm trying and that I'm so very sorry for what I did. But it's a lot more difficult to escape the past than I realized. I found that out with Stef's miscarriage." She sighed. "I feel like that log we watched out in the surf not long ago. A big log, sloshing back and forth, as helpless as a toothpick in the waves. And then disappearing in an undertow. I feel as if *I'm* caught in an undertow of the past that won't let go."

He reached over and squeezed her hand. "None of us is ever worthy of forgiveness. It's God's gift, because of what Jesus did for us. And only the Lord can lift us out of the undertow of wrongdoings, past or present. He doesn't demand that we scrub ourselves in some cosmic bathtub before we can come to him. He just wants us to come."

*Oh, Ethan, you just don't know . . .*

"There's a verse in Romans," Ethan went on. "'But God demonstrates his own love for us in this: while we were still sinners, Christ died for us.'" He leaned a hip against the table, head tilted. "But you made a commitment to the Lord once, and I know you read your Bible regularly then. So you surely know all this already."

"I know I made a commitment to the Lord. I accepted that Jesus went to the cross for me. But I also know that didn't stop me from doing all the wrong things I did! I just went right ahead and did them. Because I wanted my photo on magazine covers more than I wanted to follow God's will."

"There's a word for it. Backsliding."

"But it's worse than never knowing the Lord and coming to him for the first time. Our wrongdoings before that are understandable. But I didn't do wrong out of ignorance. I knew better! And I just barged ahead and did it anyway. Now I want God to know that I'm sincere in wanting to change myself and my life, and I'm really working on it."

"Yes, but you're also demanding that God accept you on *your* terms," Ethan pointed out. "You're saying, 'Hey, Lord, I'll get myself all squeaky clean, and then when I'm ready, I'll come to you.' But only God's forgiveness can make us squeaky clean, not our own actions."

"Oh, Ethan, you'd feel differently if you knew what I've done! I didn't tell you everything. I did something much worse that anything I told you about."

"Do you want to tell me now?"

"No!"

"Then just talk to the Lord about it. It's between you and him. There's no wrong so unforgivable that the Lord can't forgive it. Just don't let pride or shame or stubbornness or anything else stop you from taking it to him."

Angie swallowed raggedly. She could step into Ethan's arms. For all his blunt words, she could see the loving concern on his face and know that he'd hold her close and never ask her to tell him about this hidden wrongdoing. She longed to take the easy way out and do just that.

"But I have to tell you. Because my ambition took me much further astray than you know. Because this concerns you too."

Apprehension jolted Ethan as he looked at the pain and despair written on Angie's face. *I don't want to know this.* He tried to detour her. "Just talk to the Lord."

"No." She straightened her slumped back with determination. "You remember that last night before I left Phoenix for New York?"

*Oh, yes, I remember.* He'd spent many an hour in prayer talking to the Lord about that night. A night he'd also had to call on the Lord's strength not to remember with guilty desire.

"I was so excited about New York and becoming a model. I ached for it. This was my big chance, my dream come true. But at the same time I didn't want to leave you behind. And you—"

"I know about me," Ethan said. "I was afraid of losing you, and it scared me more than anything had in my life."

248

"And we both know what happened."

"It isn't something I'm likely to forget."

They'd gone out for dinner. More than he could afford, but he'd wanted to make that last evening together memorable. An expensive restaurant, candlelight, an attentive waiter, and a table overlooking the artfully piled rocks and waterfall of the lushly landscaped grounds. Yet halfway through dinner, they'd both realized that the restaurant, even though dark and quiet, wasn't where they wanted to spend the final hours of their last night together for weeks or months.

Another thought had hit him as he'd watched Angie across that candlelit table, so beautiful in her white summer dress, her shoulders tan and her long hair in an elegant French twist at the back of her head. A thought he'd dodged but couldn't avoid any longer. *Maybe it won't be just weeks or months before we're together again. Maybe she'll never come back to me.*

They'd skipped dessert. He'd driven his old Chevy out to South Mountain Park, several miles outside the city. He'd parked at a mountainside viewpoint among desert saguaro and ocotillo. No other cars were around on that hot summer weeknight. Witch-finger streaks of lightning flashed off to the north, silently illuminating the dark silhouettes of distant mountains like brief glimpses into some other world.

"We've had so many good times hiking out here, haven't we?" Angie asked as they looked down on the lights of the city. She sounded wistful, as if those good times had already receded into the past.

"Free fun," he said lightly.

"Is that why you brought me here, to remember all our good times?"

"Maybe I just wanted to prolong our last evening together. Not let it end."

She reached over and touched his cheek lightly. "Oh, Ethan, I'm going to miss you so much. I'm not sure I can stand it."

He wrapped his arms around her and pulled her close. "Then don't go. Let's get married. We won't wait for your graduation or enough money or anything else. We'll do it right now, as soon as we can get a license."

"I don't want to go away. I don't want to leave you! But I also desperately want to go. Can you understand how I can feel both ways?"

She moved her head as if searching for his eyes in the darkness of the car, but he couldn't help noticing how she'd sidestepped his urgent proposal. They both wanted to get married, but they'd never before discussed when.

"I'm afraid you'll go away . . . and never come back."

"That can never happen," she declared. "I love you! I want to marry you more than anything—"

"Almost anything," he corrected. *Not more than flying off to New York and becoming a model.*

She laughed and stroked his cheek again. "Okay, so I want to do this. I really want to do it. It's the kind of chance half the girls in the world would walk through walls of fire for. But it's just a for-now thing. Being a model isn't forever. They toss you out when you're . . . what? Twenty-five? And we won't be apart all that much. You'll visit me in New York, and I'll come back here whenever I can."

He wanted to believe that. Angie spoke as if she believed it. Yet an emptiness inside told him it was never going to happen. He knew nothing more to say than what he'd already said to keep her from going. He wasn't sure he even had any right to try to hold her back. He touched her hair, smoothing it, and brushed his lips across her temple. "We'll manage," he whispered.

She clung to him, her assurance unexpectedly vanished. "Oh, Ethan, I'm scared!"

"Scared?"

"Scared of New York. Scared of modeling. Scared of finding out I'm not good enough. Scared of failing. Scared of losing you!"

He was tempted to draw back and say, "Yes, that's a possibility. Things like that happen when two people are apart." Would that frighten her into changing her mind? But he couldn't do that to her, not even to keep her from going. "You won't lose me."

He kissed her, tenderly at first, trying to reassure and comfort her. But something ignited between them as they kissed. Fear and love and the knowledge that this might be the last time they were together for a long, long time electrified their need and blazed into the kind of passion they'd always kept under careful control, saving it for marriage. Until now, when they both wanted to be closer on that last night, closer than ever before, close enough to be one . . .

Afterward he'd taken her back to her apartment near the college. They hadn't talked much then, and in the morning he'd driven her to the airport. "I'm sorry," he whispered just before she boarded the plane. "I always meant our first time to be on our honeymoon."

She smiled and kissed him on the corner of his mouth. "It's okay. I love you."

"I love you too. So much. You'll call me when you get to New York?"

"Of course."

But it had been more than a week before she'd called. By then, he was frantic with worry and fear and anger but also so glad to hear from her that all he did was tell her how much he missed her. She apologized and said she missed him too, but her bubbling excitement about photography sessions and staying in a crowded apartment with three other models and seeing Central Park and the Empire State Building and meeting Christie Brinkley told him otherwise.

Now, standing beside a battered table in a tiny Julesburg house, she said, "New York was everything I'd hoped for. Scary and intimidating but so big and new and exciting and full of so many wonderful possibilities. I'd known before I got there that I was fortunate, coming already connected to a good modeling agency. Then I saw how many girls came on their own and were desperate to get where I already was, and I realized just how fortunate I was. I got caught up in this whirlwind of getting my hairstyle changed and my jiggly thighs firmed up and my posture improved."

"And then they sent you off to Paris."

"Training, they said. Five of us went. To get the kind of experience we needed to make it to the supermodel status they planned for us. And then, just a week after I got to Paris . . ." She paused, and her chest lifted and fell. "I . . . went to the doctor."

"You were sick?"

"I was pregnant."

The word hung between them like something alive. *"Pregnant?"*

"The doctor said I was six or seven weeks along. Although I didn't need him to tell me that since I knew to the minute when I became pregnant."

Ethan knew too.

"I was devastated. Being pregnant meant the end of everything. If I'd been an established model, I could've managed a pregnancy. Other successful models have. But I was just starting out. The agency wouldn't waste time with me if they knew. They'd have dumped me the instant they found out."

"You're telling me—"

"Yes. I became . . . unpregnant."

His mind dodged around the meaning of Angie's words. He tried to reinterpret them. "You had a miscarriage, like Stefanie?"

"I had an abortion, Ethan. An abortion."

He shook his head, desperately not wanting it to be true. She went over and stood by the window. Her shadowy reflection in the dark pane looked fragile and defenseless. She dipped her head, hands clasped into a peak beneath her chin.

"I didn't tell anyone except the older woman who acted as housemother to us. She was the one who told me what to do, what doctor to go to. I guess I wasn't the first desperate young model she'd helped. And it wasn't difficult to get an abortion there in France. They had the RU-486 pill. A preliminary visit to the doctor, two more visits for the pills, and another final checkup to make certain it was all . . . complete."

"Just swallow a pill, and in a few minutes it's all over?" She whirled to face him. "No! I cramped—" She closed her eyes and touched her abdomen as if she could still feel the pain. She fumbled for a chair at the table and slumped into it. "Terrible cramps for two days. And I bled for almost a week."

He felt her pain and took a step toward her. Then he stopped, the moment of compassion freezing as shock waves kept rolling through him. They'd created a baby together. And Angie had killed it.

"I kept telling myself that I hadn't done anything awful. It wasn't illegal. And millions of women had abortions."

He'd been gritting his teeth, trying to keep from saying anything, but now the words burst through his barrier of control. "You could have told me. I'd have done anything for you. You know that! I'd have come to Paris and gotten you . . . anything. This was our *baby*."

She didn't argue, just went on in a monotone voice. "I told myself other things too. I even got self-righteous about it. God had made a big mistake. Why hadn't he given this baby to some couple who desperately wanted one? Why make me pregnant? If he hadn't done this to me, I wouldn't have had to do . . . what I did. So it was all his fault."

*Blaming God.* He swallowed. *Been there, done that.*

"But I couldn't hold on to that, because I knew it was just rationalization for my own wrongdoing. Then I kept telling myself I was only six weeks along. It wasn't really a baby yet. It was just a . . . medical condition. Tissue." She swallowed convulsively and looked down at her hands.

"You seem to have done a lot of talking to yourself."

"You know the old saying. Talk is cheap."

"This didn't bother you afterward?" He meant it as a question only, but he heard the accusation in his own voice.

"Can you really think that, Ethan?"

No. Not tenderhearted, caring Angie. But she'd *done* it, and his image of a tenderhearted Angie wouldn't at that moment gel with the news he'd gotten. He'd thought he knew her; now he could only wonder if he'd known her at all.

"I was sick to my stomach for days," she went on. "I couldn't eat. I told my supervisor I had the flu, and I stayed in bed and cried until my eyes were almost swollen shut. I couldn't sleep. And when I finally did sleep, I had nightmares."

He swallowed, hurting with her. *But she'd gotten over it,* he reminded himself. *Gotten over it and gone on to that glittery life she'd craved.*

"The man from the modeling agency who supervised the girls came to me and said if I didn't recover soon from this 'flu,' then they were going to have to send me home. Which would mean I was through. For a few hours I was ready to go. Nothing mattered. Then the house-mother came and reminded me that what I'd done had been so I could be a model. I'd made the sacrifice. I'd paid the price. So I should claim the rewards."

The reward of having her face and body in ads and on magazine covers. At the price of a baby's life. Their baby's life.

She rubbed a knuckle across the tears sliding down her cheek. "I told myself it was a sensible trade-off. The doctor had assured me doing this wouldn't affect my future ability to have children. I was young and healthy and could have all the children I wanted when the time was right. Just like they told Stefanie. It wasn't as if I'd done something . . . permanent to my body."

"So you convinced yourself what you'd done was right."

"No! I never convinced myself of that. But I knew that the only way I could go on was to hide it all in a secret place inside me and build a wall around it. And that's what I tried to do."

"So this wasn't a part of why you quit modeling?"

"I guess in a subconscious way it was part of my quitting. But I'd . . . walled it away for a long time, and the up-front reasons for my quitting were what I've already told you. I thought walking away from them would set me free. I kept reminding myself that the past was behind me. But it wasn't. It isn't. *This* is there. It feels like . . . a shroud around my soul. An undertow dragging me down."

He saw a vision of Angie down on her knees in the Harrisons' bathroom, scrubbing bloodstains and crying. He saw her washing her hands as if she were trying to wash away a filth too strong for soap and water. Now he knew it wasn't just Stefanie's bloodstains she'd been trying to wash away.

"And then Stefanie had her miscarriage," he said.

"Yes. Stefanie had her miscarriage," Angie echoed hollowly. "I knew how desperately she and Ryan wanted the baby. How loved and cherished it already was. It made me see, as I'd never truly let myself see before, that what I'd done had taken the life of a baby. My baby."

255

*And mine. Except that I never had a choice in the decision about whether it lived or died.*

Angie's head slumped as if it were too heavy to hold up. "I look back and I'm sick about what I did. Stef called her pregnancy a gift from God. I had a gift from God too. But I threw it away. I made that deliberate choice. I threw my baby away. And I keep thinking, after what I did to my first baby, how could God ever trust me with another one?"

Ethan swallowed. Again he could see how she was hurting—he felt in his own skin and bones and heart how she was hurting. And he couldn't ignore that he wasn't innocent here either. If he'd had more control that night, none of this would've happened. So it was his responsibility too.

But he'd gladly have borne the responsibility of their baby. He'd have done anything to marry her and bring their baby into the world. Instead, she'd kept her secret, kept silent.

He grabbed his jacket and stumbled toward the door.

## 27

ngie listened to the car back out of the drive-way and roar away. The sound faded before it reached the corner, but she didn't need sound to know which way Ethan had turned. Not south to the motel to stay the night. No, he'd turned north, headed back to Eugene. Putting as many miles between himself and her as possible.

She didn't blame him. It was too much for him. *It's too much for me too.*

Her legs felt oddly boneless. She slumped to the sofa. She knew Ethan was a loving and generous and compassionate man, a man who tried to live the faith that he believed in. But the truth about her pregnancy and what she'd done to end it had struck him like a lightning bolt to the heart.

And here it was. Heartbreak. Because she was in love with him again. And he'd walked out.

The phone rang. She ignored the first four rings, then reluctantly reached for the phone. Ryan, of course. She forced a false cheeriness into her voice and spoke before he did.

"Yes, brother dear, I know. I said I'd be over. But there isn't so much as a mouse squeaking around here, and if there were, Keyhole would pounce on it. I'm staying here tonight."

"I don't think that's a good idea. This nut with a gun may try again. I'll worry. So will Stef."

Angie didn't want to worry them. Stefanie had been under far too much stress and strain already. But she couldn't go over there now. She needed to be alone. "I'll keep my cell phone right next to my pillow, and if anything goes bump in the night, I'll call instantly, okay?"

"Okay." Ryan didn't sound convinced, but he also apparently recognized that neither argument nor persuasion was going to budge her. He changed the subject. "Hey, I've been doing a little more sniffing around on the computer. I can't find anything about a car dealership recently for sale in the Las Vegas area. I checked with several agencies that should know."

"Oh? I suppose it could be something less than a big car dealership. Maybe Steve's buying a used-car lot or junkyard or something and just upgraded it in the telling."

"Yeah. Could be, I suppose."

"Look, Ry, I'm really tired, okay?"

"Sure. Get a good night's sleep." Yet, ever perceptive, he asked, "Hey, is there something you aren't telling me?"

"Ethan was here. We had a little—" A little what? Disagreement? Argument? No. No disagreement or argument about the wrongness of what she'd done. They were fully agreed on that. "I'm just feeling kind of . . . down."

"I'll come over and we can talk."

"Not right now, okay? I just need to be alone and think."

Ryan paused, then finally said gruffly, "I'll call you in the morning."

The house was silent after she put the phone down. The revelations in Amelia's journals, which had seemed so mind-boggling a few minutes ago, now felt distant

258

and insignificant. Keyhole had drifted into purr-less sleep. The wind was silent, no bushes whipping against the walls. Even the refrigerator's familiar hum was stilled. Alone. Silence. All the time in the world to think. *And what will thinking accomplish? Will it change the past? Erase what I've done? Turn my selfish ambition and my relationship with Burke and the abortion from wrong to right?*

*Bring Ethan back?*

*No.*

All the wrongdoings, all the mistakes she'd made in her life flooded over her now. The air seemed short of oxygen under the flood, and she struggled to her feet. She went to the window and shoved it open, unmindful of the cold dampness of the air rushing in. She breathed deeply, expanding her chest until it hurt, but still she couldn't seem to draw enough cleansing air into her lungs.

*Because fresh air isn't going to cleanse me.*

Neither were her own efforts to clean up the wrongs in her life and make herself presentable to God. She'd tried, and the past was still there in all its wrongness, dragging her down, pulling her under.

Ethan had laid it all out for her, partly with words from the Bible, partly with his own words of deep-held beliefs. *While we were still sinners, Christ died for us. If we confess our sins, he will forgive us and purify our unrighteousness. Only God can lift us out of the undertow of our wrongdoings and mistakes.*

So why was she still caught in that undertow?

Her pride. *I can clean up my life, Lord. Just watch me.*

Her stubbornness. *Then, on my terms and my timing, I'll come to you.*

*Oh, Lord, I'm sorry.* Angie slumped to her knees on the floor and leaned her forehead against the windowsill. *Sorry for all the wrongs I've done. Sorry I hurt Ethan. Sorry for what I did with the gift of life you offered me. Sorry I thought I could walk away from everything I've done and make my life and myself all clean and worthy of your forgiveness. Because I can't do it. I'm asking for your forgiveness now, Lord. I'm asking you to take me back into your fold, even with all the stains of ambition and abortion still clinging to me.*

She heard no forgiving words booming down from on high. She saw no visions of angels carrying her sins away. But she felt the constricting bands around her lungs and her heart loosen and fall away.

And she felt the wrongdoings and mistakes of the past that had long dragged her under lose their strength and set her free.

## 28

ngie woke early and pushed aside the curtain covering the window above the bed. The sun wasn't yet above the forested hills to the east, but the sky was blue and cloudless. Like a fresh page waiting to be written on, a day on which to compose a new beginning. *My new beginning.*

She sank back to the pillow, feeling a heady combination of exhilaration and joy rising above a foundation of serenity. Exhilaration and joy in the knowledge that she was home at last, home with the Lord. Serenity because the past truly was behind her now. Not forgotten, no. She'd never forget the wrongness of what she'd done. But forgiven.

Yet an inescapable sadness rolled in and eddied around the joy. Ethan. Ethan, striding toward the door with that shattered look on his face, as if his heart had just been ripped apart. Ethan, stunned and hurt and angry. Ethan, out of her life.

*Oh, Lord, help him deal with this. Not for my sake. I can't ask that he'll come back to me. Not now, not ever. That's hoping too much of any man, after what I did to his child. But for his sake, Lord, so he won't be eaten up with anger and bitterness, help him find his way through this. Ease his pain, please.* She swallowed down the pain clogging her own throat.

The phone rang. It couldn't be Ethan. No, of course not. He was probably already heading to the Eugene airport for an early flight back to Phoenix. And there was no one else she wanted to talk to.

She sat up and reached for the phone on the nightstand anyway, hopeful in spite of herself. "Hello?"

"You okay, sis?"

She leaned back against the pillow and forced herself into good-morning banter. "Yes, worrywart brother, I'm fine. No gunshots, no prowlers, no things that go bump in the night. Nothing."

"Just checking. How about coming over for breakfast? Stef's making blueberry muffins."

"Bait to lure me into going to church with you afterward? Or maybe you just plan to get out the handcuffs and drag me off?"

"Whatever works."

"The blueberry muffins are very tempting. But I'm planning to make French toast myself."

"Really? I wasn't sure you even knew how to make toast, let alone the French kind."

"I guess you're surprised, then, at the culinary talents I'm developing. And I have another surprise for you."

"What's that?"

"You don't have to bribe me to go to church. I'm coming on my own. See you there." Smiling lightly, she hung up before he had a chance to get past a sputtered "Wh—?"

Church! How she'd missed it. God's presence wasn't confined there, of course. He was everywhere. Here. Right now. But there was something special about meeting him in his house of worship. A praise song rose out of memory, as if it had been just sitting there waiting for release, and she hummed it as she showered and blow-dried her hair. She was just finishing a breakfast of French toast and strawberry preserves when the phone rang again. Even as her head again told her it couldn't be Ethan, her heart jumped, and she ran to the phone.

"Hello?"

"Angie, I've been thinking."

The words were what she wanted to hear, but the voice saying them was not. "Oh?" she murmured to Steve.

"About that place the nutty old fortune-teller said Amelia hid stuff."

"She didn't actually say Amelia hid anything. Just that there was some place she called her 'hidey-place.'"

"Whatever," Steve said impatiently. "Anyway, I think she may have been talking about that area under the stage at the Nevermore, back there by the big furnace where we opened the little door. It's the kind of place I might've used as a hideout when I was a kid."

"You're right about her hidey-place. Actually, I went there last night. I found a whole box of Amelia's old diaries and journals."

"You went there alone? I thought we were in this together. I wish you'd told me so I could've gone with you." Steve sounded annoyed or accusing, maybe a little of both. "Is there anything interesting in them?" he asked.

"Actually, yes." She gave him a brief rundown on the two versions of Vance Spohn's death, both of which revealed Amelia herself as Steve's father's killer. "Of course, neither of the versions may be a factual account of the murder. It's possible they're both just scenarios Amelia dreamed up because she thought they'd be more book or movie worthy than an anonymous robbery."

"But all this fits in with Madame Zorrich saying Amelia wouldn't give her the name of someone she wanted to contact on the 'other side.' Amelia wouldn't dare identify Vance Spohn by name if the reason she knew he was dead was because she'd killed him."

"Yes, that fits," Angie agreed. "But one of Amelia's stories says your father killed Vance Spohn, and the other says she killed him. So at least one of them has to be imagination. They can't both be true."

"But one of them must be true, because my father was definitely killed. Which means we should get over to the Nevermore and start looking for a body. Or whatever may be left of one after thirty years."

"I suppose we could do that this afternoon. But this morning I'm going to church."

"Church?" Steve repeated the word as if it was not a familiar part of his vocabulary. "What time does that start?"

"Eleven o'clock. It'll be over at noon. We can go after that."

"Actually, I can't. I got a call last evening that there are complications with my purchase of the car dealership, and I'm going to have to run down to Vegas for a few days. I need to get out of here as early as I can, so I can't wait until this afternoon. It's only a little past 8:00 now. We can look around down under there and be done in plenty of time for your church thing."

Angie felt a moment's uneasiness. Had Ryan's Internet snooping caused Steve's problems on the purchase? But honestly, that wasn't the real reason she hesitated. She just didn't want to crawl into that musty, claustrophobic hole under the Nevermore this morning. She'd wakened feeling as if she were basking in the sunshine of God's love, and what she wanted to do now was get out her Bible and read for a while before heading to church.

Steve's impatient voice interrupted her hesitation. "This is important to me. If Vance Spohn's body is buried under the Nevermore, it tells me one of those stories is true. And Amelia murdered my father. It's what I came here to find out."

264

"Okay, I guess I could go over for a while now. Although that's a big space under there, and it could take a long time to search all of it. If we don't find anything now, I'll just have to go back by myself later."

"I didn't realize you were so gung ho on church."

"Sudden change of direction in my life. You should try it."

He ignored the suggestion. "What are we going to dig with?"

"I have some garden tools we can take."

"Okay. Good. I'll pick you up there at the house in about fifteen minutes."

Angie started to protest that she'd rather meet him at the Nevermore, but Steve had already hung up. She carried the shovel and smaller garden tools from the backyard around to the front. She added the big flashlight to the pile. Morning sunshine sparkled on the damp grass, but the fall air was chilly, and she knew that dank space under the Nevermore would be even more chilly. She went back inside for a jacket and gloves. Still with a distant hope Ethan might call, she dropped her cell phone in a pocket of the jacket.

"You seem a little jittery," Angie said on the drive over to the Nevermore. Steve was tapping the steering wheel and jiggling the seat belt strap and scrutinizing the sparse Sunday-morning traffic as if suspecting each person might be the one who had shot at him. "I guess you'll be glad to get out of Julesburg."

His quick laugh also sounded nervous. "Well, it's not every day I set out to dig for a dead body. I wonder what's left of one after thirty years?"

"I think we may find out." She turned in her seat to face him. "Will you be coming back to Julesburg after you get things settled in Vegas?"

"If we find Vance Spohn's body, probably not. If it's there, I'll know then who killed my father, because both of Amelia's stories say she did it. The body will prove one of the stories is true."

"How do you feel about Amelia being the killer?"

"Surprised, of course. But I guess I don't have to worry about justice for her as a murderer."

"That's true. But one thing doesn't make sense." Although, with so many other things on her mind, Angie hadn't really thought about this point until that moment. "If Amelia was the murderer, why is someone afraid of our investigation? Why was my house searched and both of us shot at?"

"Good question. Could it have something to do with the newspaper rather than the murder? Maybe you ruffled some feathers there?"

"Newspapers are always ruffling feathers, but I don't think I wrote anything inflammatory enough to make someone get out a gun. And even if I did, that wouldn't involve you."

Steve shook his head. "Beats me. Actually, I'm going to be glad to get out of this backwater burg. Did you tell your brother or anyone we were going over to the Nevermore to look for a body?"

"No. I figured we'd see if there was anything there first."

"Good idea."

Steve parked the blue sedan in the weedy parking lot next to the Nevermore. Angie unlocked the theater doors while Steve got the tools out of the trunk. They carried everything across the lobby and around to the pit encircling the old furnace. The shovel Angie was carrying snagged on the gold satin curtain, leaving an ugly rip. No matter, of course, since she planned to junk both curtain and screen as soon as possible.

She was glad she'd worn her heavy jacket. The theater felt cold even before they opened the small door into the space beneath the stage. The usual scent of dank air and raw earth rushed out.

"So, if you were going to bury a body under here, where would you put it?" Steve asked.

"As far away from the door as possible, I suppose." Angie knelt down and arced the beam of the flashlight around the dark space. They had come here to try to find a long-buried body, but it wasn't until now, when she was kneeling at the entrance to the dark hole under the stage, that the full reality of this Sunday-morning jaunt hit her. She shivered from something more than cold. Had Amelia once dragged a murdered man's body through this very opening? And they were going to dig it up . . .

*No, not dig it up,* she reminded herself hastily. *Just find out if it's really here. Then call the authorities if it is.*

But maybe it wasn't here. Maybe the journal stories were just more of Amelia's weirdness, and all they'd find would be bugs and spiderwebs. She preferred that thought. *Think of this as a wacky escapade, like in a movie. Spunky young reporter doing her stuff.*

"She'd probably put the body away from where the pipes and wires are, in case someone came to inspect or maintain them," Steve suggested.

"Right."

"But the farther away from the door she buried the body, the farther she'd have had to drag it," he added. "That wouldn't be easy for a woman."

"Myrna told me Amelia was strong as a mule. She'd have to be really strong to overcome your father with a knife. So she probably could've dragged a body wherever she wanted."

"Yeah, I guess that's true. Or maybe it was my father doing the dragging, since one of Amelia's stories said he killed Vance."

Angie glanced from her kneeling position back at Steve. He hadn't yet gotten down on his knees to follow her. "Are we stalling about doing this?" she asked.

Steve laughed, but the sound came out close to a titter. "Yeah, I guess maybe I am anyway. Ol' Amelia must've had nerves of steel."

"You want to hand me those tools?"

Steve hesitated, as if he were having second thoughts about this whole project, but finally he handed her the tools one by one. Shovel, trowel, garden claw. "Okay, let's get it over with."

Angie set the tools inside the opening, braced her nerves, and crawled through. She immediately bumped her head on an overhead joist and fought an instant wave of claustrophobia. Her hands clenched into fists, and she forced herself to stretch and flex them. She squatted back on her heels and put on her gloves, less from the chill than from a squeamishness about touching bare earth that held a body. *Remind me I never want to become a cave explorer.*

The flashlight offered a surprising amount of light in the enclosed space, but it was a light that seemed to conceal as much as it revealed. Long shafts of shadow angled out from the upright braces, and pipes and wires looked like long tentacles slithering overhead. The corners and spaces between the joists were almost like sponges, swallowing the light.

"I hope the batteries in the flashlight don't give out," she muttered.

Steve was beside her now, his big frame even more cramped than hers in the low-ceilinged space. "Where'd you find her diaries?"

"Over there." Angie angled the flashlight toward the open box. "It's probably as good a place as any to start."

The first thing they discovered when they tried to dig next to the box was that the shovel was almost useless. Given the low ceiling, the handle was too long to drive the shovel blade into the dirt in the way shovels are usually used, and all they could do was slide it at an angle that dipped no more than a couple of inches below the surface.

"That isn't going to get us anywhere," Steve said in disgust. He tossed the shovel back toward the opening and grabbed the trowel.

They crawled around on hands and knees, Angie moving awkwardly with the flashlight in one hand and the garden claw in the other. Spiderwebs hung between the joists and webbed the dirt, and within moments she was swiping them out of her hair and off her face and mouth. She grimaced and shuddered when a live spider squirmed in her hand.

She stopped here and there to scrape the dirt with the metal claw. The surface of the bare earth was rough, but it was harder than it looked and covered with almost unbreakable clods. Out of the corner of her eye she saw something scurry along the foundation. Shivery fingers also scurried along her nerves. She wanted to make some lighthearted comment to ease the tension, but the situation was rapidly losing any aura of "wacky escapade."

"This may be a wild goose chase," Steve muttered. "There's no telling how deep she buried him. We might have to dig a foot deep in every inch of the space under here."

"Amelia, or your father, if he was the one doing the burying, wouldn't have had any better luck digging with a shovel than we did, so I doubt if the body is buried very deep. Maybe just a shallow trench, with dirt scraped up over the body."

"Maybe not even buried. Maybe just hidden in a corner somewhere."

Angie jumped when a spider ran across her hand. Another bump on the head. But she didn't feel so cold now. A nervous perspiration dripped unladylike tracks from under her arms and across her ribs. The French toast lay in her stomach like clods of the hard earth.

"Here's something!" Steve said.

He picked it up and held it with squeamish delicacy between thumb and forefinger. Angie moved the light closer.

"A bone," she said. It was slender and tiny, no more than an inch long. "I . . . I guess feet have a lot of tiny bones, don't they?"

"There's more."

Yes. More bones scattered over a couple of square feet of earth. All tiny and delicate, most even smaller than that first one. And finally, a tiny skull.

"A mouse," Angie said. She didn't want to titter, but she did. Thank goodness she hadn't dragged the police under here to find mouse bones.

They kept crawling. By unspoken agreement, they stayed close together. Angie's hand hit a rusty piece of pipe. Broken glass. There weren't many rocks, but Steve put his knee down on a sharp pebble and exploded with a curse word. She paused once to tap an upright support with her metal claw, expecting the wood to be soft with decay, but the thud was hard and solid.

"I should've brought Sherlock," Angie said suddenly.

"Sherlock?"

"My brother's dog. He sniffed out a body in a burned-out building once. He might've been able to help us here."

"After thirty years, this body can't be more than bare bones. Nothing much to sniff . . . hey, what's that?"

Angie moved the flashlight to where Steve had pointed. Not more than a yard ahead of them, something lay half-buried in the rough dirt. Something like a globule of blood.

## 29

hey crept closer. Angie found herself instinctively holding her breath.

Not blood. Impossible. But what was it?

"Hey, it's a ring!" Steve scooped the object out of the dirt and rubbed it against his sleeve. He cradled it in his open palm and, under the glare of the flashlight, the gem glowed like a red eye staring up at its discoverers.

Angie's cold fingers touched the base of her throat. "Amelia's journal said she gave Vance Spohn a ruby ring. This must be it. It belonged to her father, I think. But if she gave him her father's ring, why would she kill him and drag his body down here?"

"Maybe she gave him the ring and then found out he was cheating on her," Steve suggested.

"Could be."

"Or maybe it was Harry Llewelyn who killed him. That was Amelia's other version, wasn't it? But I'd lay money on Amelia doing the dirty deed herself. In any case, the ring wouldn't be here unless Vance is too." Steve rubbed the ring again, adding a gleam of gold to the ruby eye.

"No matter who killed Vance, if he's buried here, it almost certainly means Amelia was the one who killed your father later."

"Right. She was one tough cookie." Steve tried to put the ring on his finger, but it wouldn't go past the joint. He slipped it in his pocket and started scratching with the trowel in the dirt around where the ring had been. "I wonder if ol' lover boy Vance had anything else valuable on him?"

Something a dull whitish color poked out of the dirt Steve was scratching aside. Angie used her garden claw to retrieve it.

A bone.

Angie didn't touch the bone, but even without gloves, Steve picked it up without hesitation. He held the small bone in his palm and poked at it with a forefinger.

"Another mouse bone?" Angie asked.

"I'd say it's a finger. Or part of one."

Angie stared at the small bone with a mixture of revulsion and fascination. Was this the finger that had once held the ruby ring, a symbol of Amelia's love?

Steve set the bone aside and started digging deeper. Only a couple of thrusts of the trowel exposed several knobs of grayish bone with longer bits of bone attached to some of the knobs. He stopped and examined them.

"The knuckles, I think. The hand must've fallen apart over the years. Or maybe mice or rats chewed on it."

Angie stared at the knobs. A hand. A fingerless hand. A chill from the earth beneath her knees felt as if it were flowing upward through her body, congealing her blood as it moved, turning it sluggish in her brain.

"Rodents probably carried off some of the bones," Steve said. "But the main part of the skeleton must still be here."

He dug around the knuckles and exposed two larger bones, both long and narrow.

"Now we're getting somewhere," he said with satisfaction. "Those have to be the bones in the forearm. I broke my arm once, and I remember something about two bones in there."

The words of some strange old song echoed in Angie's mind, something about the leg bone attached to the hip bone, hip bone attached to the back bone. Something close to hysteria danced around the edges of her brain.

This was what they had come for. This was what they were searching for. Vance Spohn's bones. Yet the actual discovery made her frantic to abandon this dank hole, to claim space and sunshine and life. Her lungs felt breathless, but she didn't want to breathe here, didn't want to take in the stale air around a murdered man's bones. She squatted back on her heels, hands gripping her thighs to steady herself.

What had seemed a bizarre possibility in Amelia's journals was now all too real. Bones. A ring. The Nevermore had harbored not one murder but two. And here, hidden for thirty years, was the body of one of the victims.

Steve didn't appear affected by any of this, not even the possibility that his own father was a murderer. He had distanced himself, she realized, now referring to Harry Llewelyn by name rather than as his father. Eager curiosity appeared to have overcome his earlier uneasiness about searching for a skeleton. Neither did he appear to notice how the discovery was affecting her. He just kept digging, and in horror she realized that in a minute or two he'd expose the skull. She had the peculiar feeling the hollow eyes were already staring at her, staring right through earth and death and time.

She grabbed Steve's arm. "Stop! Don't dig anymore."

"Why not?"

"It's time to go to the authorities. We don't want to disturb evidence here that might help them make positive

273

identification of the body or provide clues about the death."

"It was thirty years ago," Steve protested. "What does it matter now who killed who?"

"Who killed your father thirty years ago mattered to you, or you wouldn't have come here! C'mon, we'll go back to the house and pick up the journals and take them and the ring to the sheriff's office."

"That ruby could be worth a bundle. What's the point in just handing it over to the cops? Odds are one of them will rip it off for himself."

Angie didn't bother to respond to the question or the snide comment about the authorities. She was glad her short partnership with Steve Llewelyn was over. She was finding him less likeable all the time. "Let's just get out of here."

Steve briefly looked as if he might keep digging in spite of her protests, but he finally shrugged and kicked dirt over the bones he'd exposed.

Flashlight in one hand, Angie crawled back toward the opening. She was surprised when Steve pushed ahead of her and reached the small door before she did. He grabbed the discarded shovel and tossed it through the opening, then shoved his broad shoulders through while the clang of the shovel hitting the furnace was still reverberating.

"Hand me the flashlight and the other tools," he said from outside. In the glare from the flashlight, his hand appeared in the opening.

Angie handed out the two garden tools, but she held on to the flashlight as she stuck her head and shoulders through the opening. The beam showed Steve from the waist down, feet slightly spread. It struck her as an oddly belligerent stance. He apparently didn't feel any need to offer her a gentlemanly hand in assistance through the awkward opening.

"Okay, that's far enough."

"What?" Angie asked. She was still on her knees, awkwardly half in, half out of the opening. She peered up at him.

"I said that's far enough. You don't need to come any farther. Stay where you are."

Puzzled, Angie turned the flashlight beam upward. She could see Steve full length now. Something metallic reflected a dull gleam in his outstretched hands.

She blinked in astonishment. "Steve, what in the world . . . ? What's going on? Did you hear something? I don't think anyone could've followed us in. I'm sure the front door locked behind us—"

"Yeah, it locked. All safe and secure. I checked it." He smiled, and the angle of the flashlight gave a skeletal cast to his cheekbones and forehead. "Just you and me and the resident spook in here now."

"Put the gun away. Please. You're making me nervous." She pushed a knee through the opening. "The police can handle everything now."

"I told you that's far enough! Don't come any farther."

Angie pulled the knee back, moving carefully, because his voice had risen as if nerves were squeezing his vocal cords. And now she saw that the gun was not simply held like a protective guardian in his hand. It was aimed.

At her.

Angie was almost as much puzzled as alarmed. She could see the gun wobbling slightly, as if Steve was having trouble keeping his hands steady. "I don't get it. What's going on?"

"Don't ask questions."

"If someone is pointing a gun at me, I certainly am going to ask questions!"

"You already know too much."

"I don't know what you're talking about! I don't know any more about these murders than you do."

"Maybe you aren't as smart as we figured. Maybe this wouldn't even have been necessary." The gun lowered a fraction of an inch, and the glare of the flashlight showed an indecisive crease between his pale eyebrows. "But Burke said you weren't some dumb blond, and that we had to do it. You'd figure things out sooner or later, if you hadn't already." The gun jerked upward again. "Get that light out of my eyes," he growled.

Angie lowered the flashlight beam to his waist. "Burke? You know Burke?"

Several scattered observations rushed together as if suddenly yanked by a strong magnet. Steve's nonchalant attitude about not finding his parents' graves at the cemetery. His impatient, sometimes almost bored, attitude during the interviews with Lillian Feldman and Madame Zorrich. His indifferent attitude toward the fact that Amelia was undoubtedly his father's murderer. And the way he'd now started calling Harry Llewelyn by name rather than "my father."

"You're not Harry Llewelyn's son, are you?"

"No."

"Are you any relation at all?"

"No."

"You never saw anything in the Las Vegas newspaper about the Nevermore or Harry Llewelyn or me."

Steve took one hand off the gun and swiped his palm across his thigh. Nerves, she realized. Nerves that had nothing to do with an old skeleton and long-ago murders. Nerves because of . . . what?

"All I did in Vegas was pick up the rental car and this gun. And all I knew about ol' Harry and his son before I got here was what Burke told me from reading something he picked up in your office." He sounded pleased with himself, as if deceiving her with so little to go on was an accomplishment to be proud of.

"Then I conveniently came up with a guess that there'd been something about the Nevermore in a Las Vegas newspaper, and you jumped on it."

"For which I thank you." In the shadows lurking above the beam of the flashlight, his head dipped in a nod of thanks. "Saved me from having to come up with some unlikely story about just passing through town."

Angie felt as if she were frantically cutting and shuffling lines to fit a complicated layout for a front page of the *Herald*. She shifted and rearranged, but nothing made sense. And the word that kept jumping out at her was one that simply didn't belong. *Burke*.

"Burke sent you here because—" She broke off, bewildered. "He's angry because I wouldn't marry him? Angry enough to want you to *shoot* me?"

That brought a rough laugh from Steve. Except he wasn't Steve . . .

"Burke offered you a good deal. You should've grabbed it. But you turned him down."

"I don't get it." Icy sweat trickled across her ribs, and raw instinct told her that her only chance was to keep Steve—or whoever he really was—talking.

"Okay, cut the chatter. I didn't come here to draw diagrams and spell everything out for you."

He steadied his stance and leveled the gun. She could feel the target dead center on her forehead, as if a bull's-eye were engraved there. Her life didn't pass before her eyes. Even as fear riveted her muscles, all she could think was, *Why?* "You came to Julesburg to kill me?"

"And a stupid comedy of errors it's been." He sounded annoyed. "One screwup after another. Up there at the cemetery looked like a perfect place. Private and isolated, a great place to hide a body. And then along comes Ms. Busybody with her armload of trash and her gab about imitation daisies from Wal-Mart."

"How inconvenient."

"Then I decided an 'accident' would work, you falling over the guardrail into the ocean. But no, you wouldn't get out of the car, and I figured if I tried to drag you out, it'd be just my luck for a state police car to pull up right alongside me. Then I spent an entire day looking for an isolated place to stage an accident on a trail hike. But you weren't interested in a hike."

"How very . . . humorous."

"Yeah. Well, maybe you had to be there."

"So then you shot at me. You missed."

"How was I supposed to know a lousy handgun was no good at that distance?" He tilted the gun in his hand, looking at it as if disgusted with its shortcomings. "And then I had to put a bullet hole in my own car so it would look like someone was after both of us."

"With the gun you're holding now?"

"I figure that's a nice touch to keep the cops busy. They'll be all excited when they find the bullet in your body came from the same gun that put the bullet in my car. If they aren't too dumb in this hick town to figure out it was the same gun."

"So you decided to do it here. In the Nevermore."

"Right. And it does seem fitting, doesn't it? Sort of a full-circle thing." He sounded pleased with himself again. "Maybe there is something to those old stories about disaster happening to anyone connected with the Nevermore."

"You're connected with it too."

"Only for about five more minutes."

Angie swallowed. "Do you plan to . . . bury me down here?"

He paused as if he hadn't thought that far ahead. "Yeah, I suppose I'd better take time to do that."

"Eventually the bullet and the gun it came from will be traced back to you."

"No way. Burke had a reliable source in Vegas. No record of this baby anywhere."

*Why does he keep talking?* Desperate as she was to keep him from pulling the trigger, why wasn't he simply doing it? He was jittering from one foot to the other now, though he managed to keep the muzzle of the gun targeted on her. Once he bumped into a piece of metal jutting out from the old furnace and actually jumped. Nerves. Yes. But more than that . . .

"You really don't want to do this, do you?"

"Maybe not," he muttered. "But it has to be done, and I can do it. I will do it."

Psyching himself up for it. Digging for dead bones hadn't bothered him—planning this was what had jazzed his nerves on the drive over here. He was talking tough, but he appeared to have a definite squeamishness about turning *her* into dead bones. She desperately tried to play on this small weakness.

"I thought we were friends."

"Sometimes friends are expendable."

"Who *are* you?" she asked.

"That's my business."

"Burke hired you to kill me?"

"You ask too many questions."

"I should think that if you intend to kill me, I'm at least entitled to know who you are and why you want to kill me!"

No answer, just a quick, nervous inspection of the gun in his hand. Angie was too unfamiliar with guns to know what he was checking. Ammunition? Safety lock? But she was certain about one thing—even though he wanted her dead, he was reluctant to pull the trigger.

*Talk, girl! Stall him!*

"How did you find out what Harry Llewelyn's son's name was?"

"We didn't. Burke figured if we couldn't find out what the kid's real name was, probably no one else could either. So I just picked one. Steve has a solid, honest ring to it, don't you think? Though I started getting jittery when you told me your brother was a private eye, not just an arson investigator like Burke thought. And then when you said he was checking up on me, I really got worried."

"Burke seems to be running things."

"We're partners."

*Partners in murder. But why?* "But you're the partner sticking your neck out here in Julesburg. Look who gets stuck with the murder charge when you're caught. Not Burke."

"Yeah, well Burke already did his share. He wanted me to do it the same way he did. He was good. But I . . ." He swallowed, and the jerk of his Adam's apple made a peculiar jump of shadow against his throat. "I figured out early on I didn't want to do it the way he had."

*The way he had.* Angie stared at him and the gun with a rising sense of horror. Surely he couldn't mean what it sounded like he meant. Burke had his flaws. He was ruthlessly ambitious. Possessive. Controlling. Self-centered. Vindictive. But surely he wasn't capable of murder.

"If you're telling me Burke killed someone, I don't believe you!"

"I'm sure Burke would be touched by your faith in him," he mocked. "He did it all right. Up front and personal. Though he said she fought like a wildcat. I'm not going to mess around with anything like that, even if it does make Burke a little . . . unhappy."

"Anything like what?"

"Using a knife. Stabbing."

It was too unreal. Burke killing someone. With a knife. Yet even though murder was also the intent of Steve— no, *not* Steve—he obviously found stabbing repulsive. She remembered his reaction when he'd first learned his "father's" death had been by stabbing. It seemed he preferred a sanitary distance between himself and his victim. Angie tried to make him think about the knife and repulse him further. "What kind of knife did Burke use? How big was it?"

"I don't know." He waved the gun impatiently to dismiss the questions. "He didn't draw diagrams for me. And the knife doesn't matter. It just had to be done, and he did it. Same as I'm going to do this."

"Burke . . . killed someone." She leaned her shoulder against the opening, trying to digest the truth. "Who—who did he kill?"

"Oh, come on, Miss Model-Turned-Newspaper-Editor. You know."

Somewhere in the back of her mind, the terrible suspicion churned to get out. She held it back. *No. Surely Burke wouldn't do that . . .*

"Your nosy little Asian friend, of course."

Angie's mind reeled as the truth she'd been holding back washed through her in sickening waves. Kristi. Stabbed. A question mark carved on her shoulder to throw suspicion on a ready-made killer. A body dumped in a dirty alley.

By Burke.

"But why?" She couldn't keep the anguish out of her voice. "Why would Burke kill Kristi? How could he do it? He hardly knew her."

"She knew too much. Just like you."

"I don't know anything!"

"That isn't what Burke thinks."

"So who are you?"

"I guess it doesn't matter if you know now. Jordan Riker."

"Burke's partner in the investment company." She cast around for further memory of what she'd overheard on that Bahamas trip when the two men were organizing the company. It had something to do with Australia. Burke had flown down there several times.

"Yeah. You and I've talked on the phone a time or two, remember? But we never met."

No, they hadn't met. Burke had been careful to keep them from meeting.

"Burke really chewed me out when he found out I'd hired your Asian friend. But it was a little late by then. She already knew too much."

"So Burke got . . . rid of Kristi. And now you have to get rid of me."

"That's about it."

"Burke's orders?"

"We're partners. He doesn't give me orders."

He said the words confidently, yet a nervous twitch of his jaw muscles belied the statement. With sudden intuition, Angie knew Jordan was also afraid of Burke. Burke could kill, and Jordan knew it. Jordan had to kill her or face the consequences with Burke.

"But why? I don't understand why either of you want me dead. I don't know anything about the company. All I know is that Burke told me he'd gotten out of the company months ago!"

"If you believe everything smooth-talkin' Burke tells you, then you really are a dumb blond." Another switch of gun hands and wipe of sweaty palms. "And if you're dumb enough, maybe we wouldn't have had to do this."

With a feeling rising toward hysteria, Angie desperately wanted to proclaim her dumbness. *Look at me! The proverbial dumb blond! Let me tell you a dumb blond joke. There were these three blonds, see . . .*

Angie felt like she might really be a dumb blond, because she still didn't fully understand what was happening. "You don't have to kill me. I don't know anything."

"Maybe you didn't. But you do now."

She swallowed. Yes. Now she knew Burke had killed Kristi. The knowledge still seemed unreal, but she had it. A knowledge that signed her death warrant.

She switched tactics. "Burke called you wimpy. He said you were weak. Addicted to gambling, and that's why he got out of the company."

Jordan laughed. "I'll have to have a little talk with Burke about character assassination."

"I don't understand why Kristi had to die."

Jordan rubbed his sleeve across his sweaty forehead, but the gun didn't move from its target. Angie's neck was beginning to ache from looking up at him through the opening.

"Kristi was a smart cookie," Jordan said. "She figured out what we were doing. None of our other employees did. Or maybe they were just greedier and more interested in their big commissions."

"A scam."

"People want something for nothing. It's their own greed that gets them in trouble. We weren't running out and grabbing their money. They were sending it."

"They thought they were investing it, but you and Burke were stealing it."

"It might've worked. There was a chance." Jordan sounded injured, as if she were unfairly denigrating an upright business venture. He kept the gun in his right hand and dug in his shirt pocket with his left for the cigarettes he always carried. It was an awkward process, using only one hand, but he managed to extract a cigarette, put it to his lips, and flick the lighter to start it. Apparently, with murder on the day's agenda, he wasn't worrying about the slip in willpower.

"So what was the deal?" Angie asked. "What was the scam?"

"What difference does it make?"

He sounded belligerent, but he was still putting off the final moment. In spite of the pain in her shoulders and neck, she forced herself to keep her eyes locked on his. So long as he was talking, maybe she still had a chance.

"It must've been a clever scheme," she suggested.

"Yeah. We bought this big ranch down in Australia for a few bucks down and sold shares in it. It might've worked. There was a chance we'd hit oil on the ranch."

"But you didn't. And if you had, you and Burke would've kept the profits for yourselves."

"There hasn't been any income from the ranch except a few lousy bucks from those stupid sheep, so we've used money from new investors to provide good income for the old investors and make them think everything's going great. They were happy little campers. For every new client an old client brought us, they got a reward of more shares. And if those people brought in more people, the first clients got shares on that too. People are naturally greedy, you know. They were busting a gut to spread the good word and make themselves more shares."

Which were as worthless as the ones they'd bought. "A type of pyramid scheme," Angie said. "But the company's in trouble now. My brother found out from a friend on the Internet. Someone who said the income from his investment stopped."

Jordan laughed. "Depends on your point of view. From ours, everything's fine. Going right on schedule. Now it's time to wind things up and get out. No one will ever know Burke was involved, and I'll take my share and skip down to a little spot I have picked out on Martinique. No more New York for me. I hate the place."

"But why Kristi? Why *me,* if you're getting out anyway?" Angie tried to stay calm, but she could hear the desperation in her voice.

"Dumping the company doesn't mean we're home free, not if the details get out. There's big bucks involved here, and I don't like to live cheap." Distaste creased the tanned skin between his blond eyebrows. "I ate enough Texas grits and beans as a kid to last me a lifetime. And no way am I going to get sucked into jail time just because some greedy investors lost their money."

"But Burke surely never needed money bad enough to cheat people out of it!" But even as Angie said the words, she knew they weren't true. Burke would always need more money, any way he could get it. Money was the heartbeat of his life.

"And if it ever got out that Burke was involved in this," Jordan went on, "his whole career as a stockbroker would be down the drain. He's been skimming names off his brokerage company's client list so we'd know who to target with our pitch."

"And the two of you thought Kristi was going to blow the whistle."

"Somehow she got into our confidential computer records. We're pretty sure she made disks. We don't figure she did that just for the fun of it."

"When . . . when did Burke kill her?"

"You'd told him you and Kristi were having dinner together. He got her that same night. Picked her up just outside her apartment with a story that he needed to talk to her about a problem in his relationship with you."

*Yes,* Angie thought bleakly, *that would work. Kristi was always so caring, so eager to help a friend.* "And then you made up the story for the police about her quitting the job."

"And it worked, of course. Like a well-oiled wheel. But Burke figures you either have the disks or know where they are, because you and Kristi were so close. You're also the only person who knows he's actually involved in the company."

"But I don't have any computer disks! If Kristi made them, I have no idea what she did with . . . them."

Her claim had begun with the forcefulness of truth, but it faltered as she remembered back to when Kristi had asked her about getting a safe deposit box. *I suggested a bank to Kristi. Maybe I do know where those computer disks are.*

Jordan caught the incriminating stumble and immediately jumped on it. He stepped forward, cigarette dangling from his lips, both hands on the gun. "You know something."

"No, I don't!" Desperately she tried to divert him. "If Burke wants me dead, why isn't he here killing me?"

"Wouldn't work, after he came here once. Someone might remember him. But he searched your apartment in New York. Easy enough for him to do, of course, since he already had a key."

Angie remembered Cate complaining how Angie had "gone through" her things before she moved out of the apartment. That hadn't made sense before; now it did. And Kristi's uncharacteristically messy apartment. "He searched Kristi's apartment too, didn't he?"

"Of course. First place he looked. And then he went through your house here too."

But Burke couldn't have searched her house! He was in New York when the break-in occurred. Maybe Jordan was lying about all this. Maybe he was here on his own, and Burke wasn't even involved.

Jordan smiled as if he was following her thought process like a freeway line on a road map. "Who knows where a phone call's coming from? Fooled you, didn't he?"

Her temporary hope that Burke wasn't involved plummeted. Burke had spoken as if he were calling from New York, but he could've called from anywhere on his cell phone. And then, when he arrived, he simply made up that oh-so-believable story about driving up from San Francisco.

"Burke called me from right here in Julesburg. And then came and searched my house when I told him I had a meeting. How did he know where I lived? I didn't tell him."

286

"Actually, I think he called from that little town just north of here. He got your address from the helpful girl at the newspaper office who gave him your phone number. Not that searching your place did us any good."

Now she remembered something Burke had said that had slipped by her at the time. *That dump you live in.* Of course, he knew it was a "dump," at least by his standards. He'd searched it.

But there was another inconsistency in what Jordan was saying, an important one. She jumped on it. "But Burke asked me to marry him!"

"Like I said, he gave you a chance. You blew it." Jordan tilted his head and regarded her thoughtfully, as if he were evaluating her dumb-blond status again. "Burke cared about you."

"But now he wants me dead."

Jordan shrugged. "He'd rather have done it the other way. He figured that no matter what you knew about the company—or Kristi, for that matter—if the two of you were married, you'd keep your mouth shut."

"He figured on buying my silence by marrying me." *Yet why shouldn't he think that? That was the Angie Harrison he knew.* The knowledge sickened her.

"Not exactly a big sacrifice." Jordan grinned, his appraisal now slyly suggestive. "But when you wanted no part of it . . ." The smile disappeared, and he lifted one shoulder in another dismissive shrug.

"Everything you told me was a lie, wasn't it? The story about working outside the country for several years—"

"I had to offer some explanation of why there were no records on Steve Llewelyn anywhere, in case someone checked. Like your nosy brother did. And I really was out of the country when I flew down to Australia a couple times."

"Buying the car dealership in Vegas was another lie."

"A flagrant lie," he agreed.

She remembered one of the few points in his character that had made her warm toward him. "You don't even have a cat, do you?"

"Actually, that one's the truth. I do have a cat. Ol' Macho Man is quite a guy. We're buddies. I'll take him to Martinique with me. And another truth is that I really do hate New York. I'm also quitting smoking." He spit out the cigarette that had burned down to lip level and ground the butt into the concrete with his toe.

"But why keep the whole farce going? Why bother to go back in there and dig for a skeleton today? Why not just shoot me the minute we were inside the Nevermore and get it over with?"

"I got curious about whether there really was an old skeleton buried down here. It's kind of intriguing, you know. Maybe I have a secret desire to be an archaeologist or private eye or something."

Angie surreptitiously moved her arm so she could see her watch. 11:35.

The movement didn't escape Jordan's attention. He held his own watch into the light to see the time. "Too bad. Looks like you're missing church."

By now Ryan and Stefanie would be wondering why she hadn't showed up at church. They'd be disappointed. But they'd have no idea she'd come here to the Nevermore. No idea she was trapped in an opening into a dank space under the stage floor with a gun aimed at her head. She could feel the small lump of the cell phone in her pocket, but at the moment it was as useless as a clod of dirt from the ground behind her.

"Okay, that's enough talking," Jordan said roughly, as if he'd made up his mind to get it over with. "I guess it would be better if you came out of there."

Angie stalled. "I thought you didn't want me to come out. I thought you were going to shoot me right here."

"I changed my mind. Come out. And turn around."

288

He was still squeamish about doing this. For all his talk about killing and his obvious lack of feeling about Kristi's death, he was squeamish about pulling the trigger now. Especially when she was looking at him.

"No," she said. "I'm not coming out. I'm not turning around. If you want to kill me, you're going to have to do it with me looking at you. And you looking at me."

She realized this was a dangerous game. All he had to do was meet the challenge with a squeeze of his finger on the trigger and she'd be dead. He couldn't miss at this range. But she had nothing to lose by being stubborn.

"I have to kill you," he muttered.

"You can't get away with it," Angie said.

That remark seemed to firm up his resolve. He laughed. "That sounds like a line out of a bad TV cop show."

"But it's true. You'll be caught."

"No, sorry to disappoint you, but I definitely can get away with it. I doubt I'll even be suspected when you're found dead, but, if I am, I was registered at the motel as Steve Llewelyn. Where I've already checked out, by the way, so as far as anyone knows, I've left town. The car is rented under the name of Steve Llewelyn. I'll turn it in at the rental agency as Steve Llewelyn. At that point, Steve Llewelyn vanishes into thin air. And Jordan Riker? Who's he? No one is ever going to connect him with any of this."

He was right. Angie could see no loopholes.

"You really should've married Burke, you know. It would've made a happy ending for all of us."

"Not Kristi."

"Well, that's true," he conceded.

To think that at one time she'd wanted to marry Burke sent a spasm of nausea churning through her stomach. To think that she'd once thought she was in love with him.

*Oh, Lord, how could I have been so wrong?*

"Of course, it's possible it'll be months or years before your body is found. Look at how long ol' Vance has been moldering down here. Maybe archaeologists will dig you both up a thousand years from now. But Burke and me, we're definitely going to get away with this."

## 30

*He's going to do it. He's going to pull the trigger.*

Angie's throat thickened with anger and fear as her eyes locked with Jordan's. She felt the past envelop her once more. Her relationship with Burke, now rising up to plant her in the pathway of a bullet. Not free of all the mistakes she'd made and wrongs she'd done after all . . .

*No, that isn't true. The past is behind me. You freed me from it, didn't you, Lord? No matter what happens now, you lifted me out of the undertow.*

Jordan held the gun in his right hand. He extended his left to her. "Give me the flashlight."

Angie hesitated, her first reaction an instinct to hand it over. Her second instinct was to yell "No!" at him. *Go ahead and shoot!*

Instead she leaned forward as if to obey the order. But instead of giving him the flashlight, she flicked the button and plunged them both into darkness. At the same time, she grabbed the garden trowel lying on the concrete and threw it. She heard Jordan's grunt of pain when the trowel hit the target. She squirmed back into the opening beneath the stage and scrambled away from it.

Their exploration hadn't taken them around to the far side of the furnace. *If I can get back there, with the furnace between us, maybe he can't find me.*

She bumped into a wall she hadn't realized was there. There was no way around to the far side of the furnace. She was trapped on this side. With Jordan. She crouched against the wall. The blackness around her was like a coffin. She fought the thought, fought a deadly urge to turn on the flashlight, anything to relieve the blackness that clawed at her as if it were alive. Something touched the back of her neck. And crawled . . .

She stifled another urge to scream and brushed the crawling thing away.

Silence.

*Where is he? What is he doing?*

Maybe he'd just cut and run, figuring that his only choice now was to head for his car, pull his disappearing act, and get out of the country.

"Angie?" The voice came from the opening, soft and persuasive. "Hey, you know what? You're right. I can't shoot you. I guess I'm just not a killer type after all."

She didn't move, barely breathed, to keep from giving her position away.

"Look, c'mon out. We can settle this another way. You know where the computer disks are, don't you? Just tell me, and that'll be the end of it. We'll make it worth your while to forget you ever knew anything about Burke being in the company and what happened to Kristi."

By edging forward a few inches, she could make out a faint outline of the opening, barely paler than the blackness. A smidgen of light must've been filtering behind the satin curtain from the sconces in the seating area of the theater. A dark bulk filled most of the square.

"C'mon, Angie, I can't wait around here much longer."

She didn't answer. Like an explosion, the sound of three shots in quick succession ricocheted around the low-ceilinged space. A pause and then three more shots. She heard a bullet thud into a joist just to the left of her head. Her mind reeled with the noise. How many shots did the gun hold? Whatever revulsion or squeamishness Jordan had felt about stabbing her or pulling the trigger with her gaze locked on his obviously did not extend to killing her with a bullet in the dark.

She detected movement in the shadowy shape blocking the pale square. Was he backing out? Reloading? Planning to blanket the dark space with a web of bullets until one connected? She edged farther down the wall. If she could get behind one of those uprights that braced the floor overhead, maybe it would give her some protection.

The pale square suddenly vanished. A thud, then a louder clunk. He must've shut the door and leaned the concrete block against it to brace it shut again.

The claustrophobic blackness closed in on her. It pressed into her lungs and stole her breath. It clamped around her heart and squeezed it into a thousand beats a minute. It invaded her brain and took control of her thoughts. *I'm trapped here, trapped with Vance Spohn's bones . . .*

She pushed away the darkness in her mind. *The darkness is out there. It's not inside me. Inside me is the light of the Lord.*

She forced herself to think rationally. She was temporarily trapped in here. Jordan was no doubt already running out to the car, probably as panicky as she was.

But no. She could hear footsteps overhead, as if he were moving back and forth. Doing what? She heard more clunks.

Then silence.

She waited, counting off the seconds. *A thousand and one, a thousand and two, a thousand and three . . .*

She forced herself to wait until a full three minutes had elapsed, then crawled along the wall toward the door, although in the utter darkness she wasn't certain where the opening was anymore. She stopped to listen again. Was she mistaken? Could he be waiting outside the door, planning to cut her down the moment she tried to get out? Or just send a hail of bullets through the closed door the second he heard a noise?

Or maybe he hadn't closed the door on her. Maybe those weren't footsteps overhead. Maybe he'd come *inside* and closed the door. Maybe he was in here with her. Just waiting for her to panic and make a noise or turn on the flashlight. Her skin crawled with the thought that any moment he might reach out and touch her.

She squatted back on her heels and listened, her hand wrapped around the flashlight handle so she wouldn't panic and accidentally hit the button. Now she could hear something, a puzzling sound. A kind of crackling.

She waited, then inched forward again. Every few inches she put her hands against the wall, feeling for the door. It had to be along here somewhere . . .

After taking a steadying breath, she risked a brief flare of the flashlight. Yes, the door! Here it was. From inside, the outline was more obvious than it was on the painted wall outside. She flicked off the light and pushed against the door. Pushed again, harder, throwing all her weight into the shove.

No movement. Nothing. The door felt as if a hundred nails held it. But Jordan hadn't had a hammer and nails. And she'd heard no pounding.

Then she realized what he'd done. What the overhead footsteps meant. He'd carried more concrete blocks from the pile in the corner and stacked them against the door.

The realization of what that meant rolled through her in another wave of panic and choking claustrophobia. She'd never be able to push the concrete blocks aside. And there was no other way out. No one else knew she was here. She could be trapped for hours, days . . . weeks. Trapped with Vance Spohn's bones . . .

*Lord, please!*

She took a long breath. Okay, she was trapped. Maybe for a considerable length of time. It was unpleasant here. Scary. Claustrophobic. With spiders and mice and maybe something larger of the rodent variety. But Vance Spohn's bones were no threat. And, given enough time, she could scratch her way through that wooden door with her fingernails if she had to.

Then a scent joined that faint crackling noise. A crackling that now wasn't so faint.

She raised her head and sniffed

And knew she wasn't going to have hours or days to scratch her way out of here.

## 31

*T*he scent grew stronger.
Smoke.
The crackling grew louder.
Fire.

Jordan Riker's final solution. He may have had qualms about killing up close, with his victim staring him in the eyes.

But he could kill.

There was plenty of trash in the old theater to fuel a blaze. It would only take a quick flick of a cigarette lighter to set it off.

The Nevermore burns to the ground, cause undetermined. Angie's burned body is found in the rubble. "Steve Llewelyn" is gone, checked out of his motel. Perhaps, the authorities decide, Angie lit a match when she was down here on her foolish investigation of a thirty-year-old murder.

Burke and Jordan get away with their crimes.

The realization rolled through Angie like a surging avalanche. Her mind reeled as if from a direct blow of one of the concrete blocks. Heat roared through her body as if the fire were already licking at her skin.

*I'm going to burn to death.* Sweat pooled at the base of her throat and dripped from her clenched fists. *I'm going to burn to death . . . alive.*

Panic released her muscles, and she knelt at the door and hammered the door with her fists. "Let me out! Let me out!"

She heard a loud crash. Had the metal ductwork of the old furnace collapsed? Or the roof? Now she heard a sudden whoosh and roar. The sound reminded her of a bonfire as its flames shot upward, as if it were some enraged beast. Now the beast was here, on the loose. After her.

She felt the boards overhead. Warm? She couldn't tell. Her fingers felt numb. How long before the boards burst into flames and crashed down on her?

She flicked the flashlight on. No need for caution about light now. She forced herself to shut off the smell and the roar and to study the door. *Think. Think!*

Only one way out, and this was it.

*Strength, Lord, I need strength.* She braced her bottom and elbows in the dirt, bent her knees, and put her feet against the door. *The back and legs are stronger than the arms,* she remembered her personal trainer once saying to her.

*Help me, Lord, help me push.*

She strained until her back and stomach and leg muscles quivered uncontrollably, strained until her neck felt as if it would explode with the effort, strained until her eyes felt as if they would burst from their sockets. The door didn't budge. She lay there spread-eagled limply against the dirt. How many concrete blocks had he stacked against it? A dozen? More?

The smell was acrid now, although smoke hadn't yet penetrated her prison. She tried to calm herself with rational thoughts. Smoke and flames tended to move upward. Wasn't that what Ryan had said to remember about a fire? Stay low. Crawl to safety under the smoke.

Crawl to safety. If only she could.

*Undertow*

She forced a hopeful thought: the whole theater above might burn and leave the stage floor standing. Such odd things happened. If she had to be trapped anywhere in the Nevermore, here, next to the raw earth, was probably the best place to be.

Until the roof collapsed on the stage. Maybe it had already collapsed. Maybe that was the crash she'd heard. Light flickered through a crack in the floor toward the front of the stage, up toward the curtain and screen.

Fresh hope flared, and she crawled toward the dancing flicker. Maybe the floor was weak there. Maybe she could break through and climb out.

No. Not a crack. A hole. The fire was burning in the floor now. To get out that way, she'd have to climb up through the fire itself. She backed up again. Something bumped against her hip.

Her cell phone! She slammed a palm against her forehead. She'd been so panicky she hadn't even remembered she had it.

She held the flashlight between her knees, aimed it at the tiny phone, and frantically punched 911. Would it work from under here? Yes. A ring. An answer. A human voice!

"I can't explain it all now, but I'm trapped under the old theater, the Nevermore, and it's on fire and—"

"Slow down now, please. You're where?"

"Please, don't ask questions. I'm trapped! Send a fire truck, please! To the Nevermore."

"This is in what town?" The woman sounded skeptical.

Angie forced herself to remember that this 911 number covered the entire county, several towns. And they had to have proper information before they could act. Yet she couldn't stop herself from yelling, "Julesburg. Julesburg! The old theater. It's right on the main street. It's burning, and I'm trapped under the stage!"

"I know the theater. It's been closed and locked up for years." Now the 911 operator sounded reproving, as if she

298

suspected Angie was trying to pull a hoax. "May I have your name, please?"

"My name doesn't matter! The theater is burning, and I'm trapped in it—trapped under it!"

"There's a penalty for making a false report, you know."

Disbelieving, Angie pulled the phone away from her ear and looked at it. She forced herself not to throw it against a wall in frustration. She forced herself not to scream.

"Look, I know you get crank calls. I know you get false reports. But this isn't one of them! My name is Angie Harrison and I'm the editor of the *Julesburg Herald* and I'm buying the old theater. And it's on fire and I know it's an unbelievable story but I'm trapped under here. Please help me!"

Something in Angie's tone or words got through the woman's professional wariness. "Okay, we'll dispatch a fire truck immediately. Don't panic. Hold on." Angie heard the woman yelling something to someone else. "Now, you say you're trapped *under* the stage in the theater—"

"Yes, at the rear of the building. There's a door at the back, between the building and the wooden fence, but I think it's nailed shut."

"Okay, we're going to get you out. Stay on the line and—"

Another crash. Angie jumped and hit her head. The crash above her wasn't as big as the earlier one, but this time the floor around the flickering hole collapsed as something plunged through it. Flames shot up around the edges of the larger opening.

She'd dropped the phone when she jumped. She frantically searched the ground with the flashlight beam until she spotted it. Was the light getting weaker?

But maybe the flashlight didn't matter now, because the light from the fire was strong enough to reach every corner. The flames crawled along the floor like some hungry monster nibbling with a fiery mouth. She stuck the phone in her pocket and scrambled backward.

But the fire had eaten through the floor behind her too. Reluctantly, with nowhere else to go, she crawled toward Vance Spohn's bones.

She brushed dirt from the phone and held it to her ear. The connection was broken. She started to dial 911 again, then stopped.

The 911 operator knew she was here. Either the firemen got here in time . . . or they didn't.

Another hole opened overhead. A few more minutes and the floor would be a fiery sieve.

*Lord, I'm glad I found my way back to you before this. I'm glad I didn't wait, trying to clean up my life myself. I'm glad I know what's beyond this. Thank you. It's so much more than I deserve.*

She didn't feel calm. She wasn't resigned. Terror and fear still licked like internal flames around her mind and nerves. Her mouth felt dry, her throat thick. One part of her mind kept another prayer going even as she thanked the Lord for his loving forgiveness. *Lord, will you help me get out of here? I'm asking for your mercy.*

But another part of her knew that God had his own plans, and maybe getting her out was not one of them.

Then a peculiar thought came to her. Not many people knew when they only had a few minutes left to live. *What do I want to do with my minutes?*

*Talk to Ethan.*

She yanked the phone out of her pocket and angled it to the light. With her finger poised over the tiny numbers, her heart sank. The uselessness of this small miracle of technology struck her like a door slamming in her face.

Connection took a number. And she didn't have one.

Where was Ethan now? On his way back to Phoenix? Or already there? He may have caught a flight. Yes, he could've caught a flight last night. Right now, he could be on his way home from church in Phoenix. No, the time was an hour later in Arizona. Maybe out to Sunday dinner then.

Her thoughts about time and place were muddled, scrambled like pieces of a jigsaw puzzle, but she knew that wherever Ethan was, he was doing his best to put her out of his mind and life.

Tendrils of smoke from burning debris that had fallen through the floor snaked along the boards overhead now. She grabbed a tissue out of her pocket to cover her nose and mouth. Something came out with it.

Disbelievingly she stared at the small white piece of paper.

Ethan's business card. She remembered stuffing it in her jacket pocket the night he'd given it to her at the house.

Was it an incredible coincidence that she was wearing that same jacket now? Or a final mercy from God?

## 32

*T*he cell phone rang just as Ethan was pulling out of the gas station. He braked and picked it up, ready to slam it down again. At this point, client or store problems would just have to wait. He had matters more important than a computer crash on his mind. He growled a hello.

"Ethan, this is Angie. I know you don't want to talk to me, but don't hang up on me, please! I don't have much time, and there are some things I have to tell you."

Her voice sounded strange—panicky?—and odd noises surrounded and muffled the words. A roar. Traffic? Ocean waves? No, something different than either of those. And her breathing sounded as if she'd been running hard.

"Angie, I can just barely hear you. What's going on? Are you okay? Maybe my car engine is affecting the reception. Give me a second and I'll step outside—"

"There isn't time. There are things I have to tell you. First, Burke killed Kristi—"

"What?" He stopped with one foot outside the car door. He couldn't be hearing right. Angie was telling him her stockbroker boyfriend had killed Kristi. That didn't make sense.

A horn honked behind him. He glanced in the rearview mirror, then slid back in the car and pulled over a few feet so cars exiting the station could get around him.

"You have to tell that to the police. Burke killed Kristi. The Question Mark killer didn't do it. Burke did. The DNA should prove it. He and his partner were running a scam with an investment company, and Kristi figured it out." She suddenly went into a fit of coughing.

"Angie, what's wrong? Are you sick?"

"Just listen. There isn't much time."

That was the third time she'd said that. What did she mean? Why wasn't there much time?

She cleared her throat and went on. "Kristi made computer disks that tell it all. I think they're in a safe deposit box in a bank in New York." She named a bank, coughed again, and then repeated the name of the bank.

He scribbled it on the back of a receipt he'd stuck in the ashtray. "Okay. Got it."

"Next thing, there is no Steve Llewelyn. At least the guy who came to Julesburg claiming to be Harry Llewelyn's son isn't him. He's really Burke's partner, Jordan Riker. He came to Julesburg to kill me."

She was talking so fast he could barely catch it all. Was she rational? Burke killing Kristi. Someone named Jordan coming to kill her. It all sounded anything but rational. Could she be . . . high on something? Wandering in some kind of hallucinatory haze?

"The rest is about me. If you . . . care."

"I care."

"I did what you said. Wait, I have to move."

Unidentifiable sounds followed, the clearest one the scratch of her labored breathing.

"Angie, where are you? What's all that noise?"

"After you left . . . I guess it was last night, wasn't it?" She paused as if recalculating time. Another fit of coughing. "I took it all to the Lord, Ethan. Everything I've done, all the mistakes and wrong choices I've made. I finally got it through my head that it was exactly as you said. Only the Lord can clean up my life and set me free of the past."

"If you've taken it to the Lord and asked for his forgiveness, then you *are* free."

"Yes. Spiritually. Physically, it's a little more . . . complicated." Rustles. Thumps. "It's getting warmer in here."

*Warmer?* "Angie, what's going on?"

"I don't want you to worry about me. Though I guess worrying about me is probably the last thing on your mind." She made what started as a cynical-sounding laugh, but it turned into a gasp and cough. Then her hoarse voice strengthened. "God and I are all squared away. We had a long talk last night. And I'm safe in his arms now."

That made sense. But nothing else did.

"Angie, I don't understand what's going on."

"My past with Burke is what got me into this. And even though the Lord forgives, there may still be consequences here on earth for what we've done."

Yes, that was true. But what on earth was going on?

"Jordan and I—only I still thought he was Steve this morning, of course—came to the Nevermore to look for Vance Spohn's body. Then Jordan set it on fire."

"You mean he accidentally set the theater on fire?"

"No, no accident. He lit the fire and then braced the door under the stage shut."

An unthinkable possibility roared into his mind. "Angie, where are you?"

"I—I'm here, trapped under the stage. Vance Spohn's skeleton is down here too, did I tell you that? So take Amelia's journals to the police too. There was a ring, the ruby ring Amelia gave Vance, but Jordan got away with that."

She sounded as if she were rambling now, her thoughts losing focus. Yet he no longer thought she might be hallucinating under the influence of some drug. No matter how incredible it all sounded, it was real. The Nevermore was burning, and Angie was trapped under it.

"Angie, you've got the cell phone. Call the fire department! Call the police! No, I'll do it—"

"I did call them . . . I think." Another pause, as if she wasn't certain. Then, in a more positive tone, "Yes, I called 911. They're sending a fire truck."

"Can you hear the siren? Are they coming?"

"I can't hear anything but the roar of the fire. And things crashing and exploding."

He realized that his hand holding the cell phone was trembling, and cords of fear and helplessness banded his chest. Angie's life in danger, and he was miles away. Nothing he could do. Nothing, nothing, nothing!

*But you aren't helpless, Lord. Do something for her, please! Get that fire truck there on time!*

"There has to be some way out! Don't give up. Look around! Maybe there's another door."

"It's getting smokier. And now the wall over by that big old furnace is on fire. Have you ever noticed how alive a fire looks? And acts? As if there's really a living force inside it." She sounded spacy now, as if she were detaching herself from a nightmare.

Frantically he tried to envision that dark space under the stage. Tiny door, raw earth below, low boards overhead. The decayed box Amelia's journals had been in, over there by the wall of the concrete foundation.

No way out. Unless . . .

The foundation. He pounded his thigh. "Angie, I just thought of something! The foundation around the edge of the building. Look for—"

Another noise, not so much a crash as the clink and rattle of disintegration. As if the phone were crumbling. A few broken words came through. "Ethan . . . sorry . . . I love you . . ."

Then silence. Dead silence.

## 33

ngie threw the phone when the hot ember hit her hand. She screamed when another one struck her sleeve and burst into flame. Frantically she rolled on the earth, unmindful of hard clods, to stop the flames from engulfing her. From somewhere nearby came a half dozen small explosions. Cans? Bottles? Instinctively she coiled into a protective fetal position, knees drawn to her chest, head buried under her arms.

Something ran across her ankle. A frantic squeaking.

Strangely it was revulsion at the touch of a rodent more than another series of explosions that sent her scrambling toward the farthest corner of her burning prison. She jammed her shoulders into the angle where the low walls of the foundation met, and watched burning debris fall on the patch of ground she had just vacated.

*Last stand, Angie. Backed into a corner. Nowhere to go from here.*

She kept thinking about something Ryan had told her once, that bodies don't really burn up very well. *So is this where they'll find my body, crammed in this corner?*

Another part of her mind answered those desolate words defiantly. *But the Lord is in control.*

Smoke hazed the space now. It burned in her eyes and nose and throat. She went into another coughing spell that left her gasping and weak. She tore a ragged piece of fabric from her sleeve and covered her nose and mouth. Her hand hurt where the ember had burned into the flesh, and the heat closed around her like an oven warming toward the broiling stage.

She wished she'd had the chance to tell her brother that she'd truly come back to the Lord. Maybe Ethan would do it.

Sweat ran down her forehead and into her eyes. She swiped it away with the sleeve of her jacket, then realized the ridiculousness of a jacket here in this furnace. She stripped it off, hit her burned hand, and felt tears join the sweat in her eyes.

She squirmed deeper into the corner. Sweat plastered her hair to her scalp.

*Lord, I know everything is going to be okay after all this is over, that I'll be with you. But right now I'm so scared. I'm sorry I fell so far short of what I might've done with my life. I'm sorry for how I hurt Ethan. So very, very sorry for how I treated the life you entrusted to me.*

She remembered those men from the Old Testament whose faith had saved them from the fiery furnace. Odd names. Somebody, somebody, and Abednego.

*Lord, forgive me for my fear here in my own fiery furnace. I know you saved me from the undertow of the past, and my faith is strong in the eternal scheme of things. But I'm still so scared here.*

A tiny spider scurried across her drawn-up knees. She didn't jump or flick it away. The spider must be as scared as she was. And hadn't any longer to live either.

Or maybe it did . . .

Angie straightened in the corner as the spider disappeared under a thin board attached to the foundation a few feet away. The old board was the same grayish color as the concrete. She hadn't noticed it before. Had the spider escaped to the outside?

She leaned over and slid her hand along the foundation until she touched the board. This foundation wasn't made of concrete blocks like the updated foundation under Ryan and Stefanie's house. This was something more old-fashioned, rough, with bits of grit coming off under her hand and smooth rocks bulging through the concrete. Ethan had been trying to tell her something about the foundation . . .

A vision came back to her. Ryan crawling out from under the old house, dirty and grumbling about termites. Ryan fastening a piece of plywood over the opening, muttering something about air circulation, and that maybe it should be a screen instead of a board . . .

Would the Nevermore's old foundation have covered openings too? She crawled along the concrete wall until she was kneeling in front of the board. Was there an opening underneath it? But if there was an opening, wouldn't the board be on the outside so it could be removed from out there rather than in here? Maybe this was just some kind of reinforcement for the old concrete. How was it fastened to the wall? The board was too thin to get a grip on with anything more than her fingertips. It must be nailed right into the concrete. Probably unused for decades. But it was warped, one edge lifted slightly, and the spider had been able to squeeze under it.

She scraped her burned hand on the concrete wall, trying to get her fingers under the warped edge. Instinctively she cradled the hand against her chest and tried to ease the spirals of pain.

Then she determinedly pushed the pain aside. There was much more pain to come if she didn't get out of here.

If only she had something to pry with! Dirt clods, hard as they were, were no help. What about the bands of metal around the old box in which Amelia had hidden her journals? She felt a momentary flare of hope, until she peered through the haze in that direction. No. Useless. The floor above that area had already collapsed.

She flipped over and braced her shoulders and bottom in the dirt, as she had when she'd tried to shove her way through the door. She breathed to psych herself up, the way she'd seen a karate expert do before smashing his head through a board.

A half-hysterical thought came to her. *Maybe I should try using my head instead of my feet. It's probably harder.*

Then she abandoned both psyching and speculation and went to the real power.

*Lord, I think this is my last chance. I'm asking for your help and strength.*

A peculiar sound rumbled from the direction of the old furnace. Was there still oil in it, or a storage tank down here somewhere, ready to explode?

*Okay, this is it, Lord. Go!*

She shoved her feet against the board. It didn't give. All that happened was that her body skidded backward in the dirt. Maybe there was solid concrete underneath the board. She got back in position again. This time she didn't put her feet against the board and shove. This time she drew them back and slammed them into the board.

She felt it splinter under the blow.

She swiveled and stuck her nose into the miniscule cracks. Air! She snatched a few life-giving breaths, then stuck her fingers through the cracks and tried to tear the old plywood apart. She got slivers, scratches, a rip of flesh. But the opening enlarged only by a fraction.

She changed position and slammed her feet into the weakened board.

Again.

And again and again.

Her feet were outside now. She drew them back, ignoring the pain of splintered plywood scratching and tear-ing her ankles. She hammered with one heel, then the other. The ragged hole enlarged.

She turned around and got her head through. One shoulder. Push! Then the other. Something wrenched inside her shoulder when she jammed it through the opening, but she just kept pushing and wiggling.

She squirmed to the outside ground and lay there flat on her stomach, gasping, disoriented, not quite believing that she'd really done it. Ash and debris fell around her. The fire roared behind her. Her shoulder felt as if someone had shoved it through a meat grinder.

*But I'm out. I'm out.*

*Thank you, Lord!*

Now she heard human shouts and yells. She lifted her head, seeing through smoke-blurred eyes that she'd come out at the back of the building, in the narrow, trash-strewn strip between the theater and the tall board fence that separated it from the houses on the other side.

A flicker of flame danced up one board. A stream of water hit it, spray bouncing back on her. It felt good. She wished she could open her mouth and take in a gallon of it. She crawled a few inches. Then she saw it. The front end of a fire truck. A gorgeous, big red fire truck! A yellow-hatted fireman holding a hose raised the stream of water from the fence to spray beyond it to the roof of a house on the other side. Trying to keep the fire from spreading, her fogged mind told her.

She tried to lift an arm to signal that she was here, but her muscles had turned to jelly.

"There's a door in back!" someone yelled.

Another yellow-hatted fireman. This one had an ax. He started chopping at the door. They thought she was still inside, trapped. They were breaking through, and someone was going to try to go into that inferno to rescue her! She could see him now in some kind of protective gear, lumbering up from the other side of the Nevermore.

310

She lifted her good arm a few inches and tried to yell. "Wait! Don't! I'm out here!" But she was so weak, and the words came out more squeak than yell.

The door shattered under the blows of the ax. The fireman stepped back as flames shot out the top of the doorway. Another fireman dragged the hose toward the door. The stream of water beat back the flames, and the fireman in protective gear lumbered up the steps to the door.

Another man ran up behind the one in protective gear. This one was in bare sleeves, without even a fire hat.

Ethan?

It couldn't be. Her eyes and mind were playing tricks on her. She shook her head, trying to clear the daze of smoke and fear. Ethan was in a car somewhere in Phoenix.

No. No, he wasn't. He was here, and he was going inside to look for her.

Another fireman grabbed Ethan to pull him back from the door, but Ethan wrenched away. In another second he'd be inside, where he hadn't a chance of survival.

"Ethan!"

## 34

She repeated the name, struggling to her feet with a leg that kept crumpling under her. Love and fear for him strengthened the squeak to a scream. "Ethan!"

He put a hand on the man in protective gear to stop him from plunging inside. He pointed to Angie, then jumped over the flimsy railing on the steps and ran toward her.

"I can't believe it!" He started to hug her, then saw her battered condition and scooped her up in his arms instead.

She closed her eyes. Shouts . . . another crash . . . roar of the fire … hiss of water hitting the flames. The scent of smoke still clogged her nose and throat. Fire still blazed behind her eyes. But she was safe now. No matter what was happening, she was safe in Ethan's arms.

*Only temporarily,* a voice inside her warned. *After what you did to him, only temporary safety.* But it was a wonderful haven for the moment. *Thank you, Lord.*

Ethan carried her past the firemen. "This is the woman who was trapped inside!"

A blur of words about how she got out and her need for medical attention. The feeling of Ethan moving fast, jogging but trying not to jar her. Words flung over his shoulder. "We're on our way to the hospital!"

A voice followed them. "Anyone else in there?"

Weak as she felt, Angie struggled to lift her head and speak before any lives were risked unnecessarily. "No! Don't let anyone go in there." She sank back. *But Ethan was willing to risk his life to go in after me.*

"There's an ambulance coming." The voice sounded distant, though she wasn't sure if the speaker was distant or if her mind was fading. Something more about it having to come from Dutton Bay because the local ambulance was on its way to the hospital with a heart attack victim.

*Do I need a hospital?* Angie wondered vaguely. She lifted her hand. The burn looked like a slab of badly cooked meat, but she couldn't feel it. Her shoulder too had gone numb.

"We can't wait. I'm taking her right now," Ethan said, and Angie closed her eyes again, relieved to be beyond decisions and effort.

She felt him stretch her out in the backseat of a car, carefully bending her knees to make her fit. Then she felt a not uncomfortable sway and a floating awareness that he was passing speed limits, roaring past other cars as he flew along the curves of the coastal highway. She wanted to ask him why he was here, how he could possibly be here, but speaking took more energy than she could muster, and words were more than her mind could manage. Numbness held her pain at bay, but her throat and lungs still felt raw and heavy with smoke.

Ethan didn't let her try to walk when they reached the Dutton Bay hospital. He scooped her out of the car and carried her again. She didn't feel so out of it mentally now, but the downside of mental improvement was that she could also feel every scratch and cut, every splinter and burn, every muscle screaming in her shoulder.

*I may be here for days . . .*

Yet as it turned out, after some three hours of intensive care, with pain pills, oxygen mask treatment for the smoke inhalation, shoulder and back X rays, fluids for dehydration, shots, sliver removal from her legs and ankles, inspection and treatment of her various scratches and burns, they gave her prescriptions for antibiotics and salve and let her go. "Just be sure to see your regular doctor in a couple of days" was the emergency room doctor's final directive. "Smoke-inhalation damages and symptoms sometimes don't show up for forty-eight hours or so."

Angie could breathe more normally now, though her thoughts were sluggish from the pain pills. Back in the car, when Ethan said, "Do you want to fill the prescriptions here?" it took her a moment to come up with an answer.

"No, I can do it back in Julesburg." Her voice was still hoarse, but it no longer hurt to speak.

He gave her a sideways glance as he turned the ignition key. "Do you feel up to talking? I'm still not clear on what happened today." He paused. "Or clear about Steve Llewelyn." Another pause. "Or Burke."

Neither was she clear about Ethan and his inexplicable presence here, but as they drove back to Julesburg, she gave him a halting, sometimes coughing, story of deception and murder and attempted murder. She tried to stay unemotional, but she had difficulty when she told Ethan how Burke had killed Kristi the very night Angie and Kristi had shared that last dinner in New York.

Low clouds had settled over Julesburg, obscuring the smoke, but the acrid and powerful smell permeated the air. Angie had always liked the smell of a campfire. Somehow she doubted she'd ever feel that way again.

"Your place or Ryan and Stefanie's?" Ethan asked.

Angie jolted upright in the seat. "I should've called Ryan! I didn't show up at church, and he's probably frantic wondering—"

"I called him from the hospital. I gave him about a thirty-second explanation of what happened, so he'll need more. But he knows you're okay."

She carefully leaned back in the seat, regretting the hasty movement of a moment earlier. Pain pills had their limits. "Thank you."

"So, your house or—"

"I want to go back to the Nevermore."

He gave her an astonished glance. "Why?"

"Maybe to see if it all really happened, I guess."

He tapped the steering wheel, as if he might argue with the logic of that thinking. He touched the brake at the turnoff that led to her house, but after a moment of slowing, he drove on by.

Downtown, they found a section of Julesburg's main street blocked off, policemen directing traffic to a side street detour.

"I can't get up close to the Nevermore to park."

"I can walk."

"I don't think you should."

"I need to see it," she said.

Clumps of people were still standing around watching, kept from getting too close by a no-nonsense sheriff's deputy. A smaller, privately owned fire truck from the local laser products company had joined the lone fire truck of Julesburg's volunteer fire department. Two county sheriff cars were also angled into the parking lot.

Part of the front wall of the theater still stood, but the Nevermore sign had crashed and broken, individual letters scattered like some game of Scrabble spread on the street. A section of the back wall was standing as well, and the hole the fireman had chopped through the door was an incongruous opening from nowhere into nowhere. The shake roof and siding had apparently gone up like kindling, but the misshapen lump of the old furnace was still identifiable. Firemen were pouring water

315

on hot spots, smoke rising in oddly placid curls now. Part of the wooden fence had burned, but the firemen had managed to keep the fire from spreading to houses beyond the board wall.

There was no doubt that it had really happened. The Nevermore was gone. Angie watched as something fueled a fresh burst of flame in the debris. *And, except for God's grace, I could be under all that.*

She saw uniformed officers standing by the police cars. "I need to talk to them, so they'll know to go after Jordan before he gets too far away. And Burke."

Ethan gave her a quick, assessing glance. "I'll tell them to contact you at the house later. You're in no shape for questions out here on the street."

He walked over and talked briefly to the officers. He returned with the report that they'd come to the house in a few minutes.

Angie nodded, still staring at the ravaged ruins of the old theater. "I don't really believe in that old curse of the Nevermore. But . . . I guess I won't be turning it into an office for the *Herald* now."

Ethan put his hand on her arm. "C'mon, I'll take you home."

They started back toward his car. Angie had taken only a few steps when she saw something that stopped her short. The police cars had blocked her view before then.

"Is something wrong?"

"That car . . ."

Heat had blistered and discolored the paint. A piece of burned wall lay across the hood. A maze of cracks spiderwebbed the windshield. The interior looked burned out. But Angie didn't have to see the bullet hole in the rear door to know whose car that was.

"That's Jordan's car. We drove over from my place in it."

"It is? Well, it looks like he just abandoned it there. Maybe he decided he'd be too easy to track in it."

Jordan had gone to the Nevermore planning to kill her. Doing it by fire had been a last-minute decision, but killing her wasn't. "He probably had an escape plan worked out ahead of time," she said. Still, the fact that the car was here struck her as odd. "But how does someone get out of Julesburg in a hurry?"

Ethan glanced around. "Maybe he's still here."

"Here? Why would he stick around here?"

"To watch and make sure you didn't escape before the fire got you. He probably didn't know you had a cell phone and that the police and fire department would show up so soon."

"But I did escape—"

"Exactly."

Ethan didn't spell it out, but Angie caught his meaning. Maybe Jordan Riker was still here, figuring on finishing the job he'd started, knowing he'd better or Burke might put a killer on *his* tail.

Angie had felt far too much heat that day, but yet she shivered. She glanced around uneasily, as Ethan had done a moment earlier. Was Jordan watching her?

No. Not logical. Jordan Riker had to be long gone. He'd probably already told Burke that their problem was taken care of. They would both be congratulating themselves.

She felt a sudden flare of satisfaction. They were in for a surprise. Because both Jordan and Burke would be in custody before they had any idea their murder plot had failed.

The police didn't waste time getting to the house. Two officers in a county sheriff's car pulled into the driveway just as Ethan was helping Angie to the front door. Ryan arrived right behind them. Angie suspected he was about to protest that she was in no condition to answer questions now, but she waved him off.

She repeated to the officers what she had told Ethan about Kristi's murder in New York, the Steve Llewelyn deception, and why and how she had wound up under the burning Nevermore. Except she couldn't do it all in spoken words. At times the aftereffects of the smoke reduced her voice to a painful rasp, and she resorted to writing some of it down. Even as she was still supplying the information, one of the officers ran out to the police car to radio in the information about Jordan and Burke.

When the officers left, Ryan briefly disappeared into Angie's bedroom and came out with an armload of clean clothes. "Okay, you're coming over to the house," he said. "No arguments." And not unkindly he added, "You're a mess."

Angie fingered her hair, and bits of ash and debris sifted to her shoulders. One section of hair felt short and frizzed, and dark-edged holes dotted her smoke-blackened clothing.

"How about if I bring her over in a few minutes?" Ethan said. "We have some things to talk about."

Angie could see Ryan's protective brotherly instincts jump to the forefront. "I don't think Angie is up to any more talking today."

"Actually, I'll do the talking this time. Ten minutes, okay?"

Ryan looked as if he might reject the compromise, but he finally nodded. "Ten minutes." *But not a minute more,* his look added.

## 35

*T*hank you for being here." Angie spoke formally to Ethan after Ryan left with the armload of her clothes. "I thought I was talking to you in Phoenix." She felt awkward now, remembering how she'd bared her heart to him just before the burning ember hit her hand and she'd thrown the cell phone.

She was sitting on the sofa, and Ethan was perched on an arm of the upholstered chair. Keyhole had made herself scarce while the police officers were present, but now she came out of hiding and jumped up to purr in Angie's lap.

"Actually, I was just pulling out of that service station about halfway between Julesburg and Gold Beach."

"You must've broken the speed limit getting to Julesburg—" She broke off as the geography hit her. Gold Beach was south of Julesburg, the opposite direction from his brother's home in Eugene. How had he gotten down there?

He saw her confusion. "Later," he said.

"I—I thought I was hallucinating when I first saw you. And then I realized you were going inside the Nevermore after me. Without protective gear, without anything—"

"You're not supposed to be talking." Ethan knelt on the floor beside the sofa. He touched a finger to her lips. "Brother's orders."

"I'm not sure he actually ordered me to—"

"Then my orders." He hesitated, as if reconsidering that high-handed statement. "Okay, make that my request."

Angie was grateful. Words were beginning to feel like a mouthful of those hard clods of dirt under the Nevermore, and they were difficult to spit out.

"I left here last night . . . and it does seem like a lot longer than last night, doesn't it?" Ethan said.

"A lot has happened since then."

"Yes, it has," he agreed. "And some of it happened to me." He reached for her hand, saw the bandage over the burn, and found the other hand instead. "I left here last night with a . . . with a lot of anger and hurt. I felt betrayed and shocked—"

"And horrified and sick. I know the feelings." Angie swallowed, the movement painful in her raw throat. She stroked Keyhole and blinked back tears. "I shouldn't have told you. I should've just broken off with you and spared you knowing what I'd done. Maybe it wouldn't have hurt you as much that way."

"This morning, on the cell phone, I thought I heard you say—"

"I said a lot of things."

"You said . . . I *think* you said that you love me."

"After what I did, I don't have any right to love you. Our baby, Ethan. Our baby." She tipped her head against his shoulder.

He put his arms around her and held her gently while the pain of regret that no pill could assuage flooded through her. "I'm so sorry," she whispered.

He pulled back to look in her eyes. "You know how else I felt when I left here? As if I had every right to my fury."

"You did. You do."

"I didn't stop at my brother's house when I reached Eugene. I just headed straight for Arizona."

"Driving?"

"I was too upset to wait for a plane. I wanted . . . action. I wanted to drive my fist through something. I wanted to smash and crush and stomp things."

She managed a bleak smile. "Including me?"

He answered the question with a rueful lift of shoulder.

"I don't blame you," she whispered.

"I do. But that didn't get through to me until I was quite a ways down I-5, past Medford, in fact. Then I turned around and took the highway over to Crescent City and back up the coast. I was almost out of gas when I finally remembered to pull into a station. And you called me."

"You've been driving all night?" She pulled back and studied him, noticing the lines of weariness around his eyes.

"I might still be driving, headed for Arizona, if the Lord hadn't grabbed hold of me at a truck stop café where I stopped for coffee."

"I—I didn't call because I wanted anything of you. I understand how you feel. I just didn't want Burke and Jordan to get away with what they'd done. I just wanted to say . . . good-bye."

"That was what I wanted too, as I was roaring down I-5. A permanent good-bye. But at the truck stop this couple came in, and they were furious with each other. The husband was supposed to have turned on their security alarm system before they left home. He'd forgotten to do it, and now they were going to have to turn around and go back. The wife was yelling that if he hadn't been so wrapped up in watching some stupid game on TV that he'd have remembered to do this. He was yelling back, 'Like you've never forgotten anything. Like you're so perfect. How about when you forgot to pay the water bill, and they turned the water off right when my folks were visiting us?' And she was yelling that she wouldn't have forgotten paying the water bill if she hadn't been so nervous about his crazy mother coming, and then he yelled that *her* mother drives him batty talking about how successful her other son-in-law is."

Angie wasn't certain what all this had to do with his change of heart and mind, but she didn't interrupt.

"I wanted to go over and bash their heads together and do some yelling of my own about how self-righteous they were both acting. But then it got through to me what I was doing. I'd quoted a verse in 1 John to you. 'If we confess our sins he is faithful and just and will forgive all our sins.' I'd said to you, 'There's no wrong so unforgivable the Lord can't forgive it.' "

Angie nodded. "Powerful words. Wise words. They were part of what brought me to my knees before the Lord." And what had gotten her through the ordeal under the burning building, knowing that no matter what happened there, the Lord was on the other side to welcome her.

"Yeah, but I was putting me *above* those words. I was saying the Lord could forgive you, but I couldn't. Oh, no. Not smug ol' Ethan, looking down from his lofty heights of superiority. He didn't have to forgive. He *wouldn't* forgive. I was putting myself and my hurt and anger above the Lord, setting myself up as too righteous to forgive, more righteous than the Lord himself."

He touched a finger to her lips again, stopping her from saying anything.

"So I said, 'Okay, Lord. I admit it, I was wrong. I'll turn around and go back and apologize to Angie.' If the Lord could forgive, and I knew he could, I didn't have any right *not* to forgive. So that's what I'm doing now. Apologizing and forgiving and asking your forgiveness."

"There's nothing for me to forgive you for!"

"How about my self-righteousness, my judgmental attitude, my part in what happened that night in Phoenix?" Even though all this seemed small compared to what she'd done, Angie could see that it was important to him, and she offered her forgiveness with no reservations.

"But I also told the Lord I wouldn't love you," Ethan added. "No way. I could forgive, but I couldn't love you anymore. And that was final."

Angie swallowed. "That sounds fair."

"As usual, God didn't give me a big lecture about my attitude. He didn't thunder out of the clouds or whisper on the wind or call me on my cell phone." Ethan took a deep breath. "But you did call me on my cell phone. And when I heard your voice, even before I knew you were in danger, I knew I still loved you. And when I did realize the danger you were in . . ." He lifted his hands and cupped her face. "I'll always love you, Angie. Just like I always have."

Loved her enough to plunge into a burning building to try to save her. Loved her enough to be here with her right now.

"So now I'm asking again. Did you mean it when you told me on the phone that you love me? Or was I imagining words you didn't say?"

"I said them. I meant them." She took a deep breath. "I mean them now. I love you."

Ethan grinned at her, then helped her to her feet. "Best ten minutes I ever spent," he said. And then he kissed her.

## 36

*S*moke and flames were gone now, the fire five days in the past, but an ugly scent of burned, soggy debris still hung like a morbid cloud over the ruins of the theater. Traffic flowed normally on the street, but yellow plastic tape still barricaded the site.

Angie and Ethan stood outside the tape, hands joined as they watched Ryan and Sherlock methodically work their way back and forth across the ash and debris that had once been the Nevermore.

"Is Sherlock trained for this?" Ethan asked. "I always thought he was just a big, friendly house pet."

"He isn't trained, but he's done it before. That's how he earned his name. With his detective work finding a body after an arson fire."

Low-hanging clouds threatened rain at any moment, but so far there was only a raw mist blowing in off the ocean. Droplets clung to Angie's eyelashes when she blinked. A county sheriff's black-and-white patrol car stood in the parking lot, and beyond it a big yellow backhoe. The deputy and the backhoe operator, both with arms crossed, leaned against the patrol car and watched Ryan and Sherlock, as did a handful of onlookers. Everyone was silent and motionless, as if afraid noise or movement might distract the dog from his job. Sherlock stopped, sniffed, and dug briefly in the area where the velvet drape that had fallen on Angie had once hung. Near him, a furtive ray of sunlight broke through the shifting clouds and spotlit a shard of mirror that still gleamed even after the fire.

No, nothing there. The big dog, tail waving gently, moved on. Investigators from the Oregon state police and the state fire marshal's office had come and gone. Everyone had taken a turn at questioning Angie, and the pile of concrete blocks stacked near the shapeless lump of the old furnace confirmed her story of attempted murder. Fast-moving authorities had Burke in custody back in New York, and DNA tests were already in the works. Angie and Ethan hadn't yet heard if Kristi's safe deposit box had been located and opened. Angie had turned Amelia's journals over to the authorities. And the ruby ring was still missing.

Along with Jordan Riker. He'd managed to vanish from Julesburg without a trace. He hadn't turned up at his apartment or office in New York; his credit cards hadn't been used. Burke, grimly maintaining innocence on all fronts, claimed Jordan was merely an acquaintance and that he knew nothing of his whereabouts.

Angie figured Jordan must've made a run for the nearest border once TV and radio picked up the news that she'd escaped from the burning theater. He'd know the authorities would be on his trail.

Ethan and Ryan weren't convinced Jordan had run. They thought he might still be in Julesburg and insisted that one of them be with Angie anytime she stepped a foot outside Ryan and Stefanie's house. She'd tried to scoff at their worries. Why would Jordan Riker want to kill her now? He must realize she'd already told the police everything. Wouldn't getting far away from Julesburg be a much higher priority?

Unless, Ryan had pointed out, Jordan wanted to eliminate her as a witness before he ran.

And then, on the night after the Nevermore burned, someone had burglarized the Second Hand Stuff store. Only three items were stolen: two handguns and a high-powered rifle with a telescopic sight.

Now Angie glanced up at Lighthouse Hill, which was steep and heavily forested beyond the newer condominiums. A man hiding there with a high-powered rifle and telescopic sight could easily pick out a human target on Julesburg's main street.

Uneasily she edged behind the protection of Ryan's pickup parked on the street by the Nevermore.

Sherlock had stopped again. He and Ryan were in approximately the center of the seating area now.

"I think he's found something," Ethan said.

The dog dug frantically, sending ashes into the air. Ryan knelt beside him. Angie clutched Ethan's hand. *Do I want Jordan to be in there?*

It was Stefanie who had brought up the idea that Jordan Riker might somehow have been trapped inside the Nevermore. But Angie didn't think his body was buried in the burned debris of the old theater. She didn't see how it could be. He'd had plenty of time to get out of the building after he set the fire. No concrete blocks had barred his way.

But regardless of what she thought, Ryan had offered his and Sherlock's services to the authorities. And with no trace of Jordan Riker anywhere else, they'd taken him up on the offer.

Now Ryan pulled something out of the hole. Angie tensed, a vision of Vance Spohn's bones floating in her mind. Had Sherlock dug up Jordan's burned bones?

Ryan held up the object. Angie stared at it in mixed relief and astonishment.

"Well, I doubt *that* was Jordan Riker's," Ethan said of the burned remains of a high-heeled shoe.

"Sometimes Sherlock does get sidetracked," Angie admitted.

The police officer broke into laughter. "Any time we lose a shoe back at the station, we know who to call," he guffawed at Ryan.

"Hey, we're not done yet," Ryan called back.

An erratic gust of wind swirled fallen ashes in the parking lot and ruffled Angie's newly short hair. She'd gotten it cut to even out the singed areas, the first time she'd worn her hair short in years. It felt strange but good. Another break with the past.

"Do you suppose we'll ever find any use for the lot once it's cleaned up?" Ethan asked.

Angie had decided to go ahead with the purchase. Backing out on the agreement to buy hadn't seemed fair to the owners down in California. The Nevermore had been destroyed because of Angie, and they shouldn't suffer for it. Settlement from their insurance, which they'd agreed would come to her, would ease some of the financial sting. But there would also be big cleanup costs in addition to the purchase price. Not much would remain in her bank account after that expense.

There was also no healthy stock-market account as a safety net now. At some point before his arrest, Burke had expertly cleaned out the account, and he'd apparently hidden the proceeds well. Angie wasn't glad about the loss. But at the same time, she felt an odd relief, a certain sense of poetic justice. Burke had helped her acquire the hefty account; Burke had taken it away. God probably had a hand in it too. It was another break with the past and with the ambition and material rewards that had trapped her for so long.

Angie looked over the remains of the Nevermore. "It's still the choicest lot in Julesburg." She smiled. "Estelle

Reeves at the real estate office assured me of that just this morning."

"Maybe someday Julesburg will turn into a metropolis, and then it'll be worth a fortune."

Angie smiled again. Julesburg a metropolis? Right. "Yeah, about the time we're old and gray. But maybe our grand—"

She broke off in the middle of the lighthearted statement. *Grandchildren.*

They were getting married in five days, at the little church here in Julesburg. After that they'd be living in Phoenix. Keyhole would stay with Ryan and Stefanie and Sherlock, whom she'd adopted as a kind of shaggy big brother. Angie had already arranged to sell the *Herald* to a delighted Madge on terms Madge and her husband could manage. And Madge was planning to continue the series of articles about Julesburg's old buildings that Angie had started.

God had worked out so many details in their lives. But would he trust them enough to send children and grandchildren someday?

Ethan looked at her, his gaze sober. He knew what she was thinking. "I don't know," he admitted in answer to her silent question. "But I do know we can trust him."

Yes. The ache would always be there. God didn't take away the pain of loss and regret. But they could trust him.

They turned their attention back to the debris of the theater. Sherlock had moved on and now was in the area at the edge of the stage. He started to dig again.

"Maybe he's found the other shoe," the officer yelled.

No, not a shoe this time. Ryan knelt and started moving larger pieces of debris to help Sherlock. The officer and backhoe operator clambered across the burned wreckage to help. An almost palpable sense of tension emanated from the scene.

"What's happening?" Angie asked.

"More than a shoe, I think."

A few minutes later the backhoe operator started his machine and lumbered out to the spot. With precision and surprising delicacy, he moved debris away from the area, apparently working around something in the center that Angie and Ethan couldn't see. The officer went back to his car to use his radio.

In a few more minutes, the place exploded with activity. More officers, one with a camera. The county medical examiner, the local volunteer fire chief. A crowd appeared as if a loudspeaker had blared the news that something big was happening at the Nevermore. A collective gasp went up when four officers went waist deep into the hole and came up carrying something bulky.

They loaded the blackened lump into a police van. It was body length but strangely shapeless. Angie stared at it with a sick knowledge of what it was and how, but for God's grace, it might've been her.

Ryan and Sherlock, both blackened with ash and debris, came over to where Angie and Ethan stood. Ryan wiped his gloved hands on his pants. Together they silently watched the van pull away.

"Jordan Riker's body?" Ethan asked.

"Somebody's body." Ryan gave the big dog a long stroke on the head. "The medical examiner uncovered part of a foot."

Angie clasped her arms around her body. She hadn't wanted Jordan Riker to escape justice. She hadn't wanted him free to take aim and cut her down with a bullet. But even for a would-be murderer like Jordan, to die like this . . .

"But the body looked so big and strange," she said.

"It appeared to be wrapped in something." Ryan frowned, obviously puzzled. "I've never seen anything

329

like it in any of my arson investigations. Almost like a shroud wrapped around him."

A shroud.

Angie reeled in a dizzy moment of understanding. "The old satin curtain across the screen," she whispered. "One end was drooping, ready to fall. I heard a big crash . . ."

The Nevermore had gleefully claimed another victim.

The *Herald* missed publication of one week's issue when it changed hands, the first missed issue since the four months in the seventies when editor Harry Llewelyn had been murdered.

In her first edition as the new owner and editor, Madge Edelson wrote about the attempted murder and the discovery of the burned body encased in the twisted remains of a satin curtain. The news story contained only brisk facts, including that the remains had been positively identified as those of Jordan Riker. Another separate article said two juveniles were under arrest for the break-in at Second Hand Stuff.

Madge also wrote a short editorial. Stefanie, without comment, mailed a copy of the newspaper down to Angie and Ethan in Phoenix.

Angie and Ethan, on the patio of their home in Paradise Valley, read it together.

Some people believe in the tales of a curse or a ghost or an evil spirit lurking in the old theater. Others scoff at such stories as superstitious nonsense. Your editor makes no claims either way.

There is, however, no denying that the list of disasters connected with the Nevermore is long and tragic. It started with the original owners, Warren and Althea Swarthout, who died when a tree in the parking lot blew over and crushed them. It went on to the deaths of Harry

Llewelyn, Vance Spohn, Amelia Swarthout, and death or injuries to many others. All of these can no doubt be passed off as no more than tragic coincidences. But was Jordan Riker's death a mere coincidence? Or was it the last act of the Nevermore, taking final revenge for the fire that ended its existence?

*I don't believe in the curse of the Nevermore,* Angie thought. *I don't believe a building can make some dying act of revenge. And yet . . .*

"We can be thankful the Lord is more forgiving than that," Ethan said quietly.

*I can believe that.*

Write the author:

Lorena McCourtney
P. O. Box 773
Merlin, OR 97532

Visit the web site:

http://www.lorenamccourtney.com

Have you read the earlier books in The Julesburg Mysteries series?

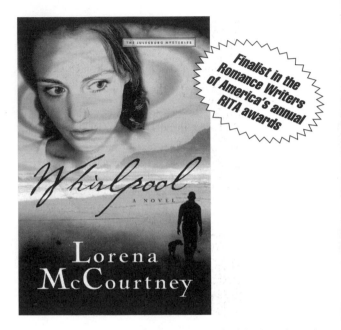

The woman who stole Stefanie Canfield's husband is dead. Stefanie is accused of killing her. Did she do it? Even she isn't certain.

ISBN 0-8007-5776-9

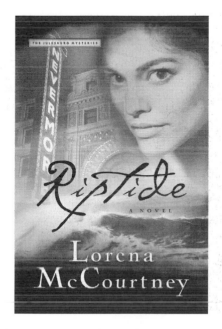

Newly reunited twins Sarah MacIntosh and Julie
Armstrong plan to buy Julesburg's old theater, the Nevermore, and turn it into a mini-mall for artisans and
craftspeople. But bad things happen to people who get
too involved with the Nevermore, as Sarah and Julie find
out when a chance encounter with a robber at a con-
venience store sweeps them into a riptide of murder and
danger.

ISBN 0-8007-5777-7